Liberty's Dawn

Art Theocles

12/22/2013

ART THEOCLES

Liberty's Dawn

Book One of the Liberty Trilogy

iUniverse, Inc.
Bloomington

Liberty's Dawn
Book One of the Liberty Trilogy

iUniverse books may be ordered through booksellers or by contacting:

iUniverse
1663 Liberty Drive
Bloomington, IN 47403
www.iuniverse.com
1-800-Authors (1-800-288-4677)

ISBN: 978-1-4697-5157-3 (sc)
ISBN: 978-1-4697-5159-7 (e)
ISBN: 978-1-4697-5158-0 (dj)

Library of Congress Control Number: 2012901562

Printed in the United States of America

iUniverse rev. date: 3/19/2012

To all who have defended our nation in conflicts past and those who presently defend our nation and our way of life, I wish I could do more to help during this very difficult period in our nation's history.

To my family and my parents, who have shown incredible patience with me over these past few years.

To Mike, who befriended me at a point when I needed it most, and many thanks, Mike and Stephanie, for the great prereads!

To the good Lord, for giving me everything I individually lack in life.

A Note from the Author

It is with great pride, admiration, and concern for my country that I wrote this novel about these fictional and fantastic happenings centered on the struggle that was the American Revolution. The history of the United States, present-day political and economic environments, and trepidation for our future generations' prosperity in America and our world, united with a deep respect for the colonizing people of the seventeenth and eighteenth centuries, permeate my thoughts and feelings. It is my hope that reading this fictional story set in an actual historical context will spark the reader's interest in studying the events, difficulties, and philosophies contributing to the establishment of a free United States of America.

Additionally, I wish to pay my deepest respects to and confirm my highest admiration for the people of the United Kingdom, France, and other great colonizing nations who came to this land in search of freedom and liberty. These are the people who became the founders of the Unites States of America and successfully established justice and tranquility, provided for the common defense, promoted the general welfare, secured the blessings of liberty, and established the Constitution of the United States of America. The principles underlying that Constitution continue to draw people from all over the world to our great nation.

Finally, I want to honor those people who have struggled and died before us and those who continue to serve our great nation and its citizens by dedicating their lives to assuring our nation's survival during these uncertain times. Although not perfect now or through its history, the United States of America is a shining example of freedom and liberty unlike any other. It is something to be fought for and preserved, for ourselves and our posterity.

May God bless these United States! God bless America!

... 1 ...
Days, Weeks, and Months ... and Years

MORNING ON THE YORK River was pleasantly comfortable for their tasks on this twelfth day of October 1781. The boys planned their fishing charade and wasted little time getting on station, as the days grew closer to the date of surrender. Their voyage proceeded as it had on the many days before this one—row a bit toward the French fleet, fish a bit, and become part of the scenery that would become one of our nation's defining conflicts, the battle for freedom and independence at Yorktown, Virginia.

On this day, though, the boys noted one difference as the wind blew stiffly out of the northeast; the brackish water of the river danced turbulently around their small vessel.

"It's a ship!" blurted Sid. "To the northeast ... just one, and she's British!"

A small, lone British naval vessel, apparently caught north behind the French blockade weeks before, was swiftly heading south to run the blockade in an attempt to escape to the freedom of the Chesapeake and the open seas.

"It's suicide," remarked Nik. "That captain doesn't have a prayer running this armada." Nik could see that the French fleet had expertly begun forming up for the engagement.

"They are making incredible time!" John now nervously warned. "If we don't move quickly—"

Ba-boom! Boom! ... The northernmost French vessels were already firing on the incoming enemy vessel.

"Options, guys?" asked Sid with the full realization that they would be at the center of the battle in mere moments. The British ship had used the stiff wind and wind direction to move at an incredible rate of speed down the York River and was now almost engaged with the French fleet nearest to the boys' position. There was no time for the boys in their small boat to move out of the way; the battle was upon them. They could see elements of the northernmost French fleet turning southward, adding their fire to the area.

The French cannons were firing from the front and toward the entire right side of the boys now as they secured their rifles and gear onto the small craft; the noise was deafening. The heavy choking smoke of gunpowder and the concussion of the close cannon fire was utterly debilitating to the boys, as the naval barrage continued to spray its deadly reports into the skies above them.

"We weren't counting on this!" yelled John.

"Row, row!" yelled Sid as each came to the disturbing fact that they were now directly in the path of the fleeing British vessel and the French cannon fire. The concussion and fire that the British vessel had experienced down the line of the French fleet had altered its course slightly south, putting it on a collision course with the boys' small craft.

"Holy—" John yelled. "It's headed right for us! You might have finally succeeded in killing us this time, Nik!"

Sid was still yelling for the boys to row as Nik quickly finished the tie-off of his gear and screamed, "Prepare for a broadside hit! Jump out of the right side of the boat! It doesn't look like—" Just then, the burning British vessel rushed past the boys, upending their craft and tossing them into the river.

The boys desperately attempted to surface as the pull of the fleeing British ship forcefully and uncontrollably towed them under the murky, cold river water. They managed to pop up together about a half mile down river, hanging on to their overturned craft, while the detonation and sinking of the British vessel finalized well beyond them. As water dripped down his face into his eyes and mouth, Sid took a deep breath and asked in an extraordinarily calm voice, "So, how did we get into all this again?"

□ □ □ □ □ □ □ □ □ □ □ □ □ □ □

July 14, 2009. It was just another day when Nik began his morning like any other in the past 775 days—wake up, get the kids to school, and kiss the wife as she leaves for work. Morning coffee from his favorite coffee establishment was a must—it wasn't a famous, upscale latte institution, but a corner gas station that happened to brew a good cup of joe. The daily visit to this venue checked another box for Nik as he meandered through these days; it gave him all sorts of folks to talk to about all things present-day. Nothing seemed to be out of bounds, conversation-wise, at the shop—politics, religion, taxes, what open job might appear soon and where, why the hell oil was so expensive, who was making all the money with it, and most of all, the day's pending weather.

Nik, a middle-aged, not-so-slim, tired-looking man of Mediterranean descent wandered into the gas station entrance and was greeted by his friend and shop manager Shana (pronounced *Shay-na*), who was always happy to see him—or so it seemed, he guessed. "Hey," Nik openly greeted anyone who cared to listen. "How's it goin' today?"

The greeting was typical and general and always seemed to draw the same response from most people: "Same stuff, different day" (SSDD), which made Nik chuckle.

"Any job leads?" someone asked.

"Nah," grumbled Nik, "SSDD." This conversation could, depending on the mood of the crowd, only last a few minutes, or it could draw out to an hour or so. Finishing up at the coffee shop, Nik headed back to the house in a quiet area in the flats of eastern North Carolina.

Home, a small country house a few miles outside of town, provided all sorts of opportunities to keep him busy, none of which he was really all that excited about availing himself of. He was a product of what some have called "The Great Recession" or "The

Recession of 2008"—or 2009 or 2010 or something like that. Nik regularly embroiled himself in the news of the day and the financial mischief of the US and world markets and concluded, after trying to make a little headway in the stock market, that it was all rigged and that the normal person (or the "little guy") was just plain screwed. Nik had often told his compatriots at the coffee shop that "it's like bringing a knife to a gun fight" or "a pistol to a cannon battle" or something as equally badly weighted, unbalanced, and bleakly depressing.

Day after day, Nik had watched decisions made by current "leaders" on issues that, in the past, were clearly covered by the rule of law that we enjoyed in this country for more than two hundred years. Their interpretations of basic American ideals were what most Americans found, well, just plain un-American.

```
Sid:  yo
Nik:  yo
Sid:  How goes?
```

Sid, a long-time college buddy of Nik, started the morning text conversation off the same way every day, as he was also in his own sort of "place" those days.

```
Nik:  SSDD
Nik:  it doesn't change
Sid:  Yeah, I hear ya
```

Sid, a fairly fit, tall individual of northern European descent, worked for a large techno conglomerate on the other side of Raleigh, North Carolina, and was having a tough time with the typical corporate mumbo jumbo that was, unfortunately, inundating the way all of American business did things those days. Nik, having been in local and corporate management for a large, multinational pharmaceutical firm, tried to talk Sid through some of the more exasperating situations that had him—how should we say?—screaming in colorful metaphors.

Nik was always a straightforward, hands-on sort who didn't enjoy the "fun-ness" of the modern business protocols and shenanigans. Honestly, Nik thought all the modern "better ways of doing things" were an utter waste of time and effort. He didn't have a problem with modern tools or technology, but scorecards, scrums, tollbooths (all terms used in modern project management arenas), endless meetings, and anything to do with the modern human resource process were utterly worthless to him (and, in his opinion, to everybody else as well). Not to mention the "modern work and labor" methodologies that had folks losing their jobs in droves as one person picked up the tasks for three or four people in the name of efficiency and the almighty buck. He tended to think all the savings ended up in some top manager's pocket as a bonus—a bonus on the suffering of some out-of-work slob.

Nik believed in the free market but also understood that greed and stupidity drove the free market to a place that none of us should ever go. Yes, there was a balance, but the absurd justification for the just-in-time, last-minute manufacturing decision making that had occurred in businesses in the recent years to save twelve cents per thousand dollars off the bottom line was the thing of B- or Z-type management horror stories. One simple interruption in the supply chain immediately caused shortages, outages, and potential loss of life in some cases—all for twelve cents. This was clearly an oversimplification but painfully factual.

```
Sid:  Shooting this weekend?
Nik:  maybe?
Nik:  let's see if we can get clearance
      from the towers …
Sid:  Yeah, LOL (short for laughing out
      loud)
```

The "tower" reference, a modern-day code shared by all middle-aged males who matured (or tried to) in the late nineties, was, of course, the loving reference to wives and families involved.

Sid was a bit of a gun collector, World War II stuff mostly. Nik was generally along for the ride and had a couple of modern rifles.

If anyone asked when they were at the range, Nik always referred to Sid as "the gun guy." Nik enjoyed shooting targets and was generally satisfied to simply hit the poor, unsuspecting scrap of printed paper at whatever range they chose for the day. He went into each day at the range with little expectation and laughed about it most of the time. Sid had some military experience and shooting training and, all-in-all, really enjoyed the history of the weapons themselves. Nik had a passion for history, admitting to all that he was not an expert by any means, but he was one who really enjoyed knowing our history on the planet we call Earth and, more specifically, *our* nation's history.

They regularly attended the local gun shows to see what was out and about in the world of firearms and such. There was something strangely addictive about the gun show experience—the many smells; the other "interesting" folks looking around at the items and wares for sale, auction, or raffle; and, ah yes, the enormous assortment of dried "meat" products of every shape, size, and flavor. Sid usually had a part or piece he needed for one of the older weapons he had, and they spent a very long time picking through all the booths and displays for whatever Sid might require or whatever caught Nik's eye. They tried to avoid the shows in the hot summer months, as the hosting venues often didn't handle the air-conditioning needs very well, especially for a place as warm as Raleigh, North Carolina; they strongly disliked the heat and humidity. For Sid and Nik, cold weather was a treat!

Every once in a great while, Sid nudged Nik into purchasing something new for the range experience and was the general antagonist for Nik's growing collection of modern firearms. Nik commonly referred to Sid as "a bad man" (for enticing Nik into spending money). It went both ways with the two men and was generally a source of great jocularity. The happenings of our modern times were a subject Sid and Nik spent a lot of breath and energy on.

As always, the ever-communicating chat network remained an open line of communication throughout the day—not the traditional teen chat method but "the more refined kind of chat" that streamed text as data instead of just an SMS (short message service) text. Nik chuckled about that explanation openly and had many compatriots among the chat waves—far less than your average teenager, but for someone in his early forties, he had plenty to waste away the day. Friends and colleagues from jobs past texted Nik throughout the day with stray comments about this or that, always stirring at least a three- or four-line back and forth. Most of the conversations were in good fun, some were worthy conversations about real things, and some were just simple daily commentary on the annoying items of the day. Everyone needs that in these times.

```
John: Yo, what you up to?
Nik: SSDD
Nik: it doesn't change
John: Yeah, too much work here
John: Not enough people
Nik: yup, same story everywhere
Nik: it sucks
```

John was a friend of Nik's from the local area. They had met some thirteen years before and had become friends through working together and some family interactions. John, an average-looking American male from the south, was in the medical industry on the information technology (IT) side of things, trying to keep folks happy. Nik had led some project and technology support groups in the past and understood the impossibility of anyone in IT ever being able to please anyone on the business side of anything. You could be making marshmallows, fishing hooks, nuclear warheads, or a pooper scooper you use in a cat box. IT folks were forever the redheaded stepchildren who *always* got the blame for everything wrong with a business, which was utter garbage.

```
John: people just want more and more!
John: with me and what army?
Nik: Yeah, I hear Ya …
Nik: gimme a job, I'll help
John: I wish
Nik: Wahoo! Do more with less!
```

```
Nik: What a great motto
Nik: geez
John: it's a crime is what it is!
```

And so the day's conversations persisted—every day, week after week, and month after month for the past twenty-five months for Nik as he endeavored to find a new job or career.

As Nik moved through the common day with the news or financials blaring in the background, a daily cleanup around the house commenced. Yes, in all fairness, it didn't always happen, but something got done no matter how small. The past few weeks had brought warmer weather and little annoying gnats; they were maddening! Nik endeavored to figure out (almost daily) where the little pests were coming from and tried to end their existence once and for all. The process ended up with the same angry rant; he would throw his hands up and move on to vacuuming or dusting the TV, which seemed to spew terrible news minute after minute. Again, twenty-five months of that would drive a man to crazy things. Thankfully, Nik didn't have any crazy vices; his definition for substance abuse was drinking a two-liter bottle of soda in one day. So how crazy could it really get?

```
Sid: Dude!
Sid: Beowulf!
Nik: lol
Nik: maybe
Sid: BOOM!
Nik: Yes Sir!
```

What Sid was referring to was the last purchase Nik had made at the gun show. Nik, being one "who wasn't going to have a collection exactly" wanted to "you know … have something to cover the spectrum," as it were. He had the standard close-cover protection of a dependable 9mm and .45-caliber pistols; he had the "standard" tricked-out, railed-up, two-stage triggered AR-15 from last year and was looking for something, you know, a little bigger. Nik fell quickly for the idea of one of the AR-type rifles that fired a

.50-caliber, pistol-type round for maximum "wow and effect." This was warmly and affectionately referred to as a Beowulf assault rifle! Yes, for all you literary types, Beowulf, like the story and the hero it's named after—that's on purpose.

```
Nik: maybe John would come too?
Nik: would also need tower clearance …
Sid: LOL … Yeah
Nik: I'll ask
Nik: Dude!
John: Yo
Nik: Shooting this weekend?
Nik: me, u, and Sid
John: I wish
John: I can always ask?
Nik: Uh, try and tell … k, ttyl (short
      for "talk to you later")
```

That night the typical answer came through—it's fine, we all get it, it's our duty. We are husbands and fathers; we need to be there as much as we can.

```
John: Yo
Nik: Shooting this weekend?
John: Um, no … lots of family stuff …
John: Got clearance to game for a bit …
Nik: well … ok … when and where?
```

Yes, folks, in the year 2010, thirty-eight- to forty-four-year-old men got together and challenged each other to computer network gaming. Commonly known as a LAN party, you log on to a first-person shooter game of your liking, virtually run around any kind of scenery or scenario, and blast each other's characters, commonly referred to as "killing pixels." Others were contacted, the gaming was set, refreshments were purchased, snacks were devoured, and good play and fun were had by all.

As Nik, Sid, and John were hanging out and cleaning up the computer area in Nik's basement after the session, Sid blurted out, "So how about a boys' outing?" As the two desk-plumped, out-of-shape, computer professionals glared at him like he had lost his mind, he added, "Steak, campfires, and some good, safe mountain firearm fun!"

Okay, that sounds much better, Nik and John thought. "Geez, you had me scared. I thought you were talking like hard-core, back-country camping, hard work, exercise, and horrific laborious tasks like that," explained Nik.

Sid admitted that there might be a little of that, but it'd be fun!

Oh boy, thought Nik.

John was good with it, as he was quite the outdoors sort; he fairly regularly fished and hunted, worked with the scouts, and such. Nik, on the other hand, well, not so much. He loved the outdoors between twenty-five and fifty-five degrees Fahrenheit with little to do but hang out, collect firewood, make campfires, and eat things cooked over said campfires. Yes, Nik was *not* the Daniel Boone or survivor-man type; weirdly and bizarrely resourceful, mind you, but mountain-man-like—absolutely, positively *not.*

Sid just laughed, "C'mon. Ask the towers for a couple of days in the fall, and let's do it!"

John smiled, Nik sighed, and Sid went on his merry way. John slapped Nik on the back, "Well, you're in it now!" And with that, he laughed—*a lot.*

Nik yelled, "Well, weapons practice, bacon, steak, and campfires are good! What could be bad about that, right?" He waved to his friends as they drove away.

... 2 ...
Life Rolls on and Best-Laid Plans...

THE TRIO MOVED FORWARD on planning for the outing, and life was just one day following the next. Nik continued looking for work, Sid and John continued to hate what they were doing for work, and they complained about all of it as an ongoing conversation. In those typical days, weeks, and months moving forward, Nik would tinker with ideas he had for all sorts of things involving a new career or a revolutionary way of doing something, anything in the hopes of generating an income. He believed that things like generating power, locally defeating the effects of gravity, getting rid of houseflies, and eliminating the gnats outside should be trivial and very easy. After failing on all of those endeavors, he screamed, then chuckled, and then moved on to other annoying points of life that continued to constantly buzz around him.

The news of the day had the United States moving toward a socialist/Marxist type of government and environment with bigger and bigger government and less and less freedoms for its people. The rhetoric that said Americans weren't intelligent enough and needed the government to take care of everything for them bothered Nik to the core. Sure, he wanted folks to get help when in need, but assistance to the point of dependency was simply a crime, and he believed that human nature meant people tended to accept the easy way out.

Nik wondered what the founders of our nation would think at our clear abandonment of the Constitution and the ideals for which it was written. "The Rule of Law" and "We the people" had become ideas that the present Democrat and Republican parties had blurred by a socialist-progressive movement that encouraged segregation and separation of classes instead of the American approach of freedom for all. Yes, the ideals had stumbled in the last 234 years, but by 1900 or so, things were on the way to being just wrong. Theodore Roosevelt and Woodrow Wilson began the Great Progressive Movement and set the United States back sixty years in many social and political aspects. Wilson resegregated our military and used the ideas of separating the classes for devious purposes where the socially and intellectually elite would rise to save the poor, unintelligent folks from their "own stupidity."

Taking advantage of the next fifty years after Wilson, the progressives used crisis after crisis to promote their agenda and warp constitutional America. All through this, Americans rejected the efforts of the progressive movement as best they could, but in the end, a little piece of the contamination stuck; over time, it grew. The free-market system promoted diversity, growth, and religious freedom. Yes, some individuals or businesses might fail, yet anyone had the chance to do, to figure out, and to prosper. Nik searched for a way to make a difference and failed at that as well—over and over again.

```
John: So when we going?
Nik: where …
John: Boys' outing?
Nik: oh, I don't know
Nik: when's good?
John: C'mon, it's November …
Nik: Well, at least we won't be hot!
John: Well, get with Sid and let's go!
```

As much as Nik hated to maintain the idea of the trip, he knew Sid and John would really enjoy it. Besides, it was only for a few days, it would be cool and dry outside, how bad could it really be?

North and South Carolina's western foothills would be nice this time of year; all the leaves would be off the trees, meaning they'd have great visibility of the hills and valleys. Nik also dreaded the ribbing his wife would give him, because she and the kids loved to camp and constantly had to deal with his resistance to it. He knew she would laugh at him for sure.

```
Nik: Yo
Sid: Yo
Nik: So, John wants a date for the
     outing
Nik: when's good?
Sid: Um, I dunno … late in the year now
Sid: After Christmas probably
Nik: K … I will look at the calendar
Nik: Jan 14-18?
Nik: yo
John: yo
Nik: Jan 14-18?
```

Nik finally heard back from the guys sometime later.

```
Sid: Sure, clear from the Tower
John: K, good date, let's go.
```

"Crud," Nik quietly sighed. Yes, his wife and kids laughed at him for about two and a half weeks.

... 3 ...
Off We Go ... Oy!

IT'S AMAZING WHEN SOME simple things are planned how weirdly they get screwed up and sent off course. It took the boys six months, after all the discussion, to finally figure out when and where to go "enjoy" the outdoors and to actually go do the activity.

Nik didn't have issue with all of this, but the thought of camping or being outdoors for any amount of time, whatever the weather, kind of drove him to retch. Yes, a campfire was great! It was great as long as at the end of the day he could go inside, have a hot shower, drink a nice, cold soda, watch a football game in a nicely temperature-controlled room, and sleep in a comfy bed. After all, it was the year 2010, for God's sake!

Alas, the dates arrived, and they were off. Sid was driving, and they plotted a course for an area of gorges and craggy terrain in northwestern South Carolina.

"Dude," Nik said, "how the hell did you pick this place out?"

Sid laughed and explained that it was an area with open camping, hiking areas with some cabins, and the ability to have and target-shoot at an outdoor range in the woods. Nik just shrugged. They all laughed at the amount of stuff that was in the vehicle. There were plenty of packs, certainly too many for the few days they would be out for, but let's face it, these guys were not seasoned long-distance thru-hikers who would be on a trail for six months. They were going to a cabin with the ability to pile their extraordinary amount

---

of provisions up and spend as much time as they needed sifting through it all to find whatever they needed and ignore the other 90 percent they didn't need. They had the ability to carry one-quarter of the junk they packed that would never be a necessity.

Sid announced, "Better more than less." Again, they all laughed.

Sid, being most concerned with the firearm fun, added, "Plenty of guns and ammo for a boys' weekend!" He figured that it would be a good opportunity to use all the partial packs of rounds he'd had for the past fifteen years. "It's like spring cleaning," he explained.

John had thought about bringing his hunting rifle, but they weren't really going to be able to hunt exactly. Instead, he bought some ammo for use with one of the automatic rifles Nik or Sid had included in the mix. Nik, having only a few weapons, brought them all—two rifles and his .45 caliber pistol—along with all of the ammo he had for days of range fun. Included in the assortment of supplies was cleaning equipment for all calibers of weapons; Sid was a little—how should we say?—relentless when it came to keeping his weapons clean and in good working order. Nik had always figured that modern alloys would be fine for the time, a very long time really, and it wasn't like they were going to shoot through thousands upon thousands of rounds of ammo. Nik had good intentions that were fairly valid, but, as always, Nik defaulted to Sid for the knowledge on *all* gun stuff.

During the ride, John pulled out a new GPS he had purchased, and he fiddled with it for a while. "What's going on with that thing?" Nik yelled back to him. "Is it working?" He said that because if a computer geek was messing with something for that long, it wasn't right. Nik knew it was the final straw when the instruction book hurriedly appeared out of nowhere with a frustrated snarl at the same time the word "dammit" raged from John's general direction.

Yup, things had gone from bad to worse. Just then, Nik wondered why they were headed the way they were. "Dude, how the hell are you getting down there?" he finally asked Sid.

Sid, expecting this from Nik, said, "This way. It's where John's GPS said to go."

"Um, have you noticed that the gizmo of topic is now in pieces?" asked Nik.

Just then, John piped up. "No, it's all good ... back in perfect working order!"

"Let me see that thing," Nik snapped as he grabbed the GPS and turned it on. He expected to see something in North Carolina pop up on the screen. Instead, he quickly explained that according to what he was looking at, they should be comfortably in downtown Toledo right about now.

Sid burst out laughing, and John yelped a very loud, "Huh? Give me that thing."

"Just kidding, just kidding," cried Nik. "We're good."

They were heading down I-85 south into Greenville, South Carolina, and from there, they would head west then west/northwest up into the hills. Along the way, everyone had commented on what they knew of the area—big sports truck plant, all the financials in the Charlotte area, historical sites that abounded just to the north and south of their route, and, of course, places to eat. They had packed plenty of packaged things such as beef jerky and chips, and as standard fare, Sid insisted on a fine selection of MREs. Nik and John chuckled a bit at the thought of crunching on an MRE and agreed to make them a special reserve for Sid. A cooler was present with all the finer items of a good campout—steak, hot dogs, more steak, a few eggs, and bacon, and yes, more steak. A "suitable meal" stop was in order for any good boys' outing, so before they headed off any of the main roads, a good steak house was found, and linner (a combination of *lunch* and *dinner*) was ordered.

The meal was grand, and a large amount of time was spent discussing what had been packed for the four-day escapade. The sampling of household items was impressive, and Nik and John were duly impressed how all these items were actually included as Sid reiterated that the details were top secret.

"Um, what the hell are you talking about?" blurted Nik. He continued to ponder and invent items in his mind that could be magically dehydrated and stored for later use; a simple drop of water would be all you needed to reanimate the item to its full, usable size and stature. Belly laughs and a continuation of the general foolery had begun to draw looks and sharp shrugs from the surrounding tables. Okay, it was like they were a group of college sophomores goofing around in their college town's local establishment; Sid and Nik remembered that from their days in college. Today, as thirty- and forty-somethings, they tended to want to go offer some fatherly advice to such "deviants." Oh my, how things change with time.

Sid continued on with a myriad of other conversation headers, including the surprises he had for the trip. Nik wondered with a raised eyebrow, and John, who was so easygoing, simply nodded and said, "Cool." Sid was already showing some signs of life outside the compu-bubble he called work. Work for everyone had been increasingly difficult as the economic times progressed into a complete disaster, except for Nik, that is, who had been out of a job for a very long time. His struggle had been more emotional than situational. Where Sid and John had been bent by the winds, pressure, and weight of the ever-increasing workload and requirements of their respective positions, Nik had existed in the vacuum of human resource hell—a realm of try this, try that, and maybe they will hire … oh, that position has been cancelled. It was all Nik could do to keep from screaming at the online job boards every day—oh wait, he did scream at the online job boards every day.

John, who had not yet loosened up in the brief time he had been away from his medical IT hell, should also certainly benefit mentally by time away from peers and managers yelping about this or that. Sid and Nik hadn't spent too much time in the outdoors, not that four days counted as any kind of extended period of time, but it was more than they would usually think about. John went on regular camping outings with his kids, so this outing would be a walk in the park.

John inquired, "So about the range this place has—"

Sid quickly interrupted.2 "It should be great, it goes out to seven hundred yards, I believe, and there will probably not be a soul around!"

Nik, like a smart-ass, added, "Yeah, it'll be like an empty golf course, which is the only way to play golf, by the way." He was being serious. There was nothing more frustrating to Nik about playing golf (other than his actual golfing ability) than being rushed through the golf course by some country club snob who lives, eats, and breathes the game and believes he/she owns the very blades of grass beneath your feet.

This spawned the conversation about the range Sid and Nik would go to in central North Carolina to shoot. It was a nice place, and there weren't too many people around to bother you or hold you up. A lot of older gentlemen, veterans of America's wars abroad with great stories and a desire to try anything new might turn up at the range. Sid owned a lot of the firearms these guys had used in previous wars, and Nik had the Beowulf, which always spurred a smile from the old guys.

"I've shot every gun that has ever come to this range, but I never shot one of those," they would say with a smile. And then they'd add, "Can I fire a couple of rounds through it?" You could hear the "pleeaaase" sort of trail out of the wind. Nik always said, "Sure. Take a few shots."

Nik was happy to have the good interaction with the older military folks; it made him feel like he was helping out somehow. John, unfortunately, hadn't been able to go to the range with Sid and Nik, so this should be a great getaway for him.

"Okay," said Nik, "let's get this show on the road." His tone, however, sounded as if he meant to say, "Oh, Lord. Let's get this thing started, so it can end."

The other guys knew his tone and laughed about it. Nik was one of those guys who dreaded most things until he got involved in whatever it was. Then he was okay for the most part. Sid and John knew their friend very well and knew what to expect from him. Nik was the common thread, friends with Sid and John from different jobs, and he was hoping this outing would get Sid and John a bit closer.

"You can't have enough good friends," Nik proclaimed as he struggled to get out of the booth at the steak house. "Note to self: as an aging and overweight American, let's get a table next time!"

Sid and John chuckled as they paid the bill and proceeded back to the truck. "Onward and upward!" Nik commanded.

... 4 ...
Are We There Yet?

THE ARRIVAL AT THE cabin area was smooth and eventless; the roads were in good repair and clear of any traffic. The cabin was right where it was supposed to be, outfitted with a campfire ring, picnic table, lockable cabin door, and garbage cans with the proper bear-proof covering. There was a trail labeled "spring" with a blue arrow headed down a dirt path to the west and another trail labeled "Devil's Bald" pointing up past the spring trail toward one of the surrounding hilltops to the north. Additionally, a third trail clearly headed off to the southwest, and the boys found it odd that it wasn't marked.

Nik bounded a few feet down the unmarked trail and came back with the simple report, "Well, it's dark and steep."

"Whatever." John shrugged. "Maybe it's an old trailhead that doesn't actually head anywhere anymore."

"Well," said Nik, "we'll have the next four days to look around. Let's get all this stuff unpacked."

Sid already had half of the provisions and goodies out of the truck and was way too excited for any normal computer-type who had found himself out in the woods.

"Is he always this way?" John asked Nik.

Nik replied, "Only when he is being sneaky."

"Oh boy," gasped John.

"Not to worry," said Nik. "I am sure it'll be good, whatever he's got up his sleeve. It takes a lot to get him going like this these days. Whatever it is, he'll be really happy to pull it off."

"Now I'm scared," said John as he smiled and carried the cooler out of the truck.

As it neared six o'clock in the evening, the guys had finally emptied the truck of its contents and had everything arranged out in the cabin. "Geez, guys, what the hell are you expecting up here? A war or something?" John was commenting on the assortment of arms he was looking at and the amount of accompanying ammunition.

"Well," said Sid, "I had a lot to clean up, and you're looking at all the odd packs and boxes of ammunition I had lying around. Anyway, some of that is for Nik's toys."

"Yeah, yeah, go ahead. Blame the novice," blurted John. It was an assortment that would impress any Special Forces folk, and it was all in the name of finally cleaning up Sid's collection. John smartly asked, "And how, pray tell, are you going to carry all this to the range?"

"Well, *we* are all going to carry it, and I have a surprise to facilitate just that chore!" proclaimed Sid.

Nik had begun working on the campfire (his favorite camping thing to do) while the other two were chatting back and forth and straightening up some stuff. Nik had combed the perimeter for some sticks and firewood with good results and had pulled out some of the bacon to "test" the fire with to see if it was a good enough campfire to work with. It was really an excuse to break out the bacon and get a jump on breakfast.

John came out and commented to Nik about his "cannon," referring to the Beowulf rifle. "What the hell does any of us need with that?" he asked.

Nik just chuckled and said, "I dunno, but it was a good deal, and it puts very nice, crisp half-inch holes in paper targets! You never know what you'll need when you need it."

John responded, "True, but geez—it's overkill. Don't you think?"

At that moment, Sid strolled out of the cabin donning his new surprise—an all new camouflage getup with all the bells and whistles. It had more pockets than anyone had ever seen. Sid proclaimed, "This forest/jungle camouflage, fully reversible to desert/dry-grasslands scheme gear has enough pockets to carry everything and anything we would ever need for a month out in the woods. At this moment, I am carrying almost a thousand rounds of ammunition, and you can't even see it. Plus, I can barely feel the weight of any of it!"

He was correct; the clothing was reinforced with a zero-weight composite banding system that distributed the weight so evenly that it really looked like the provisions weren't even there. The clothing totally supported all the weight and the bulk of the provisions. "Would you believe that I am basically 75 percent loaded?" Sid added as he began to run around and jump up and down just as easily as anyone normally would.

"Nice!" said John. Nik was also impressed, as none of them were in any kind of shape to crisscross around the place like Sid was currently doing, let alone with all the weight he was carrying on his person.

"That's not all," said Sid. "I have a set for each of you just like this one—ranger hat, boots, pack, and all!"

"Have you lost your mind?" Nik blurted.

Sid laughed and proclaimed, "If we are going to have a boys' outing, let's give it a theme! If we are going to burn through all of my hoarded bits and packs of ammo, let's do it in style!"

"Oh my God," Nik sighed. "He has lost his mind after all."

John simply said, "Cool," and followed with, "So where did you get these instruments of manly packing-ness anyway?"

Sid quietly explained that, "These little gems are *top secret*, and if I told you where I got them, I'd have to kill you."

Nik yelled, "Oh my God! You're insane." With that, he began to counsel John that Sid, at times, could be the king of cliché.

"Well, you know a man has his sources!" cried Sid.

"So when do we get our secret spy, special forces, super hero outfits, Sid?" inquired John.

"Soooooooooon," said Sid. "Ooohh … ooohh, something else! Hold on!" Sid blurted as he dug into another pack he had tucked away the evening before. "Check these out!" And Sid produced two sets of identical radios.

They looked like the typical handheld radios that had fifteen or twenty channels and were great for all sorts of outdoor events. With a sound of a letdown, John noted, "They look like the radios I bought my kids last year."

Sid sprung from his position and said, "Precisely! That's what they are supposed to look like!"

Nik interjected. "Oh brother."

Sid went on to explain that the little radios could transmit, receive, and scan millions and millions of frequencies, *all* in the military bands of the world. "These little babies aren't your average camp, eco-tree-hugger playthings, no sirree," he chuckled.

John and Nik just looked at each other and simultaneously gasped, "Cooooool!"

Sid had certainly pulled out all the stops for this outing, and he spent the next several hours smiling and laughing at all the items he was showing to the boys and proclaimed, "I am already feeling more relaxed!"

Nik had gone back to the cabin with a chuckle and started a small fire in the fireplace, as he expected the temps to dip down to around freezing after seven or eight o'clock that night. He watched Sid unpack all sorts of things onto the bench that was meant for a fourth and fifth bunk. The cabin actually had bunks for ten people and was really a good-sized place. The provisions used all of the spare bedding areas for piling and categorizing their junk, supplies, and everything else. Again, the enormity of all they had brought was beyond explanation or belief.

It seemed like each item was neatly covered by two of the three compatriots, and Sid was thrilled. "Listen, this will give me a great opportunity to really plan and configure where to put all this stuff!" he said.

Nik and John looked over at him and wondered what the hell he was thinking and where his mind was going. "So, you got a plan, man? Um, we are going to be here for a few days?" commented Nik.

"Yes, I know," said Sid. "But listen, how cool would it be to get *all* of this arranged and normal supplies set in our packs and onto our persons. You … we would be set and ready for anything! We could just leave everything intact, forget getting our stuff back to whoever; we'll just replenish it all whenever. We'll tell the wives we fell in the lake or something." Sid continued to ramble.

They all started laughing, "So your plan is to get everyone all set up with part of everything here, so we all are as completely 'battle ready' as possible? Completely outfitted with whatever we could possibly need?" asked John.

Sid calmly and authoritatively proclaimed, "Yes."

"Okay," said John. "Cool."

Nik laughed and recognized his friend Sid using this type of exercise as a form of unwinding, and Nik explained to John of Sid's OCD-type way of "working out the demons."

It was Sid's intent to have every member of the party have basically some of everything they had brought, and they brought plenty. The total cache of supplies included many forms of normal everyday things you would find in the modern medical/first aid kit—pain relievers, anti-inflammatory tablets, allergy medication, sinus medications, antibiotic creams, and cold tablets by the bottles; there were even medications for back pain and serious pain.

"So, who brought the serious pain meds?" Nik inquired.

John smiled and said, "Well … I have back stuff sometimes, and when it goes bad, really bad, one of those things and like ten hours of sleep takes care of it very nicely."

"Okay," Nik said. "Sounds good. My wife can throw her back out sneezing."

John responded, "Oh, I've done that!"

Sid started back into the conversation. "You know, once I get this stuff situated in the pockets and packs, all you guys will have to do is keep updating the meds and refill the consumables, and you'll have the setup forever."

"Or until I get too damn round for the clothing," grunted Nik. The group sighed and sank a little on the unfortunate reality of an ever-larger, growing population. Other items Sid had to work into the "system" included the items from the all-purpose range bag, including field cleaning items and post shooting wares. The final component of "other miscellaneous items" included some of the nonperishable food stuffs, small building and construction items (rope, string, and small wooden dowels), small blades, small tools, and the list went on. Ammunition was located on all persons and in surprising quantities—all dispersed for evenness of weight and balance.

The backpacks Sid had as part of the garment set were made of a similar build and material. What would appear to be metal-type ribbing (actually a composite Poly-Kevlar-Boron mix) supported the sleek shape of the pack and gave it great strength and support. The amazing thing about the packs was the dimensions of the packs themselves; only around two or three inches thick, the packs covered the whole of the individual's back and partially wrapped around his sides. Nik, on a quick glance, figured the approximate volume to be something around sixteen or eighteen cubic feet, give or take a cubic foot. That was a lot of carrying volume, and Nik hoped Sid didn't fill the packs, as there was just no need for it all to go walking around with them. The larger items went into the packs along with some ammunition, canned items, a larger blade, and just everything else they carted out with them that would fit. Nik was tired, John was tired, and Sid was on a mission. Nik and John turned in, while Sid plotted and planned the packing for the "mission."

... 5 ...
Let's Go

THE GUYS WERE IN no great rush to wake up. They were up early by most standards for a weekend, but 7:45 a.m.—no big deal. Nik looked up and asked Sid, "So ... how long were you up?"

Sid groaned, "Eh, I saw 3:10 a.m., and then everything got kind of fuzzy after that."

Nik also groaned, "Oh, man, three and a half hours of sleep. Dude, you're going to be dead tired today."

Sid simply said, "Nah." And then he got up to go work the fire and get all his toils from the night before laid out for the others.

John sat up and said, "What are we doing here again?" and laughed.

Nik fell back down and proclaimed, "Um ... don't say that." And then he quickly added, "Bacon!" With that, the day had begun.

Nik rolled out of the bunk and went to help with the bacon; he liked it chewy and didn't trust Sid to not cook it to a piece of carbon. John was the last to rise and was fairly lethargic, which was uncommon for John; he was quite the outdoors enthusiast. He awoke and was soon up and about, hurriedly getting over to the cooking area to join the fun. Conversation revolved around the day's hiking destination and what firearm they would choose to fire first.

John explained, "I'll shoot whatever ... you guys and your military motif."

"What are you talking about?" Sid gasped as he shouldered his railed out, laser-sighted, flash-suppressed, and heavily compensated M1A rifle.

"I don't know what you're talking about," Nik added as he also armed himself with something that John couldn't exactly identify the day before.

John asked, "What the hell is that? I can almost—no, I can put my ring finger down the throat of that barrel!"

Sid jumped in and proclaimed, "That, my friend, is a nicely tricked-out, .50 caliber semiautomatic rifle, fondly known as a Beowulf rifle."

John simply rolled his eyes and replied, "Ah, yes. So that's the rifle you were talking about." *Who and what army do they think we are going to engage here in the middle of nowhere?* he wondered to himself. He only thought this, as he didn't want to take the fun and joy Sid and Nik were clearly having with their Rambo moment.

Breakfast was a feast—bacon, coffee, English muffins and butter, sweet rolls of some sort, and more. The group didn't stuff themselves exactly; they just ate enough to slow their departure way down. After a few minutes, Sid told his compatriots of a small headache that he just noticed but assured them that it was small and was no big deal. After a few more minutes, the time had arrived to don the "Rambo outfits," as John called them, and be off on their adventure for the day. Sid had laid out the gear with great care and great detail in line with what everyone had for provisions. All sets of gear had been thoughtfully prepared with amounts of supplies and ammunition, divided out in accordance with the weapons being carried or used by each person.

Nik approached his gear with an OMG (oh my God) moment; he wasn't really into playing dress up. This wasn't really dress up, per se, and he knew that, as he really appreciated Sid's good intentions. He certainly didn't want to be a killjoy; he just figured they would scurry over to someplace to shoot, have some fun, and wander back and have dinner or whatever. *Not a big deal*, he thought to himself. *Put the stuff on, go with the flow ... have fun and don't worry about anything.* Nik had traditionally been what most might call a stick-in-the-mud, a conservative, unadventurous type who was certainly not happy or comfortable being outdoors and doing "weird" things. Sid, who had known Nik for many years, knew this and reassured him, saying, "Dude! Try it…. You'll be amazed!"

Nik shrugged and conceded, "Okay, man. Here I go."

Sid continued to reassure him, "Trust me; you'll love the new duds!"

John, on the other hand, was very intrigued and jumped into the task of suiting up. He quickly put on the fatigues that Sid had supplied, began fitting the ties, and making sure all the proper adjustments were made. "These are amazing!" he exclaimed.

Sid informed him that he was wearing more than ninety pounds of gear and asked how it felt. John said with a grin, "I can't even feel the weight. I mean, I feel some weight but not ninety pounds!" John was in disbelief until he started rifling through all the pockets and attached satchel pouches. He found things he knew and other things he did not. "I have rounds that I have no idea what gun they even go to," he proclaimed and laughed.

Sid quickly injected. "Well, that information is part of the 'need to know basis' category!" Sid continued explaining to the others that his gear weighed in at around one hundred fifteen pounds, and Nik had around ninety pounds as well. Nik looked up and weakly protested, mildly inviting Sid's, "*Trust me!*"

Nik grumbled, "Okay, okay." John and Sid laughed.

Sid knew that Nik kind of hated the entire new clothes thing, and he understood Nik's annoyance. Yet, he knew Nik would have a fine time once he engaged and embarked on the fun. Sid tried to get John to help as well, but John had no idea what the problem was. Sid just explained, "That's just the way he is."

Nik finally got his gear on as John jovially laughed, "Man, what war is waiting for us to show up to?" Nik, now feeling better about it all, was very comfortable with the entire new outfit on his person.

Nik proudly announced, "This *is* amazing! I can't believe it…. It almost makes me feel strong!"

"I told you," said Sid.

"Yeessss! He told you," yelled John.

To which Nik responded, "Yeah, yeah."

Once again, huge amounts of laughter rose around the campsite.

Nik looked through his pack, pouches, satchels, and pockets, intently identifying where his ammo was and how much he had before moving it to positions that suited his accessibility needs.

John noticed this and inquired, "Does it make a difference where your ammo is?"

Nik responded with an uneasy grin and a longer-than-expected pause, "I guess not ... just seemed like the thing to do."

"You're crazy!" John blurted out before turning to tell Sid about the observed actions of Nik.

Sid looked at John and said, "Really?" John nodded. Sid chuckled and said, "It's nothing. It's just Nik; you know how he is." John shrugged, and went about collecting the last of his stuff.

"Nice touch, Sid. All the items will stay dry in their own little water-tight bags. Good thinking!" Nik continued.

"You're right, you know. Sweat can ruin something as fast as rain, and the packs are waterproof as well," Sid informed them.

The group made their way to the trailhead and looked at each other. Sid asked, "So what do you think?"

John proclaimed, "Let's get going!"

Nik paused and looked at the three of them and muttered under his breath, "We look ridiculous!"

Sid walked ahead and shouted with a smile, "I heard that."

A few minutes later, Nik inquired, "Sid, how's the headache?"

Sid, a bit up the trail, waited for Nik to catch up and told the pair that it was still there. Nik wasn't too concerned and blamed Sid's all-night setup shenanigans as Sid chuckled and said, "Not to worry." Nik asked Sid if he had taken a couple of pain tablets. "Yeah, about an hour ago, and by the way you sound like my mother," Sid replied as he held his head and smiled slightly.

They hiked on, and the views were stunning! A foliage-free landscape allowed them to see all of the hills, most of their features, and a huge amount of details that are rarely spotted during the rest of the year. The boys stopped a lot to look at the views and, well, rest a lot. The three were very quick to point out they were just out-of-shape, middle-aged computer slobs and that the loads they were carrying weren't the problem. John explained to the group that his gear was so well supported by the setup of the pack and garments that it had to be their state of physical fitness; they all agreed—they were horribly out of shape.

Nik reminisced out loud about the thoughts many years ago of potentially performing a thru-hike of the Appalachian Trail with his wife. Those thoughts of so many years ago were met with shrugs and moans, because they understood such a trip would mean hiking more than two thousand miles; none of them could imagine anything like that kind of physical dedication these days. The elevation was increasing, and the terrain was getting a bit steeper and more challenging. As they walked on, Sid and Nik had stopped and were quickly joined by John; they were looking at their campsite from a much higher vantage point, and Sid pointed out an old trail and where it led. The old trail moved off to the southwest and from this high point revealed its jewels—a series of caves, gulches, and gorges. In unison and with excitement, the three exclaimed, "That's where we are going tomorrow!"

Nik spent the next few minutes rubbing his eyes and proclaimed, "Damn, they aren't as good as they used to be."

Sid thought this very strange, as Nik had always had excellent vision. "Weird, Nik, you having issues with seeing the distance. You damn near have the eyes of a test pilot."

John needed some clarification on that and shrugged. "Huh?"

"Yeah, at one point he tested like 20-8 and 20-10 eyesight. He could pick out objects from, like, thirty miles away practically," Sid explained.

Nik piped up, "Just had them checked, and they were as good as always. Dunno what's going on today. Maybe it's because of weird sleeping conditions? Too much moisture as a result of sleeping outdoors? Who knows."

"So," Sid asked, "I wonder why the bald we are supposed to turn right at is referred to as Devil's Bald?"

"Good God," Nik responded. "There could be a million reasons why it's called that. Could be witch lore, elf lore, crazy religion lore ... Who the hell knows?"

John, who was walking right next to Nik, asked, "What did you say?"

"Huh?" Nik asked, perplexed. "You know—witch lore. You are right next to me. Didn't you hear me?"

"Yes … well, no," a confused John muttered. "Must have water in my ears from when I washed my face or something."

"Maybe we are gaining in elevation. You need to pop your ears or something?" Sid queried.

Nik followed that up with, "Nah, we certainly are not gaining that quickly to do that to your ears. I tell you, it's from sleeping outside!" The boys noted the ever-growing number of "who knows" and medical questions and comments piling up on the day and wanted to end that streak right away!

"Okay, guys, let's regroup a bit," Nik blurted out. "Shake out all the cobwebs. Let's try and focus on what we are doing. Sid, where the hell are we going again?"

Sid looked at the trail map and said, "Over there," as he pointed up the trail. "About two miles … kind of up and over the bald and just a little to the west. We'll find Tracers Trail. It'll bring us right to the range."

"Okay, let's get going," mumbled all three members of the group.

A mile farther up the trail, there were more places to stop and look at the surroundings. All was going well at this point with the gear and the hike, but the pesky problems with headaches, blurry vision, and dramatically reduced hearing continued and worsened. Both John and Nik were claiming that the surroundings had begun to darken; Sid didn't notice that but was really struggling with his headache and sat down for a bit as he held his head.

"Apply gentle pressure to your temples and the base of the back of your head. It has worked for me in the past, a kind of acupressure that seemed to work on some occasions," Nik suggested.

At this point, the boys were secretly, independently thinking it might be wise to head back to camp, chill for the day, and try again tomorrow. Nik, wanting to make Sid feel better about the situation, said, "Well, honestly … we are not in great shape, but I'll tell you I am not feeling the effects of the load we are carrying. Something else is going on." Sid appreciated that, especially from a normally grouchy Nik, and agreed; something just wasn't right.

"So weird," they mumbled and discussed, and then everything subsided. Sid stood up and felt a bit better—not perfect, but better.

Nik, after shaking his head a few times and having a sip of water, seemed to get a grasp of his senses. Jon simply stood up and said, "Okay, I'm good." So they continued up the trail.

Hiking on for around a mile, they found more spots from which to view the scenic vistas of the surrounding hills and felt they had passed the odd problems. Now they were jovially conversing about blasting targets and plinking various iron and metal objects set out to provide more audio verification of their hits. They had the gear for a mock three-gun tournament, and supposedly, the shooting area had accommodations for this kind of fun. Pistol, rifle, and shotgun—well, one shotgun. They'd need to figure out exactly how to execute their fun with only the one shotgun.

"Not far now, guys!" yelled Sid from up ahead. They were quickly approaching the bald as they pushed toward the last turn to the summit.

"Devil's Bald," chuckled John. "What possessed anyone publishing a map of an area to name such a thing Devil's Bald?"

"Yeah," added Nik. "Eh, someone was bored one day at the office—who knows." Sid had gone ahead and wanted to reach the bald first for no particular reason, and Nik told John, "Sid likes to be at places first when outdoors and 'on an adventure.' It's like 'king of the hill' kind of fun for him."

As John and Nik rounded the turn, they could see the bald's clearing and the bald itself, but no Sid. *Hmm, maybe he is off in the woods taking a bio break or something,* thought Nik. The two stopped and looked at each other and paused for a second. John yelled out, "Sid! Sid! Where in the hell are you?"

They listened and moved a bit more up the trail, and then Nik froze and said, "Shh ... did you hear that?"

"Hear what?" John inquired shortly and then froze himself.

"Um, what was that? Wait! That was Sid!" blurted John.

The two had heard a ghostly, drowning sound from up ahead. They looked intently and took off running up to the summit of the bald. With no sight of Sid, they went to a full-speed sprint toward the top of the hill and the clearing of the bald.

And that's when it happened.

... 6 ...
Into the Abyss

NIK AND JOHN, MOVING at their fastest possible speed up to the bald, ran into what can only be described as a brick wall. They entered an effect that hit them like a ton of bricks—no light and heavy in density with windless forces that leveled them like a tsunami rolling over a small island in the Pacific. Blackness enveloped the bald, and Sid could be seen on the ground just as Nik and John were flattened by the forces in the effect. Now all the medical issues that the boys had experienced earlier were in full play and absolute.

John was basically completely deaf and speechless from confusion; Sid was on his back and side holding his head in cutting pain, balled up in some form of whole body cramp. Nik was utterly blind and senseless and out of breath from the impact he had taken on the fall to the ground. The boys were themselves a type of light source in the total and stale blackness of the effect. The waves of disturbance in the effect were akin to a strong, dense fluidic wind, but they were somehow electromagnetic or electrostatic in nature and were erratically pushing them around the bald in every direction.

Attempting to pull John, Nik tried to roll to where he thought Sid was positioned to no avail. "Over here!" Sid screamed weakly. Nik, doing the best he could to navigate with John in tow, went in a completely wrong direction. John, just trying to stop his movement, grabbed Nik and tackled him in a forward-moving direction. To those of the boys who had the ability to hear, a sharp and intently loud screeching then moaning bellowed out in the turmoil of the effect. The sound was as if the heavens themselves were being ripped, torn, and mutilated from the very space that was their reality of heaven and earth.

Panic was an understatement as the boys flailed in the hopeless task of trying to control where they were moving in the effect. As luck had it, in John's pushing around Nik, they careened into Sid. With the combined weights of Nik and John added to the cyclonic action within the effect, they very forcefully bounced in a definite direction—one that could be assumed would knock them off the mountain itself.

Boom! A deafening, astral event, audible even by John with his hugely reduced sense of hearing, blasted the boys away from the effect and immersed them in a split second of cerebral super flash of images and sounds and realities, some unseen by man's eyes for hundreds of generations. The events after the deafening crack could only be described as the action of someone force-feeding the contents of twenty thousand movies and documentaries into their minds in the blink of an eye. The audio and visual information was mind-numbing, and after the "playback" or "download" event was complete, the boys' minds were in total shock from the overload.

A silence fell over their senses as if their cerebral circuit breakers had all been tripped. The boys felt immobilized from their brain stems down to their toes, everything tingling now as they lay motionless. It was like death, or an absence of anything, static-electric numbness was all around them. They had apparently hit the ground and were stunned to the point of not even being able to groan. They remained motionless, as if paralyzed, and honestly, none of the three even tried to move. To the boys, it really felt as if their electrical systems were shorted out; nothing in the higher function areas seemed to work, and the three were momentarily good with just "being."

The utter silence of it all yielded itself to a far-off, intermittent, fuzzy booming sound, which, in their state, was hopelessly unrecognizable and without definition or substance. After a time, someone whispered a simple "yo" somewhat unsuccessfully, and then there was silence again.

"Uh," Nik moaned, trying to catch his breath. "No ... move." He struggled to get the words out of his mouth. It was like the breath had been knocked out of him, and he just couldn't regain it. He lay still. Sid heard Nik's grumble and just couldn't respond. John was not heard from, and honestly, the three were out of commission with no comprehensible understanding of their surroundings; they weren't even sure the others were nearby. They were utterly defenseless, immobilized, and unable to do anything about it.

After quite some time, the three were able to slowly pick up their heads and look from side to side. Great relief found them when they were able to see each other and minimal communications was possible. "Um, you guys okay?" John quietly inquired.

"Dunno," whispered Nik.

"Broken bones?" John whispered back.

"No. Sid, you okay?" Nik quietly inquired.

"Uh, I guess. Aches, whole body, head ringing," he offered.

The three were on their backs looking straight up into what was apparently an early evening sky. Sid quietly muttered as he remained very still, "Five o'clock? Five thirty?"

"Looks like it. Dunno," Nik barely whispered now.

John muttered, "Humid? Trees ... wrong?"

The boys fell back into paralysis or sleep or unconsciousness or whatever state they were in, and they just couldn't get out of the funk of whatever had happened. They just lay still and let the effects wear off. Sid had the passing thought before submitting to the weakness of the yet-unexplained event, "What a terrible way to spend our vacation."

Nik awoke to a very unfamiliar sound—the same sound they had heard in their seemingly never-ending paralysis. It startled him, but somewhere in his head he could figure that it was a ways off and probably not a danger. "Clear thought!" he muttered loudly. "I can think!"

John and Sid both whispered, "Quiet."

Nik, still lying down, looked around to the strange reality; the boys were in a very small clearing of underbrush on what looked like a small bluff or ridge (he couldn't tell for sure). Nik quickly figured they had tumbled off the bald and down the side of the hill opposite from where they had run. He tried to roll over in an attempt to get up while Sid and John scooted closer to Nik.

"Quiet, and don't move too fast or too much," Sid proclaimed in a muffled voice.

Nik whispered, "What? Why?"

Sid quickly informed Nik, "We have problems." And helped Nik up only to a sitting position and slowly peeled back a fairly heavy thicket to expose a scene that none of them could explain. "That sound, what is that sound?" Nik asked.

"Shh," John snapped in a whisper. The scene that lay before the three was one of utter impossibility. Nik, not exactly awake, darted his eyes around and looked at exactly where they had rested for the last who-knows-how-many hours.

"It's hot!" murmured Nik. "Where are the mountains? There are leaves on the trees."

"Yes, I know," said Sid. "Try and stay quiet; you took a heck of a hit."

John, now grabbing Nik, strongly whispered, "What is that?" pointing to the scene that he and Sid had unveiled for him to see through the brush. Nik, looking back at the scene, muttered some illegible noises. "Trouble, um, tired ..." And then Nik lay back down.

He did not land well, thought John, as they allowed the thicket to cover over the scene they had been witnessing. That scene needed to be analyzed by all of them, so they were trying to have Nik study it as well to hopefully try and explain what was happening. John figured that it would wait; it had waited this long, after all. *If we only knew how long "this long" was exactly,* he thought to himself.

Sid, no worse for the wear at this point, sat there reviewing his person and what was around him. John, also reviewing the surroundings, noted the immensely thick plant life and forest surrounding them, as well as the intense humidity. They didn't move around too much, but John had located a small stream at the back of the thicket where some plants and grasses were growing. He understood and communicated to Sid the fact that they had somehow moved locations, and it appeared they were somewhat more south in latitude and certainly at a lower elevation than when they had been in the mountains hiking.

John's watch pointed to 7:43 p.m. with a date of January 16. It certainly didn't feel like January, as it was probably around eighty degrees Fahrenheit and quite humid. After a time, Sid scouted a bit more about the thicket and found it to be a defendable and well-covered area, one that they felt they could stay in for a while without worry of being discovered or surprised by anyone. John, also doing some scouting, was looking for items they could use for a very small makeshift campsite—twigs, rocks, and logs that weren't too rotten or wet. He somewhat nervously continued to rummage around when Sid edged over to him. "Yo, man, what's up?" Sid asked John.

"Well, I don't know … we need to get ourselves together," John murmured.

Sid informed John, "Um, we are not where we were. You know that, right?"

John stopped rummaging, looked at Sid, and admitted, "I know." The tension in the air was building; they both knew it and were becoming agitated.

Sid said, "Okay, let's just relax and chill for a bit … or however long it takes." John agreed tensely.

"Charleston," Nik proclaimed sitting up slowly.

Sid and John swung around and in unison asked, "What?" If it were any other time, Nik might have thought it hilarious—not so much this time.

Sid moved over to Nik to inquire about his condition. As he did, John queried, "Did you say *Charleston*?"

"Yes, as in South Carolina," Nik replied bluntly while holding his head.

John quickly whispered, "What in the hell are you talking about, Nik?"

Nik matter-of-factly answered, "I have seen that exact scene in a dozen history books, pictures, and articles." Nik, continuing to hold his head and rub his temples, muttered something about noise and cannons and the British.

John sat back and chuckled, "Landed much harder than we thought, huh?"

"Yeah, I'd think that as well ... but—" said Nik.

"But what?" Sid probed.

"Well, when we got here, the 'booms' we heard ... those were cannon reports from the boats in the harbor."

"Harbor? What harbor!" blurted John. "We are in the mountains. I think we're in the mountains.... Well, we *were* in the mountains." His voice stepped down from an absolutely sure tone to totally unsure meek whisper of his voice.

"Yes, I know all that, and I'm with you," Nik answered. "But look around." His voice sounded understanding and tired.

Sid interrupted. "It is moist here, and we can smell salt air, like we are near the coast."

John agreed. "Like the temperature, the humidity, all of the leaves on the trees—we can't explain any of these facts. It makes perfect sense if we didn't know that a really short time ago we were in the mountains!"

Nik explained that he had been lying quietly for several hours just trying to put together what he was hearing from Sid and John, what they had shown him, and anything else his senses could tell him about their predicament. He apologized to the others for just lying there, as he was now feeling better, although he was still tired and really sore.

Sid and John answered again in unison and in an understanding fashion, "No problem."

Sid insisted. "Okay, we have to stop doing that," and strained a small chuckle. "Okay, listen," he continued. "It's basically dark out now. Should we just stay here for the night and figure out what we should do in the morning, or should we move somewhere else?"

Nik and John quickly agreed with. "We stay here ... at least we know a little of what is immediately around us!"

They were all still very tired from whatever they had been through, so as best they could, the three made makeshift places on which to sleep out of some leaves and others materials from the thicket. They incorporated some of those NASA-made space blankets that had been modified by the military for durability and that Sid had included in each members pack.

"Um, tell me this," John said, "wasn't the British takeover at Charleston in like the 1700s?"

Sid interjected, "Do you really want the answer to that?"

John, now fully realizing what he just asked, quietly whispered, "No."

After a long pause, Nik, not talking to anyone directly or in particular, said, "In May 1780 the Continental Army, ridiculously outnumbered, lost the city in a siege that lasted a bit over a month. Forty-six hundred or more American colonists went missing or were captured—not a good scene."

Sid proclaimed reassuringly, "I'm sure it's something else. Let's just stay put a while, and we'll look at it all with fresh eyes tomorrow in the daylight."

... 7 ...

To Coin a Phrase ... "We Ain't in Kansas Anymore"

MORNING BROUGHT A BRIGHT, clear day with plenty of sunshine, a slightly cooler breeze and temperatures, and a new sound in the distance that was unfamiliar to the boys. Sid quickly knew what the sound was. The three quietly and slowly peered out of the thicket from where they had Nik looking several nights before.

"The sound of people shuffling or marching," Sid said, as he pointed to a not-so-far-off column of people.

John excitedly jumped and yelped, "Oh my God!" He looked through Sid's binoculars toward the city. "Look at the harbor! It is a harbor! The ships! They're Bri—those are Brit—those are British ships!" With that, he fell backward.

Sid's face turned sharp as he attempted to catch the almost-back-lurching John. He took the binoculars from him and looked for himself. *What have we gotten ourselves into?* he thought.

Silence fell on the camp again; each man's mind was running a mile a minute, trying to come up with any logical answer for what they were seeing. "None of this makes sense," exclaimed Nik. "Let's take as long as it takes to figure it out. I'm not even sure where to start, but let's just try and slow down ... don't panic."

A minute later Sid asked John, "You panicked?"

"Yeah, I'm pretty panicked," John responded. Nik agreed.

John, now quite distraught, asked Nik, "So what is the date?"

Nik, trying to think straight, peered out over the view of the line of people leaving the city, the British flags blowing on the ships in the distant harbor, and the city itself. "Um, wow.... I am trying to remember ... early May ... May 8. No ... May 12? Yes! May 12."

A pause yielded the next obvious question, "And the year?" inquired John.

Now a huge pause came from Nik—not because he didn't know or was trying to figure the answer out, but because he was having trouble even saying it. "The year is 1780," Nik slowly responded to his friends.

"There is no way we are sitting hundreds of miles from where we were in the year 1780!" blurted Sid.

"Dude, I am with ya.... I know, what do you want me to say?" Nik complained. "Look at that!" he added, now pointing at the scene displayed before their eyes.

Sid, understanding (hoping) all that Nik was saying was a working theory at this point, responded, "Maybe it's a huge reenactment of—"

"No way," interrupted John. "I have seen those before. This ain't that.... And if it is, they win the award for the best damn reenactment company in the world!"

The intermission between disbelief sessions had the three stowing their space blankets, sharing a single MRE between them, and discussing the situation. It was just incomprehensible to them that they were actually on the verge of settling on the conclusion they were discussing. Two degreed engineers and a near self-made computer genius were actually theorizing that they were somehow transported to the year 1780, just outside Charleston, South Carolina, as the British Navy and Army were taking the city. It was just too much for these guys to accept. They sat, they observed, they sat some more ... and the day went by.

Finally, John spoke up. "Look, as crazy as it sounds, I think Nik is right about when and where we are. I know I am repeating what we have already said, but let's just take as long as we need to figure out what we need to do ... about everything. Okay?" They all agreed, but what were they to do?

The present working theory and the realization of what they were looking at spawned a group-wide request to inventory what exactly they had with them.

Sid proclaimed, "Well, we have everything a very well-stocked modern sundry shop has ... and then some!"

Nik tried to cheer the mood up a notch or two. "That is awesome!" he proclaimed.

Sid continued. "Rifles, ammunition out the wazoo, no shotgun—that's probably lying where I dropped on the bald. Man," he said after a long pause, "that was an expensive shotgun too!" Sid rambled on for a bit with a frown on his face.

John confirmed Sid's findings regarding the contents of their packs and said, "We are good for a bit anyway. Just a ton of medicine tablets, several sewing kits, and some things I can't even figure what they could possibly be for."

Nik, again trying to reassure the group of something positive said, "See. It's looking up already!" In his mind, however, he thought, *Man, oh man, where in the hell are we, how did we get here, and how do we get home?*

Wanting to get his mind off that last thought, Nik asked John, "Hey, man, you have the only manual (wind-up, non-battery-powered) watch here, could you reset the date to May 12?"

"Sure," John responded meekly. "No big deal, but are we really sure we are on May 12 ... 1780?"

Sid was still very intently watching the city and the surroundings and concluded that they were fairly safe on the small bluff or hill or whatever it was they were sitting on. Nik thought that Sid had already reached that verdict before but gave him the thumbs up, giving his full confidence to Sid's assessment. That assessment was, in fact, very correct, and nightfall came quickly with all of the action and excitement. The time had truly flown by with all the deductions and conclusions being formed; they had also calmed down a little as they were trying to convince themselves of some ideas that could be grasped and held on to. There had been no lunch that day, because it had gone by so quickly, so they all shared an MRE for "linner." Nik wasn't hungry at all, and the others were only slightly interested in food, so it didn't take long for them to settle in for the evening.

Lying down now and talking quietly, a plan was forming from the continued observation of the apparent British takeover of Charleston. It was agreed that they had just witnessed the shelling of the city with cannon rounds by flagged British vessels—nothing like the 70mm shells of the modern-day naval ships—and, oh yes, these ships were wooden vessels doing the attacking! They assumed the date to be May 12, 1780, and as ludicrous as it sounded, they were alive and well in the middle of it all. They were concerned for their families and wished they could blink to be back in the cabin on the hillside in January 2010.

They were very concerned about their situation. If, in fact, they had somehow slipped back in time—none of them could even say it—were they ever going to find their way back? Some of these thoughts and questions just couldn't be asked right now.

Nik did ask, "Do either one of you guys know of any high ground near Charleston?"

John smartly responded, "Yes, and we are camping on it."

"Oh, brother," Nik said with a smile.

"Okay, let's get some sleep and get something done tomorrow," Sid replied. The others agreed and turned in for the night.

This night was not a peaceful time. The boys were quiet throughout the night, but the sounds of the events occurring some miles away were very haunting to the group. After all, it was a battle on the mainland of their United States of America. They still weren't even sure "where" they were, let alone "when." When! It was simply crazy to think that "when" was even a question here.

Nik thought about what their next move should be. He vaguely remembered some of the measures the British took after the victory at Charleston. He knew that they set up garrisons in places basically radiating out from Charleston to the north through North Carolina to Virginia, but he was unsure exactly where. Concerns for their very existence now came to mind—food, water, cleanliness, sickness, and the list went on. Were they really in 1780? Really? How did that happen? It clearly had something to do with the crazy experience on the bald, which wasn't something any of them could explain. He figured he didn't want the group to dwell on that, as it wouldn't be productive and could certainly drive them crazy—or worse, apart. The latter being far more of a problem.

No, Nik thought, *if we are in the year 1780, there will be no splitting up of this group … ever!*

Nik knew it would take all of them together to survive this and get home. He figured if they were in or around Charleston and they knew where they had been in the mountains, maybe they could return there and go back to the hills where they tried to go camping—but to do what, he wasn't sure. Further considering the 1780 theory, the theories of time travel, warping time-space, and slipping into neutral space all played in his mind as he hopelessly tried to figure a way out of their situation. Nik wanted to wake up in the morning and tell his compatriots that he had all the answers, but he knew that was simply not possible. Again, he knew it was going to take them all to survive this and get home. He needed to drive that point through to the group in the morning.

Nik, of all of them, knew that he would be the most miserable and the worst of the "campers" if, in fact, they were out in the wilds of nature for an extended period of time. Their lives would be radically different for sure, and if, in fact, they were actually in 1780 with no magical device to get them back home, their lives had already changed in an unnatural and dramatic fashion—one that Nik didn't want to think about. He thought of his kids and his wife, and he was not a happy man; he also hated sleeping outdoors.

Sid's mind ran wild as he lay down on his self-manufactured, "leaves and brambles" mattress. He was also thinking about all that had occurred during the past several days, and his mind turned immediately to the security of the group, hoping his friend Nik wouldn't freak too badly being out in the outdoors, especially if it would be for an extended period of time, which appeared to be the case. He knew his friend well when it came to these conditions and had faith that the severity of their predicament would and/or could keep him on the straight and narrow.

Sid thought about the 1780 theory. Assuming it to be valid, care would have to be taken on all kinds of subjects, and he knew that Nik would be able to help the group through those thought processes.

Sid also knew that John had plenty of outdoor experience—hunting, fishing, and the like—so those areas were covered as well. Sid saw no way out of the situation, except he was unsure of the actuality of the 1780 theory and predicament. *Really? Thrust back in time somehow from 2010 to 1780? C'mon!* he thought to himself.

Sid had hopes of it all being a huge reenactment event, but the odd events leading up to their seeing what they actually saw, and *not* being where they had begun this trip, made those hopes slight at best. It sincerely appeared as if they had slipped through something that moved them away from the mountains and into this warmer, low country climate. He was relatively sure that his family (and the others' families) were okay; this was something that they were dealing with in the immediate moment. In 1780? Who knew? He felt that an assurance on his part would keep the other two in a better frame of mind. Sid didn't know John nearly as well as he knew Nik, but he had the sense that even in these extraordinary circumstances, John would remain fairly calm. He wasn't sure what he thought of it all; he knew that everyone was certainly on edge and, thus far, in a stable frame of mind.

John lay on his side, and as he watched the glimmers of light off in the distance through the brush and brambles, he wondered what he was actually looking at. He was looking at the city they had witnessed getting barraged by what Nik described as "red hot shot," a type of cannon round that did more burning than blunt object destruction. The flicker of the occasional light could have been a campfire or the small fire of a burning building; John didn't know. He knew one thing, though—if that was Charleston, and they were in the year 1780, he was not prepared to deal with any of it. Or was he? Were any of them? After all, they had several rifles and pistols—*modern* rifles and pistols—ammunition up the proverbial yin-yang, and a couple of friends he knew who were wired for this kind of a situation in one way or another.

All those years of strategy games on their computer systems— hours and hours, days and days, over years and decades. They had played these exact types of scenarios. *It's crazy to think about,* John thought. With all that in his head, he suddenly felt quite a bit better *if*, in fact, they just witnessed the actual fall of Charleston in 1780.

Oh boy, John thought, *just imagine the possibilities! Okay, I know outdoor survival; I can help this team survive! I know Nik will certainly welcome that help; he can't stand camping. Oh no! This could send him over the edge for sure!* John's mind reeled. He was sure he could help make an extended stay outside better for everybody. *After all of those weekends and extended three- and four-day stints with a bunch of eight- and nine-year-old Cub Scouts, this should be a piece of cake,* he chuckled to himself. He thought of his family later in the evening and figured they were okay. The group wouldn't officially go missing for some time, if they were even lost at all. Who knows? John figured they would work it all out tomorrow or wake up from this crazy dream. With that, and the grandeur of all he had just spent hours thinking about, John went to sleep.

... 8 ...
The Thicket

MORNING BROUGHT A DAMP moistness that nobody liked. "Yuck," said Nik, "I hate being moist in the morning. I hate sleeping outside! We're still here, huh? Tell me we're all in the same dream—" Nik rambled on.

Sid laughed quietly as he fully expected the immediate complaining from Nik and expressed his entertainment from it all. John went along with Sid, as he knew Nik liked being the humorous complainer. He also knew that Nik, in fact, hated anything and everything having to do with sleeping outdoors and on the ground. John made a small fire, and the three sat around it as Sid siphoned off and filtered some water to make some tea; he had some tea bags in one of his many pockets.

The three enjoyed some hot tea, and Nik joked about not having paid the proper taxes to King George for this spot of tea. Sid broke the ice on the more serious subject after sipping some tea, "So, I see we are still here."

John and Nik nodded, and Nik followed up with, "Yup."

Sid continued. "Soooo, what are you thinking?"

John looked at Nik. Sid looked at Nik. Nik looked up. "Um, why the hell are you looking at me?" Nik asked.

Ten or twenty seconds went by, and John explained, "Well, you're the closest thing we have to Carl Sagan right now, and we

---

need an answer." A pause yielded to a sort of painful chuckle and more sipping of their tea.

"Well," Nik started, "I figure if we are where and when we think we are, then we have some work to do."

"There's an understatement if I've ever heard one!" blurted John, not trying to be annoying. "We need to figure out how to survive, we need to not be discovered for who we really are, and we need to really *figure out* how to get back to where we came from."

Nik immediately thought to himself, *No, really? Idiot! How stupidly profound was that? Idiot!*

Sid quickly agreed, while Nik and John both looked at him with odd looks. "Well, we need to eat, drink, sleep, live, think, and function without dying out here," explained Sid with almost a pleading tone.

"Yes, I totally agree," said John. "It sounds like we are in full agreement that we are now members of the Colonial American people of this, um, country.... Are we?"

Nik moved a little closer to the fire and said calmly and quietly, "For now, we are just us. Until we can get a better look at everything, we need to stay right here where it appears to be safe and somewhat protected and figure the whole living thing out." He looked at John and Sid and continued. "If we *are* in 1780 and *are* just outside Charleston, South Carolina, we need to talk, and I need to explain some detailed history to you guys—if I can remember it all."

Nik continued to look at John and spoke again. "And you need to tell us about living outdoors, hunting, fishing, traps, shelters, not going frigging crazy out here." And then he laughed. "And you, laughing boy," (a comical passage from a cartoon that Sid and Nik often referenced) Nik added as he peered at Sid. "We need a defensive plan; we need to know *all* about the weapons we have and the possible uses of said weapons on possible targets of this time."

"Now you're talking," John excitedly proclaimed.

Nik quickly put his hand out. "No, no, *no*! We have to be super careful not to be seen, let alone become actively engaged by or with any forces—on either side. We have to be ghosts, spectators, souls who must not be seen, heard, or spoken to! We have to stay out of the way of the people and events of this time and not affect so much as a colony of flies." Nik's face was completely red, and he was out of breath from whispering so quickly. "Really," Nik added. "It's so important."

They all understood, and John whispered, "I know, yeah, I know. I was just saying—"

And Nik quickly and gently retorted, "I know, man. I am right there with you. I know the thoughts that have gone through your mind, believe me. I was awake all last night just thinking of the possibilities. It's mind-boggling."

The group talked about their plans and developed a schedule for the next week, dividing up chores and things to do based on their skills and strengths. Time would certainly be spent cross-training the others to get everyone up to speed on what each was weak on. The guys took it easy on Nik, as he had a higher learning curve and lower tolerance when it came to all things outdoors. One thing he could do well was start a fire. Nik employed modern chemistry to get things burning and honestly had nearly twenty ways up his sleeve to get it done. Common items from Sid's packed stores, which all of them had, could be used in various ways to create flame. This was good, because fire was a huge necessity!

One idea Nik tried, which he had read about in some obscure text, was "the aspirin flint" method. It was a miserable failure, but it made them laugh more than once. They deemed it more important to have the aspirin for medicinal purposes more than anything else. John stopped as Nik looked intently at the aspirin he had mangled in the process and seemed to be fixated on for an inordinate amount of time.

"You okay?" asked John.

Sid moved quickly, with some concern, to the others to see what was happening. "Yeah," said Nik. "It's just this aspirin. You know, it won't actually be invented for another 110 years—roughly, you know. It boggles the mind."

Sid let out a Nik-like "oy," and John added a "yup, oy is right."

Nik began to collect kindling, some Spanish moss from the trees, and other things that would burn well as kindling. He found some southern birch that was shedding its bark; it would be great for use as kindling, because it was loaded with oils and a type of flammable waxy coating. Nik, as a habit, always packed a good supply of magnesium shavings. Used in conjunction with a good flint sparker, most commonly used for welding (yes, Sid had packed four of those as well), magnesium could ignite even the dampest of material to create a fire. Some items in their medical packs were also available to create fire; all in all, they were in good shape for creating fire as long as they had enough material to fuel an extended burn wherever they ended up.

The three were forming an intense bond and a great sense of teamwork; they were learning each other's tones and understood the nuances of each other's speech patterns. In their solitude, they were beginning to realize that they were all they had; there was no one in this time to turn to—they were it. The group reiterated the fact that they wouldn't and couldn't ever split up for anything, and that played out over and over in the short time they were there in the thicket.

John had mentioned, "You know, you always see in movies these stupid people saying, 'Okay, let's split up and look for whatever, and we'll meet back here in a certain amount of time.' Stupid! That is stupid!"

They made a habit of checking on one another, continually looking around their perimeter and slightly beyond, not wanting to be discovered or surprised by anyone of whatever period of time this happened to be. They always whispered and were as quiet as possible at all times of the day and night. The protection of the thicket was like their training ground for what might face them in the coming days.

John spent time devising small traps for rodents and varmints. He came up with a type of trip noose that he could use to snare birds on the branches of the trees while they were landing.

"Ingenious!" commended Nik. After all, birds are birds; they all taste like chicken. Everyone likes chicken, and there isn't a bird on the planet Earth you can't eat! John had previously found a stream on the backside of the hill near the back of the thicket, and with Sid's help, they created a small canal and collecting pool fed by the stream that they then directed to the far-right side of their encampment. This was an immense improvement to their living arrangements. In short, John and Sid had quickly and efficiently added running water to their thicket-bound encampment.

John made bows and simple wooden arrows for a quiet form of hunting small prey; he was bound and determined not to have the group go hungry. Nik was overjoyed and very complimentary of all the food-gathering techniques John had been working on. John had also identified edible grasses and berries for something to eat other than meat. Bread and carbohydrates would be a bit of a challenge, and no one was up for the lichen flour, hard-tack-type bread Nik had described in great depth and planned to try. John proclaimed he'd eat his shoe before he ate lichen flour bread. They all agreed, and abandoned the bread idea, even Nik.

Nik laughed and said, "That's fine. Shred the idea of a genius. If you don't want nasty-rock-sticking-lichen-scum-flour bread, see if I care." He sarcastically and disingenuously shook his head. The fact that they were humored through this entire time made Sid feel better about their developing situation. John said he'd figure out a flour source; stone grown and dried lichen was officially out!

Sid had spent his time scouting just a little further outside the thicket, still within sight of the others but just a little beyond the perimeter they'd previously had. He found viewing locations that covered every direction and available elevations. A few of these vantage points were even up some very large trees that were probably a few hundred years old, giving the group the ability to see a little farther in many directions. He deduced that they were about three-quarters of the way up, and basically on, the southeast side of a small hill facing Charleston and the harbor.

"Not that it really makes any difference. We are in 1780. What the hell help is it going to be anyway?" Sid murmured to himself. Nonetheless, he surveyed the entire area immediately outside of their thicket, making sure not to go too far away. Sid remembered Nik's words: "We have to be ghosts, spectators, souls who must not be seen, heard, or spoken to! We have to stay out of the way of this time and not affect so much as a colony of flies."

Sid understood this very clearly, returned to camp after some survey time, and had some water that they had boiled and let cool.

After the slightly extended survey of their surroundings, he began to look over the weapons and provisions. Sid slowly and carefully stripped down each rifle and checked the major parts for damage from the fall they had taken during their initial arrival. He also affixed the two bayonet-mountable knives they had for the rifles.

John, observing this, asked Nik and Sid, "Bayonets? What for?"

"Well, we have them, and we probably don't want to be firing these things off for just any reason," Sid answered. "If we need to, we can stick things."

"Okay, makes sense," John said, satisfied with Sid's answer.

Sid continued his inspection and preparation of the weapons and related his extreme comfort with their load by exclaiming, "Guys, this is great! We have thousands of rounds of ammunition, blades, enough cleaning supplies for a long time, as long as I don't get to cleaning crazy. Honestly, we are all set with respect to firepower." He would fill the team in on what they had to work with later in the day—or week or month, for that matter.

Sid also spent his time setting some perimeter alarms of sorts—snap traps, which would pop or crack to alert them of anything large trying to walk into their Shangri-la. Nik and John asked to see the alarms and their locations so as to not trip themselves by accident—best-laid plans, right? Nik and John would both be found tripping over them several times in the days to come.

With a lot of what he could think of done, Sid sat at the campfire and played with one of the radios he had shown the others. He was the only one who had actually brought one, so the possibility of using them among themselves was out. Then again, they would never be apart far enough to need them, so he couldn't be too mad at John and Nik for forgetting theirs. Knowing there was absolutely nothing to hear on the radio, Sid released the squelch setting and began to listening to the empty airwaves, frequency after frequency, over and over again. It was mesmerizing to him. And then he turned it off. He knew that there was nothing to gain by listening to the scanner, but it connected him through time to a place and epoch he could relate to.

Sid wouldn't believe the craziness they were experiencing if he weren't in it himself. There, on the ground, was a humid, wooded area overlooking a distant city that hadn't existed in this form for some 230 years.

"Two hundred and thirty years," Sid muttered before being startled by Nik.

"Huh? Oh, sorry," Nik exclaimed. "It's okay, man. We are all thinking the same thing, you know."

John wandered over, now joining the gathering. "So what do you think?" Sid asked Nik.

"Well, we're doing okay with food, thanks to John the 'bird god.' Water is okay. Supplies, thanks to you, Sid, are okay. Direction, however, is still up in the air," Nik recounted.

John assured the others that he was sure they would figure something out. Sid added, "Nik, I know your look. You either have or are working on a plan to move us somewhere."

Nik's single raised left eyebrow confirmed that he had indeed been working on a possible plan of action. "Kind of," Nik admitted. "I need to fill you in on what I remember about all of this in the next few days."

There was a short pause followed, and then in a sarcastic tone, John added, "A history lesson! Wahoo ... *not.*" Sid just laughed, but Nik was obviously a little surprised. John reassured Nik, "I'm with you, man. We are in 'it' in a seriously bad way, and we need all the help we can get.... You know me; I want to be as light as possible." John sounded honestly apologetic.

"It's all right," Nik said. "I know you were just trying to help our moods. It's good, and we need that. It'll help our sanity. Don't stop, okay?"

John replied, "Okay," and smiled.

... 9 ...

A Present History ... and What of the Future?

"So," Nik began, "we believe we are in the year 1780. We think we have witnessed the fall of Charleston, South Carolina, to the British, and we have been here for eleven days living ... well, living ... what can I say? So, it's May 23, 1780." A hugely long pause hit the group as Nik waited for someone to say something.

"And what are we doing?" asked John.

"We're living," Sid exclaimed.

Nik, feeling that John would have wanted something more, added, "Thanks to your outdoor skills, John, we are eating and drinking well and not suffering at all." He continued. "Sid, thanks to your ridiculous packing of everything except the kitchen sink in 2010, we will have many modern items, necessities, and comforts we would otherwise not have in 1780. We would have probably and surely suffered badly without them. All in all, we're really not in horrible circumstances." Another long pause from the group lingered through the next several minutes.

The past eleven days had been pretty good for the boys. John, the outdoorsman of the group, had spent much of his time catching things for his group to eat, cooking (he really enjoyed that), and helping keep the mood light. He especially wanted to keep Nik entertained, as Nik was most often buried in a small pad of paper

---

trying to brain dump everything he knew of this time period and the area they were in. Nik's mental strain looked painful, and John (thinking Nik was far too serious about it all) wanted to keep his spirits up. John was accepting the "where" and "when" of the situation and was bound to make the best of it. From the time travel conversations the boys had the previous week, John thought all of what they left behind in 2010 was paused in a sense. He thought of his family, as they all did, and believed in the "frozen future" theory. This kept them all dealing with the fact that they might be 285 miles and 230 years from home.

Sid knew the whole situation was just beyond description, and he too wanted the morale of the group to be as high as possible. He honestly didn't know where to go from here, so he concentrated on the defense of their area and remained vigilant. He created a map of what he could see of the area and ventured out just slightly away from the thicket to get more details. His map was certainly not large by land mass, just a general layout of the very immediate area and some details he felt were important to him in his defense endeavors. Every night he reported to the group anything he may have added that day, including trip lines and piles of sticks, which, if disturbed, could warn them of an intruder. He also made note of any elevations or natural features of the surrounding lands that might be important for them, either to watch from or retreat to if needed.

Nik wanted the others to feel better about the actuality of their situation, and after almost two weeks of trying to figure out how to survive away from, well, home for lack of a better word, he wanted to bring to light their successes and the great job they had done so far. He knew that once the everyday stuff became normal and relatively easy and painless, the reality of their predicament might begin to weigh on their morale and bring them down. The truth was that Nik himself felt pretty worthless through all of this; he certainly tried to help out with the others' endeavors and ideas, at times showing his resourceful attributes. He considered himself a generalist of everything and an amateur historian.

Sid, John, and Nik were now all sitting down. "So ..." Nik began. The looming and charged pause led to the conversation of wanting to know the answer to the looming $64,000 question: "What are we doing, and where are we going?" And they were now looking to Nik for the answer.

"Well, man," Sid said, "you started off with 'so,' and I know that beginning, and I know that tone in your voice. What's our course?"

Nik looked a little surprised at the question, and John quickly interjected. "You know more about all this history stuff, and you have been working pretty hard thinking about it. You have shared some of your notes with me; you really should have been a history teacher. Piss on computers; I think you missed your calling."

"Maybe," responded Nik. "I'm not sure how all the interaction would have made it with kids, though."

Nik unfolded his hands, held his head for a second, and began, "So ..." Sid smiled. "We think we know where we are, and we think we know when we are—not trying to beat a dead horse. I think we need to make our way to the area where we were trying to camp in 2010."

John and Sid shrugged their shoulders and agreed. They each wondered why this hadn't been discussed before today. *Nik clearly kept his thoughts to himself on the subject*, John thought.

Nik continued. "I thought of a bunch of options for us and just couldn't get off this one. I need to go over some historical events, but I think that if we can get back to that area, we can hide out, stay away from the present-day happenings (thereby not affecting the natural flow of time and its events), and live on."

Sid nodded and wondered when one of them was going to ask about getting back to 2010, and then John raised his hands. "So, any ideas how to get back? To 2010, that is?"

Sid laughed, although he knew that he damn well wouldn't have asked that question. "You beat me to it."

Nik laughed, because he also realized that he wouldn't have asked. "Glad you asked that question!" Nik blurted out.

John sat up straight, thinking that Nik had an answer and then slumped back onto his log when instead Nik proclaimed, "First, some history!"

Sid quietly chortled, "Ha!"

Nik asked his compatriots to get comfortable. There were groans from Sid and John. "So," he began for the third time, "the British, after the fall of Charleston, set up lines of defense that consisted of outposts radiating out from the city. The lines from a place called Ninety-Six, South Carolina, past the city we knew as Columbia to a place called Camden, South Carolina." Nik was now drawing a map in the dirt, and a really terrible one at that, to show Sid and John what he was trying to have them visualize.

"These lines didn't take long for the British to form, so we are probably not going to be able to totally avoid them," Nik continued. "The next British line of defense, if you want to call it that, is up near where we were camping over to a place called Cheraw, South Carolina; it's south and west of where we knew Rockingham, North Carolina, to be. So, we have some obstacles to overcome, but I don't think that an army can cover the landscape in 1780 like we could in the Civil War period, let alone in 2010. In my humble opinion, we wouldn't stand a chance in our time avoiding detection, but here and now, we shouldn't have too difficult a time moving unnoticed unless we get careless."

Sid looked at the map and said, "Cool, are there any sites to see along the way?"

John's eyebrows rose. "What are you talking about, Sid?"

Sid continued. "Well, we are in 1780. Maybe we can pick up some historical knowledge for when we get back to 2010?"

Nik's voice got softer, almost a murmur. "Well, there may be opportunities, depending on how long we're here and where we end up."

John continued to inquire, "Like what? You're going to let us know when something is coming up. Right, Nik?"

"Of course. C'mon, man, I want no surprises for any of us. What I don't want is for us to be tempted and get ourselves, and the history we knew, in trouble," Nik explained. "I think we are going to see more than we actually want to see, quite honestly. What we see might dictate a course of action for us; there may be opportunities for research and certainly absorption of happenings and occurrences that no one has seen for more than two hundred years! So for now, we leave in the morning for our 2010 camp area."

"How far was that again?" John meekly inquired.

"Um, my best guess," answered Nik, "is 245 miles, plus or minus twenty or so."

John rolled his eyes, and Sid added, "We have all the time in the world, like 230 years, right? We'll just move at our own pace."

Sid asked Nik about battles they might need to know about as John listened intently. Nik explained that he'd think on that and let them know what he could remember, but he really wanted them to focus on the trip to the 2010 campsite and assured them they'd get the lowdown on all the battles and whatever details he could remember about those battles.

That night was spent stowing gear and picking up their camp in plans to move out the next day. They were all a bit gloomy about that in a way; they were apprehensive about moving out of their little protected zone where nothing seemed to bother them or know they existed. They certainly would return to this site to regroup if any serious problems arose in the next week or so in their travels. This became known as "camp-1780" or "C-80" for short, and likewise, the campsite where it all began in the hills of northwestern South Carolina in their time (2010) became "C-10."

... 10 ...
Set Course to C-10

THE NEXT MORNING CAME early with great anticipation and, honestly, some anxiety. They were leaving their bastion of safety for unknown parts north and west. Needing to know if anyone was around, Sid took a few minutes to check out the area for any Colonials or British, or anyone else for that matter. Over the past days, there had been very little in the way of human sightings of any kind, and all of these were pretty far off with no chance of detection.

There was a natural avenue out of their enclave, and that's the way they planned to leave. So, with an "Okay, let's go!" they were off. Travel was going to be a task they would build up to, and they all knew they would be slow at the start and stopping a lot for breaks. Like the trek up to the bald, they had their rifles on their backs, semiautomatic pistols on their sides, and fully loaded pouches and packs within reach. They were ready for anything, but their physical condition and the weight they were carrying would certainly slow them down for a few weeks until they built up their endurance, stamina, and themselves.

Their course would take them on a skirting path around *any* civilization they might encounter. In the heat of summer, they would try to take advantage of whatever streams or water they could find.

"We need to watch the water routes," Sid pointed out. "Just like us, everyone else needs and wants to be close to the water for life itself." Nik and John agreed and pushed on. They stopped often, looking and listening, making sure of their course, and listening for potential hints of humanity ahead of them. At this point, they were just plain paranoid.

John looked back now at the place they landed and came to realize where they had been. It really wasn't that high up after all. They had actually climbed only slightly, basically about fifty to seventy feet above sea level to where they were now. From this point, they were looking slightly down at their thicket. It was fairly well hidden, even from this vantage point, and they wouldn't have been easy to spot if they had stayed there through the summer months for sure. They were now headed away from Charleston, and for that, they were pleased. The greater the distance they could create between the British and themselves, the better.

Their frequent stops accommodated the out-of-shape men, and they were sure they would be in better shape soon, as they were now headed on a roughly 245-mile hike into the unknown. John huffed and puffed, "Two hundred and forty-five miles, are you kidding?"

Nik piped in with, "Man, you are in twenty times the shape I am. You can do it!" He smiled between deep breaths of air. As time progressed, a few *oys* could be heard from Nik, along with several choice curse words from Sid and John followed by a curse from Nik.

Footing was crucial. They needed to make sure that every step was placed as well as possible with the concern of not twisting an ankle or something worse. They would all stop at various times for a foraging break. At these junctures, John would try to snare dinner, Nik looked at what was of use around them, and Sid scanned for people or threats. They were all pretty pleased on this initial day of hiking, minus the physical exertion and utter exhaustion.

They stopped relatively early when they found a nook in the woods that would make a good overnight camp, and honestly, they were all spent. Nik built a small fire; John had snared a bird and picked some edible items along the way that day. Sid scouted a little distance from their camp to make sure nothing else was around and reported an "all clear" when he returned. They were all hungry; dinner wasn't a feast by any means, but it was sufficient and satisfying.

"I will certainly shed some pounds doing this for the next … who knows how long," Nik commented.

John, probably just waiting for this chance, came out with, "Yes, we can call it the Nik-Sid-n-John Revolutionary Diet!"

This was met with groans of sarcasm from Sid and Nik. "That was just so sad," moaned Sid.

"Yes, I know," John admitted as he put his head down in apparent disgrace and then smiled.

The boys understood there would be days of feast and many more days of famine. They had done well living off the land at the thicket and had some items from their time that they were going to save in reserve for as long as possible in case of an emergency or dire circumstances. They also realized that they were going to get used to sleeping on the bare ground or fabricating quick bedding out of something from their surroundings, as their space blankets were not going to last long with prolonged, everyday use. These went into the emergency item stash on their persons along with any other 2010 items deemed "for use in dire need."

Sid questioned, "What defines 'dire need'?"

Nik shrugged his shoulders. "Well, space blankets for really cold weather and MREs and beef jerky for starvation—that kind of need."

John added, "Makes sense."

"Just checking. Gotta know these things, you know?" Sid replied.

"I know, and honestly, I'd rather eat the bird tidbits John catches. They are just downright tasty!" Nik added.

Sid quickly complemented John and reaffirmed the "bird god" status to him. "Yeah, man, I have to admit, the little buggers aren't bad. They are tasty for sure, but not very big."

John closed the complement session with, "And really easy to clean up for dinner, and that's important. Yes sirree!"

They sat down and laughed as it began to get dark. Nik requested of John, "Hey, man, its May 24. You might as well set your watch to the correct date for us. We can semicalibrate the time come the next equinox or solstice or whatever when it comes around."

John replied with a smile, "Already did—did it yesterday night when we agreed to go on this march."

Sid sat back and commented, "A well-oiled machine—smooth, quiet, and efficient." He also smiled, as if to totally forget about the reality of their situation, or try anyway.

Nik understood his friend's thought process and his ploy for dealing with the bitter realities and went with it, adding, "Let's not get too confident, and let's keep our heads in the seriousness of the arena we are now playing in." With that, he smiled and threw some crumpled-up leaves into the small fire they were enjoying.

As the three lay down to rest before sleep, they looked up at the stars. Nik commented that the constellations looked the same as they did in 2010. He went on to say that it took millions of years for the constellations to move around in the sky. Sid quickly added, "I knew that!" John chuckled. The chatter of their conversation waned off fairly quickly to utter silence as they began listening to all that was alive around them in the cool, early summer evening surroundings. They would make a practice of going to sleep armed, or at least more armed than they had in the past twelve days in 1780.

In the thicket, they were certainly armed and vigilant, but here they felt much more exposed for obvious reasons. They always had their pistols near them, but now each would have his pistol with him as he slept. Sid was good for coverage in the thicket, and again, it just seemed very safe there. The silence was briefly broken as they all quietly conversed about all that had happened, including their brief time in the thicket and how they were now out in the open under the stars, before finally falling asleep for the night.

As tired as Nik was, his head was reeling again in thought, and sleep was not coming easy this first night. He went over his plans in his head, as temporary as they were, based on the unknown nature of what they were hiking into. He wanted to make C-10 in good time but certainly didn't want to rush and/or make mistakes getting there. He was so focused on not disturbing the history that they knew, where any of their actions could change anything of what they knew, it almost drove him crazy. Nik knew he sounded like a broken record to the rest of the group but felt he needed to keep up the awareness as to not grow complacent and sloppy.

The next morning brought overcast skies and humidity. The boys woke up to aches and pains after their first complete day of hiking with their full complement of gear and all the glory of the exercise. Oh yes, and finally a complete day of hiking where they didn't get warped to some far-off year on the calendar. "Ugh," said John, which was followed by "Double ugh, I think," from Nik.

"Yes, this will take some time," admitted Sid. "No big deal; we'll do fine." He was trying to convince himself and the others.

"We have plenty of time to get to C-10," said Nik. The one-night stays would be great for not having to pack up a huge amount of stuff before they trekked off in the morning, and the boys were good with that.

They traveled along a route the second day that dropped slightly in elevation and flattened out sometime after noon or one o'clock in the afternoon. There were no sounds or signs of humanity in the area, and that was comforting to the group. They stopped by a stream on one of their many breaks, and John and Sid were successful in catching several fish.

"These will make a great dinner," Sid whispered. The rule of thumb for communicating during their travels was to whisper or use low, quiet whistles. They didn't want to generate any loud noises if they could help it—just one less thing to be conscious of or worry about. All they needed was for someone to hear them and wander over to see what was up.

"Honestly," John admitted, "I'd be scared to death coming face-to-face with someone from this time."

"I know, what would you say? Where would you begin?" said Sid.

Then they looked to Nik, and Nik, looking surprised, said, "I have no idea … let's just not have the problem, okay?"

"Okay," smiled John, and again, off they went.

They stopped a few times to get their bearings, looking and checking ahead and side to side. "Guys, we will get into a more casual rhythm for scanning our way and being sure of our position as we proceed along," Sid explained. "It seems like work now, but it'll become second nature soon enough."

"It is a bit nerve-racking," John admitted. They were in a flat, marshy, mushy area that was okay to walk in but wet, and again, they felt exposed and out in the open. This was going to be the general terrain for a while, and they were all waiting for the first body of water that they'd have to traverse. It would be a river most likely; they would walk around a pond or lake, but a river would be different. They would have to hope for a shallow spot, low rain totals, something—even the production of a raft might be needed.

John changed the subject with, "Ya know, there is so much stuff to think about with our predicament. It's overwhelming!"

Nik interjected. "Don't worry about it. Let's concentrate on walking, getting to where we want to go, and not hurting ourselves doing it."

Sid followed up. "We'll get there safe and sound, undetected, and all will be well with the world."

"Yeah, in the year 1780," John remarked in a smart-ass tone.

"Details, details," Nik grumbled. This back and forth generated chuckles from Sid and John, which then made them all laugh and kept their spirits up. Honestly, they were in it! There was no "beaming" back home unless it happened as suddenly as it did to bring them to the year 1780. They needed to find the humor in whatever they could and discuss their worries among the group; they would have to be their own therapists.

They found a cluster of trees and decided to stop for the night. They were not enamored with the location and basically built the smallest fire possible to cook the fish over, huddled around it, ate, leaned up against some trees, and got some sleep. It was a no-nonsense campsite with the "stay ability" of only one night. The fish was great—a little boney, but tasty. Nik complimented John and Sid on their expert fishing technique, to which they smiled and proudly replied in unison, "No problem, man."

There wasn't anything to see in the sky this night, as there were heavy clouds building. "Looks like our first real rain is going to get us tonight," Nik said.

"Yeah, with no real cover either—crud," complained Sid.

"This flat, zero-cover area is going to piss me off," exclaimed John.

"Welcome to the lowlands of South Carolina," said Sid with a grumble. Around two thirty the next morning it began to lightly sprinkle, and they could see thunder and lightning off in the distance; the rain never did reach them that night.

Morning brought more aches and pains, and a round of ibuprofen was distributed. Sid remarked, "These things are going to get a lot of use here in 1780!"

"Amen to that!" John added.

Nik asked Sid for the small binoculars, because he wanted to look around for some higher terrain. After a time, he admitted, "It's hopeless; we just have to walk out of this flat stuff!" He continued with his thoughts about their course and plan moving forward. "We want to basically walk another two or three days west then turn straight north, see where that takes us. We are looking for a particular river. If we can find it and follow it northwest, it should lead us to the approximate area where C-10 was.... Well, the foothills in the area of C-10 anyway."

"Sounds like a plan," said John. "Did this river have a name back in 1780?"

"Well, I think it's the Santee River, but my South Carolina geography isn't that sharp," admitted Nik.

They continued moving along, skirting a few small tributaries and crossing some others with ease. The westward push brought them onto firmer ground and areas with more tree cover. Nik was surprised that they had not crossed any roads or paths, and he wasn't sure if they had just been lucky or if there wasn't anything out there. Who knew? So went the next five days, quietly walking, looking around, being careful, camping, and eating on the little they could find; all was going well, aches and pains aside. The aches and pains were slowly and predictably becoming less bothersome as the days went on and the miles piled up. Over the past several days, the boys thought they could hear some sounds in the distance to the north and east, but they didn't even think about looking into them as they stayed the course and quietly pushed on, making sure not to draw any attention in their direction.

They pushed west and then north until the eighth day; there they found a nice stopping location and a very defendable campsite to settle down in. "What do you say we rest here for a day?" inquired Nik. The others shrugged their shoulders and agreed.

Sid said, "Good by me. We saw some water to our south, not sure how far. We might want to visit?"

John murmured, "Well, let's see what we can find around here, food- and drink-wise, for the day we are here. I'm sure we'll have time to camp at an area with more water than a stream, no?"

Nik shrugged and stated, "I'd rather keep a tight path, don't really want to stray too much from our general direction."

Sid quickly agreed and thought to himself that he wanted to keep the group's minds busy. "We have enough to worry about; we need to stay on course," he pointed out. "So what do you think we heard a few days back?" He added this to change the direction of the conversation.

Nik shook his head and simply said, "Don't know." They hadn't heard any shooting, thankfully, no screaming, no cannon fire—just what sounded like muffled voices. "After all," Nik continued, "there are people spread all throughout this countryside. It would be odd for us not to see and hear folks. I just don't want them seeing or hearing us."

Nik figured, and hoped, that they were between the second and third rivers or tributaries (he had no idea what their names were) west of Charleston. He had them on a west/northwest, zigzagging course hoping to find the place where the third one turned north. This is where they would turn north to meet the river he thought was the Santee. He wasn't exactly sure how they would know it was the Santee, but they'd deal with that problem when they came to it.

The group unpacked a bit; it was nice getting the rifles off their backs for a longer period of time than ten or twenty minutes. They sat down in the cool shade of the trees and relaxed for a while.

"So, Sid, I was thinking," said Nik. "I was thinking about the rifles. Could we make something to mask the true look of them? Like a wooden shell or something?"

Sid nodded his head. "I guess. We could shape a wood cutout to cover the rails and such. Sure, it could be done. Of course, it would take some time to do."

"Okay, let's think on it," Nik responded.

Sid sat up and pulled out his radio/scanner and turned it on, squelch off, for the entire group to hear the static of millions of channels of dead air. "You didn't—" John started, but Sid quickly interrupted. "No, not expecting to hear anything. Just listening."

Nik sensed a turn in mood and jumped in to curve it somehow. "Yes! But wouldn't it be something if that thing somehow worked through the tear in time-space? That would be interesting."

With that, Sid turned the radio off and stood up. "Okay, what are we doing? We need something to sleep on, and we need a fire." And off he went to look for supplies for those endeavors.

John was busy looking around for water, and Nik began to get a small fire going, so when Sid came back with some wood, it'd be already to go. After a time, Nik also began gathering some wood for the fire. They had learned one thing—they couldn't have enough firewood. Sid came back with what the group needed for mats to sleep on and some wood to burn. Nik had also helped John get some water to begin to boil for drinking water for the next few days.

Around the campfire, lying down, Nik did a morale check. "You guys doing okay?" he asked.

John murmured, "I guess. How are we supposed to be doing?"

Sid said, "Well, doing okay. Wish we knew what the hell was going on."

Trying to be positive, Nik said, "We'll figure it out. Let's get some sleep."

Sleep came quickly that evening with the sense of security from the campsite and the general exhaustion from walking. John was trying to figure out how far they had walked over the past eight days and concluded that he had no idea. He figured they would keep walking until they found C-10. How would they find it? It's not like there was a sign or anything. The hills would all look the same. *Ugh*, John thought.

They had decided to leave the next day and continue their trail training. They hiked for several weeks and practiced their skills in moving through the remote countryside as undetected as possible, continuing to adapt to their surroundings. Then one day, on a day that appeared most pleasant, serene, peaceful, and sunny, the group came upon a site that would pique their interests and dampen their moods.

... 11 ...
A Cold Reminder of What Was

JUNE 22, 1780. THE boys were moving through the central rolling landscape of South Carolina. They had been skirting what they had thought was a trail for several days and had purposefully stayed far away from it, camping for a day at times to observe the happenings of the area around the trail. But they hadn't seen or heard anyone for quite some time now. John commented that it was a bit eerie. They'd had countless sightings and witnessed many groups and folks of the time moving around and living their lives. The boys remained in the shadows, in the background, invisible to the people of the time. After all, they were hiding; they didn't want to be noticed.

On this day, though, they stumbled across a site that caused them to stop and think. They were drawn to a spectacle in the woods, a scene directly out of a fairy tale gone wrong. The group lingered on the outskirts of a sight they watched for hours and could not draw themselves away from ... the scene that lay in front of them. They spied on the landscape, keeping quiet and out of sight, utterly moved and spooked by the specter that presented itself. They carefully surveyed the surrounding areas, hoping not to find any unfortunate victims and hoping for a clear and understandable reason for what they were now observing.

Sid used their bird whistle signal to get the attention of Nik and John. He motioned to release the security on their sidearm holsters

---

and form together farther back in the woods, about one hundred feet behind their present positions. They were now well back from the trail and farther away, looking straight at what had stopped them for this now very long period of time.

"It looks wrecked. I wonder if they got out," John whispered.

"Not sure. Quiet down.... Did you see anyone?" Nik added in an even more hushed voice.

Sid broke the tension with the eventual question, "So ... are we going to take a closer look?"

"Hmm." Nik pondered.

A few more minutes went by. John kept a lookout behind them as Sid continued to survey the scene in front of them. Sid suggested that they set up a small camp near some downed trees deeper into the woods, stay fireless for now, and wait to make sure no one was around. Tomorrow, if it all stayed quiet and abandoned, they could move in for a closer look. This plan of action was agreed upon, and they quietly went about creating a small "stealth" camp for the night.

What the boys had stumbled upon was a ramshackle homestead that appeared to have been recently sacked. The structure of the home was still smoldering, collapsed where the fire had done its worst destruction. The yard and farm areas appeared to have been recently worked, and there were some domesticated farm animals out of their confines. They only had a glimpse of the animals, as they were standing off from the scene for obvious security reasons. The sense of a struggle was in the air, but there were no signs of it from their distant observation point. It was clearly their paranoia that was driving these feelings, and it was what probably kept them from going in to investigate the scene that day. The boys watched the homestead for the rest of the day and into the evening and searched the surrounding areas fairly well, which yielded no leads, no incriminating tracks, nothing.

Nik admitted, "If we saw something that was suspicious, would we really know it was suspect? I mean, it is 1780. There aren't car tracks or anything leaving the scene of a crime!"

They admitted they probably weren't exactly the seasoned detective types, and they would simply have to do their best. The three compatriots had completely circumnavigated the property without as much as a sound from the destroyed homestead. There were no stirs or signs of any life except for the loose chicken pecking around. Additionally, there were stables of a sort, crude but functional enough; however, there were no signs of any livestock anywhere on the property. Returning to the campsite, the boys relaxed a bit and tried to find peace in the fact that they saw absolutely nothing menacing at or around the scene, except the burnt-out portion of the house.

"Well, I would say there isn't anything to worry about there," commented Sid.

"No, not much to see for sure," added John.

Nik said, "We'll check it out tomorrow."

Sid admitted, "It's a nice place for a homestead—a little hill to one side, stream to the west, not really sure where the trail goes, but—"

John nodded and said with his voice trailing off, "We'll check it out tomorrow.... I wonder what this place looks like in 2010." And with that, they sat back for the evening and rested.

... 12 ...
The Homestead

THE NEXT MORNING WAS warm and slightly overcast. The boys were up bright and early and left their camp set up, because they were planning on staying for a few days to explore the wreckage of the homestead. These plans could obviously change at a moment's notice, depending on what transpired through their investigation and the day. Nik suggested that they enter the homestead property from the opposite direction of their camp merely for perception purposes. The idea was that if they were noticed moving closer to the scene that lay in front of them, the observer of their approach would have a false notion of their point of origin. Sid and John made fun of Nik for being "so damn paranoid," and they laughed at him for it.

Nik just shook his head. "Go ahead. Laugh it up," he said. He wasn't angry and enjoyed the fact the he, with his concern (irrational concern, probably), could entertain his friends to the extent they clearly were.

Entering now from the north side of the property, they circled the house and looked for evidence of recent human activity other than the smoldering beams of the house. They went to the stables and stall(s) and figured there were a horse or two, a cow maybe, and the chickens that they saw every once in a while darting all around like it was a game or a secret quest for the next piece of food.

"You see that," John added, pointing to the chicken waddling quickly across the yard. "That's going to make a very nice dinner or two."

"Well, we'll see," said Nik. "Let's make sure that this isn't still someone's home, and they just made the unfortunate mistake of leaving with a candle burning or something when they left to go hunting or into town. I don't want to be here eating someone's pet or livestock, or whatever a chicken is to a farmer, when they return to their now burned-down house. They'd see us and assume we did all this. And, yes, I don't want to have to try to explain 'us' either," Nik rambled on.

Sid muttered with a smile, "Yes, the burned-down house and chicken leg in our hands we might be able to handle, but the 'us' part, I'm not so sure."

John added with a smirk and in his best antagonist voice, "I prefer the wings, honestly."

"Okay, okay. Stop! Enough chatter," Nik begged as he walked off to the field area between the stable and the main house.

John looked at Sid. "Touchy! Touchy! Isn't he?" he noted.

They stood at the main house looking at the front porch. On the left, part of what was apparently the dining area was burned down and collapsed, while the kitchen on the right looked intact. The upstairs looked in decent shape, other than the piece over the dining room; nothing more could be discerned without entering the home.

"Do you remember seeing a back door to this place?" Sid asked.

"I think so," John quickly answered, and off they went around back. There was a back door, and it was locked. Not knowing how the locks were constructed in 1780 and not wanting to break in, they went back around front and pondered going in the front door, which they hoped was unlocked. They waited several minutes and decided to enter the house and look around. They also agreed they were not going to yell, "Hello, is there anybody home?" They simply didn't want to make that much noise. John, surprisingly to Sid and Nik, decided to remain outside for the time and act as a lookout.

They all thought that was a good suggestion, but a bit puzzling coming from John.

Sid and Nik went to try the front door and found it to be unlocked. They gave each other a surprised look and cautiously opened it, entering slowly with their pistols now drawn with a round chambered. Nik leaned to the left toward the only slightly smoldering and collapsed area, and Sid went right into what appeared to be the kitchen. John now pulled out his pistol and chambered a round. They were ready now—"ready" for no apparent reason, but ready nonetheless; they just felt a bit spooked by the events now playing out.

Sid looked into and entered the kitchen, noting it did not have another exit; it was simply a single room. He gently looked into some of the cabinets and was impressed with the craftsmanship, functionality, and layout of the room and its furnishings. There was some sort of a stove of a very small size in the left-hand corner with a type of stovepipe or oven box-like area that appeared to protrude up and/or out of the home somehow. He really wasn't sure what he was looking at, but he knew it was some sort of fireplace/cooking appliance. It wasn't exactly a fireplace and by no means was it a wood stove as they knew it; he guessed it was an early version of a cook oven heated by wood fire that one day might become an early version of a wood stove.

Nik asked, "You okay, man?"

Sid responded, "Okay here; all good so far."

Nik walked into the room to the left and looked upstairs and at the sky above. Looking around above him first, he seemed to be peering into a bedroom, although the bed and one set of drawers had careened into the downstairs area due to the fire and were partially burned. The bed, which had fallen against the farthest corner of the house's outer wall from the entrance of the room, was burned and lying atop the dining room table with the drawers mostly spared from the fire. The area wasn't hot from the smoldering furniture, and Nik decided to investigate the fallen dresser while he was there.

"Sid, give me a minute while I look at something in here. Let's not split up, not yet anyway," Nik asked of his friend.

"No problem, man. I will hang here and wait for you," said Sid as he walked up to the dining room entrance. Sid did briefly look up into the remnants of the bedroom above and then down the hall he was standing in. John walked up to the front door and asked how things were going. "Okay, just looking around," Sid responded.

Nik was now looking through the contents of the dresser drawers that were spread out on the floor due to the fall. "Anything interesting?" asked Sid.

"Not from what I can see," said Nik. "Some papers, clothes I guess, a small empty box—nothing for now. We may revisit this later. Let's look at the rest of the house first before we look at anything in detail."

As the two began to move toward the back of the house, John stuck his head in and said, "Can you guys make this fast? I am getting the creeps out here."

Nik and Sid responded, "Yeah, man. Give us a few more minutes." With that, the turned and moved down the center hallway.

They found two more rooms as before, one on each side. Again, Nik went left, and Sid went right. A quick glance left by Nik revealed an area that looked like a living room with some chairs, a fireplace, and a kind of burlap throw rug. Sid quickly peered up the stairs and looked into the room that was directly behind the kitchen. It appeared to be a type of storage room with many boxes and bags of things, but it would need a real inspection to know what was in them. He figured they could look at it when they were more comfortable and secure about the house, their solitude, and their surroundings. They met back at the stairs and inspected the back door with its eighteenth-century locks before heading up.

Yup, it was locked all right—a solid block of wood jammed into a fitting on the wall that resembled a latch. They decided to leave it secured while they proceeded up to the second floor. Nik took the right-hand side, which included the burned-out and collapsed bedroom that he had seen from downstairs and the back room behind it. Sid looked into the left two rooms, both front and back. All of them appeared to be bedrooms, and the two back rooms were very small due to the pitch of the roof toward the backside of the house. There was nothing of much interest to look at and a more in-depth inspection could be done of these areas later.

Sid and Nik returned out the front door to see how John was doing. He was crouched down near the front support of the porch. "What's up?" asked Sid.

"Just exposed. I'm freaked out just sitting here on the porch of this place, like I am out in the open waiting to get picked off!" complained John.

"No worries, man. Let's get back to our little place in the woods and hide away for a while," Nik said, trying to make John a bit more relaxed. They once again utilized the north side of the property for their departure route and walked around to where their encampment was just south and slightly west of the homestead.

John, feeling better now, tried to explain the sense he had on the porch of the home. He conveyed his emotions so well that Sid and Nik began to feel a bit nervous. Nik told John that he understood and that it was because they had been basically walking around, keeping very hush and under cover for the past several weeks.

"It is totally understandable," Nik explained.

Sid also admitted that he felt a huge degree of apprehension and anxiety looking around the homestead. Nik also figured that it because the house was such an odd and haunting site the first day; they had no idea what might have gone on there, and for that, there lurked a sense of foreboding. The fact that they were poking through it like some sort of scavengers (which they weren't really doing) made them feel all the worse. They had become comfortable in the woods from the past forty days of hiking, hiding, camping, and sleeping outdoors, and the confines and the damaged home simply made them nervous.

They felt they could build a small fire, and the fire they built was just that—a *very* small campfire. Nik had built it without things that might create a large amount of smoke and reoriented the camp now to give them a clearer view of the homestead while remaining mostly hidden. The fire was on the far side of the encampment, monitored and kept small by Sid for security purposes. If one were to smell the burning wood fire, they might figure that it was the result of the still-smoldering structure of the house over at the homestead. Nighttime conversation included topics of who might have built and lived at the homestead, what really happened there, and where did the people who lived there go. Eventually, the conversation ended the same way all questions in 1780 seemed to end: I don't know.

"Oh well, we try and answer these questions, and we only come up with more questions," John sighed.

"No big deal. Get some sleep. We'll hit it in the morning!" encouraged Sid.

The next day was glorious. It had cooled down over night, the sun was shining brightly, and there was a fresh, sweet smell in the air in contrast to the previous day's humidity and damp forest odors. The boys had planned on a reconnaissance mission to reach a little farther away from the homestead to see what was around. The boys really wanted to know just how far civilization was from their location; they certainly didn't want to get involved in it at all, but they wanted to know where the boundaries were so they could be conscious of them. They planned on being gone from their encampment for only a few days but still took everything with them. The hike was good; there was water along the way and several high vistas from which to look around. The good weather allowed them to assess the fact that they were on remotely traveled paths and that no one had been on the trail to the homestead for a fairly long time, or so they assumed. It appeared that the trail they originally shadowed on their way in was cut specifically for the homestead property, a long driveway of sorts, very long at that. All they could figure about the fire at the homestead was that it had been an accident; there was simply no evidence of any foul play.

They returned to the homestead after a few days and decided to repair the structure of the house as best they could. They gravitated to this as a clear diversion from the past weeks of hiking; they really didn't know why they were going to embark on a project such as after-fire home repair at the homestead! Maybe they felt some draw to it, as they were homeowners and missed the housework. Who knew? They had previously found building materials back near the animals, which may have been left over from the original construction of the house. The damaged area really wasn't very large, and John thought they would be able to complete the work in a fairly short time.

"It won't be perfect," admitted Sid, "but it'll be a roof over an eight-room home."

"What about the trail? Do we want to leave it open and passable?" Nik asked the others with an answer hanging on his breath.

"What are you thinking about?" inquired Sid.

"Well, as it is, you could get a horse or horse-drawn carriage roaring down that path, and we could be caught totally by surprise, not really a great position for us to be in. No?" Nik lobbied.

"I see your point," said Sid.

John piped up quickly. "So we drop a dozen or so trees across the trail; that'll solve the problem," he said with a smile.

"Okay, let's do that first ... tomorrow," said Sid.

"Deal," said Nik.

They stayed together, as usual, and inventoried the building materials they had at their disposal. They found some tools and some fasteners of the day, always keeping an eye on the trail into the homestead areas, rifles close and pistols holstered but at the ready. Camp had a light feeling that night, and the boys were simply pleased with the thought of the upcoming home-repair project. It really gave these middle-aged homeowners an escape back to the concerns and rigors (if you call them that) of their lives back home. It was also something that would give them a break from the rigors of 1780. All of the "required tasks of the day" in 1780 included sneaking around, remaining very quiet all the time, walking a lot, and maintaining the overall judiciousness of each and every day in the unknown of the times of the American Revolution.

"A break in the action. That's what it's going to be!" John said exuberantly.

They laid out the beams, the roofing material, and the support boards they'd found stored in the stable near where the work would be done. The boys now wandered down the trail, staying in the woods, of course, and began scoping out which trees would be the easiest to drop across the trail to protect them from a fast-moving approach. There were three major clusters of trees they would target the next day. Although it appeared they'd be somewhat short on tools, there were some saws, axes, and a hammer scavenged from the shed. They figured the job wouldn't take too long, and they were excited to get started the next day.

Back at their camp later that evening, they talked for a short time about the next day's events repairing the house. "Are we looking to stay here and move in?" Nik inquired.

Sid shrugged his shoulders, and John simply said, "Dunno, but let's fix it and see how we feel. Are we in any great rush to go anywhere in particular?"

"No, not really … just wondering. It'll be a great diversion for us for sure," said Nik.

Sid, holding his head now, added, "Who knows, maybe we fix it up, and if we can't figure out what the hell to do in this time, we come back to live out our lives right here. Talk about lost in time … geez."

John, now trying to pick up the mood a notch or two, added, "I don't know about all that, but let's have fun with it. We can bang a few nails or square peg things or really odd-looking square fasteners or wooden dowels or whatever. If we stay, we stay; if we move on up to C-10 to look for answers there, that's okay too. If not that, we'll do something else."

Nik wanted to say something, sensing some frustration, but he was unable to figure out what to say. Instead, he just added, "Let's allow a few days to go by. We'll figure it out; we always do." The others nodded, and they all agreed to get some sleep.

The next morning had the boys up early felling trees along the trail. The hatchets they found worked quite well, and they were able to make an utter impassable mess of the trail to the homestead. The cuts the boys inflicted on the timber with the short strokes of the small hatchet heads looked a bit—no, a lot—like chew marks from a small animal or maybe a bear or something. Only the closest of inspections would give someone the idea that these trees were purposefully cut down. This was certainly by accident; the boys couldn't have fabricated these cuts if they actually tried. It was just dumb luck. Mission one complete!

Mission two began with Nik taking a rifle and standing guard around the property, while John and Sid worked the high areas of the construction. Nik had real issues with heights and would be better off being the lookout until the second floor, floor joists, flooring, and roofing struts were put into place. John and Sid did a fantastic job that day and were able to complete all the framing they needed. While Nik was half surveying, half guarding that day, he scuffed around the grounds, stable, and shed areas to see what he could see. He found eleven coins on the property that day; six were minted in 1776 and were quite large, much like silver dollar size. The others bore a 1773 mint date and appeared to be made of copper or bronze and were smaller in size. The larger of the coins were clearly labeled "Continental Currency" and were made of a heavier metal of light color, probably made of pewter or maybe even silver. He had read about these and actually had recently seen pictures of them in coin books when he was thinking about purchasing silver coins for investment purposes (in 2010, of course).

The evening came quickly and they were all tired—Nik from standing around all day, Sid and John for busting their backsides up on the structure of the house. Nik told the others about his coin find of the day. "These are normal tender in 1780, but in 2010 … Dudes, we'd be rich; not filthy rich, mind you, but I bet these are probably worth anywhere from five to two hundred thousand dollars a piece in the condition they are in. I am not kidding," continued Nik as he passed around the coins. "Look at these things; they are in near mint condition."

"Cool," said John.

"Well, if we ever get back, we'll be good!" Sid exclaimed with a grin.

The conversation then turned to the subject of "getting home," and it wasn't a cheery a discussion. They theorized how they might find some hints of their chronological displacement at the C-10 bald. The discussion ended rather abruptly with Nik scratching his forehead and saying, "I don't want to be a killjoy on this, but there is no reason in the world—or universe, for that matter—to think there is anything at that hunk of rock that will give us an idea of what happened to us. After all, the event that tossed us back in time won't occur there, at that spot, for another 230 years.

Unless we think that spot is somehow a fixed location for some vortex or rip in time and space, it's just a hunk of rock on a hill. A hill in the northern hemisphere on the small, rocky, molten-iron-cored, insignificant planet we call Earth located in a backwater solar system in an even more backwater fringe of a spiral arm of the Milky Way galaxy. Not a lot of promise, guys. I hate to be a downer, but—"

John, with his head now spinning, simply and comically replied, "Okay, you can shut up now." They all chuckled slightly as they settled in for a night of rest. Nik apologized and listened well into the night to the noises of their surroundings.

The next morning brought Sid and John to the rafters of the house to continue their rapid repairs. Because they enjoyed the construction work and the challenge of it, they waved Nik off and ordered him to go "play in the sand some more." Nik said that he could certainly help with the mud packing of the walls whenever they were ready; they were good with that, and all was calm in the world.

After five days passed, the floors, walls, and roof were secure and ready for the outside walls to be sealed. Nik got right to it with the clay and sand in the area, as there was only one bucket found to use for a preparation container. He could pack the walls with the mixture, and the home would be waterproof and airtight again. It was slow work for all, and this activity took Nik six days to complete, after which they were tired from their respective work activities on the house. Sid slept the whole first day after his part of construction was completed; John just sat and became the lookout by default, while Nik worked on the walls. The next day, John slept most of the day, while Sid acted as the lookout. He, thinking of future riches, also looked around for more of the coins Nik had found on the previous days, to no avail.

They finally finished the repairs and were doing a final cleanup when John whistled the bird sound—the alarm! "Guys, we have visitors! Let's get out of the area via the stable side! Right now! Right now!" John ordered.

The three took off after quickly triple-checking the house to make sure nothing of theirs was left behind. They were very good about only having the bare minimum with them, but they had to be sure. The house was all clear of their items, and they scampered into the woods behind the stable area. From there, they would go deep into the forest and swing around to approach their campsite from the far side, so as to not to be seen by the approaching interlopers. Once back at their campsite, they quickly and quietly moved their camp setup back to a hidden area to ensure they couldn't be seen from the homestead.

"Man, that was close," John panted. They were all lying on the ground now, looking through the cracks in the brush that covered their small sheltered area.

"I wonder who it is," Nik said.

"No idea," mumbled Sid, rifle drawn and at the ready now.

The commotion coming from the trail sounded like a male voice. He was yelling, complaining, and cursing about the trees in his way and was yelling to someone about it. A gentler voice was heard, but the words were not understandable at this point.

"Guys, quietly pack your things. I think we are done here," Nik said, still breathing hard from the run in the woods.

The group stayed low and quietly, quickly packed the few things in the camp area. Sid dispersed the fire pit and covered up the ash area with leaves. The group was moving closer now, as they pushed through the trees the boys had dropped on the approach trail weeks earlier. The male cursing the trees wondered aloud, "How in *the* hell could such a thing happen? Must be them damn beavers or something."

The other voice could now be heard clearly. It was the gentle sound of a woman's voice trying to calm down the male. Children's voices could be heard now as well as the commotion of their wagon and belongings rumbling down the trail and approaching the homestead became fully visible to the boys.

"What the hell is going on?" Sid whispered.

John stated the obvious. "Duh? They are returning home."

"Oh, yeah, that makes sense. Duh." Sid realized his clear miss of the events from the obscured vantage point and chuckled a little bit. Nik slid over to get a better view of the house as the family was just turning the corner to the front area between the planting field and the house. The boys could see the cattle and horses being walked behind the family's wagon and crouched lower to relax and enjoy the show.

As the family approached the front of the house, the mother yelled aloud, "Henry, look! Our beautiful home—it's not burned anymore. It's fixed by the grace of God! Our home is fixed; it is truly a blessing from God and a miracle!"

The children bounded off of the wagon and began jumping around excitedly, yelling, "It's fixed! It's fixed, Daddy! You fixed it! How'd you do it? It's fixed!"

The man, rubbing his sweaty, balding head in utter confusion, looked around at his land, walked around the outside of the home where the fire had ravaged the structure, scratched his head again, and muttered, "I don't know."

His wife ran up, hugged him, thanked him for the wonderful surprise, and hugged him again. The children joined in and almost knocked them over as they continued to yell. "Thank you, Daddy! Thank you!"

The woman happily commanded the children to go inside and get ready for dinner; she hugged her husband again and ran in after the little ones. The look on his face was priceless, as he was absolutely at a peak of confusion and unknowing. He stood scratching his head and then his belly for the longest time, just looking around in bewilderment. Finally, "Damn beavers!" came out of his mouth, and he went inside.

Nik rolled over and began to quietly laugh. "If that wasn't the funniest thing I have seen in a long time. Did you see his face?"

Sid quietly laughed and said, "Well, if he wasn't a believer, he sure is now!"

John sadly said, "Believer nothing, miracle nothing—we fixed his house for him. Man, I really liked that house." With a frown on his face, John rolled over on his back. Sid reminded him that the house wasn't ever theirs to stay in or claim; it was just luck that they had as long as they did to stay and work on it.

Nik also added, "And did you see how happy they were? We did good, and we got off the long trek schedule for a while. It was good for us."

The boys, all laying on their backs now, looked up at the sky and contemplated their next move, still thinking of how happy the family was returning home to a nicely repaired dwelling. A long time passed while the boys just rested in the cooling forest when a passing scent—a familiar scent—caused Nik to sit up and look around. Sid and John hadn't noticed Nik's distraction, and nothing came of it. The boys could hear the occasional squeal of the small children from the homestead and realized just how alone they were—again.

Nik stared straight up and mumbled under his breath. Sid immediately knew Nik was having a conversation with the man upstairs. He was asking for guidance. Sid could almost read Nik's mind during these instances. John, catching on, also looked up and whispered, "It's all going to be okay. We're good."

Nik, always keeping track of time, quietly added, "Tomorrow's Fourth of July, guys. Happy Independence Day. Happy fourth birthday, America! May God protect it—and us!"

... 13 ...
Onward and Upward

THEY SLIPPED AWAY IN the early morning hours on that Independence Day with mixed emotions. They were still sore from their manual labor and were sad to leave the "wonderfulness" of the homestead. They each felt great knowing their toil had made that family so happy with the repairs of the home. The kids, who reminded the boys of their own kids, were exuberant for the house's complete state of repair instead of the burned-up and exposed state it had been in when the boys stumbled upon it. The boys had all agreed and thought for a while that the home might be a place to stay for an extended time, or at least until they could get a grasp on what had happened to them and how to possibly reverse it.

Again, even though they were all fairly intelligent, they knew a solution back to 2010 was not in the realm of possibility trapped, as they were, in 1780. Hell, a normal person couldn't travel through time in 2010. How could they really expect to solve the problem now? Alas, Nik, Sid, and John could still hang on to the hope that somehow, something, or some combination of things, could reverse the process. This drove them on; it was the reason they originally planned a route back to C-10. They were back on course now and thinking clearly on that overarching mission: return to C-10 and look for clues to the rift in time they had fallen through to put them in this time. All Nik could think about right now was "Hup, two, three, four. Hup, two, three, four," as they marched on and on.

The next few weeks were basically uneventful with very few sightings of people and only an instance or two of some close-call situations, which were successfully avoided. The summer storms of July in the southeastern colonies were typical of this time of year. The boys, thinking back to the Raleigh area of 2010 North Carolina, constantly blamed "the damn global warming problem" and then burst out laughing. They remembered the proponents of global warming and climate change who always blamed man and his many evil vices, like the massive consumption of fossil fuels, pollution, deforestation, even the very process of breathing—blah, blah, blah.

"Screw those idiots. It's as hot and as cold and as wet and as dry as it has always been and will ever be until the sun goes nova or a meteorite slams into the planet, killing all of its inhabitants," Nik loudly ranted. "Experts—ha! And I am the king of England! It's all a money-making agenda, I say! In 2010 all this global warming is a money-making fantasy! It's all an agenda to take the money from the folks from one part of the world and distribute it to another part of the world, for 'fairness.' What in the hell? That is simply ridiculous!" He broke the code of quiet for more than a moment during his tirade.

John laughed and rolled his eyes as they continued to hike. "Here we go," he said. "Dude, we are so far from that now. Let it go. If we get back to 2010, we can tell them just how wrong they are."

Sid laughed even louder. "I can see that.... 'So, by the way, we just vacationed at the 1780-Charleston club, and we noticed the climate sucked just as bad then as it does now.' Ha! That'll go over well, as we're loaded into the little white truck."

The conversation died off as they began to climb some small hills. The boys felt they had made it more than halfway to their destination at C-10. They didn't really know that for a fact, but they did arrive at a larger, meandering river, which was conveniently and comically labeled with a small wooden sign: the Santee. They chuckled about this, because Nik had wondered how they might be able to identify the correct bodies of water. But there it was—a sign, nicely placed right where they emerged from the tree line. It was truly an uncanny coincidence and a huge relief to the whole group.

With this good fortune, they followed the river to the left, basically west-northwest. Nik figured (and hoped) they would soon reach the higher elevations of the central and western Carolina hills. They successfully navigated "the big lake" (Nik couldn't remember the name of it) and slipped past the British outposts around the city the boys knew as Columbia. Nik wasn't sure what it was called in 1780; it might have been Columbia or something else, but they neither knew nor really cared about the name. They were basically going to try hike up what, in 2010, would become the I-26/385 corridor, missing Greenville and veering west off into the hills. C-10 was up there somewhere near the caverns and gorges.

July's storms brought the dog days of late July and early August. There really wasn't anything that stood out during the group's run up to the mountains except one very interesting encounter somewhere well northwest of Greenville, South Carolina. The boys were easily hiking along—they were fed, hydrated, and not too sore; their spirits were relatively high; and all was good in their world. Nik had backed off of his not-so-quiet concern of making sure they kept a quiet, low profile and all that went along with it. Sid and John understood the credo of the group, which was now fairly concrete, but they had grown a little tired of it all. Nik, up until about a month previous, continually reminded John and Sid about their stance on the globe and very often drove home the imperative with, "We can't change or affect anything or anyone. Let's not be seen or heard, blah, blah, blah … quiet down!" He reminded them so often, in fact, that it drove Sid and John crazy.

The event that unfolded on a lonely trail in between mountain passes (big hills, really) was an encounter that would test the group's resolve to their previously agreed upon credo of noninterference. Spotting a water source high on a hillside, they climbed off their track to camp for the evening. It was a glorious place to stay, and they really thought about just making the site their new base of operations. But as events had it, the boys, from their newfound campsite, witnessed what could only best described as a 1780s western-style, mountain pass hold up.

From their elevated, off-trail hideout, the boys watched a family of six in their wagon, animals in tow, as they traveled down the trail to the southeast. The boys figured the family was headed to Greenville, South Carolina, when a group of four men came out of the trees and intercepted them on the trail. This event was occurring south and east of their campsite, but in their eyes, it was all much too close for their own good. In the spectacle that unfolded, the men closed in swiftly on the family and their wagon. The men were very large compared to any of the folks they had observed in the past six months. John thought they might be fur trappers, because they had big packs that looked like they had fur on and around them. They might have been of German or Nordic descent; the boys really couldn't tell, but they theorized that the pack size may have made them appear bigger than they really were.

In the family's party, there were two men, one woman, and three small children. The newcomers to the scene, the "mountain men," moved swiftly to the family's position on the trail, causing an immediate confrontation—a bunch of yelling, some scuffling, and then the two men in the family party were dropped hard and very quickly. The boys were motivated to jump up and do something, but before they could act, Sid stopped them. "Did you see how they just did that?" he pointed out.

John said, "Yeah, they hit them. Let's go!"

"No, no—the technique. These guys are trained killers. Get down!" Sid warned.

"What are you talking about, Sid?" Nik inquired.

Sid continued, "Did you see how they dropped those guys? I have seen that technique used or demonstrated somewhere before.... I just can't—"

"Yeah! World wrestling or whatever it's called in 2010—now let's go kick their eighteenth-century bully asses," John interrupted.

Nik grabbed John's sleeve. "I'd like to, man, but we just can't. Remember?"

The beating on the trail continued, and the two males of the family didn't have a prayer or stand a chance. The kids were screaming and the woman was crying and holding the kids close to her, while the four mountain men tore their belongings apart. The family's men lay motionless on the ground; it was just a horrible sight.

Nik asked the others, "What would these guys need from those folks I wonder? They look more than capable to get or do whatever they might need, ya know?"

John grabbed Nik and said, "Are we going to let these guys kill those folks?"

Sid interrupted and said, "Is there really a choice?"

John, now jumping to the wrong conclusion, replied, "There ya go. Let's roll!" He grabbed his rifle and readied himself.

Sid grabbed John's shoulder and quietly commanded, "*No!* You misunderstood.... You know we can't interfere here. How do you know this didn't really happen?"

John, now realizing their role—or, more correctly, their lack of a role—replied, "Well, I know, but ... I don't know at the same time."

"None of us know. That's the cross we bear," said Nik. "I'll tell you what. If these guys really look like they are going to kill someone, we'll engage them, okay?"

Sid, his head now leaning off to one side, inquired, "How is that not interfering, Nik?"

"Well, if that family dies, I couldn't live with myself.... So, to hell with it. We rip the bad guys!" declared Nik.

"Sounds fair," acknowledged Sid, bringing his head back to an upright position.

Nik put his hand on his friend John's shoulder. "Well," John replied, "I'll buy that for a dollar!"

"Okay. You good?" Nik asked once again. "Okay, good. Now let's see what happens." Rubbing his temples, Nik was really hoping to get a break in all of this by not having to get involved in the outcome of the events now unfolding.

As the boys tried to calm down, the events continued to play out. The woman and kids continued to cry, the family's men were still down on the ground and apparently unconscious as the mountain men continued to pour through the wagon's contents. Nik fumbled with his rifle and quickly informed Sid and John, using his scope with the laser range finder, that they were about 577 yards from the scene of the conflict. They had three rifles that could effectively reach, but with this information, reality set in. Their skills would certainly be tested at this distance. Each man loaded his already prepared ammunition clip and positioned himself in a prone position for the potential engagement. The scene began to look grim, and the boys were now getting nervous as the mountain men corralled the woman and children and dragged the two men over by a large rock on the far side of the trail. Sid offered up some advice to Nik and John. "With these rounds at this distance and elevation to the targets, aim high by"—an abrupt pause muted any surrounding sound for a moment— "four and a half inches."

Nik and John acknowledged the tactical information with a simple okay.

The mountain men, who were now talking among themselves, were yelling and occasionally waving their hands. Just then, the largest of the men drew a huge knife and waved it around. John gasped, "Holy—"

Sid quickly requested, "Weapons free?" He paused, waiting two more seconds and then repeated his request. "Weapons free?"

The answer to Sid's request would initiate the confirmation to release the safeties on their rifles, which would, more than likely, produce a "fire" order and commit the boys to armed combat in the year 1780—230 years in their past.

Nik, watching the chaos down on the ground in front of him, his head spinning with rage, confusion, and a loss of control of his own thoughts, quickly regained his composure and now calmly said, "Weapons free. Release your safeties. Please wait for my commit order before firing."

Sid and John were good with that, and the quiet, unimposing sound of their weapons' safeties softly sounded—*click click click.* Would this be the first ballistic encounter for the group in 1780? The mountain men grew louder, and it appeared as if they were having a moment of internal strife between themselves. It appeared that one of the huge men was trying to force an issue with the other three, but it wasn't entirely clear at this distance. Through the barely inaudible yelling, Nik quietly asked his friends, "What language is that?"

The distant argument was just too faint; they were simply too far away to make out any part of the conversation. They knew it wasn't English, not the King's English, and not French.

"No idea," Nik murmured.

Then the moment of truth arrived as the big man walked over to one of the men on the ground, picked him up by the hair on the back of his head, and raised his sword-like knife.

"Hold," Nik slowly and sternly whispered. "Don't let him do it; keep him from doing it, please." It was almost as if Nik was giving a request to someone. Nik really didn't want to shoot anyone and was struggling with the fact that they might now have it forced upon them in very short order.

Sid quickly whispered and informed the group, "The angle is good. We have the angle."

At that instant, with a herculean lurch, the big man threw the man across the trail and roared in apparent disgust. His roar shook the boys from more than five hundred yards away. The mountain men, now yelling, ran off into the woods and up over the hillside to the north. Sid kept a bead on them through the scope of his M1A, while Nik and John, as if totally spent, collapsed within their prone positions and then rolled onto their backs in total relief.

"Oh my God," Nik gasped.

John was breathing so hard that he was almost panting. "That was sooooo close, holy—" he said, his voice trailing off.

Sid, now on his back as well, reported that the mountain men had disappeared over the hill to the north. Sid also noted that he just wanted to run to C-10 and get out of this area and then reminded the others to please engage the safeties on their rifles.

Nik admitted that he nearly pissed his pants and was completely soaked with sweat from head to toe. John tiredly responded, "That makes two of us."

"Who were those guys? And what were they doing?" asked Nik, wanting to have an emotional outburst but resisting with all of his remaining strength. The others had no answers, and they were all pretty unnerved and very agitated.

"Bandits, I'd guess," John muttered.

"Pretty impressive bandits, I'd say," Sid responded with a deep breath. For hours, Sid continued to scan the area of the incident and as well as the direction to which the mountain men had ran. "No sign of the bad guys," he reported.

The family tended to the man who had been thrown like a rag doll to the other side of the trail, picked up their belongings, and moved off down the trail toward Greenville, South Carolina. The man who hadn't been thrown across the trail was now driving, while the rest of the family tended to the other man, who now had a bloody wound on his head. At this point, the boys had no idea of the guy's condition and resigned themselves to never finding out.

"Well, in some strange way, a disaster was averted—by the grace of God, I think. Let's get rolling; what do you guys want to do from here?" Sid asked.

John started, "Well, I liked it here until all that."

Sid added, "We need to get to C-10 and figure out what to do from there. I just hope there are no people there."

"I second that," Nik added.

"You want to leave now or in the morning?" queried John.

Sid wanted to leave immediately but suggested they get their water boiled over a small fire and their stuff collected. He also added, "We'll post a guard tonight—three short shifts, just in case."

The guys were happy they had made the decisions they did and believed they executed on them fairly well. "So, Nik," began Sid, "why were you the final call on the fire/no fire decision earlier?"

A long pause went by as Nik pondered his answer. "I dunno. You're the gun guy; John is the hunter guy; maybe that leaves me to do what I do best?"

"And what might that be?" inquired a smiling John.

"Shooting my mouth off, of course," replied Nik.

"Ha!" Sid chuckled. "Well, you have a point there!"

John laughed. "Yup, you can't argue with that fact," he said as he continued to snicker and sat down to get some sleep during the first shift of the evening. The night came and went without so much as an owl hooting overhead and in the morning, the trio began the footrace to C-10.

... 14 ...
Okay, Let's Try Again ...
Onward and Upward!

THE BOYS, ON THE move now for better than a week, were approaching the mountains of northwestern South Carolina. They could see what they thought was part of the Blue Ridge Mountains, but honestly, they didn't know exactly which mountains they were looking at. Nik was rambling on about moving west a bit until they approached a big body of water; at that point, it would be time to turn and proceed north. He described a valley area that he remembered from the maps he had looked at in January 2010 before their trip. He wanted the group to head north and northeast after turning at the big lake to move through a large valley.

"This valley would narrow out," as Nik explained as he remembered, "and toward the end of the narrowing valley, a set of creeks would give passage to the west up to the area of their ill-fated beginnings in 2010."

"You think?" John jabbed.

Nik smiled and started, "Okay, Magellan, your sextant; oh, better yet, go ahead break out your GPS. Ahhhhh, psyche—no GPS; hell, no satellites for it to use even if you had one. Remember? 1780."

"Yeah, yeah. Go ahead, pull the 'back in time' nonsense on me. Man, oh man, sometimes I miss the modern conveniences," John admitted.

After several more days, including some days stumbling through a few valleys, the group came to what they thought was the set of creeks that ran by the C-10 campsite. The theory was that if they followed those streams up the mountainside, they would be able to find that flat area on the side of the hill where the cabin was. They knew the cabin wasn't going to be there; they were just talking from what they knew from the 2010 frame of reference.

It didn't take them long to scamper up the creek rise, and as they looked at the potential courses up the hills, they became confused. One by one they navigated the creeks into and up the hills looking for something that looked familiar.

Sid mentioned to the group, "I don't think it has to be the exact spot, just a nice place to set down and set up house." Nik and John agreed, as they all darted up and down the south-facing sides of the hills running along the creeks.

A few hours later, they found the promised land! Sid said, "Up here! Guys, up here!"

"Really?" John yelled.

"C'mon, Sid, you can't find anything!" Nik laughed.

Sid responded, "Nik, have you been telling John lies again! Really, this is it! Really, c'mon!"

"Okay, okay. We're coming, geez." John laughed as he ran up the hill to where he thought Sid was but got lost on his way.

Nik shook his head and taunted. "No, over there. Oh, wait; he's over there. Wait, up there!"

With that, Sid began complaining. "Guys! What is wrong with you?"

They finally climbed up the right path to where Sid was located and looked around, and then they looked around some more. "Ya think so?" asked John.

It certainly looked different. After all, it was 230 years earlier, and the area was just a wooded forest; there was no clearing, no cabin, nothing. "Well, we could start clearing the area? We'll see what it looks like after we do a little work on it," Sid said meekly.

They all agreed and started to clear some of the underbrush and small trees away.

"Remember how we got to the bald and the water. Those will make good landmarks in order to figure out where we actually are," added John. They worked long enough to make a small camp area and decided to go down to the stream where the water would be in 230 years. On the way down, each wondered if it was there at all in 1780, but together they were pretty sure they would be able to find a small stream somewhere around the area. If worse came to worst, they could use the creek for water.

They found a stream located just above the camp area, and John excitedly described how he wanted to create the running water setup they had back at C-80; he was truly inspired! They figured it would be very convenient and would work on it because they could use it for as long as they were there, which, at this point, could be a very long time. The canal idea also gave them their first big project to work on in the first days at C-10, and tasks like this tended to get their minds off their current situation—at least for a little while. While John was concentrating on the canal, Sid began collecting larger logs with the hopes of building a cabin. In the time between collecting the logs and actually using them to build a shelter, the logs would act as a set of walls for their encampment. Fortuitously, in the haste of fleeing into the woods a couple of months earlier, the boys had mistakenly taken the hand tools they had found and used to tackle the construction on the homestead.

The exertion of the day caused them to sleep soundly through the night and awaken late the next morning. John went off to continue his work on the canal system; he really wanted running water close to their encampment. Sid and Nik continued logging and creating the spaces for the specific camp areas; the fire, cabin, cleaning area, and so on. Nik thought the boys needed to look for Devil's Bald at some point, but for today, he wanted to survey around the camp and just to see what he could see. He found an area he thought might have been where they had driven in; obviously, there wasn't a road in place, but with considerable clearing and 230 years, it was a possibility he could envision. It really wasn't important to them to find the exact spot of C-10, just somewhere close that was secluded, defendable, and had all the ingredients they needed for a long-term stay.

The now-forming camp had a backdrop of a high ridge, defendable and sturdy; a mudslide would cause a serious issue, but that was unlikely with all the overgrowth of the mountainous area. Nik climbed up to check on John and his dreams of a canal only to discover John had already carved out an almost 150-foot water route for the future canal and had partially routed part of the stream into said canal route. John was sitting on a downed tree looking at the run; he looked frustrated.

Nik chuckled. "What's up, man?" he asked.

John went off. "The damn water isn't flowing down the length. What is going on with this thing?"

Nik looked at the run of canal and commented, "Well, give it some time, be patient. The water will run as soon as the ground gets saturated enough; at that point, it'll flow quite nicely."

John knew that, but he complained about the time it was taking and figured here in the mountains, the ground would be plenty wet enough to facilitate a water-flow faster rather than slower.

"Be patient; we have plenty of time," encouraged Nik. With that, they returned to camp where they found Sid sitting down absolutely winded and just worn out.

John, with a clearer head, told his compatriots, "Okay, we need to pace ourselves, guys! We have plenty of time. Let's not kill ourselves!" They agreed and all sat down for a rest.

"John's correct," admitted Sid with a smile. "We have to pace ourselves."

Nik continued, "Guys, John has it right. Let's just calm down. We very likely have a lot of time here, and, after all, we just got here. If it takes us two years to make all this the way we want it to be, it'll be okay. We have trudged more than 245 miles to get here. Along the way we saw some weird stuff and a lot of nothing as well. Let's just gear down, relax, and take our time."

At that moment, the laws of physics, nature, and gravity turned on Nik. John's waterway finally saturated sufficiently, providing a healthy torrent of cool, fresh, mountain water in all its glory, hitting Nik square on the top of his head. Sid and John erupted in hysterical laughter, as Nik looked up and held his hands. He shook his head, which was now awash in the flow of their newly formed canal. "See, I told you—just needed some time."

The boys spent the rest of the evening setting up a small temporary shelter, as it looked like some rain was coming in. The night was cooler than they had experienced in the past months and was very quiet. The boys continued talking about their plans; the subject of what they wanted to do or accomplish kept coming up. Yes, survival and all that, but goals from here moving forward seemed to become more difficult. Or were they?

"We do need to think about the winter, though, Sid," Nik commented. "And we definitely need that cabin you are thinking about."

Sid smiled, nodded, and said, "Let's get some sleep; we'll get up and solve the world's problems tomorrow." Once again, sleep came quickly with all the project work the boys had started on, and all was grand with the world—at least on this night.

The next morning had the boys waking up late again, and honestly, they were fine with it. Today they decided they wanted to attempt to make their way to the bald, if they were even actually in the correct location. They couldn't be sure given the overgrowth and really unfamiliar surroundings. They were also going to help the water flow become more of a flow and less of a waterfall. For that, the canal needed a small v-channel cut into it, especially at the side of the hill where it dropped down to the campsite. They would need to add a rock base to help it along and reduce erosion for the length of its path. This wouldn't take too much time with all three of them working on it, because a gentle flow was much more desirable than the somewhat raging waterfall they were experiencing now; besides, it was very loud. All this would be taken care of by nature and physics over time, but they didn't want to wait, and they would rather speed up the process for their sake.

"There we go—us horrible humans changing all of what nature gave us. Man, do we suck!" Nik joked, clearly stabbing at the ridiculous stance of those lawmakers in charge of American politics in 2010. "Those idiots would give a dead deer the right to an attorney for you having shot it as a hunter! What sense does that make?" Nik continued.

Sid chuckled and responded, "Just another way for the lawyers to make a buck, man, nothing more. It's all agenda."

John, now standing up after carrying some rocks and falling over, added, "People actually supported this kind of thinking in the administration? Really?"

"Oh, yes. Pure joy and politics in the year 2010," Nik said, now shaking his head. After completing the plumbing modifications, they moved on to searching for the bald.

They had talked previously about this hike and agreed to take everything with them on the off chance that maybe, just maybe, the effect would somehow know they were coming and allow them to step through it for a return trip to 2010. Nik clearly had his doubts about this, but who knew? Without the trail present, they struggled to get their bearings. After most of the day was spent hiking, assuming and conjecturing on their direction to the bald, they decided they had made too many turns to be on the correct path, so they turned back to the camp. The day's experience was thoroughly frustrating, and discussion began regarding trying again tomorrow. Frustration won the evening, however, and their conversation would turn to more constructive ideas.

The camp was quiet that evening from the disappointment of not finding the bald. Sid and John hoped in the back of their minds that they would be able to step through a magic portal and be home—really home, in 2010. Nik didn't have much thought about this, but he wanted to be hopeful for the others. He felt deep down that there was so much more to all of this; bending time for a man, or three, to pass through requires extraordinary energy and science or, more likely, supreme nature or even divine intervention. Nik also had a hard time believing that the effect they went through was natural, but once again, no one really knew. Honestly, he had about as much real knowledge on the subject of time travel as a small child had about quantum physics, and Nik knew it. He wasn't kidding himself, and he tried reminding the group that they had absolutely no chance of thinking their way back to 2010; it just wasn't going to happen.

Sid queried the group, "You guys doing okay?"

John jumped in first and said, "Yeah, tired tonight."

"Me too," admitted Nik.

"Yeah. If we can't find that stupid bald now, we will probably be able to find it after the leaves drop off the trees." Sid wanted to get the group's morale up.

"For sure. That's a good point," replied John.

Nik finished. "Remember, we have however long we need."

It grew silent again. The wind picked up a bit, and again it cooled off nicely, making for a very comfortable evening. Sid, apparently not wanting to go to sleep, said, "You know, we did a good job on that house at the homestead. We fixed it up really well."

"Quick too," added John.

Sid continued. "I really want to get a cabin built for us here. I want to work on that tomorrow. Is that okay?"

Nik and John both responded with, "Yeah, man. No problem."

John wanted to assure Sid that they were all enthusiastic about it and said, "Let's do it. It'll be fun, and we deserve a real structure to live in!"

Nik followed up with, "Absolutely!"

Nik was concerned now; he had wanted to do whatever he could to get the group feeling better about whatever was kind of bringing them down. It was a difficult balance that the three of them handled very well. One of the members was usually off a bit emotionally, and the other two were there to pick him back up. Uncommonly, when two of the boys were in a funk at the same time, the single outlier had a job on his hands to cheer the others up, usually with good success. They always had a triangle of emotions going, and if they were ever all three in the same mood, it was most certainly on the happy, positive side of the spectrum. The rarest condition would be when all three were feeling down in the dumps simultaneously. When this happened, it got really quiet, and time was required to work one of them "out of it" to pick up the rest. They were simply a good team!

They had worked very hard to get to their present location, but the homestead episode was a little bit of a letdown for them. It wasn't theirs to take or have, but they had somehow convinced themselves it was abandoned. After several minutes, Sid, in a sleepy, talking mumble, murmured, "Cool," and then began to snore.

John ended the evening with, "Let's make this place our home base—make it as comfortable as possible and figure out what the hell to do about bending time back in our favor."

Nik agreed and rolled over and went to sleep. John tossed and turned all night thinking of the reality of their situation. He missed his family, as they all did, and was having trouble getting them out of his head. He remembered Nik's advice and thoughts on it: "We humans can't remove ourselves from the singular time line in which we exist. There is no way for us to comprehend a reality of multiple time lines except for the 'what-ifs' or the 'well, before we were here's. These are concepts of reality—either present, past, or otherwise—not time on the singular line we exist in. We don't exist yet as we did; our families don't exist yet; no one we ever knew exists yet. Do not mourn what doesn't exist yet. Celebrate that we didn't drop into some astral hole and disappear forever. The fact that 'we are' means there is a chance that we will be again. Does that make any sense?"

John still had trouble understanding how that helped. He remembered what he had in 2010—his wife, his kids, his pets, and on and on. Yes, it was 1780. Yes, no one they had any relationships with was alive yet, but they did! They were! They will! It annoyed him immensely, and reminiscing on these things, he fell asleep angry.

The next morning John told Nik that he thought Nik was wrong about time and space and all that. Nik said to him, "You're probably right, but I strive to explain things as best I can as a simple idiot mortal from one time thrust back 230 years into history. As someone living in the woods where even taking a dump is literally a pain in the backside. As one of three old, fat dudes in the middle of a conflict that, honestly, is very scary...." Nik continued talking for the next twelve minutes before he ended with "... so what do you think?"

Sid, on the ground now, laughed almost uncontrollably at Nik's uncanny ability to ramble on and on for what seemed like forever on a subject. Sid, still laughing, turned to ask John, "So … what do you think?"

John rolled his eyes, scratched his head, and said, "Oh yeah!" And then they all laughed! John then asked, "Aren't we building a cabin today?"

"Yes we are!" piped up Nik. He then looked at Sid and screamed in his best drill sergeant voice. "Get up, soldier! What in *the* hell are you doing on the ground laughing like a small, wet-behind-the-ear child for? We have a cabin to build!"

Sid, who continued to laugh, stood up and saluted Nik with a silly, salute-type gesture and ran off into the woods to continue cutting lumber for the cabin.

"You guys are crazy," mumbled John as he pulled the small brush and weeds from the camp area.

Within days, the trio had a frame laid out for a very decent-sized cabin. The cabin had three very small bedrooms, a kitchen/living room area, and a small extension where the door would be placed. The small extension was sort of mudroom, a place that would serve as a "between area" from the inside and the outside later in the year. Additionally, there would be door on either side of this little mudroom.

The next few days saw full walls, and the following week, a roof was added to the structure and was being thatched with branch shingling. Finally, at the end of two weeks, their cabin was complete in a very basic fashion—walls, roof, and door. They hadn't ventured anywhere in that time, except for a little light hunting and food collection. They'd worked very hard and finally had a place to call home.

A fireplace was cut into the structure in the front room and was fashioned after what the boys had observed at the homestead. After the cabin was basically complete, it gave the boys something solid to build the fireplace onto. The boys had talked for a long time on exactly how they were going to get the fireplace into the cabin and settled on a method that they thought would work the best. Their methodology went something like this: Rocks were collected from the surrounding creeks and broadly piled at the base. They were then secured by a mud, clay, and grass mixture to make a type of cement. It took days of stacking, mudding, and lighting fires in the fire-pit/fireplace, which helped solidify and dry the cement mixture that held it all together. This had really taken the longest of all the tasks to date and was completed about a week after the basic cabin had been finalized.

The cabin was built just in time to avert nearly a solid week of constant rain. The roofing was very effective, and the areas that needed some reinforcement and added cover got the attention they needed. The fireplace was kept hot to further solidify and cement in all of its building components; the boys were worried about the excessive rain taking down their newly assembled fireplace and chimney. This early test was perfect for getting their new home all set up for the coming winter and the combination of rain, dirt, sand, grasses, and clay from down by the creek gave them the perfect weather and materials to get the job and all the fine-tuning done in one shot. The extended rain also gave the boys plenty time to mud-seal the log walls just like Nik had done back at the homestead.

Nik had been working on a makeshift cover for the camouflage the boys were wearing; just in case they ever had the need to be seen, they would look like everyone else. He had picked up the burlap throw rug from the homestead to use as a kneeling pad during his work there and forgot to put it back. He spent hours splitting the many layers of burlap from the rug and was making poncho-like cover-ups for them. He coined the name of these cover-ups as "burlaps."

Sid had turned his attention to creating covers for their rifles out of pieces of wood and bark. He carved these covers out of the very plentiful small pines that covered the southeastern landscape around the valley floor near C-10. He was able to mold the covers with carved fittings, which sort of clicked into place on the rails of the boys' rifles. These would cover the rifles with nicely shaped wood panels. This was a very interesting idea for them, and the job was executed perfectly by Sid and his small carving knives from his massive store of items from 2010. Now their modern weapons would resemble weapons of the day, sort of. Needless to say, there would be very few folks in 1780 who would ever be able to pick out their rifles as anything other than normal from a distance, and more importantly, the wood covers simply took the attention off the items as a majority of rifles had wood on them in this time period.

John had also been working the "tailoring roles" with Nik during these past weeks. He had worked on a particular piece of the outfits Sid had provided for them, and he did it somewhat secretively. He had removed the Velcro patch depicting the American Flag with its full complement of fifty stars from his shoulder and experimented with some berries he had found. These berries looked and tasted like blackberries, although they were considerably smaller than blackberries. He used them to create a type of ink or paint that he then applied to fabricate a thirteen-star field from the existing fifty, not the known and popular circle of thirteen stars, but one that was unique to their team. He worked his patch until he was able to get the ink to stick, and then there were thirteen white stars clearly displayed on the patch. John presented his modified patch to the others and, with their approval, began working on their patches.

The patch was very interesting, because, looking at it, you knew there were fifty stars present, but it appeared as if the thirteen were clearly strong and more present; the other thirty-seven seemed to exist as "stars in waiting"—waiting in the wings to be eventually and rightfully uncovered as the "nifty fifty" they knew and loved from the year 2010.

"Very cool, Dude!" Nik said to John.

Sid followed it up with, "It's like we are prophets or time lords or something, boldly flaunting the thirteen stars and the blue-grayed-out placeholders of the future thirty-seven."

John nodded his head and said, "Thanks, guys. We've done a ton of work these past several weeks, and it was good for us to have our little side projects."

The rains subsided, and the weather cooled off. It was a refreshing change for the group, and the boys were hoping for an early autumn and an untypically warm winter in the mountains. A "warm" winter in the mountains was loosely defined by the boys as temperatures in the thirties and forties; this was a very optimistic and unlikely hope, but they all surely welcomed the cooler weather, as the heat and humidity of the summer months had worn on their nerves. A day or two of relaxation and "getting their bearings" was in order. Now that the cabin was built and the canal was engineered and running beautifully, they wanted to explore the caverns to the southwest. Then they really wanted to try to find the bald from which they were spit off of four months ago—or 230 years from now, whichever might be appropriate.

The caverns they were now searching for had been spotted briefly in their trek to find C-10 just a few weeks before. The boys also remembered the map they had pondered over as they were driving to their eventual camping spot in 2010. Nik had theorized that the old, spooky-looking, unmarked trail they had seen at their campsite in 2010 was the approximate way down to the caverns. It wasn't long before they were slipping and sliding down the hills and across swollen creeks to the area where they believed the caverns to be. They looked around a few of the caves and caverns that they found and noted defensible positions where they could retreat to in case they had a need in the future.

"What would make us retreat into these?" inquired John.

Sid, wiping the blood off a scratch he suffered while descending down to the area, answered, "Not sure, but it's good to know it's here just in case."

The boys continued looking for a while and poked around the area only to discover a source of very fresh, very cold water in one of the caverns. "Also a good sign," commented Sid.

Nik was distant in thought and appeared to be somewhere else on this journey, so John nudged him and asked, "What's up, man?"

Nik just answered, "I want to get done here and go find the bald."

With that, and the fact that Sid was satisfied with the cave and cavern exploration, John exclaimed, "Let's go!"

... 15 ...
Devil's Bald Revisited

THE BOYS HAD DONE a little looking around during the collection of materials for the cabin and thought they may have located the correct course to take up to the bald. It wasn't the same as moving up a trail that had existed and been traveled and maintained for many years in 2010. It was truly virgin ground to them and probably most other white men; it would take a little time to figure out and navigate their way to where they thought they were going.

The boys developed a system for marking their trail and progress during their search. This way, if they had to make several attempts to find the bald, they could keep track of the correct paths and dead ends. It also kept them from getting lost in the process. This wasn't like their previous trek from Charleston; it was a mission of seek and return, whereas before it was move forward and keep moving forward to C-10. They set out, cutting a small tree every so often at Sid's height to mark their trail. If they failed the first time, they would then mark their trail on their next attempt by cutting the same tree at a lower height.

It was midmorning, and the boys basically made it out to be a vacation day. Armed and vigilant with only some of their gear (the rest was hidden in a secret area under their cabin), they began to make their way up the hill. They hadn't seen a soul in this area since arriving those many weeks ago, and they were fairly confident of their "home sector's" security, or at least absence of population.

They moved on course up the hill, briefly checked out the canal, and then continued on course to—well, they didn't know exactly.

"That way," said John. They worked their way up a hill that offered some of the visual overlooks they thought they vaguely remembered, but as the trees were still full of their summer foliage, they really couldn't see much other than the most immediate scenery of their wooded location. They did stop a lot on this trek, not because they were winded or tired but for the careful comprehension of their surroundings. They laughed about the shape they were in now and the sharp contrast to how they were last time they thought they were in this area. They had walked themselves into a shape probably unrivaled by most in the year 2010. They were stronger, had more endurance, and were thinner by about forty or fifty pounds each, and they were certainly much better for it in so many ways.

They didn't know for a fact if they were even on the same hill they had hiked almost eight months ago. On one of their breaks, Nik inquired of his compatriots, "So, anything, guys?"

The others knew what he was talking about; Nik was asking them if they felt okay. They deduced many months ago that the medical issues the three experienced on their hike to the bald in 2010 had something to do with the impending "effect" that had set them on this journey back in time and away from their location in the mountains. The symptoms appeared to attack the individual's strengths—Nik's vision and John's hearing. Sid was the exception. The "attack" on Sid, and they deemed it an attack for some reason, seemed to go after an old injury and his entire nervous system. This was all a theory, of course, and they really had no clue what it was all about.

"Nope, I feel fine," said John.

"I'm good," Sid added.

There was part of each of them that wanted to feel some effects. They still hoped deep down that some sort of childish storyline would play out, and they could "jump back through the portal" and be home again in time and space.

"Well, which way now, guys?" asked Nik.

"Let's go this way," Sid suggested as he pointed up the hill. They moved up the hill, stopping every once in awhile to let Sid cut a sapling. He'd then bend it over unnaturally so it was sticking the opposite direction of everything else growing in the forest. They looked back and could see their course very easily from the cut, bent trees Sid had been fabricating.

"Good job, Sid," John commented as Sid took a bow.

The group moved up the hill, and the forest grew denser as they continued. This couldn't be compared to their trek in the winter of 2010—all the leaves simply obscured everything. It was a quiet, pleasantly tepid day, and they found it easy to wander and just enjoy their walk in the woods. They truly couldn't imagine that anything could go wrong on this day—and to this point, they couldn't be any more correct.

The group approached a small, flat area where they had a choice of directions; one would send them downhill slightly, and one would send them uphill and to the right. They all chose and felt the uphill course was correct, and Sid looked anxious now.

"What's up, man?" Nik asked. "What are you thinking?"

Sid looked intently up the hill and broke out into a cold sweat. John moved to his front and looked at him straight in the face as Nik unstrapped his rifle from his back and moved to a defensive posture.

Sid quietly said, "This is it.... It's up there."

"You sure?" John asked. "There is a lot around that wasn't here in the wintertime."

Sid quickly responded. "No, no ... this is it. I ran ahead of you guys and was looking at where I was going. You guys came running up for me, from what you told me, trying to save me from whatever it was that we fell into. You probably didn't get a good look at anything."

"True," admitted John. The boys looked around. They all now had their rifles out and ready for, well, something ... anything. After twenty minutes or so, they decided to continue up the hill and see if the bald was actually up there.

Nik started digging in the pockets that covered his jacket and pants as Sid and John watched with amusement and wondered what their friend was doing. "Are you looking for that golden time warp device I gave you to transport us back to 2010?" Sid asked him.

Nik, who had been struggling with a very difficult pocket on the side of his body, finally retrieved the prize to offer to his friends. Wanting to make a gesture of "good luck," he held out three, still vacuum-sealed meat sticks he had saved for a special occasion. He then announced, "With these delicious, delectable morsels from the future, I ask the powers that be to show us some truth about all we have been through!"

The others laughed, unpacked their clearly worn and abused snack sticks from the future, lowered their weapons, and enjoyed the greasy, overly chewy, "meaty" snacks. They wiped their hands, and with a "Wow, that was good," they proceeded to raise their rifles and walk up the hill.

The group fanned out and walked apart from each other along the width of the woods. The idea was to not be clumped together walking out onto the bald to potentially be picked off by some yet-unknown force. Yes, they were on edge and might have been overreacting a bit, but considering their reality of the past eight months, it was better to be safe than sorry.

Nik spotted a thinning area up ahead, used the bird whistle to alert the others, and pointed to where he was looking. Sid looked through his rifle scope and didn't see anything of interest. Nik now used his hands to ask the others how they felt. The others gave the thumbs-up sign and began to walk again. They arrived at the end of the thick portion of the woods and slowly moved through the perimeter to take a look around. There was nothing of interest there, which was a relief in a way, but the boys were hoping to see something that might explain their situation.

"Crud!" said John. "I really wanted to see an obelisk or pyramid or something so we could say, 'Ah, that's the culprit!'"

Instead what they saw was the bald, the lonely piece of rock rounding out the top of the hill, devoid of trees or anything of any appreciable size. The group spread out around the bald and looked for any clues, anything at all that would give them promise of a way back through time to 2010. There was nothing, not so much as a scratch on the rock, a tingle to the skin, an itch on a forehead—nothing.

Sid stopped sneaking around now and slung his rifle onto his back. "Nothing here to see," he sighed. "Why we were apprehensive about this again?"

Nik secured his rifle onto his back and wandered over to the spot where he believed they'd gone careening off the hill to land in 1780 some four months ago. He saw nothing.

John walked over and asked, "Is this where I pushed us off?"

"I think so," replied Nik.

John laughed, "Well, I tried."

"You did good, man!" Nik said.

"So where do we go from here?" asked Sid.

"Home, gentlemen. Home," implored Nik.

They slowly walked away from the bald, looking back and hoping that something would still show up, but there was no change. They would visit the bald on and off through the next few weeks, looking to see if anything might appear different—nothing did.

... 16 ...
A Decision to Serve History

SEPTEMBER 14, 1780: "GENTLEMEN, I proclaim that we are officially members of the American Colonial population and now truly persons of the eighteenth century," Nik announced. "As standing members of said Colonial peoples of America, I think we need to watch history unfold!"

"So, what are you thinking?" asked Sid.

"Well, I propose hiking out to a place called Kings Mountain and setting up an observation post. We will sit and watch the American militias kick the tar out of Major Patrick Ferguson's army on the battlefield there," Nik proudly proclaimed.

"So, is that all we are going to do?" asked John.

"I don't know. I just figure we could look and maybe write down what we see. Talk about a history lesson," replied Nik.

"So when do we leave?" Sid blurted.

"September 21 of this year of our Lord, 1780," Nik announced. "We will set forth into history!"

John followed with, "Nice!"

They planned their trip and made sure they had all the provisions needed for their excursion. They would leave in six days and secure all the doors and windows of their cabin. This was quite a task. They hadn't designed or built any way to secure the structure yet, so it was back out into the woods to gather more materials for construction. They would build a top cover for the fireplace, shutters with locks for the windows, and a locking mechanism for the front door. This door-locking mechanism posed the greatest challenge; the final assembly became a puzzle-type device where sticks acted as knobs that had to be turned the proper direction in the proper sequence to successfully open the door. It took almost the whole six days to get it oriented and working correctly.

Three nights before they left, the boys sat down and talked objectives. They wanted to understand exactly what they were getting into and why. It was basically an observation and documentation mission, so there shouldn't be a reason to get involved or have anyone see them. The forces on the field would be fully engaged in their own affairs and should never have an opportunity or need to see the group. John inquired about aiding the Colonial forces in any way. Nik explained that historically, the battle would be over in about an hour, and the American militias would score a quick and decisive victory. That's why Nik picked this battle; it was a key win for the Americans and was, or would be, an utterly lopsided Colonial victory. Because of these factors, the boys should not be tempted to do anything but sit back and watch history come alive and unfold before their eyes.

Sid asked, "Do you foresee any issues that might have us fighting in any way?"

"No," Nik reassured Sid and John. "Historically, this was, er, *is* a slam dunk. Based on the forces on the field, the Colonials will easily win, with a 100 percent assured positive outcome of an American victory. The British were simply outclassed, outgunned, and outmaneuvered that day."

On the last day before the departure for Kings Mountain, the boys hung around restlessly. Sid played with his scanner/radio and listened to the obvious and typical 1780 dead air on all frequencies. John pondered the canal while they were gone, and Nik poked at the fire. John asked if he could get some help in closing the canal off for their trip. "There's no sense for this to run while we are gone, right?" he explained.

Sid and Nik agreed; the life expectancy of the canal could be drastically extended by not having water run through it when it wasn't needed—while they were gone, for example. They left camp to take care of the canal, and Sid left his radio set to auto scan. Normally this wasn't a big deal; it would simply and effortlessly scan through the millions of channels of dead and open air. However, on this evening, with the boys gone to work the canal, they missed a cold and ghostly sound in the forest: "Я понимаю, товарищ [I understand, comrade]." The words screeched over the small speaker of their scanner/radio.

Upon their return to the cabin, Sid noticed that his radio was still on and complained. "You know, I am such a bonehead. I left the radio on! Huh, the automatic scan stopped. That's odd, and it's a weird frequency it stopped on. Bizarre! Oh well, probably dying batteries or something."

John added, "Yeah, weak batteries sometimes make my police scanner back home stop scanning randomly. It's no big deal."

Sid made a note of the frequency, turned the radio off and packed it safely away. With that, the team went to sleep in preparation for the morning start to Kings Mountain.

... 17 ...
Let Us See What We Can See

THE APPROACH TO KINGS Mountain was ordinary, and no one would ever imagine what was about to happen here in the coming days—nothing more than a dirt trail, just like all other trails they had either walked or seen in the past five months here in 1780. After all this time, the boys were still amazed at the lack of buildings, structures, and roads.

"Dirt, dirt, and more dirt," wailed John, quickly cupping his mouth as he realized he was being really loud. "Sorry," he added quietly.

"It's all right, man. We haven't seen or heard a soul in days," replied Sid in a quiet voice.

The date was October 5, 1780, and the boys were going to look at the area where, in a week, they would see one of the key turning points in the American Revolutionary War. Their plan was a simple one—set up an observation post far off the battlefield and just watch what transpired. Nik knew the history and assured the others they should be in no danger at the extreme range from which they would be hidden and observing. Sid and John honestly didn't care about danger at that point, and they knew they would be quite far away from the action. Sid was fairly confident that the weapons of the day, even if misfired in their direction, wouldn't reach them. "Even with a stiff tailwind," he chuckled.

Nik described the actual battlefield as a sort of "raised mixing-spoon-shaped, plateau-type piece of real estate." John was less than impressed. "What the hell kind of description is that?" he heckled.

"Well, that's what I remember, because, honestly, it was stupid that the British got themselves pinned up there," Nik explained.

"Maybe they thought it was a good, defensible place, being the high ground and all," Sid suggested.

"Yes, but accessible on all sides, as I recall," Nik noted. "Did they think there wasn't a chance the Colonial forces could conjure up enough men to basically surround them?"

"Who knows?" said John. "It apparently didn't work out so well for them, though."

"No, not so much," Nik said, his speech trailing off.

"Oh boy, I don't like the sound of that," said Sid suddenly.

"Sound of what?" crackled Nik.

"Well, whenever you trail your mouth off on a thought like that, it usually means something just popped into your brain that I, um, *we* won't like."

"Well," Nik started.

"See, I told you," yelped Sid.

"Well," Nik said, revisiting the previous question-and-answer session they had just finished. "Why would the British stick themselves up in a place like that? Doesn't seem like a decision the best fighting force on the planet would make. Really, think about it."

"Maybe they just had a bad day," John suggested.

"Maybe, but it just doesn't add up," grumbled Nik.

Sid asked John, "Don't you just love it when he gets twisted around something?"

"No, not really," John replied meekly. "It just means something bad is going to happen."

Sid laughed. "You have a point there."

"So you're telling us something else caused them to make a horrible miscalculation?" Sid was now pressing Nik for additional thoughts on the apparent British stupidity.

"I don't know," Nik admitted. "It didn't make much sense to me reading the historical account back in high school. Now is no different. Is it possible that the guy in charge ate a bad meal, threw up all night, and couldn't think straight going into the day of battle? Hell if I know," said Nik in a most comical fashion.

John laughed. "You have a magically nasty way of expressing yourself sometimes, Nik."

"Yeah, it's a curse," Nik said with a smile.

"I've listened to this nonsensical dribble for a lot of years. Honestly, it never gets old. He makes up more stuff than most comedians, and it has always kept us entertained," admitted Sid.

The hike continued, and they began to slow down as they approached the general area, making sure no one was around before getting to the top of the "mixing spoon" plateau. They arrived at the base of the plateau and began their ascent. It wasn't a hard climb by any means, and they made sure to stick close to whatever tree line might be close. Nik didn't want the group to stray too far from the southern tip (or the end of the handle of the spoon), because he knew there were folks in the area from both sides looking out for the other's forces.

Nik explained, "The Colonials in this battle were basically a hodgepodge group; they hadn't been trained by the military but were true militia, hunters, trappers, backwoodsmen, and marksmen. These guys were very good shots with their weapons. Some of their weapons had a bore length of forty-five inches—huge and very accurate with an excellent range for 1780."

After quickly looking at the area where the British would be camping and then the site where they would eventually be attacked and defeated, the boys moved off toward the south and the place where Nik had figured they'd make their "observation post."

"So, what's the plan?" Sid inquired smartly, as they were making double time to the southern portion of the plateau.

John, looking interested and curious, listened intently to the next words out of Nik's mouth. "Well," Nick began but paused for a long while before stating the obvious. "We observe."

John, utterly let down, scratched his head. Nik continued. "We know what is supposed to happen. The British camp right over there after leaving a place called—um, I forget." After another pause, it came back to him. "Gilbert Town. Gilbert Town, that's it. Anyway, after Gilbert Town, they came here. The Colonials got wind of the encampment and rushed groups of militia from the north, south, east, and west to this very place where we're walking. The fact that the Colonials knew they were here tells me there are spies or informants in the area, which is why I think we should stay out of sight."

Sid just shook his head. "Who knows this stuff?"

John quickly interjected. "Um, our friend the history book. 'Nuff said for me; let's go."

As they picked up the pace to their destination, John inquired, "So, what's this observation post supposed to look like?"

Nik replied, "A big pile of downed trees."

Sid laughed. "Well, that's inventive."

"Yeah, I don't figure we have too much time to get undercover, so a well-built hut wouldn't make sense. We couldn't build it anyway; therefore, a pile of downed trees. Basically, it's an igloo made out of trees and branches, a—"

"Yeah, we got it," interrupted Sid, trying to slow the continuation of the obvious.

"Yup, crystal clear. You're good," rambled John as he rolled his eyes.

"One more request?" asked Nik. "Once we get to the wood line down there, we lose the burlaps and go camo in the woods. It's time to disappear."

Sid and John agreed. "Yes, sir!" they said simultaneously.

They reached the southeastern tip of the plateau, and Sid looked around. "So, right here?" he asked Nik.

"Well, kind of," Nik said. He then walked over to the edge of the drop-off and pointed down the ledge about two feet. "Right there," he added.

The three peered down the ledge, which was more like a hill going down in a rather steep grade. "We'll dig out a V-like channel and put logs across it to create a little floor. Then we can take down some trees and make a crude frame structure to then set branches on. We'll use other foliage on and around the base."

The other two looked at Nik like he'd just eaten three candy bars and was on the ultimate sugar high, jabbering away uncontrollably. "What?" Nik stopped and inquired.

"Nothing," John blurted. "I just can't believe you came up with all that so fast."

Nik explained that he had been thinking about a plan for this observation shelter for the past two weeks. "It all looks a little different from what I remember reading, but ..." He continued mumbling about what he thought he remembered about this time and the pending battle.

Sid interrupted with some laughter and started to inquire about posting a lookout during the construction of their shelter. Each of them thought it was a very good idea based upon the possible spy problem Nik had previously theorized about. They worked through the rest of the day and most of that night to make the observation shelter perfect. It literally looked like a pile of trees—their own little thicket away from it all. The pile of brush that was now their observation station was almost assuredly not going to draw any attention from folks with war and killing on their minds.

Sitting in the observation post, John asked about the whole floor V-canal construction and its purpose. "When it rains," Nik explained, "it'll give the rain somewhere to run off other than the floor of our little abode here. I don't want to sit or sleep on a wet, muddy floor."

"Rain? What rain?" Sid looked at Nik like he was crazy and continued. "We've had great weather. Maybe a few quick showers, but nothing earth-shattering."

Now John proudly sat up like he and Sid had the upper hand in the "overworked design" of their hut. Nik just smiled. "Yeah, yeah, maybe we didn't need that. Yes, it was a complete waste of time. You're right," Nik stated, still smiling.

John slumped now. "So what does he know that we don't?" he asked Sid.

"I don't know, but whatever it is, we'll find out. I'm sure of it," murmured Sid.

Nik asked if they could get some more branches and stuff on top of the shelter, to which they all agreed. John acted as lookout this time. Sid also suggested they think about not using fires from now on until the events came, occurred, and ended, and they found themselves alone again in the quiet of this area. They all agreed with a nod and a shrug.

The temperatures of early October on this end of the North Carolina-South Carolina border were very nice—temperate days with cooler nights, but all in all, it was very comfortable and pleasant. The boys reminisced about the summer months, the hiking, the extreme heat, and the bugs; they decided that these were better weather days for sure. They spent some time collecting things they would need when they were hunkered down, including water, grasses, and berries. Whatever John caught in the form of meats, they quickly precooked to have for their time in the observation hideout.

All was going very smoothly, but as the three were carefully foraging for items, Sid invoked the warning bird whistle and motioned for all to get down and come together. Nik wondered what Sid had caught sight of through the binoculars as he moved stealthily and quickly to the others.

Sid whispered, "About a half mile, maybe a mile south and a little east ... looks like an encampment, and a pretty well-hidden one at that. It looks like it's hidden on purpose, and it's pretty big from what I have seen so far."

"Hmm," pondered Nik aloud. "Who are they? Can you tell?"

"It's at least a day before we are supposed to see anything or anybody from either side. Why don't we collect what we can and get packed into the shelter?" John suggested.

"I second that; sounds like a real good plan to me," added Sid.

"I third that motion," said Nik.

The rest of the evening was spent securing their position and "learning" where the peep holes were so they'd be able to easily navigate them for observation of the future happenings. They hung their rifles on the walls, about a third of the way up from the floor of their shelter and got comfortable for the long haul. Sid wished he had acquired at least one pair of night-vision apparatus for their trip and mumbled, "I won't forget next time!"

"What?" John asked him.

Sid said, "Nothing. I'll tell you later."

Wanting to lighten the mood a bit, Nik offered up, "Oh yes, and by the way, it's going to rain like the seven hammers of hell sometime soon." He then smiled.

John just trailed off a, "Great." Nik also informed the boys that they would really need to be utterly silent, as the British tents would be very close to the south, just down the hill. Sid and John wondered what other surprises were in store for them on this trip.

The next morning brought a good day with high clouds and more company. "Well, there they are. Behold, the British," Nik whispered. Peering out of their homemade thicket, they saw the exploratory lead scouts of the British troops under Ferguson's command. They were at extreme range on the southwesternmost point of the plateau and well down the hill.

John whispered. "Just like you said, Nik."

"Yeah, they probably arrived last night sometime after dark, and the main body is probably just over that hill to the south," Nik continued. "Man, I am nervous!"

Sid gently asked about the camp to the southeast. "So who are they? Americans?"

"I don't know," Nik admitted. "Not Americans, though; they ended up basically running here from all directions all night and day on the sixth and seventh. I don't know who they are,"

John offered up his own thoughts on the matter. "Well, do we wait and see, or do you want to slip away tonight?"

Nik, admitting he was spooked, said, "Well, I'd be lying if I said I wasn't freaked out by all this; this is a serious battle coming up, and sitting here makes me really nervous."

Sid didn't understand the mixed signals. "Well, we can go; we just have to avoid that force to the southeast of us," he pointed out.

"No, we need to stay," Nik insisted.

Sid, not trying to challenge, repeated the obvious question as he pointed off to the unknown and hidden encampment. "So who is that down there?"

Suddenly, abruptly, and rudely changing the subject, Nik coarsely asked Sid to give them a rundown of what they had for firepower. Sid was now really confused. He thought Nik knew exactly what they had for rifles, pistols, and ammunition. They had carried it all for more than 320 miles as they trekked through South and North Carolina these past five months! Was Nik cracking up? John also looked a little confused but didn't say anything.

After a short time, Sid figured out his friend's "check tactic"; it was one of Nik's methods for stalling for a moment to ponder something. Sid proceeded with his request. "Well, we have two AR-15s. Yours is scoped to four hundred yards; mine is scoped to three hundred yards. We have ninety rounds of ammunition for them in magazines and ready to go. We have the M1A, which is scoped to five hundred yards with eighty rounds loaded and ready to go, and we have the 50 Beowulf, iron sighted to one hundred and fifty yards with forty rounds loaded and ready to go. There's also plenty of boxed and clipped ammunition left for us to use after the magazines are emptied."

"No, we're not leaving," Nik, equally as rudely as before, quietly blurted.

"Oh boy!" John mumbled.

Sid interrupted John's moment of expression and asked, "Okay, what's going on, Nik? What are you thinking?"

Nik appeared to be in a little contained frenzy. "Okay, we wait.... We wait. I have to calm down," Nik said with a slight smile now. "Let's watch the Brits put up their encampment, and let's watch this thing play out." Sid asked Nik if he wanted to sit down, and Nik responded by admitting, "I need to. Can you watch out, guys? I've got to think."

"Uh, yeah. Okay," they agreed. John realized they were in a small, confined area, and he didn't want to make Nik any more crazy than he appeared to be. At his first chance, he whispered to Nik, "I am going to talk to Sid about you now. Is that okay?"

"Yeah, man. No problem," Nik said with a smile.

John moved over to Sid. "What the—" he started to ask, but Sid stopped him short of completing his thought. Sid explained that Nik's request for a status update was an attempt to pause, so he could start working on a problem. He now needed a minute to start thinking about it. "To him, time was really short for a plan," Sid said.

"Plan? Plan for what?" John inquired.

"Not sure," Sid murmured. They sat in silence for hours as Sid and John looked out to the north, east, and west. Nik peered to the southeast toward the unknown encampment. Then Sid looked up. "Oops. Who do we have here?" he asked.

The others didn't see anything as yet. And then John spotted it too. "Uh-oh, a British—"

"Mounted cavalryman," Nik said, completing John's thought.

Sid and John looked at Nik. "How did you know that?" Sid asked.

"*It's a trap!*" snapped Nik as quietly as one could with panic in his voice.

"Okay, what are you talking about now?" John demanded.

"A trap," Sid said. "Those guys on the horses are going to defend the troops on the hill here, but history tells us that the British were defeated here."

"Yup," Nik said, "they were." Nik paused again. "But that history hasn't transpired yet; that history isn't history yet. I was afraid of this!" Nik steamed.

"Afraid of what?" John asked. "What are you talking about? How could any of us know anything about what was going on? We are just here, no one knows were are here, and we aren't affecting anything." And then John ran out of things to say.

Sid chuckled a bit. "Time is messing with us, isn't it?"

Nik nodded. "It would appear that way," he said. "We know what's supposed to transpire in *our* official, historical time line, and we know as we whisper among ourselves that history, or at least some of the history we know, is proceeding as it's supposed to. But these guys on the horses—these guys are devastating to an unsuspecting militia force. They will slaughter those Colonial ground forces if the Colonial leaders don't see them coming. If the militias don't know the mounted British are there, they will most certainly get flanked and wiped out."

A silence grew in the hideout again as Nik got up to look at the forming encampment. The lone horseman, now off his horse, was conferring with some of the men at the encampment. This encampment was now filling with a few British regulars and a majority of Tory defenders of the crown.

The boys sat down and started to discuss ideas on what was going on and what they should do. "So, we sit and watch the battle?" Sid asked.

"Sure, and what if it ends in a British victory when a defeat was the clear result before?" Nik inquired.

"Well, maybe something happens that makes the British lose," suggested John in a hopeful manner.

"Not with light dragoons in play for the British; light, heavy, any cavalry is a bad deal for the colonies," explained Sid. Sid also kept a lookout on the various positions as the sun started to set in the west and the clouds thickened overhead. The boys knew that the American militias would be forming up on this hill sometime tomorrow and would attack around three o'clock in the afternoon. They also knew that it would only take an hour for the battle to be over, based on their history. All bets were off if the mounted British forces were allowed to engage their American targets, and that was just the honest truth. "What to do" would be the looming question they all pondered.

The dark of night took over as the boys listened and quietly discussed options and scenarios. The sound of nature around them was quite loud on this fall evening, so any noise they produced was masked very well by the volume from the bugs, frogs, and everything else buzzing around them in their evening surroundings. As they discussed possibilities, the scenarios were whittled down to several options, depending on what the observed forces did the next day. Most of the scenarios had the boys following their original plan—observe and do not interfere. The decision to get involved was extremely difficult, and the situation for interference had to meet some very strict conditions.

Sid and Nik devised a set of rules that would protect their positions and status while giving them the ability, albeit statistically very small, of engaging the British dragoon force if need be. Their rules of engagement (ROE) were as follows: (1) they could and would engage the mounted British force only, and under no conditions would they extend their weapons reach to the ground forces of either encampments; (2) they would only engage the mounted British force if it was actually and clearly advancing on an unsuspecting American force; (3) they could engage if, and *only* if, the fight was engaged at the British main camp and/or main battle location at Kings Mountain. In other words, the British on the hill and/or the American forces must be actively shooting for the boys to fire their own weapons. The boys' weapons could not be the only weapons firing on the field, *ever*, in any theater where they might engage; and (4) Finally, once they engaged a group, there must be no survivors. Engaged forces must not be able to report anything about the boys, their position, their numbers, their weapons, or anything else about them.

Sid got done outlining these conditions to the group, and there was the expected silence. Nik noted that their timing would need to be impeccable and that they would need to pick their targets quickly and dispatch them even more quickly. John raised his hand in the midst of discussion and stated a good point. "Um, none of us has really practiced any of this ... *ever*. We've only had a glimpse of our firing arcs out of our shelter here, because we were not going to be engaging anything. Where will the horse guys even be for us to shoot them?"

"All good questions, and that's why our timing will be so important," Nik said. "If all else fails, we can just default to doing nothing." And with that, John changed the subject and asked Nik and Sid why their reinforced NASA space blankets were woven up in the ceiling of their shelter.

Nik laughed for a moment and said, "Wait for it."

John looked at Sid and said, "Ooooh kaaay." Thirty or forty minutes later, nature dealt them a pouring rain.

The rain was coming down in torrents, and their shelter, made of downed trees two or three inches in diameter, was holding up in grand fashion. They reveled in the "river under the floor," as the water began to run off the hill right down the V canal they had engineered several days before. Nik proudly smiled, and Sid patted him on the back. John congratulated Nik on his keen knowledge of history and all of the bizarre details he brought to the table.

At that very moment there were American militias from all over, in every direction, literally running to the area in a hurried march to engage these encamped British forces. The boys were there as well—waiting, not knowing, a lot like the British and the Americans. What would tomorrow bring?

... 18 ...
This Isn't Proper History. How Will We Explain This?

THE NEXT DAY BROUGHT an end to the torrential rains and a quick awareness and tension of what was yet to be. The boys were awake early and somewhat nervous as they continued going over all the potential situations that would potentially see that day. They all felt that somehow they would now be thrust into "this affair," and somehow, deep down, they felt some patriotic compulsion to protect their country and their history. They stared at the modified US flag patches on their arms. The clear option of "do nothing" was certainly on the table and always seemed that it would be the correct thing to do in the context of the continuum of time and space. Their rules of engagement were very specific and clear—well, as clear as they could be now that their emotions had started to build in anticipation.

"I had a conversation last night," Nik explained to Sid and John. "I spoke to the Good Lord and asked him for guidance. I tell you guys, I have never been let down, you know." Nik stopped as his eyes began to flood a bit.

In support of their position and his friend Nik, Sid added, "You have told me that a couple of times before. I certainly believed you then, but this makes me believe you all the more now."

John, knowing Nik was fairly spiritual for an American of their day (and not in an evangelical way) was surprised at his present emotional state. He wondered if Nik knew something about this day that the others didn't know. Nik quickly apologized, wiped his eyes, and moved to look at any potential movements on either side.

It was ten o'clock in the morning now, and Sid asked Nik if he had any details on the lineup of the Colonials before the battle. Nik began by explaining what he remembered (keeping in mind their perspective of the battle from their observation post); the Colonials built forces on all sides of the hill, more on the right side than the left.

John said. "Maybe this undocumented force might naturally concentrate on that side?" The others agreed. Sid noted that they may want to put two of their three rifles on that side of their outpost, just in case the charge came from the mounted force more on the right.

"Yes," Nik said, "the .50 and the .223. And the M1A on the left?"

"Good mix," confirmed Sid.

"If the situation meets our ROEs, who fires what?" inquired John.

Sid thought a while but wanted to leave Nik with his scoped AR-15, because he thought Nik was a natural lucky shot with that weapon. He would use the Beowulf .50-caliber rifle; if it really came to shooting the British mounted force, he would like to use the biggest slug they had and hoped to use it to hit multiple targets at once. "You know, to stretch the ammo," Sid added with a smirk.

They also had more open firing arcs on the right side, so Nik and Sid would man that side of things. And John would get the M1A on the left side, as the firing arc was much smaller and couldn't really fit two shooters. Again, they were betting that a larger force would be on the right side anyway. The .308 from the M1A round on the left would serve up a punishing blow and should easily handle that side of things if their hunch was correct.

John, not wanting to offend, returned to Nik's emotional moment and asked, "Nik, are you afraid?"

Nik waited a moment before he answered. "Afraid would be too strong a term, just very concerned about all this. This could mean everything about the future of what we know of our history."

John said he understood and wondered if their actions would truly change anything. Maybe, in fact, their actions, as they theorized, would maintain the historical time line as they knew it.

It was now eleven thirty, and the tension continued to build. Sid looked intently at the battlefield for signs of the coming American forces—none yet. Nik nervously checked to see where his clips were and then looked to the right of their post, riveting his attention south to the "other" British position—no movement yet. He felt that if they didn't see the mounted forces moving forward, they might not even know about the coming battle. Maybe they would move off and miss it altogether. Could that be how history rights itself? Nik chuckled as he thought to himself that he wasn't looking to avoid a fight exactly; it wasn't actually their fight to engage in anyway! None of them would be "of draft age" for two hundred or so years, plus or minus a decade.

"What are you snickering about over there?" Sid asked.

Nik explained his last thought. John, understanding what Nik was thinking, said, "Maybe it's not a trap; maybe they'll move off, and history will be what it was—or is—or whatever."

"Maybe," Sid acknowledged.

John added with a huge smile, "Nik, for once, I want you to be horribly wrong and completely off on this thing. I want to laugh at you, make fun of you, and call you a spiritual alarmist with a sense for nothing!"

Nik quietly laughed and agreed. "I hope I am wrong, and I hope you give me a hard time for it for the next 230 years!" He was trying to be light now; they all were. John checked his ammo, looked left, and tried to settle in with his weapon for the long wait of the afternoon.

1:55 p.m. Sid looked for the Americans to the south and west, Nik looked north for British, and John looked to the east and south for anything. A few minutes went by, and Sid almost lurched from his stance. "Look!" he exclaimed as he handed the binoculars to Nik. "Way off in the distance over there."

Nik whispered now. "There they are, right on time—our militias."

John moved over to look, and Nik handed the glasses over to him. "Whoa, ragtag-looking for sure."

Nik quickly moved back to his north-northeast perch. Some time went by, and Nik asked the time. "2:13 p.m.," John reported.

"So," Nik murmured, "let's load our first clips."

John slowly replied, "Really?"

Sid, already efficiently loading his first clip into his rifle, breathed. "Okay," he agreed.

"Yes, *if* we need to use them, it'll be a split-second decision," he continued. "This thing should start around three o'clock." The boys watched the Colonial militias form up around the hill south of where the British were now loosely stationed.

The British looked as if they were preparing for an attack, and because of Nik and his description, it almost looked to all the group like it had read about the battle in the history books. Sid reported these occurrences, and calm formed over the group. Sid, not wanting to be surprised with anything, asked Nik, "Anything to the north, Nik?"

"Nothing yet," Nik answered.

The minutes went by painfully slow. Nik's hands and arms were sweating now, Sid was rocking back and forth, and John was biting his nails. They all rechecked their clips for the umpteenth time and noticed that the battle area began to get louder with yells, hoots, and generally annoying clamor.

"Oh boy," gasped John.

"Yup, it's going to start," commented Nik nervously.

"Well, let's see what comes," Sid quietly added. A few more minutes, and it looked like the battle of Kings Mountain was about to foment, and minutes later, off it went!

The militias were in full advance now, and a few shots erupted. This was not the amount of shooting that their rules of engagement would allow them to begin firing, *and* they presently had no targets. Nik, constantly looking off to the north and east, reported that he had no contacts. Sid confirmed that the west was clear and continued to glance at the battle on the hill. John reported that he had no contacts and snuck a peek at the battle to the north of them. "Wow," he said. "It happens slower than I thought."

Sid commented, "It isn't modern warfare, for sure."

3:17:45 p.m. The battle at Kings Mountain was now in full swing. The American forces were fully engaged with both sides firing at will. There were no forces in the British camp to the southeast of them, and there was no evidence of them anywhere. Nik commented, "Okay, we have enough weapons fire now. Stay alert and clear on how much gunfire is happening; don't fire if it quiets down."

Nik quietly and meekly suggested, "Weapons free?"

"Weapons free," replied Sid and John.

"Still no contacts," John said. Sid confirmed, and Nik began to agree but quickly stopped.

3:18:48 p.m. "Wait.... Oh man ... here they come!" Nik reported with surprise. "Oh my!"

"Oh my God!" John gasped.

"You have ten or twelve on your side, John!" Nik reported.

"We have more than twenty, " Sid gasped with a hushed tone!"

"Holy—" Nik gasped.

The mounted British forces were moving right past their location—thirteen on the left where John waited and thirty-seven on the right where Sid and Nik were stationed. "Wait.... Listen.... Wait," instructed Sid.

The sound of the battle continued, and the dragoon forces were now surely headed for the battle on the hill, and they were not moving at a very fast pace. They seemed really relaxed, as a matter of fact. "They are waiting for the Americans to be fully consumed and looking forward ... and away from their approach! They want to catch the Americans by surprise and from the back!" said Nik, seemingly almost out of breath.

"Nik, you were right! It's a trap!" John replied.

"Okay, they are almost here. Don't fire early; let them get just about even with us," instructed Sid. "Steady ... steady ... lots of gunfire out there, a lot of noise. We're good to fire."

3:18:57 p.m. Nik glanced at Sid and quickly ordered, in the most muffled bark of a command he could muster, *"Fire!"*All the fury of their modern weaponry began ripping into the unshielded British mounted force. There were fifty targets moving at one to two miles an hour; they passed directly in front of and through the boys' firing arcs. They were between ninety and 175 yards away from the boys when the firing began.

The dragoons stopped and scrambled for an unfortunate split second in and among the boys' fire. The utter surprise to the dragoon forces, which the boys were now engaged with, would certainly aid in their utter destruction as the boys' rounds effortlessly destroyed their targets, some two and three at a time. Sid's shots were obliterating his targets as the .50-caliber rounds exploded through anything they hit. Nik paused for a split second, making sure the battle on the hill continued and then quickly returning to his firing pattern. He was targeting the farthest cavalry first then bringing his fire into the closer targets.

John skillfully dispatched his targets and was pleased with himself and his success. It was truly a gory scene; the reality unfolding was an absolute massacre. The British were completely surprised and naturally outgunned. Additionally, the boys weren't even sure the British ever got a shot off in their direction. John, now having completely and successfully rendering his designated group ineffective, remained on the lookout for any other targets. He also kept listening to make sure the battle volume stayed high enough to cover their actions. He looked off toward the battle on the hill and saw that the rout that Nik had previously described was, in fact, occurring.

"It's happening, man. We are winning the day!" said John.

Sid quickly added, "Yes, sir!" Then he sharply yelled, "Nik, one got out! He's heading away from us at about ten o'clock, three hundred yards!"

"Damn! Sid, trade targets! Get that guy in close!" ordered Nik, talking about the one last dragoon on the ground within seventy-five yards. Nik then aimed out 290 yards at the runner and quickly sighted him in.

"Get him, Nik!" pleaded Sid. "Shoot now!"

Nik, having lined up his shot as best he could, squeezed the trigger and landed his shot. The fleeing dragoon received the shot to the base of his neck, exploding his skull, decapitating him, and killing him instantly. His headless corpse collapsed to the ground where he stood.

"Oh God," gasped Nik. Sid, having dispatched the closer target, listened for activity and looked to make sure that there were no more mounted units fleeing or otherwise.

Nik scanned their battlefield for moving targets and realized the savagery of their actions. John looked, listened, and slowly turned as he noticed a bayonet poking into their outpost from the hill side of the fort. "Holy—" he screamed.

The boys, looking in disbelief at the weapon protruding into their hidden, protected zone, were almost in shock. John, rather recklessly, pulled his pistol out of his holster and fired three rounds blindly into the brush of the shelter wall that made up their fort. He clearly landed his shots, as the bayonet fell out of the fort, and the moans of a dying man could be heard no farther than seven feet away from them.

In the distance, the battle continued and grew even louder. Sid, now moving to the back of their fort, pulled his pistol, stuck his head out of the shelter, identified the already fatally wounded British soldier, and immediately ended his life with two more well-placed rounds. He came back in, holstered his sidearm, and picked up his rifle again. They looked at each other, the battle on the hill, the southeastern approach to their position and stayed quiet.

It was 3:21:02 p.m. Their battle lasted just a little longer than three minutes. They worked on a little shelter repair as they witnessed the American victory at Kings Mountain. There were no indications that their escapades were noticed, no looks in their direction, no patrols sent to investigate odd noises or occurrences. They sat silently and looked at what they had done—dead men, dead horses, all dead, utterly destroyed. The severity of the wounds they had inflicted were typical of those a present-day weapon could do to the human body, but the ease and speed at which death was dealt absolutely stunned the boys.

They continued watching. It was now 5:45 p.m., and the battle was long over. It had lasted only sixty-five minutes; the cleanup on the battlefield had begun. Nik theorized that the Americans wouldn't stick around long, and they would soon whisk themselves and their British prisoners off under guard, possibly as early as that evening. No one came for the dragoons; the silence of *their* battlefield was eerie and haunting. Nik feared there might be survivors on their lines, survivors they might have to deal with that evening. They may have to kill again this day. This was not to be, however, because all of their targets were dead on the field—motionless, quiet, and at peace.

The boys remained as quiet as possible for the rest of the night as they slowly and deliberately collected the brass casings from the battle and accounted for every one of them. They fired a total of eighty-two rounds in three minutes and dispatched fifty-one targets, including their visitor at the end. Their ammo distribution for the day consisted of twenty .50-caliber rounds, twenty-four .308 rounds, five .45-caliber pistol rounds, and thirty-three .223 rounds.

Sitting quietly, John finally broke the silence at around eleven thirty that night. "So, how did it go?"

Sid answered, "We did well, I think. We won; the Americans won."

"Yup, that guy at the end was scary," Nik added.

With a smirk on his face, John asked, "The guy at the end was scary? It was all scary!"

Nik shrugged. "Well, yeah, but that guy was scary. He was way too close. I'm not sure what else to say. We needed to make sure we continued … well, 'we' may not have 'been' if the Americans lost that battle today. I am sure of what I knew; I'm tired, and my brain hurts. There are fifty-one dead guys out there that no one knows about. We need to figure out what to do with them before we leave this place," Nik explained.

Sid quietly said, "We can't just leave them there, exposed. We'll fix it; this is war, after all. Guys, close your eyes and rest." They all quietly agreed and only partially closed their eyes that night, while listening to the sounds of the cool evening chill. Nik inaudibly asked for forgiveness for what they had done that day. He felt chilled to the bone and held his head in his hands.

Sid was up early; John had joined him quietly on the field. He asked John to act as a watch for him while he dragged the deceased British soldiers into a pile near a small ravine immediately northeast and down the hill from the group's outpost. Nik woke up last and watched the others for a while until he figured out what they were doing. He looked to the battlefield on the hill for activity; all he saw was a wrecked camp and trash, no people. He scratched his head and scanned the rest of their surroundings before exiting the shelter. He moved down to the ravine and began to dig it out, making it wider to accommodate the fifty-one bodies they were planning on burying there. John came over and informed Nik of their plans and told him he would trade tasks when Nik got tired.

"Thanks, man," Nik said. "I need this right now; it'll be therapeutic."

Sid came over a bit later and asked Nik how he was doing. Nik said, "Okay ... we need to get this done today and leave tonight or tomorrow at the latest."

Sid nodded and added, "We'll get it done. And we'll leave, but where to?"

"Dunno," Nik admitted. "I'll think about it as I dig. You think on it too, and we'll talk later. Ask John as well, because we'll need everyone to give input into our decisions from now on."

"Okay," said Sid.

When Sid crossed John's path, he mentioned Nik's request. John nodded in agreement. As John came back for lookout duty, Nik, wanting to joke a bit, said, "Hey, man, I don't want to get my ass shot off digging my first mass grave! Keep a lookout and shoot whoever might want to put me in it, okay?"

John laughed. "I never saw you as a grave digger, man, and it's not really fitting, you know?"

Nik gasped, "I'll buy that."

John lingered and reassured Nik that they did what they needed to do and were all responsible for their actions. He continued. "No one person, Nik, is more responsible than any other; we agreed, and we had rules of engagement. They were strict and precise, and our country and our future was in real danger. It doesn't matter that we are 230 years out of time. We are Americans, and we defended our nation, no matter how young it is at this point."

"Thanks for the reassurance. I know what we did was what we thought and believed we needed to do. It's truly that simple," Nik replied, as he weakly smiled and went back to digging. He looked up again and said, "Maybe Daytona Beach?"

John said, "Huh?"

"You know, Daytona Beach—beach, speedway, fun! Maybe that's where we should go," Nik said. John shook his head and laughed. "Okay, maybe," he muttered as he headed back to Sid.

They were able to bury the bodies of the downed British deep enough to keep them from being scavenged by animals, birds, and other wildlife of the surrounding area. They also decided to leave them where they lay in hopes that the stench of death, which would soon set in, would be attributed to the dead horses scattered about their battlefield. This might keep a search for and discovery of the British soldiers from ever being initiated at this location. They had been watching all day for anyone scouting around the now quiet and pristine hillsides; no one was seen. The boys found a clean, fast-moving stream. It was still brimming with water from the rains of two nights ago, and the boys used it to clean themselves off from the day's work. Sid had mentioned that, moving forward, he hoped they wouldn't need to clean up anymore battlefields. Nik nodded his head with agreed upon exhaustion, while John ended the subject with a simple "amen."

They worked their way back to their outpost for the last night and talked about where they would head next. They all agreed that the short hike to C-10 would be fine. They had grown comfortable in the place they would go back to so many years from now as an escape from the utter chaos of the social and political realm that was 2010. Little did they know at that future time that they would end up hiking back to that place 230 years in the past to seek refuge from the chaos of that time period as well; it simply boggled their minds. They spent this final evening in their outpost among the phantoms, spirits and specters, both American and British, from the previous day's battle.

They spoke of how many time lines were potentially altered due to their actions, and John posed a very interesting point. "How do we know these guys didn't die in this or some other battle? Just because the facts of their deaths or disappearances didn't make the history books on this occasion, how do we know that they hadn't met some other fate during the run up to this battle or one before or later?

"And, the most eerie point of all," John added, "is how do we know *we* weren't part of all this all those years ago?"

Nik and Sid almost fell over at this. Nik comically yet seriously said with a smile, "Dude! And you thought I was the spooky one!"

Sid quickly leaned over looked at John and said, "Umm, you've been hanging out too much with him," and pointed to Nik. They all nodded their heads, and Nik admitted that John's thoughts were, or could be, completely valid. Nik ended with, "The possibilities are endless."

The rest of the night was spent packing the few things around the shelter. They wanted to slip away early in the morning and get clear of the area once and for all. They needed to distance themselves from the realities, old and new, of the battle at Kings Mountain.

... 19 ...
Stay Focused!

THE BOYS HAD WORKED their way through the wilderness now for almost six months, being very careful not to be seen or discovered in and among all of what was late 1780. They had done quite a job adapting to what they had to work with in that time, with a huge advantage from the modern items brought with them from the year 2010. It was a strange journey, and each one had his own specific talents and opinions to bring to the mix and they were happy to be headed back to their cabin in the mountains.

Honestly, the boys were quite pleased with themselves, still being very conservative about all the moves they had made to this point. Thoughts of "what was" and "what is" ran together now. At this point, their worlds had collided, which would pose a challenge in the time to come. What challenge, one might wonder? The battles and odd occurrences were not easily predicted by the group. Nik thought about it. He thought about it a lot and continued to worry about the group and their grip on reality individually, but honestly, a quiet calm had descended on the boys when they talked about their families and the time of the future.

Nik, quite the philosopher at times, believed their families would be okay and that they would get out of this. "Somehow" and "someway" had been discussed many times in these past few months. Sid and Nik would start endless conversations about time travel, eddies in time, currents of history, and on and on. Even John

---

enjoyed these topics, and it allowed the three to revolve together in the time and events. Through it all, some comfort was found for all of them. With all of this conversation and realization of their predicament, Nik had warned against maintaining their focus and getting complacent about their situation. Not one of them argued these points. Nik never claimed to be a prophet by any means, and he certainly wasn't perfect. He had even grudgingly felt the instances of complacency in himself, which he voiced to the others as he recognized them.

Nik wasn't trying to use probability against the team either, but he had warned about and feared of a time when all three would simultaneously blur or lose their perspective for just a moment and make a critical mistake. The fear of that moment—when in an instant of good cheer and presumed smooth sailing, one small detail was missed that could potentially expose them for who they were (souls out of time with the might of an army at their fingertips)—gnawed at Nik in the depths of his being. The boys had the courage and restraint not to use what they knew they could, but one unfortunate "miss" in their perception and the resulting action could plunge them into untold situations that might force any man to act in ways that 99.9 percent of the time would be absolutely not done. So went this day: October 12, 1780.

The boys were successful in many things, from negotiating through the fall of Charleston to scavenging for information and useful items to skirting British outposts while "gently" aiding in the events of time as they knew them to just plain navigating and surviving all that the wilderness can issue someone during the warm months of the year in the southeastern United States. They now had a new understanding of what they were capable of in 1780, specifically referring to their acts of defense on the side of the colonies at Kings Mountain to assure history, as they knew it, held true without error, mutation, or deformity. The boys had been stealthy and precise in their steps, performing well under conditions that not many from the twenty-first century could have handled. They had rationed and utilized their modern provisions extremely well and, for the most part, stayed in good states of mind through it all. They had planned camps well, kept a quiet and a light presence on the land, and done an overall excellent job at keeping a low profile.

Of course, let's be honest, a normally trained Native American scout of the day, or a well-trained Indian child for that matter, could have probably tracked them with ease—*if* they were looking for them. There was no reason to think either heads or tails about this until ... until on a prescribed and well-planned move from one location to another, the group stopped as a cold chill hit them simultaneously. They froze in their tracks. Nik, Sid, and John, in what felt like a period of many hours, slowly peered up from checking their footing and keeping hush as they progressed on their prescribed course.

They had been so sure of their progress and confident of their execution. It was what had been in their bywords all these months: make the right move, do it well, do it quietly, triple-check your footing, etc. All of these things were good training that had served them well. But on this day, while doing all the correct and proper things, they quietly and with stealth had just walked right into one of those moments when all three became blurred for just a moment, at the same moment, and without a plan to extricate them from any issue they'd misstepped into. Nik broke into a cold sweat before he could even calculate the possible cost and looked up at what they had done. John had that sick feeling and was utterly speechless, which was a good thing at the moment. Sid just closed his eyes for a split second and tried to reboot his brain and get a grip on just how they were going to get away from this.

They all knew where in space and time they were and could feel the stares piercing their bodies. Not angry or quizzical stares, just simply stares the boys wished they hadn't created. These stares emanated from folks of a different time, and these folks found themselves gazing upon something that wasn't the norm for their day and age. To make matters worse, the people who stood before the boys couldn't be easily communicated with, not that the boys could even begin to effectively explain themselves.

These stares were directed at the boys from eyes from the eighteenth century; they were gazing at the future, a future they could not yet imagine or comprehend. These individuals probably didn't even speak the King's English, let alone what mumbling or dribble might come out of the mouths of the boys. These individuals were looking at three heavily camouflaged individuals from the year 2010, donning assault rifles and semiautomatic pistols with faces half painted. Of course, these folks didn't know all that. What they did know was this: "They ain't from 'round here." (In their native tongue, of course.)

Nik's mind raced wildly as he tried to work out what exactly to do. He very quietly under his very shallow breath said, "Hold." It was the only thing he could utter. It seemed as though an eternity had passed from the start of the unexpected encounter up to this point. Nik felt there wasn't any danger, so wanting to promote a good outcome and a less offensive stance, he very slowly allowed his rifle to gently slide to his waist on its strap. John acknowledged the hushed command and accompanying action with a very low, "Uh oh." Sid just waited.

What Nik and the others had intruded upon were up to twenty-five Native American females, ranging in age from fourteen to twenty-one. The boys had been following a small brook that had abruptly opened up into a pond that was heavily overgrown on all its banks, *except* the one from where the Indian women were now in a dreamy sort of visual exchange with the boys. The eighteenth-century Native American women were on the opposite bank of the small glade and were in the middle of various chores when the boys appeared across the water from them.

John thought the looks on the ladies' faces were priceless. In fact, they would have been comical, if it weren't in the here and now with the situation that now faced the three out-of-time wanderers. The young ladies became as still as the boys but certainly more at ease with the situation. They didn't seem a bit scared of what they were gazing upon, and that's the way the boys wanted it to stay. Nik guessed that because they just weren't sure what they were looking at, it would be used to their advantage.

Sid knew Nik would be spewing a thousand curses in his racing and really annoyed and concerned mind (which he was), but he was more preoccupied with the problem at hand. Sid had quickly noted that the boys were no more than two steps from the heavy overgrowth; one more step after that, and they'd have been swallowed up by it.

Sid muttered ever so quietly, "Two steps. Two steps in—no eye contact." That was an impossible request, thought both Nik and John. The two-step thing made sense, but how could they not look at the spectacle of what was in front of them. Nothing uncouth, sexual, or anything like that, but these guys from the year 2010 were now standing in front of a group of people who no one's eyes had beheld for more than two hundred years. Plus, there was the fact that they had all already made eye contact.

Damn! thought Nik. He then repeated softly, "Slowly on three, two, one." Trying not to look at their observers, they slid back into the brush, stood in silence for a second, and then moved smartly away, trying to be careful, deft, and, most of all, swift.

They tried as hard as they could not to be loud or noisy as they moved, but they were "feeling the rush," as it were, from the encounter. They each had different thoughts on what had just happened and would certainly need to debrief about the event at some later time. No one was angry exactly, just really concerned with what could have gone wrong. Nik was probably the most irritated, which was not unusual; Sid was just not feeling good about walking into a "bridal lair," as he called it later. John was in the utter shock of the moment.

"Did you make eye contact with any of them?" Sid asked.

John quickly jumped on the remark and almost yelled, "What in the—" Sid confessed with lightning speed, "So did I." Nik just chuckled, swearing under his breath.

None of them could give in-depth detail of the scene or the event. They just knew what they had gotten themselves into that day. Who knows what had been going on there. It didn't make a difference. All Nik knew was that three dudes from the twenty-first century walked in and, not so gracefully, walked out of what looked to be a peaceful, normal, daily native happening. Nik made a point for the boys to make double time the rest of that that day, night, and the next day to put as much distance between what they had just witnessed and where they were going.

At that point, that goal was all confused, as they had basically taken an orthogonal course away from the glade (and their original path) where the Indian women were, zigzagging around some known obstacles while trying their utmost to avoid any other individuals they had heard in the area.

John then added, "Umm, we're lost, and there are way too many living things in this area!"

Sid pointed west to the hills. "We need to go that way, we need to get back to C-10 as fast as we can!" he insisted. They all strongly agreed.

... 20 ...
A False Sense

NIK PUSHED THEM LATE into the evening, and they finally found a decent, defendable spot to set up a basic bed for the night. Nik insisted on a "no fire" camp that night. Sid told him he was being a little ridiculous about it all, and Nik admitted to being paranoid but was agitated and concerned about Sid's comments after the day's events. The next morning they broke camp and continued away from the previous day's encounter at top speed. Discussions cropped up all day long about potential repercussions of what had transpired; clearly, Sid and John felt Nik was concerned about something more happening.

Already knowing Nik wouldn't make it easy, Sid queried him about his worries. "So, Nik, you okay with all that happened yesterday? What are you still thinking about?"

With a sigh, Nik replied, "Well, what's done is done."

John, playing devil's advocate, as he so often did and not wanting to listen to another Carl Sagan-type speech from Nik, added, "So what's done is done. We goofed up; some indigenous locals saw us, and we ran away. No harm, no foul, right?"

"Well," Nik continued, looking sternly at John, "that's right. We ran away. Let's hope that isn't taken as a sign of weakness, and if it is, we can be sure they won't take kindly to our little intrusion back there. Let's hope they just forget what they saw. Let's hope that if they happened to tell anyone, nobody believes them. Let's hope

---

they mistook us for moving flora. Yeah, tall weeds with eyes. Let's hope it just gets lost in the day's conversation at the wigwam. Let's hope they were a peaceful bunch."

"Umm," poked John, "and if it wasn't all of those things?"

Sid turned to John and asked, "Did you have to ask him that?"

The boys moved for the next six days, more swiftly than before and into more remote areas to stay off the beaten path and out of the way of anything or anybody. John commented that they were traveling the billy goat paths these days. They headed basically southwest and were horribly off course from the events of seven days before. Their intended destination was camp C-10; they knew they could depend on the fact that there were no people of any kind there, or so they believed from their time building their humble abode.

Sid and Nik were now sure they were heading in the correct direction. The boys made good time in the slightly cooler days of mid-October near the mountains in southeastern United States—or what would become the southeastern part of the United States. They were staying true to their mode of safe travel, watching their course, avoiding people and obstacles that would slow their progress, and maintaining sure footing. The day ended in a rocky location with bluffs and ledges off in the distance. The boys built a good encampment and found some water, and John had scavenged things along the day's travels to have for dinner. All in all, they felt they were in good shape, and Nik once again warned against complacency issues and reminded them to all stay vigilant. Morning brought a colder day, so camp was quickly picked up, and the boys were ready for their day's travel.

For a time, all was quiet and smooth. They had progressed into a type of lightly wooded field area, which was very different from what they had trudged through in the summer months or even on the way to Kings Mountain. They had been heading slightly higher in elevation, and they had assumed it was just the foothills to the eventual mountainous area of their destination. Soon the rocky fields turned into more rocky areas with little mini valleys that became tight turns and some blind corners.

John proclaimed rather sarcastically, "Goat trails again—joy of the ages!"

"A few more minutes," Sid exclaimed, "and I think we'll be out of these little canyons soon." The group didn't like the closeness of it at all, and they each thought to themselves at different points in the hike that they might want to backtrack and find another path—a trail that was more open or better protected.

They came around the next right-hand bend and walked into an area that was open on the left and had a rock face on the right. Proceeding on their course, the boys were about to experience another unfortunate meeting that they so direly would have liked to avoid. The boys, having turned a sharp corner into this area, were now confronted by a team of what could best be described as Native American men. Once again, Nik broke into a sweat, as did all the boys. Their backs were to the rocks, and they were looking at some twenty or so Native American males, clearly a party or team intent on something.

Nik murmured, "Here we go again."

The Indian team was arranged in a half circle that basically cut off the path forward and backward for the boys. The center cluster of men appeared to be the leaders of the scout team, and for the moment, the Indian group seemed calm. John thought it felt like an eternity as they all stared at each other; the rising tension could have been cut with a knife. The boys once again had on their camouflage, including a half-camouflage face-paint job (sloppily done, it might be noted). They might appear as "plants with eyes." No such luck on this meeting, as the center group of Indians talked among themselves. Obviously, there was no hope of any of the boys understanding what they were saying, as they were speaking in their native tongue.

The Indian men coarsely and coldly inspected the three closely and murmured between themselves. To the boys, the Indian team appeared very confident of their position, as they looked the boys up and down. There were two in particular off to the right of the boys who were quite a bit more agitated about what was happening and what they were looking at. These two Indian men drew an occasional sharp-sounding scream from the three in the middle of the pack.

Nik, for better or for worse, was going to attempt to show that they were just walking peacefully and didn't want any problems. Sid was more on guard this time, and they could all feel the tension building. This encounter was certainly different than the last one; these guys were armed, equipped with bows, sling-type weapons, and spears—all deadly weapons in the hands of trained individuals.

John quietly muttered, "What now?" As he spoke, one of the center pack Indians screamed something very loudly. The boys lurched back in genuine fear, and all of a sudden they felt that things were not going so well. Sid, showing restraint in the sheer fear of it all, gently unsnapped his holster that contained his loaded pistol. Nik and John, who also had holstered weapons, dropped their respective hands to them without outwardly showing they were reaching for anything. Sid was clear in his posture and was ready for whatever, and he knew he could handle anything that might come at them.

This was the moment Nik had dreaded. They couldn't properly communicate with these folks. They just want to go their own way without conflict, and these guys (especially on the right-hand side of their lines) appeared to be forcing an issue. Nik stepped forward just slightly, slowly and quietly with his hands out, palms open and facing out, below his waist. "We are peaceful. We are walking," he said as he pointed to their right, down the semblance of a trail. "It's okay. We are peaceful," he continued.

One of the agitated tribesmen to the right of them started screaming and moving around, yelling something; he jumped forward and back as he swung some form of leather whip or bridle.

"Whoa, he is pissed!" Sid whispered. And as the overly agitated male was screaming and yelling, the whole group of natives took a step back. Nik and John, now with firm hands on their sidearms, in unison, gasped, "Oh!" With that came the screaming warrior. He quickly closed to within thirty-five feet and raised his weapon, and the universe appeared to stand still.

John ducked defensively, while Nik pulled his pistol and screamed, *"No!"* At the same time, Sid quickly and expertly aimed his already half-drawn sidearm and fired once—a .45 caliber hollow-point self-defense round at point-blank range. With a round such as that, Nik thought with certain fear, *This is not going to be pretty.* The shot was very loud compared to anything the Indians had probably ever heard close up. The boys didn't have their hearing protection on either, so they thought it extremely loud as well. Nik quickly thought, *Oh great, a loud gunshot.... That'll be dismissed by the common folk of 1780*—not! The bullet struck the charging Indian's center of mass and knocked him back several yards. He hit the ground and didn't move again.

Yet again, another period of time that seemed to last for eons continued in the boys' minds. The remaining Indian men glared at their compatriot's mangled and motionless body in staunch disbelief. Sid's bullet must have hit and exploded the man's heart, because there was an enormous amount of blood now pooling around the dead man's body. The nature of the hollow-point round would cause the boys to assume that the hole in the dead man's back would be at least four to five inches in diameter.

Nik heard a deep breath from Sid and quickly whispered, "It's okay. Self-defense. Be quiet now, and let's see what they are going to do." Nik and John readied their .45-caliber semiautomatic handguns. It seemed to the boys that the ring of the shot could still be heard, probably only in their heads. John didn't know if it was the actual sound of the shot or his ears still ringing from it.

Once again, Nik murmured, "Hold."

A conversation and plenty of finger-pointing began in the ranks of the native line. Some very quick and nervous looks were being directed at the boys now, but not the in-depth inspection they had been undergoing minutes before. The confidence the natives once had was gone, and they were now all agitated, on guard, and certainly not in the controlling position they once possessed.

Nik holstered his pistol, knowing Sid and John could deal with any onslaught if necessary, and once again held his hands out in a gesture of calmness, although he was shaking from being so nerved up. John still clinched his weapon, while Sid gently and slowly lowered his still-extended pistol. Each one waited for a reaction from the tribal team that now numbered nineteen.

The apparent leader said something to his team, after which three members dropped their weapons and slowly picked up the dead man. Blood was now everywhere. Gasps and grunts came from the natives as they witnessed the condition of their compatriot—a huge, bleeding, swollen crater in the back of his corpse. Other members of the tribal team picked up the dropped weapons and moved back into the woods behind them. The leader was the last of the Indian forces to retreat back into the woods. He sharply and intently glared at the boys the entire time until he was out of sight.

And with that, the lore of the "Tree Men" was born.

... 21 ...
Home Again

THE BOYS WERE UTTERLY frozen in their tracks—*again.* Sid stated the obvious: "We have to go! Right now!"

Nik said, "I know, but I think I'm stuck." Nik was just frozen in place with shock.

John moved behind the group and patted Nik on the back. "Let's go now. We are done here," he said. "C'mon, I'll walk with ya, and Sid can watch our backs.... C'mon."

"Okay," said Nik.

Sid encouragingly piped in, "We're good. They won't bother us now; were good." He quickly located his shell casing and picked it up from the ground.

Nik wasn't quite sure of that and ended with a quiet gasp. "I'm sorry you had to shoot that guy," he said to Sid.

Sid quickly and reassuringly told Nik, "Look, we had to. We were backed into a corner; we had no choice.... It was either that, or one of us would have been stuck."

John added, "That's right.... We can't die in 1780, we can't be found here, we need to move and hide, and we need to be okay."

Nik started walking, still looking at the tree line where the last Indian, the leader, looked fiercely at them and then backed into the woods. "Man, I didn't want this to happen," he murmured.

John made sure to stay with Nik, not because Nik was falling apart but for the concern of the group. John was himself still in shock over all that had just occurred. Sid was pretty close behind, guarding their movement out of the area. He eventually took the lead and encouraged the group forward as Nik had done after the last encounter with the Indian women at the glade.

They made quick work of the hike the rest of that day, mainly driven by their own adrenaline and fear. Nik cursed most of the way wondering, *Why would they even want to follow us?* and *What were they thinking?* John was genuinely interested in the notion of trying to understand the actions of the Indians and generating conversation between the groups, but that didn't go so well.

Sid also added his thoughts now. "Well, they were curious. They should have left those two guys, who clearly had anger management issues, home with the women back at the wigwam or something."

The tension was slowly breaking, with nightfall concluding another long day of hiking well after dark and settling down to a fireless encampment. They chose to camp against a steep hillside to ensure a highly defensible position, because they were all concerned about the possible return of any Indians. Once again, at daybreak, they would begin the footrace to their home base at C-10.

The boys, having moved into their "home sector," were feeling relieved and much more comfortable. It was October 29, and the security and comfort of C-10 resonated with the group. The area of the bald, the caverns, and the cabin site just made them feel, well, at home. They approached their cabin area in full camouflage, no burlaps, no woods, and a full clip in their rifles with two or three standby clips each. They hadn't ever previously moved either in or out of their area but by one way, so naturally they followed the same path into C-10 this time. They didn't expect any issues. It had been some time since they were last there, and a lot had happened. They each had taken turns over the past week alternating a person every four hours to watch their backs as they progressed toward C-10. This action made for a slower pace, but they didn't want any more surprises, and in their collective opinion, they'd already had enough surprises this past six months to last a lifetime.

Moving through the outlet of the creek that emptied the cool mountain water into the valley, Sid began to assign particular positions as checkpoints. The outlet of the creek became "check point alpha" and wasn't visible from the boys' cabin. John theorized it might be seen in the winter months from their hideaway high up in the hills of the Blue Ridge Mountain range.

Nik commented, "Let's not make too many of these checkpoints. I'll get all crossed up in them if we need to use them in a hectic situation."

"Oh, please … stop," Sid blurted. "You are certainly capable of remembering a few location signifiers!"

John just shrugged. "Eh, we'll figure it out when the time comes."

Sid assigned locations up to "lima." Nik just shook his head and replied under his breath, "You know I can't remember anything."

Approaching the turn up to the cabin area, Sid raised his hand, signifying a stop. They silently rested, each leaning against a third of a tree while looking at and observing the wilds of their mountain area. "I'd like to stay here for a time," Sid whispered. "Just to ensure we're alone."

Nik and John agreed, holding their vigil and enjoying the quiet of the nature around them. This stance had become the standard for the group; they called it their "120-degree defense stance." Finally, after two hours, Sid stood up and nodded. "I am satisfied. You?" With a "yeah, man" from the others, they slowly made their small ascent up to the cabin. Sid had them pause one more time while moving up the hill, and they looked around for several minutes before finishing their ascent.

The cabin appeared as they had left it, buttoned up and secure. They fumbled with the awkward locking mechanism and finally remembered the combination of pokes and pulls to open it. The inside was clean; no appreciable water leaks were observed, and the walls looked sturdy and intact.

"Man, oh man, this is really nice. What a welcome sight. We get to sleep indoors tonight," professed John.

Nik, now sitting down on his homemade, makeshift bunk, looked around and thought to himself, *So, is this it? Do we live here for the rest of our days on this planet?* Nik's face was now blank, betraying his deep thought.

Sid walked over as he unpacked his stuff. "You okay, man? What are you thinking about?"

Nik, surprised by Sid, snapped his head up and looked at him. "Nothing," he said quickly.

Sid replied in total disbelief. "Uh-huh, I'm sure we'll talk on it at some point." He smiled at Nik.

John went out for a quick scout of the area and found most of the snare-and-snap bundles of sticks and twigs intact and not sprung. The snap brambles farther out from the cabin in the woods were all sprung and messed with, probably by passing deer or other medium-sized animals. Sid, with his rifle in hand, joined John after shedding some of his provisions. John informed Sid of his findings, and the two reset the brambles for no particular reason. They returned to the cabin and found Nik still sitting in the same place where Sid had left him earlier.

"C'mon, man. We need to go turn our water back on," Sid said as they dumped some dry twigs into the cold, dark fireplace.

"Okay," replied Nik. "We need water."

The three compatriots, now lightly armed and packing far less in the way of provisions and items, scampered up to the ridge to check on their stream and activate their previously entrenched canal. There was a good flow of water in the stream, and the canal quickly and thirstily accepted the contents of the diverted stream. The canal was dry and would therefore take quite some time to resaturate and return to its fully intended functionality. In a few hours, the camp and cabin would have all the water needed for normal daily operations." The three stood again, leaning on a tree in their "120-degree defense stance," and listened as they quietly observed their surroundings. The clean, crisp air seemed to refresh them with every perfect breath.

"Let's get back before dark," Sid suggested. "I don't want to be moving around in the dark. I wish I had packed three night-vision setups!"

"Battery power would have been a problem," commented John.

"Yeah, true," nodded Sid in agreement.

"Can we head back?" asked Nik.

"Sure, man, no problem." shrugged Sid as he pushed off from the tree.

John, hoping Nik was feeling okay, asked, "You feeling all right, man? Tired?"

Nik looked at John now, nodded, and replied, "Yeah, man, I'm just tired. That's all."

Sundown brought absolute darkness. The combination of a slight moon, the forest half-adorned with leaves, and the partial cloud cover that had rolled in made the darkness seem darker yet. The small fire in the cabin was burning with a gentle glow that illuminated the inside of the cabin nicely. The nighttime temperatures in the mountains during this part of October were dropping to a point where the cabin could, and would be, closed up at night so that the heat from the fire could keep them quite comfortable. The boys certainly didn't want it too warm, but freezing wasn't an option either. They arranged their belongings and settled in the common area for conversation, each of them yawning and now feeling the effects of the last few weeks.

"So, what are we going to do from here?" asked Nik.

"Ah, the question of the blank stare now comes forth," touted John, trying to sound un-John-like.

Sid sat back. "I was wondering when you were going to open your mouth tonight."

Nik, now scratching his arm, sat down and expressed his mood. "Well, it's the end of October 1780. We are, well, home. It's a nice place, our little hideaway in time." A pause came over the group as the fire crackled and filled the air with smoky warmth and a soothing glow.

Sid broke the silence with a sigh and a cough. "Well, at least we are alone."

"Yes," began John, "but we are not alone. *We* are here, and we have been through ... an indescribable time. One of us has to write all this stuff down! We are alive, we are well, and it's the time of year that I am going to bag something wonderful for us to feast on!" John sounded really excited, and his emotion worked on the others in a very positive way.

John felt his good spirit picking up the mood of the group and continued speaking with a huge smile on his face. "We'll have Thanksgiving how many years before they officially sanction Thanksgiving as a national holiday? We'll have Christmas and New Year's! This is the best damn time of year! And we are not sweating our you-know-whats off either!" With that, John sat down with command in his action.

"Whoa, dude! You are inspired!" retorted Sid.

Nik wanted to be more jovial, so he sat and watched the other two have fun with it all. John, now looking at Nik, said, "C'mon, man, cheer up. We have a lot to be thankful for."

Nik stood up and poked at the fire a bit before replying. "We do, man. We do. It's this time of year—I'm never much fun. The prospect of you trapping or shooting something on the big and meaty side, though—well, that sounds pretty good."

They all smiled, sat back, and listened to both the crackling fire and the silence of their wooden abode. Nik finally stood up and said, "Well, I need sleep…. Night, guys."

Sid nodded, "Night, man."

Whereupon John stood up and announced, "Well, if I am going to do all those great things, I'd better get some shut-eye too."

Sid waved the others off for the night and sat with the fire for a while. The planned short time turned into half the night, as his mind wandered to all corners of their adventure. He sat for a time outside and looked at the stars and listened to nature in the crisp evening of the mountains in late autumn. As he sat Indian style, snugly wrapped with his arms crossed tightly against his chest, Sid thought about a midnight stroll but quickly nixed that idea. He wasn't going to be the first to break one of the group's cardinal rules of not going anywhere without the others. The rule of staying together had been a key to their existence in 1780, and he wasn't going to recklessly disregard it now.

All earlier efforts of the day hadn't really made Sid sleepy, so he continued to meander around outside of their cabin for several more minutes until he decided to go in and play with the fire a bit. As he turned to head into the cabin, he heard a screeching off in the distance that surprised him. He was sure it was something from nature, but he hadn't heard anything like it or that loud, and it startled him. About thirty seconds later, John came out and inquired about the noise. He asked Sid what he was still doing up and why he was outside at this time of night. Sid told John he was restless and that the recent noise had stopped him in his tracks. They stayed out awhile longer and waited to hear the noise again, but not so much as a peep was heard. So, they went in and secured the cabin for the night.

... 22 ...

Happy Holidays and Merry Christmas, Gentlemen

THE NEXT FEW WEEKS were full of relaxed chores, as well as a few humorous tasks and happenings, in the run up to the holidays. The boys made some improvements to the cabin and semiwinterized the canal, hoping against all hope that it wouldn't freeze solid over the winter; this was extremely wishful thinking, as temperatures could fall well below freezing in the northwest mountains of South Carolina during the winter months.

There were many visits to the bald during this time, because John was working on something having to deal with the bald. He was being comically secretive about it all, however. Nik spent these many weeks collecting wood and carrying out all the tasks the others asked him to help with. He had figured out most "woodsy" things and wasn't utterly helpless in the wilds anymore, much unlike the way he had felt in the beginning of this adventure. There were also many trips to scenic overlooks to survey the areas in every direction around them. Not once seeing another living soul, the utter peace and silence of their surroundings was the subject of their conversations in the days and nights to come on more than one occasion.

One day, John finally announced a trip to the bald for that afternoon. The group snickered at what could only be described as

"The Great Bald Mystery: Part II," which obviously followed "The Great Bald Mystery: Part I." Part I, in the immortal words of John, was "how the hell we got here!" Yes, John was all atwitter and in high spirits; Nik and Sid didn't have a clue what he was up to.

Sid, now poking for clues to the excursion of the day, asked, "So, do we need to camouflage and arm up for this meeting at the bald?"

John looked at him with a sneer. "You're not going to get a thing out of me. We will be in no danger, and the normal camp complement sidearms will do fine."

Sid ended his little interrogation with, "Just checking, just checking. I don't want to walk into some sticky wicket without being prepared for it."

Nik just laughed. "Don't worry, man," he assured Sid. "That's what you brought me along for."

Sid and John now looked at Nik and said, "Oh no, what do you have in store for us now?"

Nik just shook his head. "It's not for now," he said. "Let's enjoy our holidays; the Revolution will wait for us for a few weeks, don't worry."

That afternoon brought their hike up to the bald with Sid up front, Nik happily plodding along in the middle, and John taking up the rear with some sort of pack in hand. Arriving at the clearing, they paused as they always did, just checking, looking, and listening to their surroundings. As it had always been in this time period, all was well, and there wasn't a hint of malevolence in the area.

"So," Sid began, "what's this all about?"

John smiled and said, "Well, it's nothing really. Just—" and he paused.

Nik circled around to look at John's face. "You are up to something, my friend," he noted. "I know that sound in you. It's your playfully devious, 'I might be up to no good' sound."

John, now feigning being offended, huffed, "Well, I never." But he quickly retreated back and said, "Okay, so I've been known to, well, play a few pranks in the past ... or future? Well, you know. Anyway, this is nothing like that. Really, you know—well, sort of." With that, John lowered his head as to look ashamed.

"Okay, so ... remember our ride up to this area?" John asked. "We were talking about this and that and why things had particular names and attributes. Do you remember that?"

Sid nodded and smiled. "Yeah, that was at the time your new GPS had us in downtown who-the-hell-knows-where, and we enjoyed that wonderful steak dinner," Sid recalled. "Yeah, I remember."

Nik now looked at John for something more. "And ..." he asked.

John darted his attention over to Nik and continued. "Well, remember I asked you how this bald got its name—Devil's Bald. We had no clue."

The guys nodded their heads to weakly confirm the happening of those many months ago and waited for the next line. "Close your eyes," John requested.

Sid and Nik closed their eyes, complaining, "Can we just turn our backs toward you?"

"Yes, yes, that's fine," John said now wrestling with something. A few bangs could be heard as if he had a large rock and was using it to pound on something. "Okay, you can look," John proudly announced. Sid and Nik turned around and came face-to-face with history—or, in this case, the future.

John had made a carved wooden sign and pounded it into the grassy area by the bald for all to see. The sign read "Devil's Bald." The boys burst out laughing.

"You ... we can't leave that there!" Sid said. "You'd be messing with history, adding *our flair* to what is ... or what will happen!"

Nik, now recovering from this somewhat obnoxious attempt at time-lording, stated, "The thing is ..." He was still chuckling almost uncontrollably. "The place *was* named that in 2010, so he isn't changing history, really. He's just helping it along, you know?"

John was now animated and blurted out with excitement, "That's right, and it's fitting, because I asked the question driving up here. So I should be able to leave my sign here."

Okay, okay, if Carl here," he said, referring to Nik as Carl Sagan again, "says it's okay what the hell do I care? I just don't want to get back to 2010 and find out we screwed something up," Sid noted.

John, who felt victorious in his lobby to name the bald, commented, "And how do we know we didn't name the bald previously?"

Nik and Sid looked at each other and then John, and they felt a chill. "We don't know," said Nik. "It's like the chicken and the egg discussion."

"I always hated that conversation," admitted John.

With that, they secured the sign post with their utmost "vim and vigor," and when it was finally steady and secure, they headed back to camp, performing a little supply gathering along the way. John went after something to eat, Nik collected some firewood in the form of some downed trees they had cut some weeks ago, and Sid ended the trip by dragging some of the timber Nik had gathered down the hill. Camp was, as always, a welcome sight, and the three just sat down to rest. Everyone yawned.

"Man, what is with us?" Sid asked. "We didn't work that hard today, so why are we all so tired?"

"Eh, no reason," John responded. "We have had our days of hard work. We're just catching up."

"Or it's catching up to us," Nik retorted.

Sid added, "Yes, probably the latter. No big deal, so we sleep. We have all the time in the world." They went to sleep early that night.

As the weeks rolled along, the temperatures grew colder, and the boys continued to settle comfortably into their surroundings. John was particularly exuberant as this particular day began, because he again had something to be especially excited about. He grabbed a rifle and proceeded up the trail about nine hundred yards to a spot he had been baiting for about a fortnight. They had previously collected some wild grains from around the area, which the boys then tried to fabricate into something edible to no avail; the seeds simply tasted nasty. They tried to grill them, smoke them, boil them, and even burn them to see if it lessened the horrid taste. Nothing worked, but as it happened, the wildlife appeared to really enjoy them, so John began using it for bait for larger, "meatier" animals.

John proclaimed, "After two weeks of baiting, I do believe I am going to score a large beast on today's hunt!"

"Cool, man," Sid replied. "Do you need some help?"

John countered with, "Not sure. I'll call you if I need you." He smiled and scampered off to the hunt. Sid and Nik kept their eyes pointed in John's direction and went about their camp business. Several hours later, a large *boom* echoed loudly through the hills and mountains. Sid looked up to check on John, trying to see if everything was okay. "I'll bet he got something," he noted. Another hour went by, and John returned, informing Nik and Sid that tomorrow would be November 25 and that he had secured Thanksgiving dinner!

"That's great news, man!" Sid rejoiced as Nik sat pondering for a minute.

John looked at Nik. "Um, dude—meat! A lot of meat! What's wrong?" he asked.

Nik, now quickly looking up, also rejoiced in the next days, or weeks, of good eating. "No, that's great. It is going to be great!"

John, now perplexed, probed further. "Why the pause then?"

A longer pause now prevailed. "Well," started Nik.

"Oh no, there is that 'well' again out of his mouth.... *What?*" Sid demanded.

"Well, I may have forgotten to tell you a really unimportant, small piece of information. Really, it's nothing. We feast tomorrow—tonight even!"

John, wanting to know what Nik was talking about, asked, "Well, if it's so minor, tell us."

Nik went on to explain that in these times, the Continental Congress actually voted every year, usually around October 18 per presidential proclamation, on the dates for the upcoming national holidays. They made their decision based on the happenings of that year and the circumstances of the day.

"And?" inquired John with a shrug. His head was down, now looking for more than this useless tidbit of information.

"Well," Nik continued, "in 1780, Thanksgiving Day was ... was actually on December 7 as I remember, and don't ask me why this sticks in my mind."

John now looked puzzled. "So," he said "there can be only one thing to do." Nik and Sid were the ones looking perplexed now as they waited for John to finish his thought. John continued, "We eat good and huge until December 7!"

Sid burst out, "Ha!" This grand plan was approved by all. So began the business of preparing the deer John had shot for all to consume. The meal was delicious, and they were able to use a supply of salt John had "borrowed" from the homestead. The salt had survived well in storage at their cabin over the past months and was the perfect thing for the quantity of meat they were able to extract from their kill. It wasn't nearly the amount a trained butcher could yield, but they did their best.

December 7 arrived, and Nik began the day's festivities with, "So, what day is today?"

The others looked at him rather smugly and said, "Thanksgiving Day, right?"

"Yes!" said Nik. "But there are multiple answers today!" In a somewhat somber tone and after a time, Nik added, "December 7, 161 years from now, the Empire of Japan will attack our forces at Pearl Harbor, and World War II will formally start for our nation."

John just murmured, "Mr. Cheery this morning, huh?"

Sid just laughed and said, "I knew that ... and no, it's not funny or cheery. Okay, your name for today is Mr. *Un*-Cheery."

"Hey, now! Don't compare me to the UN!" insisted Nik, as they all enjoyed the humor.

... 23 ...
A New Course?

DECEMBER CAME AND WENT. Christmas and New Year's Day brought a mountain of snow with grand vistas of visual peace and a still quiet, harking even further back in time to a place where "peace on Earth" was declared to all mankind. Their world was blanketed with the serene and clean white mantle of fresh snow, which insulated their world both audibly and visually. The boys looked off of the various overlooks and could see only a little snow on the distant valley floors. They figured the snow that fell on them the night before wouldn't stick around for too long unless the temperatures dropped again. If that happened, it could be a very long winter. They remained inside in the late afternoons, warming themselves by the fire and discussing various subjects, including their possible future plans for this fledgling year, which was 1781. John and Sid began this conversation with, "Nik, you mentioned some opportunities we might want to partake of. Would you like to go into some detail?" As they asked, they couldn't help but smile at him.

"1781 ... 1781 ... well, I have been doing some thinking on the subject," Nik began.

"I knew it!" John snapped.

Sid sat down and inquired, "So, anything like Kings Mountain?"

John now sat down. He didn't look quite as intent with the thought of that. "Well, I'm not sure we should do that again," his voice trailed off.

Nik, now stoking the fire and adding some logs before sitting with his two compatriots, started describing his thoughts on the year 1781. "We have several opportunities based on what happened in history." Sid and John were now getting comfortable, as they knew this could turn out to be a long, late-night history lesson.

Nik began with a mild disclaimer. "Well, I am not even sure history will play out as I remember anymore. And honestly, I'm a bit unsure of it all anyway, but ... there will be a few events we can go observe. These events are all skirmishes and battles around our little Revolution here; some are American wins, and some are British wins. It's sometimes a challenge to really know who came out victorious the moment the bullets stopped flying, but in time, the results worked themselves out.

"So, we could choose from a few battles, like the battles at Guilford Courthouse in North Carolina, Cowpens in South Carolina, a place called The Ninety-Six in South Carolina, or Eutaw Springs in South Carolina; the list goes on to the hopeful end result of the British surrender in Yorktown, Virginia. These events take place from basically the middle of this month to October in Yorktown. Although it represents a lot of hiking, we would have enough time to do it easily if it's planned correctly." Nik now paused to see if he'd get any reaction.

Sid and John pondered what they had just heard. John spoke first. "So, we should go do this? Go and observe again? That really didn't go well last time, you know."

Sid smiled. "Well, it depends on how you look at it, John. It didn't go so well for those light cavalry the British had."

Nik now raised his hand. Sid and John looked at him oddly. Then Sid, in his best English aristocratic accent, announced, "We of the two now yield the floor to the one for comments and queries."

Nik smirked and then stated, "I just want to add something to that. It might be considered having 'gone well,' as we did preserve the history we knew. What might have happened without us might have ended us completely."

"Okay, so it did go well, but we sure weren't prepared for it other than the fact that we completely dominated *our* little side battlefield and won the day for the colonies," replied John.

"Do you think all of these battles will end up like that?" Sid asked the group. "Like history is all messed up, and we have to react to change things? What would we do if we went and observed an American loss and somehow changed that into a victory? What then?"

Nik, not having the answer to that, shrugged his shoulders and added, "Why would we do that unless we got overzealous or simply got the history really wrong? No, I don't think we'll have that problem; we'll be okay. We can sleep on it and figure it out tomorrow," suggested Nik.

"I think the magic is in the planning," said Sid, to which John, in agreement, added, "We need not kill ourselves. What is the eventual end to all this?" The conversation continued. Nik now sat back and listened to the discussion; he had several plans of action they could pursue, but he wanted to listen to get a feel for what the group wanted to do.

Sid, John, and Nik continued for hours. It seemed apparent to Nik that the group felt like they needed closure on the conflict they knew as the American Revolution. They were tied to this thing now—the events that a year ago they'd only known as the history of the American Revolution, they were now immersed in. They were experiencing it in real time, living, as it were, on the ground with it. They had killed for the colonies, America, their United States. The group expressed a deep desire for closure; the correct closure was yet to transpire, with the Good Lord's help, on October 19, 1781, at Yorktown, Virginia. Nick was absolutely enjoying the conversation the three were having about their possible upcoming actions when Sid and John suddenly and simultaneously looked at Nik.

"You already have this thing planned, don't you?" exclaimed John.

Nik, now looking surprised, answered him. "Not exactly. As we are talking about it, I am piecing together potential routes for us." Nik held up a crude map of Virginia and the Carolinas. "I'm trying to figure out, you know, how we might best make it to the end of all this—alive, preferably."

Sid couldn't help but laugh. "That's good, man. I like direction!"

Nik had a sense that John felt like he was just playing the situation and, in the end, would tell them what to do, when, in fact, it was just the opposite. Nik didn't want to make any decisions for anyone else and really welcomed discussion and buy-in on whatever they were going to do. "Making decisions in a democracy or a republic is difficult," Nik said. "Some of our founding fathers said that a democracy, if left to itself, would eventually commit suicide. Yes, really, John Adams said it, I am not that funny. I couldn't make this stuff up if I tried.

"This is about all of us checking and balancing the others for our very survival, and maybe the survival of our country," Nik continued. "Yes, I have an idea of what might be right, but all of us have to agree and initiate the whole plan together, or we won't have a whole plan. Am I clear on that?" Nik now looked slightly annoyed and confused; he really didn't mean to, though.

Nik's speech brought a strange silence from John and Sid. "It's late," Sid pointed out. "Let's sleep on it."

John said, "Didn't we try this a few hours ago?"

Nik responded, "Yes, but a really great discussion broke out, and *we* had too much fun planning our next moves." He smiled as he finished.

"Sleep!" demanded Sid. John and Nik finally agreed.

Nik was up all night running through the possible courses of action in his head, but he always came back around to the one he had devised weeks ago. He wasn't dictating the route and the events to the group, and there were only two or three good possibilities for them to explore anyway. They didn't want to follow some course of action in a direction only to have to backtrack and cover two or three times the mileage to get to their next event. From their nights of conversation, Nik assumed they all wanted to see the surrender of the British at Yorktown—for the sake of closures. He was having a hard time working out the exact mechanics for actually doing that, however.

Yes, they would walk there, in some form or fashion, but the "field" would be loaded with people from the present time (1781). They had worked hard to stay away from folks. How then could they, one October day, just stroll out and join the Colonial ranks, cheering on the victory some three hundred miles away on the coast of the York River? It was a bizarre problem that he wasn't going to be able to solve in one night or on his own, for that matter. He needed to bounce ideas off of Sid and John and get an agreement on an eventual plan of action. Sid and John, now snoring pretty hard after the night's cerebral festivities, left Nik awake in the cabin playing with the embers of the fire as he continued to think.

The morning saw Sid and John wake up to a cold day and look at Nik, who still hadn't gone to sleep from the evening before. "Dude, you look like hell this morning," blurted John. He continued inquiring, seeking to make sure his friend wasn't bothered by his contriteness of the previous evening. "You know me, man. I am just trying to look at all the angles, and I wasn't accusing you of anything evil."

Nik looked up and shrugged. "No, I know, man. I just couldn't sleep."

"You can sleep now.... You look like hell!" said Sid.

"I think John already covered my general appearance, but thanks for the verification of his observation. I kept the fire going, right?" said Nik, now looking for some good to come out of his sleepless night.

"So, what did you come up with?" asked Sid.

"Do we have a plan and a course? Which battles are we going to?" John began excitedly pushing for an answer from Nik.

"I need sleep. Let's go over this tonight," pleaded Nik.

John waved his hands as he smiled. "Oh, man, you planned this didn't you?" he yelled. "You're killing me! I am ready for our next mission."

With that, Sid looked at John and asked, "Mission? Have we become an expeditionary force?"

Nik now looked alarmed. "Whoa, whoa. Take it easy. What are you talking about?"

Sid smiled again. "Just trying to see how awake or asleep you really are; get some sleep and we'll talk later." Sid went out to look at the world around them, Nik collapsed into his bunk, and John began devising plans for the day.

Sundown had the guys back indoors, as the temperatures headed down again. The fire in the hearth was roaring. Nik had prepared more mud the other day and spent the early evening packing it around the spaces between the fireplace and the cabin walls. With the huge fire now ablaze in the fireplace, the mixture was hardening nicely and would be much like concrete by morning. The monstrous delivery of firewood that Sid and John worked on all day while Nik napped would hold them for quite some time and would assure a most comfortable environment in their cabin.

John had gathered some tidbits of food from around the creek, and Sid prepared some of the last of the salted venison from the Thanksgiving feast. Nik sat down at the table with his map and some notes, most of which were drawn on large pieces of birch bark he had previously collected for either kindling or paper, whichever would be needed first. They all sat around and picked at dinner, while Nik outlined the iterations of the plans he had drawn up for them during the past two weeks. Sid and John were not surprised that a quick return to C-10 was not planned, but the realization that they would be away for almost a year made them quiet.

"I know we'll be on the move for the better part of this year, but the events happen when they happen. We can't change that fact," Nik said in an attempt to console the group.

After a few more details on the various battles and plans Nik had labeled #1, #2, and #3, John asked, "Okay, so what are we doing?"

Nik responded, "It's up to you guys. I am trying to weigh out our options and present them to you. If there are any other options, we can discuss them as well. I guess option number four would be to stay here and live out our lives."

Another silence fell over the group. Nik looked at Sid and asked, "What do you think, man? You've been quiet over there." There was another pause.

"You have a feel for this, Nik, honestly, for direction and knowledge of this time … I default to what you think is best. After that, if you get us into a jam, we'll get us out of there with all of us coming to bear on whatever trouble we are facing. Let's be honest; there is nothing to stop us in this time. If they don't know we're coming, there isn't a force on this continent that can stop us," Sid explained.

"I'd agree with that," John said. "Kings Mountain was quite a thrill; we all thought it would be interesting to see, and as it turned out, it was just as important for us to be there. So what's your next hunch tell you, Nik?"

"Guys, I didn't want this to be me telling you … *us* what to do. What do you want to do?"

"We just told you, Nik. We are comfortable with you figuring this out. We have our roles and good points, things we are good at, and you suck at everything else. No offense, but this is your strong point. We want you to guide us through our time here," John tried to explain and reassure Nik of his confidence and desire for his decision.

Sid jumped in with his volley. "You got us all the way from Charleston to here, and in between, you developed the Kings Mountain strategy. There, when all of what you and/or we had planned for the battle went to hell in a hand basket in less than ten seconds, we, and the plan, performed very well. Take my word for it, as the tactics guy, you devised it in minutes, and it was tactically sound! So, where are we going, and when do we leave? Unless we are going to stay here and sit the whole rest of this Revolution thing out, give it to us now. And, by the way, I know you better.… You've been thinking on this for plenty of time. I know, because I've known you for a long time. Remember?"

Nik was a bit stunned. "Really?" he asked.

"Really," blurted John.

"Okay, then give me a minute. I'll weigh out my ideas and let you know what I think, okay?" Nik replied.

John and Sid agreed, and John followed that up with, "Man, I am so glad he's on the hook for all this." John and Sid both laughed as Nik raised his head with a deer-in-the-headlights look in his eyes.

"Oh, you guys are a pain," Nik said as he threw a piece of crumpled-up birch bark at them. About an hour later, Nik looked up to the waiting eyes of Sid and John.

"So?" John asked smartly.

Nik now turned a map around to show his compatriots a course and rough itinerary. John and Sid moved closer to inspect their potential route and spent several minutes looking at the places and dates with some curious faces. Sid noted they were not going to head south at any point on this plan. "Hmm, all north and east to Yorktown, huh?" he asked.

Nik nodded and revealed a bit of his thought process. "Yes, this course will take us to lower elevations across what we know as northern South Carolina to Cowpens, where we hope to see an unprecedented double envelope maneuver by the Americans that will yield a quick and embarrassing British defeat. Lieutenant Colonel Tarleton, by the way, who is a pretty famous British name of the day, gets his clock cleaned. It's a huge win for the Americans. This battle, like Kings Mountain, only lasted about an hour."

John looked on at a question mark on the map and asked Nik what it was. Nik looked at the question mark east of Raleigh, North Carolina, "That is a location of potential opportunity ... May 8, 1781," he explained. "We will see the main body of the British Army and possibly Lord Cornwallis himself if history holds true!"

Sid, now interrupting to remark, asked, "Okay, let's not get ahead of ourselves. What is this here?" He pointed to an earlier point before the question mark John had been looking at after Cowpens.

"That's basically Greensboro, North Carolina, a place called Guilford Courthouse where a battle takes place and the British are victorious by the slimmest of margins," Nik said.

"Why would we want to go see that?" asked John sharply.

"Well, it's on the way east, and the royal forces took quite a pounding there. As I recall, they lost upward of 20 percent of their men, which is a huge cost in men for such a small venue. I am also curious to see how it goes; will it be a different history from what we know? Do the British win big instead of by a slim margin? Do they win at all?"

"Hmm," murmured John. "It's going to suck seeing us lose."

"As long as we lose by the slimmest of margins, it'll be okay, because that's what actually happened in our known history," added Sid.

"So really, all in all, what do you think?" inquired Nik as he sat back down and observed the mood of the group. For the first time in all these many months out in the wilderness of 1780–81, there was an air of question and a speculation that felt a little foreign to them. "It's a big decision, and we are all in it together," Nik said, now trying to eliminate any concern.

Sid, looking at the dates associated with the events, asked Nik, "So, after Cowpens and before Guilford Courthouse, quite a long time passes? What would you have us do in that, like, month and a half?"

Nik scratched his forehead and responded meekly. "I'm not sure.... Let's see how Cowpens goes and what kind of surroundings, mood, and weather we have. Maybe we stick around there and ease up to North Carolina; I'm not sure. That's the 'play it by ear' part of the plan."

"And May 8 isn't?" asked John.

"Well, that is an opportunity play—might happen, might not. We'll see." Nik, being a bit vague, added, "I just don't know how we'll fare or feel at these times; we just have to see what goes on and what our guts tell us to do."

"Fair enough," said Sid.

"Yeah, sounds like a plan, I guess," John said. He finally appeared as if he accepted and understood the plan and approach.

After some time, Sid stood up and asked, "When do we leave?"

Nik looked at John. "Well?" he asked John again.

John sat back and responded, "When do we leave?" He threw his hands in the air.

"You're sure?" continued Nik. "We can do whatever we want. Going once ... going twice ... sold to the computer geeks in the small homemade cabin in the woods! We need to leave ASAP, as we need to make Cowpens by the eleventh and get our observation area set up."

The camp immediately became astir with commotion and movement that they hadn't seen since the days of the cabin construction the previous summer. Nik watched as all the things were put in order; travel provisions were separated, and Sid checked and distributed the battle packs of ammunition to each member based on the weapons they carried. Honestly, they all felt a certain rush in the preparation for moving out. John, who was very charged now, was collecting food stuffs and supplies, dividing up what they, had and balancing the food weight among the group.

"A well-oiled machine. Ha! This is awesome!" John excitedly yelled as he went about his arrangements.

"You excited, man?" Sid questioned John.

John stopped, sarcastically said, "Nah!" and then laughed.

Nik was busy finalizing his pack as he stowed and arranged the placement of his items. "You sure seem excited about our plans, John," he commented.

John, now settled down, slightly retorted, "Yes! We are going to go preserve our history! And I, for one, am excited—as long as we don't have to dig any more mass graves. Can we be a little more selective this time if we need to 'get involved'?"

Nik now retorted, "Hopefully, we don't have to do anything but watch. That's our prime mission—to watch."

"We know," said Sid. "And we knew that at Kings Mountain and had to radically change our plans."

"Understood, and we'll do it again if the situation justifies it, but—" and Nik ended there.

"We know the drill," Sid said and smiled.

... 24 ...
C-10, You Will Be Missed

NIK, SID, AND JOHN embarked on their new mission, code named "Liberty's Dawn." It was early January 1781, and the boys were now headed to witness another one of the American Revolution's jeweled moments for the struggling young nation-to-be. Spirits were high for a moment, and then they paused to look at their packed-up and secured cabin through the snowy forest. This sight made them a little gloomy, as they had grown accustomed to their lives at the C-10 camp. They had come to feel, in a way, that it was their home "out of time," their home in the year 1781.

Standing in silence now, John asked the clear and obvious question. "You guys think we'll ever get back here?"

Sid replied bluntly. "If we survive the next ten months, we'll come home."

Nik added, "Unless time catches us first." A long pause brought a cold breeze and a snow flurry to their hillside. The silence was absolute, and they could hear the snowflakes hitting the dry leaves, now expired but still clinging to the frozen, brittle branches from which they had sprouted that past spring. The wisps of sound of a far-off, blustery wind blowing up the mountainside soothed the boys' spirits. It was stunning and peaceful and was one of the reasons the boys lingered so on that trail leading into an unknown future they had so meticulously planned.

The group, now individually contemplating their next move, recognized the expressions on each other's faces. Nik's visage became a harbinger of doom and gloom. Sid knew they would survive their travels safely but had a sense of loss for their camp and home of 1781; he looked around and felt his face flush as his eyes welled either from emotion or the biting cold wind that swirled around their faces. John saw the gloom and sadness in his compatriots' eyes and wanted to say something that would lighten the mood. Unfortunately, he himself was stuck in a similar emotional quagmire. The movements made by any or all at this time were heavy and laborious, like they were teeter-tottering back and forth, trying to make a decision to stay put or proceed onward toward their next adventure.

Nik took the first positive step ... and then a second. He was fifty feet from a still-immobile Sid and John as he called out in an abnormally loud voice, "Hey, we can execute an RTLS if the mood doesn't shift? Let's get some distance downrange and then see how we feel."

Sid looked up with a familiar smirk on his face and nodded his head. John, getting a pat on the shoulder from Sid, now moved forward. "RTLS?" John inquired of Sid, "What the hell is that?" Sid smilingly relayed to John of another of Nik's motivational tools he employed whenever Nik was at a loss for words.

"RTLS is short for 'Return to Launch Site.' It's an astronautics term meaning just what it sounds like, a deviation or execution of course on a track or course for a return to the specified and specific point of origin. He likes to break into other modes of speech when times get strange or uncomfortable, and he wants to try and change things up. I am sure he has used this before with us on this trip—in a more subtle way, of course—but he does it all the time, either with humor, an odd voice, or something."

A march of epic proportions was executed that day after the sluggish start. The boys skidded down hillsides, scurried across high valleys, and nestled themselves into a small hillside cave for the night. It didn't smell very welcoming, as it was damp with wall coverings of various forms of moss and lichen. It was still cold, even at this lower elevation and under cover, and the boys knew for a fact they had certainly grown accustomed to the comfort of their cabin home at C-10.

"Dammit! My toes are freezing!" John yelped, as Nik tried to get a start of a fire going with some kindling they had gathered. It wasn't the driest of stuff they'd ever come across.

An annoyed and now quickly cooling Nik proclaimed, "Piss on this!" He then strategically extracted, from one of his many pockets, a supply of magnesium shavings.

Sid quickly produced a flint sparker he had stowed, and Nik smiled. "You read my mind."

Moments later a rather large kindling structure resembling an igloo was assembled, which was immediately engulfed in the white flash of flame that could melt most any normal materials. A five-thousand-degree magnesium oxidation reaction started the group's fire efficiently and easily, yielding the much-needed warmth for the night.

"That is some nice stuff!" Sid said.

"Who would have thought to bring a supply of that anywhere?" John commented in a happy and gracious way.

Nik smiled and uttered, "Only an overly aggravated, slightly paranoid, wholly irritated person being made to go camping against all logic in the year 2010." This rant brought the much-needed comedic relief the group needed for the evening.

"We walked a long way today, once we got started," Nik said, beginning the evening's conversation. The phases of the day had become a pattern for the group: wake up, perform morning tasks, continue with daily routines, indulge in dinner, prepare for the night, rest and have their evening conversation, and then sleep. Sid referred to the evening conversation phase as the daily debriefing, when everything that had transpired through the day could be rehashed, discussed, and resolved if need be. This evening was no different, and the hike and cold were the main topics of conversation with a hint of what the next day would bring.

"Another day of skirting the hills, and we'll be able to head east," informed Nik.

"East to where?" asked John.

"Well, from what I can remember, there is a lake that runs east-west," Nik explained. "If we find it and walk the length of its banks, we will end up close to and just southwest of Cowpens, I think. That's a really good guess, anyway."

Sid, now looking ahead for a tactical sneak peek, asked Nik about the battlefield at Cowpens. Nik responded, "Oh boy … you are expecting a lot, Sid. I am not sure I could even begin to remember what I have read of the Cowpens battlefield. Thankfully, battles of this time period didn't involve a huge amount of tactics, which is where we would excel if we were actually fighting a battle … you know, in this time period."

Sid, not exactly seeing how that answered his question, continued, "Umm, that's it?"

John sat up and watched the exchange. He listened as Nik responded. "Well, there were woods, some flat open ground where the—"

"Yeah, yeah, I know all that. I want to know how the battle went," Sid interrupted.

Nik looked tired. "You want to do this tonight? We'll never get to sleep if I give you the full details of what we are about to watch."

John now joined in on Sid's side. "Well, just the high points," he said. "You know, a little tidbit."

"Okay," Nik said, giving in. "We are going to witness a sixty-minute battle, much like at Kings Mountain. But this time our American forces will perform, for the first and last time ever on this continent, a maneuver that resembles a double-flank action, which completely engulfs the British forces under Tarleton, sending them running in surrender. How's that?" ended Nik.

"Eh, okay for now," replied John. "We'll want more later, of course, but for now, it'll do."

Sid had to ask, even though he thought he already knew the answer. "Do you know how we are going to set up?"

Nik, now lying, answered him. "Yes, I think so … and yes, I have fall-back plans in case we need to provide some offensive fire power to ensure the historically correct result."

"Oh, now that's not fair," retorted John. "Now I am really going to be up all night thinking!"

Sid murmured in an almost half-asleep grumble. "I knew it. I knew you were working on something; you always have way more going on in that devious little head of yours."

"Good night," Nik replied, and after a pause, he continued. "I have no idea what you're talking about."

John laughed as Sid snored. Nik closed his eyes and allowed sleep to deaden his thoughts of war.

The next morning brought temperatures equal to the cold of the previous day, and Sid and John did not want to get out of their makeshift bivy sacks. "Thank God for these modified space blankets," muttered Nik. "They are pretty warm."

"Warm enough that we don't freeze to death," remarked John. The boys had wrapped and crudely secured their toughened NASA space blankets around them to form a wrap—kind of like a cocoon or duffle bag; they had to be careful not to move around too much to keep from damaging them. The boys' breath in the cold, crisp air was quite visible and filled the small cave area with a humorous fog.

Nik had assembled a small fire just to get them going with some hot water. Sid reached into a pocket on his left side and produced a single tea bag. "This is a good time for this," he said with a smile. They brewed the single tea bag with the boiling water and shared the resulting, weak brew. It was very simple; it was warm, and they all needed that kick-start on this frigid morning.

They packed up and moved out of their small cave, tromping out into the freshly fallen snow. There wasn't much of it on the ground, but an inch or two of the white stuff made the ground more difficult to traverse. They were slowly heading down in elevation as they moved to the northeast. By the end of the day, they would arrive at a location where they could, with the coming of the next day, turn east and head for the lake Nik had talked about. The day was eventless, and all they could find to eat were some frozen berries still hanging on leafless bushes along the way.

"The lake will be great!" John rattled on as they hiked. "We can catch some fish, assuming it isn't frozen over."

"That'll be a welcome change; we aren't finding much to feast on here," Nik huffed and puffed, now sounding a bit winded.

Sid, who was in the lead, raised his hand to signal a stop. The three, now scurrying behind some covering brush, were observing a crossroads of sorts. They hadn't seen a soul for months, and seeing actual traffic was almost a shock, not to mention a bit creepy and quite unnerving. There were several wagons moving along a road perpendicular to each other. It appeared to be a chance meeting for those parties navigating the roads. Sid, seeing the event through his small binoculars, now reported the passengers waved as the wagons passed each other on the small, frozen and snowy crossroad. The boys remained vigilant a long time in order to let the slow-moving, horse-drawn wagons completely exit the area and see if any others would show up on the roadways before they made their way.

John had a great suggestion. "We need some arctic camouflage for the snowy times here."

"I thought of that recently but had no idea how to make something like that for us in this time," Sid added.

John answered, "I know; it's not like we have a huge supply of bleach for anything like that."

"Nice idea, though; next time we plan an outing, we'll include some arctics ... and night vision. We forgot the night vision," Nik said, now being comically sarcastic.

Sid interrupted with, "Um, dude, we don't own any night vision."

"Yeah, yeah, details, details," remarked Nik as he laughed. The day sped by, and the camp that night was quick to form. A small fire was made, and because there wasn't a great camp to be found, they assembled a small and quick lean-to. There wasn't much discussion this night, as their long hike that day had left each one of them simply exhausted.

Several more days, including the turn east, led them to the lake Nik had talked about. They hadn't moved with great speed in the cold winds of January, and all three of them hoped the frigid weather would break soon. It aided them in a way, by the fact that they were able to keep moving without overheating, which was problematic in the heat and humidity of the summer months. Not one of the guys really became acclimated to it; they were just always hot. The cold also seemed to reduce their appetites. This might seem counterintuitive, as the human body would normally need to burn more fuel (i.e., food) to keep warm and function. They just weren't eating as much.

A very nice stopping area was located near the banks of the lake. Nik assumed this to be the lake he had vaguely remembered from the maps and knew it would take them only a day or two to traverse the distance past the easternmost side toward the battlefield at Cowpens, South Carolina. John had instructed the others to build the camp as he ran off down to the lake edge with fishing gear in hand. Honestly, the group hadn't felt very hungry, and the fact was there wasn't much on the land they could forage. They didn't dare hunt anything large due to weapons noise. Rifle reports were not an odd thing to hear, but their weapons had a much different sound than the rifle of the day.

John happily returned with a few fish, dropped them off, and ran back down to catch some more. He was having a lot of fun down at the banks of the lake, despite the cold. It had been a grueling four days of hiking, and they all needed to blow off a little steam. Nik and Sid collected firewood at a feverish pace before John's first fish delivery and were readying a fire. John, Nik noted, was getting dangerously close to the edge of the bank, and Nik was worried about him falling in. Sid assured Nik that John always "danced with it," referring to his flirting with the water. In the summer months, this wasn't an issue, but now, with this cold … well, it wouldn't be a good thing for him to fall in.

"How the hell is he catching fish in the middle of winter?" inquired Sid.

"Well, a long line down into the deepest parts of the lake, I guess? I'm honestly not sure," Nik replied.

In another hour or so, the fire was roaring, and the guys were sitting around it warming up. Their spirits were high. John had been preparing the fish on a makeshift table off a ways from the fire. This kept the fish cold and made them easier to prep in bulk. Sid and Nik were whittling and smoothing sticks to be used for skewers as they anxiously waited for dinner to be delivered. John retrieved the skewers and proceeded to mount his recent catch onto them for cooking. Waiting for the fire to die down and generated a nice bed of coals was killing them; they were hungry. Finally, the glow of the embers was right. Each had a meat-loaded skewer to cook, and once again, the time couldn't go by fast enough for the hungry group.

The fish cooked to a crispy tenderness; the smell was exquisite to the boys, and it reminded them of a home cookout over a grill or the steak house on their trip out to camping almost a year ago. They had worked on their cooking skills all this time, but this meal seemed like the best they'd had yet. Hunger was the probable culprit; they had eaten lean for more than a few days and really needed a meal like this. Fish, fish, and more fish!

"Any idea what kind of fish this is, John?" asked Nik.

John looked at Nik and said, "Nope, unless there is a fish called tasty and scrumptious." They all laughed for a moment, and John made the comment that he was going to try and catch some more fish for the next few days of travel.

"Good idea!" Sid added, as he slowly worked around some of the bones in the fish he was eating.

"It's not like it'll go bad out here; it's below freezing, and it'll last for quite a while" Nik muttered as he continued to eat.

The day wrapped up gloriously with plenty of fire, warmth, great food, and good cheer. This had been the first semirelaxed camp experience they'd had since leaving C-10. The cold was, very simply, tough to deal with, and combined with the scarcity of food, it became quite dangerous for the boys. Nik and Sid collected material they could use as bedding to put between them and the frigid ground for the night, while John went off to get a little more fishing done. Pine straw, leaves from whatever trees were around, and anything else they could find would do fine and make this night out in the cold just a bit better.

John now returned to the camp; he was cold and tired, but he'd caught a good supply of fish, which he quickly cleaned and left to freeze overnight. Nik and Sid were already sitting down for the night and waiting for John to finish, so they could all be near the fire. They had planned on discussing a little more of their plan of action for the upcoming observation mission at Cowpens before calling it a night.

John arrived completely exhausted and shivering. "Dude, sit down. You have done plenty for today," remonstrated Nik.

"I know.… I am freezing; throw another log on the fire." John shivered as he spoke. They just sat for a while as John warmed up, while Nik poked and prodded the fire, occasionally adding some logs to it to keep it going strong.

Sid decided to begin the conversation. "So, Nik, are you going to inform us of our plans going into Cowpens?" He knew the answer to the question as he and Nik had talked before John returned from fishing.

"Oh, yes, of course. It all began on one scary frightful night—" Sid and John looked at Nik as if he'd lost his mind. "Oh, wrong story. Cowpens, yes, of course." As John joked, he looked to see if he had entertained the group.

"Yeah, yeah, c'mon. I am dying to hear what peril and predicaments you are going to get us into this time!" blurted John.

"Okay, okay.… Geez, you're a tough audience. Well, we are on course and probably a few days out of the Cowpens battlefield area, maybe three days at most."

"What do you figure we'll see when we get there?" asked John.

"Hopefully, absolutely nothing," answered Nik. "I am hoping to have several days to construct our observation shelter and battle tubes."

"Battle tubes?" Sid asked. "What the hell are you talking about, and what purpose will they serve?" Sid's expression looked as if he really wanted to ask, *What has that devious little mind conjured up this time?*

Nik was now smiling. "Weeelll, if we need to intervene, we might use this design I have been thinking about for the past couple of weeks to give us a tactical advantage." Nik paused momentarily for effect. "You know, if we need to."

John looked oddly at Nik. "Tactical advantage? Umm, did you see what we did at Kings Mountain? Tactical advantage … I don't think we need any advantage!"

"True, but let me tell you what I'm thinking." smiled Nik.

Nik proceeded to describe a similar observation shelter to the one at Kings Mountain with one small addition. Nik drew a picture of the Cowpens battlefield as best he could remember it and showed where the American horse mounted force had, in their history, overrun the British troops under Tarleton. His idea and plan was to set the group up in such a way as to support that side of the British flank, and if things didn't look like they should, they could make a quick decision on what might be done.

Nik hastily created a map in the dirt diagramming the shelter, the battlefield perimeter, and three ravines they would dig, leading out from their observation shelter toward the battlefield perimeter. He continued to explain that they would endeavor to cover these ravines, forming tunnel-like passages they could lie down in and would serve as covered firing positions. This was just in case the Continentals under Gen. Daniel Morgan needed their help to make history true to the history they knew, of course.

"Kings Mountain caught us by surprise," Nik shrugged. "But we had a full day's notice that something was wrong—the dragoons. They were not there in the history we knew, and they certainly didn't attack anyone in that area on that October day in our historical 1780. No, that was strange. This battle lasts sixty minutes as well; there will be no time to sit and make some kind of grand decision if something that plain isn't laid in front of us a day before. No, we need to be ready, ready at a moment's notice."

Sid and John were now really sort of annoyed. "Ready for what? Aren't we supposed to be staying out of this and observing?" Sid questioned. John was also stammering in annoyed concern.

"Yes! And we will. I am sure that nothing odd will happen, but don't you want to be … ready?" inquired Nik, seeking to be understood.

"Well, of course we can be ready. It's just, well, it seems that we are sort of moving ourselves into the fight." John measured his reply.

"We don't have to do any of that," Nik answered back. "We all have a say in our approach, and honestly, the history and the numbers and the events have us doing nothing. Our rules of engagement will be in play here."

Sid added, "When we observe the environment and battlefield, we will revise them for what we see and what is pertinent to the engagement."

"Yes, we are a couple of days out. I just wanted to introduce you to what I was thinking and ... this is a key battle in the Revolution. It cannot be lost by the Americans." Nik emphasized the closing to his commentary.

"It sounds like a solid idea; let's see what we see when we get there," said Sid with a cough.

Camp was a little quiet that night, which disturbed Nik a bit. He kept the fire going late into the evening and into the early morning hours, because he couldn't sleep. Was he really trying to force the issue for the group to act? Did he think he knew something more about this history besides what was? To him, he was as clueless as any of the three about anything in this time. But he had formulated these ideas from all he struggled to remember and couldn't cleanse his mind of the surprise at Kings Mountain. He ruminated for a bit on all of these things as he stoked the fire and elevated both its temperature and glow for greater heat generation. Why would he contrive these plans and really detailed ideas on how to set themselves up for a conflict that wasn't theirs to get involved in? "Dammit," he murmured more loudly than he meant to at 1:21 a.m.

Sid picked his head up. "Go to sleep.... Sleep," he said before covering his head up again.

Nik now sat down and fell asleep leaning on a rock that was being warmed by the fire. It was a quiet night, and he hoped the guys would understand his good intentions about the upcoming situation as a whole. He wasn't trying to force a fight; he was concerned for the group, their country, and their future back—or would that be forward?—in 2010.

... 25 ...
The Path to Cowpens

THE MORNING BROUGHT A cold, stiff wind and pure misery. The boys packed up their camp and their deep frozen fish and almost ran to more sheltered areas a bit north of the lake. They had planned to head east along the banks of the lake and then turn north to the Cowpens battlefield area, but they changed that plan when they realized it was much too cold and blustery for lake shore walking. Away from the lake, some trees and foliage, meager as they were in January, would be an improvement over the bank of the lake where the wind had a free pass to deliver its worst and strongest blows to the group. They pivoted north-northeast in an attempt to find a wind break of any kind—trees, a canyon, deep ravines, anything would be better than the battering they were taking.

"That fire yesterday and last night sure spoiled us quickly, didn't it?" John proclaimed.

"It sure did," added Nik.

Sid was trying to take little, fast steps in an attempt to keep up some warmth. "Man, oh man," Sid groaned. "I sure am happy global warming is coming; another half a degree, and we'll have droughts and death by heat all around us! We'll have to leave the planet; we humans are sooooo evil, dirty, and nasty." This constant sarcasm and continual banter they recalled from folks in 2010 who wanted to basically see man wiped from the planet so nature could

---

be alone in its utmost glory continually entertained the group on their treks.

"What utter lies and misconceptions!" yelled Nik over the whoosh of the blowing wind. "Another way to nudge us into some other incredibly expensive way to do something that traditionally could have been done easily and for pennies on the modern dollar." Nik's complaint referred to the essence that anything that was "good" for the environment came at a significantly higher monetary cost, light bulbs being a prime example. A normal, run-of-the-mill incandescent light bulb cost less than a dollar, and if it broke, you swept it up and threw out the pieces. The new, energy-efficient, good-for-the-environment style could run you as much as ten dollars per bulb and contained mercury oxide, which was absolutely toxic to human beings and the environment. With this and many well-placed laws, a person would be *required* to leave the area and call a hazardous material team to clean up a broken bulb (at his own expense). Nik rambled on for an hour about this, as the others chuckled and shook their heads at his annoyance.

They had made some headway into a wooded area where they stopped for a minute, just wanting to pause long enough to take a good look around their new terrain. "It's cold, snowy, has some trees, and did I mention it was cold?" John piped up, knowing he might get hit with something.

"Brilliant deduction!" Sid laughed. They pushed on for the rest of the day and part of the evening, finally finding a crevice to sleep in for the night. It wasn't much of a shelter and was very uncomfortable. They slept recumbent in the long direction of the crevice, rifles in hand; they were extremely uncomfortable and hoped to make Cowpens in the next day or two where they suspected (or rather hoped) there would be woods or a forest to provide shelter.

The next morning couldn't have come soon enough, and the boys were awake and off fairly early. They felt they wanted to push now; the temperature was a bit warmer, and the wind had died down considerably. The terrain had flattened out, and there was a spring-like scent in the air.

"Let's not kid ourselves, guys. It's only like four or five degrees warmer today, and because the wind decreased dramatically and the sun is out, we are fooled into thinking it feels much warmer," Nik explained, trying to make himself and the others understand that winter was not over.

"Oh, I'm sure it's going to get cold again," John said. After all, it was January 13, 1781, and they were behind schedule! They ran that day and most of the next to arrive at the woods near the site of the Cowpens battlefield. The boys, now wearing their burlaps and woods, spent the cold dusk of the fourteenth assessing the area that they thought would become the next bloody affair of the American Revolution.

"This place is like a park—serene and quiet; it's even sort of green, considering the cold setting of winter. It seems like an unlikely place for a battle to take place, you know?" Nik commented.

Sid, looking at the tactical side of things, asked Nik where they were going to begin setting up their observation station. Nik stopped for a second and looked for a body of water, a river he had remembered that was supposed to be swollen with water, runoff from heavy rains or snows, he'd assumed. John pointed off in a direction, and after a little walking, they thought they spotted the river Nik had vaguely remembered from the history texts.

Resetting his mind's eye now, Nik indicated the direction that the British would rush in from, where the Americans would be camped in the area between the two small hills, and where he had recalled the actual battle took place. "Of course, these locations are pure guesses, guys," Nik noted, proffering a disclaimer to everything he had just shown them. He then paced out a location far off the battlefield where he thought they would construct their camouflaged, downed-tree hideout.

"Look," said John. "Look at the ground—furrows!" The boys looked down on the landscape in gratitude. What they saw was indeed a slew of furrows that were naturally shaped into the land and headed south from the battlefield area. Their shelter would be along these furrows to the south, using them to facilitate the creation of the battle tubes.

"You can't get any luckier, Nik. These things are right here and almost ready to go. Did you know these were here?" asked John.

"No, man, it's an incredible stroke of luck!" Nik exclaimed. "Providential even," he murmured in a more hushed voice. "It also means we won't have to do as much digging, which is also lucky for us since we arrived here much later than I had planned."

Sid, now looking at the area mentioned, noted, "What if we make little bunkers instead of covered tubes? There isn't much to use for all that; look around. And, honestly, I don't feel like digging. The little army shovel we have just doesn't cut it for anything bigger than a small hole or shaving away at an already-present hole or ledge. I am amazed at what you excavated at Kings Mountain, Nik. It was truly a feat!"

Nik shrugged. "It was nervous energy, I guess.... More like deep remorse and guilt," he followed up with seconds later.

Sid was correct; it was January, and there wasn't much growing around. This place looked and smelled like what it sounded like by its name—an area where animals grazed in a sparsely wooded pasture; it was not dense forest by any means. There were no signs of grazing cattle, but evidence could be found to support the fact that this was, in fact, grazing land for some large beasts. Additionally, some crude fencing could be found in certain areas of the region. There were sufficient trees to accommodate the creation of their observation hideout and some bunker-type nooks, but to fully cover fifty-five to one hundred yards of tunnel—well, that would be a severe reach, maybe even impossible. The observation structure could be built in the thicker wooded area, and the bunker units could be created up to two hundred yards closer to the battlefield.

"Sounds like a plan. It's good we are flexible about what we are doing," said John. "We should get started on the hideout construction. We don't have much time left today, but we can probably manage to down trees that we can crawl into for sleep tonight."

They selected a location with the highest number of trees in a group that they could fell into a teepee-looking pile. A single furrow led into and through the bottom of their newly constructed structure. They would be able to scurry out of the shelter to their respective and yet unbuilt bunkers/weapons positions.

"Look, Nik! A V channel for drainage!" John laughed sarcastically.

"Uh-huh," Nik grumbled, unamused. Sid laughed at him. "Let's build some blocks or gates to use on the inside of the shelter to hem up the furrow on each side," Nik suggested. "I don't really want it to be easy for something to crawl into our little shelter." They all agreed.

"Primitive" was the word for their shelter and camping conditions that night, and they went to sleep vowing a better setup effort in the morning. They did have a small fire, but they were wary about making it much bigger than a foot in diameter for fear of being spotted by some errant Colonial passerby. The contrast between Kings Mountain and this location was staggering; the cold was a serious problem, and there wasn't much they could do about it. They were able to have a fireless camp in October, but now they needed a little warmth to stay comfortable. Here they couldn't afford to get chilled. Hypothermia was something they had been able to avoid up to this point, and it made no sense to risk it now. They had little choice now, as they needed to ensure their cover. It was a long, cold night.

The morning of January 15 brought similar weather, but they were working hard on their shelter, which kept them warm through the day. By the middle of the day, temperatures had risen and exertion had reduced the amount of layers they had been bundled up in for most of the morning hours. Once again, their work created a shelter that looked like a bunch of fallen trees piled together. It was thickly walled with the branches of the trees from the inside of the structure applied to the outer walls for coverage. Fallen leaves and pine needles covered the floor of their new hideaway rather nicely, making it slightly cozier on the inside. Sid had relatively quickly and easily manufactured two portcullis-style coverings out of sticks and grasses for the small furrow openings in the bottom of their shelter.

"Dude, those look great!" John complimented Sid on his quick work.

"Yeah, let's hope it keeps out any unwanted critters or people," replied Sid.

The boys opted to work on their weapons positions the next day and decided to cammo-up and take a look around at their surroundings just before sundown. They paced out the edges of the battlefield, being careful not to run into anyone. The last thing they needed was to blow their cover, become discovered, and be tracked back to their hideout. They had been spooked a few times; in whispered voices, they discussed this and decided to cut their reconnaissance short with an immediate return to their "nest." The group adopted the name "the nest" for their observation hideout for no particular reason other than they wanted a short name for it. It did resemble some sort of giant bird's nest from a fairy tale they'd probably read to their children sometime in the past ten years.

That night brought a "gentle" demand/request from John on what they were facing in the upcoming event on the seventeenth. Sid was interested but figured they had a full day and a half to work the bunker locations and chat about the upcoming battle. Nik wanted to tell John and Sid as much as possible, and he began that night with the run up to the fight that would happen in less than two days.

"So, where do I start?" Nik began. "Two military leaders: On the American side, Gen. Daniel Morgan was assigned to annoy the British down here in the southern backcountry. For the British, Lt. Col. Banastre Tarleton. This guy was hated by the Colonials for being a bit more than ruthless. He didn't really like to have his enemies surrender to him; he'd rather just kill them on the field.

"A few days ago, around the twelfth, I think, Tarleton's scouts located Morgan's regulars and began planning the assault that will transpire here on the seventeenth. Morgan basically pinned himself and his forces in by the high waters of the river, streams, and tributaries, and I guess he made the decision to make his stand here at Cowpens, South Carolina. That said, some felt that by having the water to their backs and sides, they were protected from any potential British flank attack, which may have very well worked out in the Americans' favor.

"Morgan sent out couriers to give the word to the surrounding militias that his forces were here at Cowpens and were in need of assistance. Militias from all around answered the call. From what I can remember, they will begin to arrive tomorrow. They would, or will, camp in that area I showed you near the short hills. These militias included the Overmountain Men we got a glimpse of at Kings Mountain. It is noted in the history texts that General Morgan spent the entire night wandering the camp, telling stories of victory and motivating the men for the upcoming battle. There were even stories of him proposing a bravery competition between militias to increase their fighting performance the next day. A final report on the Colonial encampment was that General Morgan didn't get a moment of sleep that night."

John yawned, stretched, and then broke the story with a sarcastic question to Nik. "So, why did you go into engineering and computers again?"

"I don't know," Nik admitted. "I thought I liked the idea of solving problems."

"You would have made a great history teacher for sure!" John continued.

Sid added, "You should have heard him go off like this on a daily basis in 2010. You couldn't shut him up. He was so passionate about all that we hadn't learned from our history. I didn't want to know so much about all of it—until now, of course. Now it's different; now we're living it. It's is a little closer to home, you know?"

"All right, I need sleep. I'll give you part two tomorrow night— Part Two: The Day of the Battle at Cowpens!" announced Nik.

The group settled down to try for some sleep with a deep chill in the air and a small fire in their more-complete shelter. Each member of the group had that feeling again; it was an anxious feeling that wasn't really conducive to sleeping. They tossed and turned most of the night and hoped they wouldn't have to intervene in any way in the upcoming battle. They hoped for the historically correct victory of the American forces in two days, and each weighed out in his mind the actions that could end up as a possible intervention at Cowpens as well.

... 26 ...
Preparations for War

THE MORNING BROUGHT A coldness that was representative of the mood of the group. Sid and Nik had aches and pains; John felt good enough but was restless. They all stayed in the shelter, rested through midmorning, and discussed what they needed to accomplish on this day.

"What are we doing today, guys?" John asked.

Nik rolled over and began, "We need to work on our bunkers and maybe tunnels to get to them—" Rethinking what he'd just said, Nik continued. "Maybe we just concentrate on the bunkers and not worry about the tunnels. We'll see, I guess."

Sid was now moving about the shelter and getting ready to go look for possible locations for the bunkers. "You know, I liked your idea about tubes to shoot out of. I think we should work on something small and sleek we can lie down in as well as being able to use our bipods for accuracy," he said. "Not tunnels exactly, but something with the same kind of functionality. Our targets could be up to six hundred yards away. We need to be as stable as possible to be effective at those ranges."

John looked over at Sid, "Effective? We could spray the entire area and drop everybody! What's to be effective?"

Sid nodded and laughed. "True, but effective means making every shot count for two important reasons. First, we hit our targets as precisely as possible, and second, we need to preserve

---

all the ammunition we can. We are in 1781, and we are limited in what we have even though we have quite a supply with us, be stingy with it at all times. Shoot smart!"

Nik joined in on the conversation to show support for his friends' advice. "Thankfully, we are not expending huge amounts of ammunition in these encounters, and thanks to Sid, we have thousands of rounds for our seven weapons. We are set up pretty well and could carry out a protracted fight in this time if we needed to. What you said is important for many reasons, Sid; we do need to shoot smart. Imagine if we shanked a shot and hit General Morgan or, worse, General Washington if he were around!"

Sid and John looked at Nik in horror. "Okay, point taken," John noted.

"Well, you know, I'm just saying." With that, Nik ended his commentary.

Sid, now leaving the shelter, squinted from the light outside. John joined him, and Nik straggled behind. They walked over to the clearing where they believed the battle would take place. Sid paced back toward their hut and after thirty of forty minutes settled on a location where he thought they should set up their "gun tubes." He would lie down and roll around the area he was looking at, trying to make sure the group could see where they potentially wanted to shoot. He chose a spot where they could use one of the existing ravines to move from their hideout to their gun tube. The gun tube was located on a slight rise in the land, not drastic by any means, but a foot or two of elevation gave them a little clearance for choosing their targets at the four-hundred- to six-hundred-yard range.

"We need to dig this out a little," Sid pointed out. "I don't think we need to cover it exactly.... I think we will be able to crawl along this dug out ravine in our camouflage without being seen." Nik and John looked at the area and agreed.

"I like it," John said.

Nik added, "Yeah, I don't suppose anyone will venture out this far away from the battlefield." They agreed and began their work. Nik concentrated on the digging process and suggested applying some natural material to hide the excavation. Sid worked on the gun tube structure using a mini version of the downed-tree shelter. John took patrol and lookout duty. They felt it was within a day or so of the battle and wanted to keep a sharp eye out for anyone or anything. At the end of Sid's day of construction, he had created a basic pillbox. The single gunnery location for the three looked like a bushy bramble from the battlefield side and a mini half-dome structure from the side of their hideout—not exactly a "gun tube." This would serve their purposes, because, as Nik had said, "We're not married to any one idea on this, you know." Additionally, the idea of three separate positions was exchanged for this one location, because it would accommodate all three of them and provide an easier way to communicate.

They stood around two hundred yards away from their structures and stared at what they'd created. "Honestly, I can't tell any real difference from the natural surroundings," commented John.

Nik reinforced John's commentary by adding, "It's pretty good, guys. From this direction, it looks like the wooded area that surrounds the whole place."

Sid rubbed his chin. "You know, we could make this even more convincing." With that, he ran off into the wooded areas to the right and left of their hideout and pillbox.

"Okay," responded Nik and John as Sid ran off. They fanned out a bit, still keeping within a close proximity of Sid. Nik patrolled near a body of water to their east and southeast while John moved in a fan pattern to the west and north, neither of them wandered very far from the now-hardworking Sid. Both John and Nik paused at trees, peering around and blending into their surroundings. They didn't want to be constantly moving, so they moved slowly and then paused, always looking around before slowly proceeding to the next position.

Sid returned to the two-hundred-yard position after nearly two hours and looked at the scene again. John and Nik joined him and observed his handiwork. "Nice!" John chortled with a low whistle.

"You have gone over and above, man," added Nik. The boys were looking at a large number of little brambles that resembled their hideout structure and their pillbox. These were smaller and not as well formed, but to the casual passerby, these items would all blend into the landscape and look very natural. There would be no reason for anyone to come and investigate any particular one, as they all looked very ordinary and familiar scattered about this piece of the landscape.

"This should keep any possible interest in our bramble structures down to a low roar," said Sid.

"It looks great! Good idea, Sid," Nik said as he patted Sid on the back.

It was approaching three o'clock in the afternoon, and the guys decided to call it a day. Nik knew it wouldn't be very long now; there would be an American camp forming between the hills to the north, and they needed to get under cover and out of sight. They also had to figure out how they were going to keep warm on this night; if they had a fire at all, it would have to be very small. Once in the shelter, one of the boys kept a lookout through the thick branched walls, and the others tried to devise some method of keeping warm in the absence of a roaring fire. Sid pulled out a military-style fuel tab that he said they could light if they needed to generate some smokeless heat. "It will last for a few hours anyway," Sid noted.

John asked again, "Do we get Part Two of the battle history tonight, Nik?"

Nik nodded his head, indicating yes. "Yeah, man, we'll get you all caught up on what we should see tomorrow."

"Okay," John answered, expectantly rubbing his hands together. An hour ticked by before Nik, Sid, and John sat down for the evening discussion about what the next day would bring. They could hear some noise now and then off to the northwest, and soon after, a slight glow could be seen growing where Nik thought the American encampment would have been forming.

Nik sat up and peered out a very small hole in the shelter wall that faced the north. He began his talk on the battle by saying, "The essence of what I am going to tell you, to make a long story short, is this—British and American forces will meet here tomorrow. Well, they should meet here tomorrow and engage in a battle that was, in our history, considered to be another turning point in the Revolutionary War in favor of the Americans. The armies form up at roughly one thousand men apiece; the British actually had around eleven hundred men on that day.

"Tarleton was a man who didn't like to waste time with anything, especially battle, and General Morgan, on the American side, knew his tendencies for haste. The Americans take advantage of this and are successful in collapsing both sides of the British lines, forcing Tarleton to flee and surrender the field. I left a lot of details out, but the biggest British downfall was that they fell for a trap in that they misread an American fallback as a retreat; in reality, it was a planned regroup where Continental Regulars were positioned in waiting for the British onslaught. The British charged with no concern and, due to this misstep, found themselves badly out of position facing the brunt of the better-trained American force on the field."

John looked oddly confused now. "That's it?" he asked.

Sid snickered, and Nik looked at him with an almost angry stare. "Yeah. What did you expect?"

John now softening a bit, added, "Well, I figured there was more."

"There is," explained Nik, "but those were the high points."

"What about our rules of engagement? Are we going to have boundaries for our involvement?" asked Sid.

Nik now rubbed his eyes, "Yes, of course. This one is easy, and again, doing nothing is always probably our best option. Based on our decision process at Kings Mountain and the fact that we don't have some mysterious force skulking around (like the British Dragoon Force), we can take a very conservative approach and hope we just get to witness history in real time. Sid, can you go over what we laid out at Kings Mountain, minus the Dragoon stuff?"

"Sure, man," Sid began. "Well, I think this engagement should follow these rules, basically the same ones we adhered to at Kings Mountain: (1) we will only engage the British forces if and only if an event occurs that doesn't follow our known historical time line; (2) we can only engage enemy forces if the known American victory is in jeopardy; (3) we can engage if, and *only* if, the battle is in a state of full engagement. In other words, the British and American forces must be actively shooting (and making noise of gunfire) for us to fire our weapons. Our weapons cannot be the only weapons firing on the field, *ever*, in any theater we engage in; and (4) once we engage a group, there cannot be any survivors unless said enemies are at such a range that our existence would not be discovered or we simply couldn't dispatch the targets at that range. No engaged forces can be able to report anything about the group, our position, our numbers, or our weapons. At this extreme range, we probably won't have a problem with that, in my opinion."

A pause fell over the group as they digested their boundaries. "Perfect. It doesn't get any better than that," Nik complimented Sid on his review.

John nodded his head and agreed. "Crystal clear. Well said, Sid."

"So when does all this start?" asked Sid.

Nik scratched the back of his head, and looking like he was straining to recall the details, shook his head. "I'm not sure. I want to say this all goes down at sunup, but I can't remember for sure."

"Man, that's early! Well, we need sleep!" blurted John in a whispered voice.

"Yes, we need to prepare our loadouts for our weapons tonight, so we can be ready for anything," suggested Sid, now reaching into his pockets for his rifle magazines.

"For sure," agreed Nik and John.

This preparation didn't take very long, and the boys fell quiet for the long, cold night before the battle. Sid woke up during the early morning hours and ignited his fuel tab to bring their shelter to just over the freezing point. Without a proper fire, it was a truly the coldest night and morning and the boys had experienced to date.

... 27 ...
The Power in Numbers

5:57 A.M., JANUARY 17, 1781. The boys awoke to the sounds of scurrying around the areas outside their hidden lookout. Sid slowly peered into the darkness and squinted to see anything recognizable in the moonless, early-morning darkness. Nik looked out and reported several persons moving through the woods, but he couldn't make out their allegiance.

"They have moved off. Should we pack ourselves into the pillbox?" Nik informed and inquired of the group. A period of silence went by and with the absence of motion, Nik asked again in a whispered voice, "Well?" He continued to nervously look out for any additional movement in the woods.

Sid and John loaded their rifles onto their backs, and the three moved to their battle station. They quickly and efficiently covered the rear of their pill box with the brush that had been preplaced the day before for their shielded "back door." They prepared their rifles, Sid with his ruggedly scoped and sighted M1A, John with a scoped AR-15, and Nik with his precision scoped AR-15. All three of them were now prone, lying on their stomachs on the cold surface of the earth, utilizing their bipods for stability; they were ready for almost anything.

"Magazine check, please," whispered Sid.

"All set; four mags ready, one loaded," reported Nik.

John followed with, "Yup, four mags, one loaded and ready."

"Okay, I concur. Four mags, one loaded and ready to go," Sid agreed. They lay silent for several minutes, rifle barrels protruding just slightly from their brush bramble pillbox, scopes free from obstructions for a clear view of the suspected battlefield. Sid whispered, "What if we have picked the wrong area where the battle is going to occur?"

After a brief pause, Nik replied, "Then we do nothing—no worries. We'll sit tight and let the time go by, and then we'll retreat from this place and have a nice fire tonight."

At that point, a scurrying, raucous group rapidly approached their position. Were they spotted? Had they been discovered somehow? It was as if the noise was running right at them, and it was unnerving; they all felt the urge to move in some way, any way. At this point in time, all three were sharply agitated and intently fearful.

6:21a.m. There was now, without question, a small fighting force making preparations in close proximity to the boys. They were not sure whose forces were now stationed just outside their location, and they were also unsure of their mission. Were they there to investigate the boys' movements or presence? Nik, Sid, and John could hear the accoutrements of war in 1781 rustling and clanking off to their ten o'clock position. Sid reached for his pistol, and Nik, as quietly as possible, slowed him down. "Hold on … let's get a look first." John was in position to get a first glimpse of their visitors.

The sun was coming up, and the frigid, dark silhouettes of night began to give way to the cold images of the day. The boys were spying five members of the American forces who were armed with very long rifles; Sid quietly explained they were the snipers of their day, long riflemen or sharpshooters. The Americans of this time utilized, in a very effective way, an early form of guerrilla warfare, and the extremely effective tactic of targeting the leaders of an enemy force.

Nik explained in a whispered voice. "They did this now in the Revolution, and looking back at the history books, it appeared that they had forgotten this tactic when the Civil War came around. Except for here in the Deep South, Americans basically morphed back to the old, very British Revolutionary War-style of fighting in lines and ranks for some reason. Both North and South rediscovered this by the second and most certainly the third year of the Civil War.

"The idea behind these guerrilla teams was to knock out the enemy's leadership on the battlefield before the battle started and then fight on against the enemy as they floundered without direction from that now-eliminated leadership team."

The boys couldn't make a sound, and the sharpshooter force appeared to be very anxious and agitated as they stood with very intent looks of concern. Clearly excited, these sharpshooters were rather impatiently waiting for the moment they could inflict their premeditated, preemptive strike and then quickly retreat back to the relative safety of their own lines. The boys had been equally agitated as their American sharpshooter compatriots, but after a few minutes, they had calmed down, because they were fairly confident of being unnoticed and were safe for the time being.

6:47 a.m. The sun was up! The battlefield had begun to take shape in the extreme distance, and the American sharpshooters were now very still and very quiet. They were all positioned in a solid stance against some trees, and they could be seen sighting in their first targets. Moments later, five shots blared out among the quiet landscape the boys had known for the past few days. The sharpshooters dropped their rifles, picked up a second set, and quickly let loose another killing volley into the British flank. The sharpshooters picked up their spent rifles and scurried away from their shooting position as fast as they had arrived. The boys, still silent, looked at each other in awe and almost disbelief; Sid quickly returned his attention to the developing battlefield.

The battlefield continued forming, as most of the American lines could be seen off to their ten and eleven o'clock positions. The British lines had initially surged at their one and two o'clock positions, but after the lightning strike of the American guerilla fire, they eased back for a moment. John looked at his rifle as if he were preparing himself for an imminent event; Nik darted his attention all over the battlefield as well as to the areas on their sides and rear. He wanted to make sure they were secure in their position, and he was slightly concerned with the appearance of the sharpshooters.

An instant later, Sid began reporting sightings on the British side of the battlefield. "Um, Nik? This doesn't look—" It was as if they had entered yet another giant fuzzy spot in reality. Nik knew Sid was making a report on the British movements, but the reality of what he was seeing was completely fogging his mind.

How could this be? Nik thought to himself as he heard John mutter, "Holy—look at that."

6:51 a.m. The boys, now exiting the "fuzziness" of the unexpected, were looking at a massive British force moving up the field of battle, a force that was clearly at least twice that of Morgan's American field units. Sid and John simultaneously exclaimed to Nik, "There are way more of them than there are of us out there!"

Nik was trying to ascertain whether the Americans had the thousand or so expected fighters. He looked back at the advancing British mega force and shrugged. "No way," he said. "They have way more than the eleven hundred guys they are supposed to have!"

"How do you know that?" asked Sid quickly.

"I don't! But our forces will suffer a horrific defeat if Morgan doesn't get more troops on the line," blurted Nik. "John, what do you see over there in the American flank?"

John was now looking through the binoculars, scanning the rear lines of the American forces. "Well, they look a bit confused, but ... I don't know?"

7:01 a.m. Sid looked at the battlefield and reported to the others. "The lines have solidified. There seems to be a pause at the moment. It looks like the British are massing now, more on the left side—the side closer to us."

Nik picked his head up. "Pausing? That's not like Tarleton!... Massing ... waiting ... big numbers? What is going on? John, what's happening on our side?"

There was a pause, and John replied in a rather relaxed fashion. "Same," he said. "Nothing different." There was another pause, and with all the movement of troops and horses, you could have heard a pin drop in their pillbox. At that moment, Nik pulled the action back on his rifle, chambering his first round.

"Sid, what rounds do you have in your rifles?" asked Nik quickly.

Sid gawked at Nik for both the question and the energizing of his weapon. "Normal 55gr FMJs (FMJ is short for full metal jacket). Why?"

"How quickly can you rearm with green-tip, steel-core rounds?" Nik demanded.

Sid quickly rolled over and pulled out a pile of magazines from his leg pockets. "Less than a minute. Why? What now?"

Nik reached over and grabbed the new AR-15 magazines for John and gave them to him. "John, pull your mag and use these instead. What I am thinking is we are going to need a little heavier, a little deeper penetrating round for this."

"For what?" John asked.

7:09 a.m. "What I am thinking is that somehow Tarleton figured out what Morgan was planning and brought in additional forces. I have no idea how he could have figured that out; it certainly didn't happen before. And the buildup on the left," Nik continued, almost rambling, "the left—the very side where the Americans collapsed the British lines with their cavalry some 230 years ago—2010 time. How?"

Sid, chuckling somewhat, queried, "Luck maybe?"

"I have no idea," said Nik. "Are we all picked up here? In case we have to move out fast?"

John and Sid confirmed. "Yeah, all good and ready to go."

"John, you asked 'for what' a little bit ago. Well, it's clear that we are looking at a new battle at Cowpens. This battle was more than half over by now in the history we knew. It's all coming back to me now. This battle is now simmering and hasn't yet really begun, where before, it was almost over! The British have more troops, and they are taking their time, studying their American opponents. This is in total opposition to the Tarleton we read about in our history. No, this guy is different somehow; he is acting different in this reality."

"So what do we do? Blow the hell out of them?" asked John.

"Yes," said Sid. There was a long pause, and then a simple "yes" came from Nik.

8:49 a.m. And they waited.... Almost two hours went by, and the unnaturally long observation period continued. Finally, Nik broke the silence. "Sid, does it seem like the British forces are maintaining their left-side battlefield bias with their mass of troops?"

Sid checked the view of the battlefield and reported, "Yeah, still left, maybe even slightly more left now."

"Ugh," Nik mumbled. "So, if we engage here, using these rounds, try and adjust your shots for thinner, crucial parts of the body; head or neck would be best."

"Nasty, man, you are looking for hits on multiple targets with our shots, aren't you?" asked Sid.

"Yeah, that's what I am thinking. It's what we need. It's what the American side needs to see. We will need to drop a massive amount of these guys if we hope to have the Americans win this. They were, in our history books, basically at even odds with the British; they had a chance to succeed in the battle, which they did. In this reality, the odds look like two- or three-to-one in the underdog side of the aisle; I don't like those numbers, and I don't like their chances," admitted Nik.

"How long do you think we'll be waiting for them to start this thing?" inquired John.

Sid quickly shrugged. "Man, there is no telling. I can't imagine this Tarleton guy you described being able to contain himself for much longer, especially with this fighting force he has at his disposal."

10:03 a.m. The boys almost thought now that the fight wouldn't materialize on this day. The lines had grown relatively quiet and were fairly stationary with little movement on either side; it was eerie, except for the left side of the British infantry units, which appeared to be loud, excited, and rambunctious. There hadn't been any incursions into the boys' area since the early morning, and they were happy for that as they were unsure of their close-range cover. The tension was present, constant, and even though they were not trained military individuals, it was becoming strangely tolerable, almost routine. Time, which had become an item on their side in the early morning, would soon become an issue and a problem as the day dragged on. Waiting would become brutal for Sid, Nik, and John if they were to remain at the ready for many more hours; it would be asking a lot after all they had prepared for these past few days.

"I am tired, and laying here in this cold is not good. If we have to get up and run away in a quick escape move, I'm not sure I will be able to even roll over and crawl, let alone run," said Nik. As fate would have it, Nik's comment ushered in the first of several colossal booms of cannon fire on both sides.

"Holy moly, here we go!" reported Sid. The boys were instantly warming up with adrenaline, and they almost couldn't help themselves from fidgeting all over their enclosure.

"Oh man," murmured John. "Holy—" At that moment, a massive push came from the British troops along the entire length of their lines. There was huge noise now, almost groan-like, and they could barely pick out the sounds of the men falling to the speeding lead balls they were fighting with.

"The entire American front force is engaged!" reported John from his side of the pillbox. "They aren't even making a dent right now!"

The mass of the British force was moving forward with clear and decisive action and wasn't meeting much resistance. The Americans were fighting hard, but the numbers were horribly against them. "You just can't deny the numbers," Nik said under his breath.

"So when do we jump into this?" Sid asked as he released his rifle's safety.

Nik and John followed suit, and Nik asked John, "As we all engage in this thing, can you keep an eye on the American cavalry and let us know when they try to make a breakout on our side of the lines? Back in the history of it all, this was the killing maneuver that sealed the American victory. Today, well, it may be an act of utter futility and desperation. We need them to make a move for our aid to really help."

"Can do," said John.

Sid quickly reported, "We have the angle, there is plenty of noise, and there are plenty of targets to choose from. We are ready when it's time."

Nik glanced down at his magazines and began to feel ill. Even in the cold and damp, he was sweating. He knew that the likelihood of an American win at this battle, which was a clear victory in their history's reality, was almost impossible now. He wanted to just start firing but needed to see the push on the American right (the British left) to start softening up the British line.

"It's not happening, man! We need to do something, or this battle is lost, Nik!" Sid implored his friend to think faster, as the volume and groan of the battle greatly increased its intensity.

10:13 a.m. Nik, now in a profuse cold sweat, knew his friend was correct and began with a deep breath. "We need to help them see the way. Gentlemen, are you ready?"

"Check!" John confirmed.

"Ready," Sid agreed.

Nik, now taking a second deep breath, continued his cadence. "Please divide the mass on the left we've been watching. John, take the forward third toward the American line; Sid, please dispatch the rear third toward the British flank; and I will work the middle of the mass. We need head and neck shots, guys; we need each of our rounds to drop at least two of these guys, if possible. America, our country," Nik paused and took a deep breath, "doesn't have much time left this day unless we can make a difference here and show them the way. God help us and our forces on the field."

Nik, using the built-in digital rangefinder on his scope, informed his compatriots of the distance to the middle of the mass of troops on the left-hand side of the British lines directly in front of them—their targets for the day.

Nik took in another breath as he readied himself—329 yards to closest target. Nik spoke, "On three, two, one, *fire!*"

In the instant of the fire order, Sid, Nik, and John felt as if they'd entered a zone all their own. It was utterly silent to them as they dispatched death on a massive scale. Nik was shooting almost to a musical rhythm; he was floating his rifle along his targets as if the barrel were on a slide, creating a crazy eight sort of pattern. His victims fell with every fired round, and very often one or two others immediately collapsed downrange, as the rounds were successfully moving through his selected targets.

John, wielding the same firepower as Nik, was inflicting very admirable damage as his targets were evenly lined up on the front of the British lines. They were the same men who, moments earlier, had been hammering their outnumbered American enemies. John's targets were victimized by the arrangement of the day as he fired at will, his rounds often finding two or three unsuspecting British troops in parallel profile. Heads, necks, shoulders, and internal organs—the .223-caliber rounds indiscriminately screamed through their victims, slicing comrades to their immediate right.

Sid's larger and heavier .308-caliber rounds were punishing and pounding the more unorganized rear of the British lines on the left. He was becoming an expert at placing his shots to ricochet and rebound all over the British rear areas, eliminating large numbers of British troops. Nik wondered how long would they have to fire on these unsuspecting troops; the entire time he maintained his even and constant execution of their plan.

The onslaught continued without ceasing, and the boys were using their magazines at a prescribed and methodically steady pace. They shouldn't need to reach for any reserve magazines before the end of their "mission." John had cleaned up his front third of the British fighting mass and took his prescribed pause to look around their immediate area, remembering the surprise at Kings Mountain. John sounded an "all clear," and Nik thanked him for making sure they were still alone.

"No problem," John responded. "Don't need any surprises!" John also took time to look at the overall battlefield. "Guys, we have just ... it's—" John didn't know what to say about the results of their actions. "It's—" John stopped for a long pause. "We have done our share for country today; that's all I can say." He turned to the American side of the lines at the very moment the American mounted forces rode out of their rear position. "Here they come! The American mounted forces! They are attacking!" John said excitedly.

As the swift-moving American force arrived at the midpoint on the left of the battle, Nik ordered, "Hold your fire! Cease fire." He thanked John for the good news. The boys' guns fell silent, and it could be seen that the British right and left lines were buckling now. "Pick up your brass! We can keep watching, but let's get some of this up now," Sid implored the group.

The American mounted force rode into the British left flank and attacked the remaining soldiers who were still on their feet. The area was almost completely blanketed with dead British now, and the sheer horror was apparent on both the British and American faces. Nik and Sid now looked at the field of battle after picking up their spent brass cartridges.

"Man, oh man!" said Sid. "I can't believe what I am looking at!"

Nik rubbed his forehead with his gunpowder residue-covered hand. Looking over the carnage of the battlefield, he spoke to the soldiers in the field in an encouraging tone, "C'mon, wrap this thing up, guys! Win this thing!" He repeated it over and over. "C'mon, end this thing, guys! Win!"

Sid, now looking at the approximate count of fighting soldiers on the field, reported to the others. "There are now more blue and militia on the field than red. It's almost over." Minutes later, the remaining British troops were in a full retreat. John noted the fleeing Lieutenant Colonel Tarleton, or so he thought at the time, off to the southeast through the binoculars. "There he goes! Bye-bye! Ride on! Run! Run!" John called out quietly so only his compatriots could hear him.

... 28 ...
An Unwelcome Sighting

11:07 A.M. IN THIS new reality of the date January 17, 1781, the British formally fled the field of battle at Cowpens, South Carolina. History now changed forever. In this "new history," the final result was maintained—America won the day and turned the tide of their struggle, drawing one step closer to the hopeful and eventual independence from the British Crown. The group was quiet as they absorbed all that had happened around them. Nik, certainly moved by the horrendous bloodshed they'd committed, didn't feel the same as after Kings Mountain; it was different somehow, even though the end result was the same—dead British troops at their hands.

This was the second time the history they knew as true had failed them. How could it be wrong twice? How could "time" be wrong twice? Why were the British able to better plan, predict, react, and execute in this temporal go-round? Nik had so many questions and no time to ponder them; they had to plan their exit from this area as rapidly as they could. Sid was pleased with the results of the battle and decided to decompress from it at a later time. The boys began to turn their thoughts to their path away from Cowpens, and Sid was ready to help the group in any way he could to quickly succeed at this task. He collected whatever he could to facilitate this and communicated his intentions. "Guys, let's think about our exit," Sid suggested.

John couldn't believe the volume of the dead and wounded covering the battlefield. He also decided, in his mind, to debrief about this day's events at some later time and agreed with Sid. "I am with you.... Let's go!"

1:04 p.m. The boys were waiting for an opportunity to slip away, as they watched the events on and around the battlefield from their pillbox. There were mounted patrols moving among the fallen; they appeared to be surveying the results of the fight and looking for survivors, at least that's what the boys assumed they were doing. An hour or so had gone by, and John continued watching the battlefield. Nik had turned around to concentrate on their flank, while Sid watched their sides.

John quietly mumbled, "What do we have here?"

"Where?" inquired an anxious Sid.

"Over there," John answered in a hushed voice and pointed off to their one o'clock direction.

The boys were now looking, with a certain degree of terror, at people rummaging through the wounded and fallen on the battlefield. Not a surprising sight, they figured, but these people were picking up the bodies and looking at them in an unexpected fashion. At one point, the examination had the investigators ripping off uniforms and examining entry and exit wounds on the fallen. There were plenty of examples of their work out there, and they were sure the damage they inflicted with their modern rifle rounds would look very different than what was created by the typical weapon in 1781. The boys continued to watch this for a bit and soon were hit with a stunning realization.

"What are those ... oh? Guys! Look at ... look who's on the battlefield!" John frantically announced.

"No way!" blurted Sid. "Tell me I am not seeing—"

"You are," John interrupted. "You're seeing exactly what I am seeing!"

"What in the hell?" Sid continued.

Nik looked now, and his jaw dropped as he quickly scurried to a prone position on the ground as well. "Whoa. What are they doing here?"

The three were looking at the four huge mountain men they had seen those many months ago out on the mountain pass trail attacking and assaulting the family with the wagon. John murmuring with a gasp, "Look at the way they are picking up and dropping those bodies—barbarians!"

Sid quietly thought aloud, "Yes, but more importantly, why the hell are they doing it? They are really looking at those dead guys—the dead British guys—and fairly intently, I might add."

"Do you think they are looking at the wounds made by our weapons?" asked John. All the while, Nik continued to observe.

"They are throwing the hacked, slashed, and blown-up victims to the side, but our rifle victims ... they are really interested in them," Sid pointed out. Sid, with much more of a concerned sound, snapped. "Wait ... oh man; look ... they are using the bodies to—"

At that point, the biggest of the mountain men peered in their general direction. He pointed and pulled at one of his buddy's arms and pointed their way now.

"Look, hey!" whispered John. "Those guys know we are here!"

Sid interrupted, "No, *no*, calm down. They only know that someone over in this direction fired the rounds that killed those guys. We need to leave as quickly as we can! We cannot engage these guys here and now; there is no other gunfire going on. We'd stick out like the sore thumbs that we are."

"Agreed," said Nik quickly.

There was an apparent feud now going on between the mountain men—a lot of pointing and yelling in some language the boys couldn't identify.

"Wow, these guys fight with each other a lot!" noted Sid. One, no two, of them were walking away from the other two, who were now arguing and getting more agitated.

"The last time we saw this, the big one picked up someone and threw him a hundred feet," John pointed out.

"Yeah, let's leave while they are preoccupied with themselves and their anger," Sid suggested.

Nik admitted, "Well, there is nothing else to do here, and unless we are going to shoot these guys for some reason, we need to leave before they come up here trying to find out who or what inflicted all that damage out there."

3:21 p.m. Sid noted that the coast was clear for them to wiggle out of their pillbox and make their way to the hideout. They wanted to check it over one more time to make sure they hadn't left anything behind. Nik continued to look back and check the battlefield to see if anyone were following them. As they reached their hideout and loaded into it, they took another moment to look around. There was nothing amiss in their immediate area, and they pondered whether they should stay there for the evening.

"What do you think? Should we do our last night here?" wondered Sid aloud.

"Hell no! I'm not fond of that idea, knowing that those giant barbarian-looking guys think there might be something over here to look for." implored John.

"Yeah, no, we don't stay here, you're right. They know something came from this direction, and they will come looking for who or what did it. It's human nature, and by the looks of those guys, they probably believe they can beat up or murder anyone crossing their path. We don't need to be near those people," Sid explained with an added sense of pushiness.

Nik agreed. "I don't want to deal with those guys either, whoever they are, and they will come looking for us tonight, so let's leave as soon as we can—like right now!"

After a quiet and complete last check of all things in and out of the hideout area, Sid moved out first, followed by John, then Nik. They would initially head south and away from this location and then decide which direction to go after that. The sun was dropping fast, with a cold dampness in the air that had a stale odor blowing from the battlefield. The boys were now second-guessing their decision to move out from their hideout at the Cowpens battlefield, but they knew they couldn't have stayed due to the threat of the mountain men. Their position had been compromised, and their deeds were certainly discovered; if not for the war and the history they had known, they would have been murderers in the eyes of man, and they hoped deep within their souls that they would be forgiven for their sins.

"We dropped a lot of British soldiers back there," muttered John.

Sid looked back. "Yes we did," he agreed. "No official count on spent rounds yet, but we did do our fair share of damage at this engagement."

Nik was quiet throughout the hike and more worried about finding a place to get out of the cold. He also didn't want to speak of the massacre they'd just created. Instead, he pondered on it in a silent vigil in his head—he knew there was no choice for them, and he knew they couldn't sit back and allow history to be changed and quite possibly eliminate all that the boys had known from history. He knew—hoped, really—that somewhere, somehow, they would be given a pass on the forced actions they had engaged in 229 years before they innocently tried to go camping in 2010.

"I say we head back to C-10," Sid began.

John looked at him and smiled. "I hear it's a good place."

Nik nodded in agreement and continued. "We do have another key engagement we need to watch later on. I just wanted to mention that."

John stopped abruptly. "To use your words, oy. Where is this one going to be?"

"Well, if you remember our discussion back at C-10 before we left, we will be trekking up to a place called Guilford Courthouse in the area of what we know as Greensboro, North Carolina."

Sid blurted, "Oh yeah! But that's in the other direction!"

"Yes it is, but the good news is—" Before Nik could finish, John interrupted with his jovially annoying sarcasm.

"Well, at least there's some good news to all this, right, Sid? See, good news! So what's the good news, Mr. Cheery?" John's sarcasm was directed at Nik.

Nik winced a bit at the sound of his compatriot's clearly sarcastic question. "We have a lot of time ... to get ... there.... Let's just get back to the camp at C-10, and we'll talk about it there." And with that, the group marched on.

... 29 ...
Let's Make Quick Work of This!

CAMP WAS UTTERLY MISERABLE that night; it was cold! They had a very small fire and a very large amount of a "what now?" attitude bounding about in the group. Sid broke the misery, wanting to explain an obvious, simple thing, and candidly trying to break the ice. "Sorry about the small fire, guys. I just felt that we needed to keep it small until we get away from here." Sid was trying to ease into a conversation, any conversation, to uncongeal the mood of the evening.

John looked tired as he huddled around the pathetic embers and whispered to the others. "Let's make good time tomorrow, so we can have a real fire tomorrow night. That will go a long way in making us happier."

Sid nodded. "That we will!" Sid turned his attention to Nik, who was staring off into space. "Does that sound good?" he asked.

Nik nodded, not taking his eyes off the stars. There wasn't much sound from the group after that, and Sid was a bit depressed about the whole end to the day. He was certainly happy with the outcome of the battle; they preserved history—sort of. He admittedly understood that they probably killed upward of five hundred British soldiers that day. He hadn't had time to count their spent rounds yet but figured roughly six thirty-round magazines for the 15s and most of four magazines for his M1A. That's ninety plus ninety plus eighty, with many multiple hits per round—that's a lot of dead Redcoats. *This is probably why the guys are in a funk!* Nik thought.

Sunrise came quickly the next day. The boys, having been up before first light, were now moving south and west to the big lake they had camped by on their way to Cowpens. John asked again, "Are we going to walk hard today and try and make it to the other side of this thing?"

"Yes," replied Sid. "It'll be huge; we'll need to make record time, so we can have a decent fire, which will make us all feel better." As he spoke, he mimicked the request from the previous night. Sid was working double-duty trying to keep the mood of the group as high as possible in the absence of Nik adding his voice to the conversation. Nik wasn't talking in his usual manner; as a matter of fact, he wasn't speaking at all. He was somewhere else so distant that not even his old pal Sid could draw him out of whatever deep thought was consuming him. John and Sid also knew Nik was preoccupied with something, because he wasn't complaining about anything—that was truly odd.

Their progress was steady, and the weather was fair enough to keep them neither too cold nor too hot. It would help the boys make their destination in good time and on or ahead of schedule. Sid hoped they could get to wherever they were going to make camp that night with some daylight left, so they could collect enough firewood to have a great blaze the entire night. He also thought about food and really wanted to have something fresh and grilled over the fire. "Fish would be unbelievable," he gasped as the three almost broke into a run over the rolling, half-frozen landscape. Nik was feeling tired and also wanted a respectable fire for their troubles of the past four days.

John announced with exuberance, "I will collect firewood in the dark if I have to." He really wanted a good fire with plenty of heat and was sick of being cold. He had thought to himself that some freshly caught fish that he could roast over a campfire would be fabulous for dinner and insisted they pick up the pace. John, hoping for a response of any kind from his friend, said, "Nik, I'll catch us some fresh fish tonight. Wouldn't that be good?"

Nik responded with a simple, "Yeah, man. I'll get the firewood; we need some food." Nik wasn't in a bad mood, and he wasn't angry, sad, mad, upset, or anything. He was just blah. Each member of the group had bouts of this, but the timing for Nik was odd. Sid wanted a debrief session from the battle, and John expected it. Nik did too, but he wasn't talking yet, and understandably so as they were tired, very hungry, and moving hard to the west.

"We'll talk about our adventure and where it puts us in the annals of time later, okay?" Nik abruptly interjected to the conversation of the hike. Sid and John nodded and continued moving forward; they were just happy to finally hear from their friend, as brief as it was. On this day, the group didn't stop; it was a silently ordered, self-imposed, forced march that John thought of as a type of self-torture to excise the demons from the previous day's events.

Three o'clock put them at the northwestern end of the big lake on the C-10 side of their world. They had actually camped more toward the middle of the lake on their way out to Cowpens and passed that site earlier in the day. Sid and John figured they would stop there even though they had talked about making the western side that day. Nik, on only the rare speaking occasion, strongly suggested they push toward the western edge of the lake past their previous stopping point. Sid quickly figured out there was a reason for Nik's insistence and relayed his thoughts to John. Sid didn't know the reason for the push farther west, but he would gently demand to know what was up around the campfire that night.

The boys dumped their stuff and formed a camp for the evening along an embankment by the lakeshore. All members were armed with sidearms only; Sid and John went off to gather fish and firewood, while Nik headed toward a wooded area to gather some firewood as well. They were all within earshot of each other and, from the wooded edge on the northern side of the small tree area, Nik could also see back along their trail. He waited and watched for a time and was comforted with the clear air, slight snow cover, and an apparent clear trail back to the east. Nik hauled—actually, more like dragged—back a pile of firewood and watched John down by the frozen lake looking for easy access for his makeshift line. He had discovered that fish in 1781 enjoyed old and dried meat product with modern chemicals, now unhealthy for human ingestion, as a tasty treat. Little did the fish know, the delectable tidbit would be retrieved out of their fishy little mouths and used again for as long as it could be rebaited on John's makeshift hook.

An hour later, a big fire burned hot, and the sizzle of fish filled the air. The aroma was fabulous, and the moods of the three thawed. "So, Nik, What's up? You have been silently and quietly thinking about something. Spill it.... C'mon ... what's trapped in that head of yours?" pushed Sid, somewhat sarcastically but also gently. Sid, having informed John of his planned attempt to get Nik to tell them what was bothering him, now gave John the "go" sign to poke and push like he did so well.

John began with an attempt at reverse psychology. "He's fine; leave him alone. If he had something—" Before John could finish, he was cut off by Nik.

"Well," Nik began.

Sid laughed, and John was disappointed at how easy Nik broke "under the interrogation." "Oh, c'mon, man. Put up a fight anyway. That was too easy," moaned John as he tried to drive his already-made point home.

"Well," Nik started again as they began to eat their delicious meal from the lake. "Well, those guys after the battle; they bother me."

"Yeah, the big, ugly dudes looking at dead bodies and then pointing in our direction. They bother me too!" John remarked.

"Yeah," said Nik. "That's the problem."

Sid was now shaking his head. "Which part? It's all a problem— the action of picking through the British dead, the pointing in our direction, the fact that we had seen them before in their utterly brutal actions with the family on the mountain trail.... Should I continue? It's all disturbing."

"Well, yeah, all that.... It's like when I was in elementary school and you were what you were—a kid in school trying to make your way. Then there was a bully, and you wanted that bully to never know your name. When he noticed you, when he knew you existed, when you sparked his interest, then you got a certain sick feeling in your gut, and it wasn't a good one. Those guys out there—they've been bullies all their lives, and I think they most certainly know we exist," Nik concluded.

"Who the hell are they? I mean, where do you think they stand in all of this—our Revolution?" interjected John with some seriousness of emotion.

Sid sat back and added his thoughts to the conversation. "Four big dudes on the British side of the lines looking around for ... who knows what?"

Nik now squinting his eyes thought aloud, "On the British side of the lines? Just there, the American forces aren't paying any attention to them; the retreating British didn't give them a look. They aren't wearing the colors of the crown. They're just there."

A short pause yielded to John. "So ... what's the concern? I guess I'm not following what the problem is."

"Visibility," began Sid. "We just dropped a huge amount of men back there, and even if these guys are neutral, which I don't think they are, they would be seriously interested if not really, really concerned at the show of firepower." Sid scratched his side and continued. "I think theses guys are realizing that the firepower they are looking at now has only been used on the British forces. They looked at casualties from both sides but concentrated primarily on the bodies of those dead British troops, not the American forces. Yes, they initially looked at some fallen American troops, but when they noticed the distinct and specific signature results from our ballistics, they understood that something was amiss. I am sure they feel that they have identified a military force that *isn't* on the side they're on, assuming they are on the side of the British. This fact could make these four guys very dangerous, and us, a very interesting and focused subject for them."

A pause fell over the group, as the fire raged on with its warmth radiating about their camp. The conversation took a turn of sorts. "So," John began again, "we are concerned about these guys because they know we are out here?" John honestly still wasn't sure where Nik was going with his line of thought. He was trying to piece it together from what Sid was talking about, but he was hitting dead ends.

"So," Sid began, also reaching for more from Nik, "is there more?" Sid and John were getting slightly annoyed now at this drawn-out event that Nik continued to prolong. Nik could read the frustration on his compatriots' faces and, leaning forward, initiated the conversation that, in the end, he knew would cause them to call him crazy for being so paranoid.

"I feel we have exposed ourselves—not by any choice of our own, for sure—but history or the preservation of our history sent us down that path. Utterly destroying entire lines of men out there yesterday and having had four people of an unknown origin, whoever they were, looking at the results of our intervention has made us visible in a very acute and distinct fashion here in 1781. Here's the key—they identified which direction the killing rounds came from. I am afraid we could be followed."

A gasp of sorts fell quickly and not so quietly. "Oh please," John blurted. "In all of that, *we* are going to be followed? I find that hard to believe."

Sid added in Nik's defense, "Well, look how we did the last time we were seen—Native American warriors really pissed off at us. Although, Nik, your imagination might be getting the best of you, you know."

"Maybe, but I want to get back to C-10 as quickly as possible," Nik said. "Can we do that?" Sid and John both agreed, and the three went back to the fire for more dinner.

"Sid?" Nik now began to ask a very strange question. "Can you go over with me in the morning the rally points and checkpoints you made up for the approach to and around C-10? I can't remember them all and, well, I'd like to know more about them. You know, to know."

Sid shrugged his shoulders and said with a smirk, "Sure. In the morning, okay? Maybe as we walk, I'll go over them."

Nik agreed and asked for a picture as well. John shook his head now and smiled. "Always gotta make things hard, Nik. Let's get some sleep; we apparently have a heavy hike again tomorrow."

As they lay there by the fire and against the embankment, Sid started running down the checkpoints in his head. *Piece of cake,* he thought to himself and rolled over as the fire snapped and crackled embers into the night sky. John maneuvered a little closer to the fire now, as their time for sleep had officially set in, and he was very tired. Fishing was strenuous in the cold weather, but the rewards far outweighed the fatigue it brought. He also enjoyed the light show the campfire embers produced in the complete blackness of the January sky.

Nik was the last to settle down and was kept awake by a lingering concern of the mountain men. He couldn't shake the sighting of them after the battle at Cowpens, and he was more than worried that they appeared to have put two and two together and got the three of them at the end of the equation instead of four. *The only time in the universe two and two equaled three,* Nik thought to himself. He was awake well after midnight and spent some time on his feet patrolling around just a foot off their camp perimeter. He added wood to the fire to keep everyone warm and finally lay down from utter exhaustion at around 1:15 a.m.

... 30 ...
West-Southwest to Home

MORNING BROKE WITH WARMER temperatures and howling winds. Warmer meant that it actually got above forty degrees; howling meant just that—the winds were screaming through the area with gusts stronger than fifty miles an hour blowing the boys all over the place.

"Outta the frying pan, into the fire ... damn weird weather! Nik, did you order this?" John exclaimed.

"No, man, not me. You know me; I just want calm, cool, and cloudy," Nik answered.

Sid was having all he could handle with the wind and was not enjoying it. "Let's find a nice cave with a hot spring in it," he joked.

"Don't laugh; there are hot springs around the hills in North and South Carolina. I have no idea where they are, but they exist!" answered Nik.

"Well, we need to find them!" John demanded.

They pushed on through lunch and stopped around two thirty. The winds had subsided slightly, and life was back to normal for the most part. Nik looked ahead and noted, "We could push to the hills tonight and get tucked in against some cover, providing the wind direction doesn't change on us."

The group agreed to do the best they could that day but fell short by a considerable amount. They were just too tired, and the

---

stop in the middle of the afternoon put them in much more of a "let's get a good hike in tomorrow" mood. They finally stopped around four o'clock that afternoon, built a small fire, and just sat down.

"We'll do better tomorrow," John reassured his friends.

"Oh, yeah. We have been at it for a few days, and honestly, I didn't sleep much last night," Nik added.

Sid looked at Nik and said sarcastically, "You just couldn't wait to hear my rundown of our tactical positions at C-10, huh?"

Nik looked over and said, "Well, now that you mention it, let's hear it. I know it's riveting stuff, after all." John laughed now as he enjoyed the entertaining banter and began to heat up a little of the leftover fish from the night before.

"Really, you care about those?" Sid asked. Nik glared at him now, and Sid quickly raised his hands. "Okay, okay. Geez, the things that interest you at the weirdest times."

Again, John laughed and said, "You guys are like an old married couple sometimes!"

"Okay," Sid began as he counted on his fingers. "We have six approach checkpoints and twelve hard checkpoints."

Nik looked at him again. "Twelve checkpoints? Approach points? Are you kidding? Really?"

John, now adding his innocent bystander two cents, commented, "Man, I wish I had a drink and some popcorn. This sounds like it'll be entertaining to watch!" Sid and Nik now both glared at John, so John began to backpedal. "What? I'm just saying this should be, you know, fun. Fun? Ugh, what am I going to do with you guys? No sense of humor."

Sid and Nik laughed now. "We know, John. And we are glad we can bring you some entertainment," Sid added.

"Okay, back to business," Nik requested.

Sid sat down and began to draw a diagram on the ground of the area around C-10. He drew the picture oriented as if peering from the north looking south, with the valley on the left-hand side and the hills containing C-10, Devil's Bald, the caverns and caves, and the creeks on the right-hand side. There were three creek areas they had found and surveyed, the third of which was where C-10 was located. The caves and caverns, in reality, were off the second creek, but the boys approached these from C-10 along the old path that they remembered from 2010, taking a heading down from C-10 and to the southwest.

"So, the approach checkpoints run up the valley floor from south to north. I called them Approach Points or APS for short," Sid explained. "APS Alpha through Foxtrot are marked with the little stick pyramid markers, which are made up of two or three sticks tied together, and are visible from most of our other checkpoints with a scope or binoculars. APS Charlie, if you remember, is aligned with the creek that leads up to C-10. Get it? *C*—Charlie, C-10. Do you understand? Cs indicate our camp, our cabin? The checkpoints begin at Alpha, located at the point where the creek roughly meets the valley floor. These checkpoints, CHPS (pronounced "chips" for short) go from Alpha to Lima."

Nik now studied the drawing on the ground and pointed at the ridgeline CHPS. "Which ones are these?" he asked.

Sid looked and answered, "Beginning from the southernmost point, Golf, India, Juliet, Kilo, and Lima."

"And is this the bald, CHPS Foxtrot?" asked Nik, pointing at CHPS Foxtrot on the drawing. Sid nodded yes.

"Umm, so what? Nik, what do you care about this? Why are you bothering with these?" John wondered aloud.

Nik waved his hand again as if to stop John from interfering with his thought. "Correct me if I am wrong, guys," Nik started, "above APS Echo—no, Foxtrot—isn't there a more gentle rock inclination up to CHPS Lima?"

John piped in. "Well, it doesn't go exactly there; it heads more north, and after a pretty challenging climb, you sort of end up between Lima and Foxtrot (the bald)."

"All the better," Nik happily remarked. "Then we have our first task once we get back there."

"I love it when he has a plan!" Sid remarked.

John, not quite so exuberantly, stated, "Great. Another Nik task. You know, whenever you come up with something new for us to do, things usually get complicated, and we get in some sort of trouble!"

Nik now chuckled. "Hey now. Remember, it was two against one to go hiking and camping in the mountains in 2010. I just caused trouble after all that, or this—now or whenever we are."

The camp and evening went quickly, as everything was calmer than it had been the past two or three nights. Nik had appeared to have calmed down a bit about the possibility and/or worry of being followed, and the "plan" he had devised seemed to comfort him in some strange and odd way.

"We have nothing to do here," Sid pointed out. "We might just as well relax."

John was the most restless and/or energetic of the three, and he spent the evening looking around and acting as a guard like Nik had done the previous evening. He wasn't worried exactly; he just figured with the other two members happy to sit down and relax that evening, he would be more alert. Sid commonly patrolled around, and fairly often Nik had an affinity to spend time surveying their surroundings. It was a breezy evening with moderate temperatures for January, and as the darkness enveloped the landscape, the group settled down for the night.

Several days later they reached the APS Alpha marker as Sid announced, "Here we are!"

Nik looked back now at the trail they had left in the snow and on the ground they had just traversed. He scratched his shoulder and said, "Well, let's get going. We have a lot of hiking to complete from here."

John and Sid looked at each other and shook their heads, as the hike from this point would normally only take them three or four hours to reach C-10. Obviously, Nik had something else up his sleeve. He comically shrugged off the others' questions, so his plan couldn't be too off the reservation. *Or could it?* John thought. They moved at a good pace; Nik regularly looked back every so often, as he realized they were walking in a very open and exposed area, which was a rarity for them and their "keep hidden" agenda. None of them liked this wide exposure, but it was the terrain; they were simply out in the open with nowhere to run if they needed to take cover.

Sid now commented during a brief pause in the walk, "Stop, listen." It was the sound of utter silence in the valley. There wasn't so much as a peep from a bird; the wind could be heard if it gusted in the far-off hillside trees, but that was it. They stood there in the clear, crisp air for several minutes. John looked up and expressed a revelation that wasn't a surprise at all, but to the boys, it was a concept they hadn't given a thought to since arriving in the past.

"No planes, no jets, no industrial sounds," John pointed out. "I hadn't really thought about it until now. All of the things that have occurred to us and around us during our eight months in calendar time here in the early 1780s, and not a thought of something as simple to us as airplane noise."

It grew silent in the ranks of the group. After a few minutes, Sid said, "Time to keep moving ... let's get to APS Charlie. Turn left and go sit down at camp."

The group soon arrived at APS Charlie, and in an almost habitual fashion, they began fading left to turn up to CHPS Alpha when Nik yelled, "Stop!"

John almost pulled his pistol, and Sid became entirely defensive, drawing his rifle up to his side and chambering a round at lightning speed all while looking for a target.

"Whoa, sorry. Didn't mean all that," Nik said. "I just wanted us to not go left or look like we are going left."

John, now looking in C-10's direction, pointed out, "Umm, but that's where we are going."

"No, don't point!" Nik requested very firmly.

"Dude, what in the—?" John wanted to know what was going wrong with Nik—again.

"Easy. Here's what I'm thinking—hear me out, real quick!" Nik requested.

"Well, it's about damn time! You need to start telling us things, *in advance*!" John yelled in an annoyed tone.

Nik immediately began apologizing. "I know, I know. I'm sorry.... I hadn't quite figured out what I had in mind until we got to the base of the valley approach, and then I was just trying to put it all together. I just finished it when we got here. Listen to me.... You ready?"

"Boy, this better be good," answered Sid, "because you're beginning to even freak me out—and not in a good way."

"I know, and I'm sorry.... Thinking sometimes takes a little bit, especially in 1781." Nik continued to apologize. "Okay, here's the deal.... I propose we move straight up the valley and pivot when the trail gets thin after APS Foxtrot. Let's move up the ridge up there where the snow and ice have blown or melted off the rocks, so we don't leave a trail right to our home away from home and possibly our future as we knew it."

Nik's two compatriots looked at him like he had truly lost his mind, and Sid began the questioning. "Is this what you have been contemplating these last few days?"

John joined in. "This is your plan? For what? There isn't a soul around! Do you like walking? This is going to add like, another—" But before he could finish, Sid stepped in again, "Do you really think we need to do this? Really?"

Nik was taken by surprise by the grilling, and he now felt really awful about his idea. He waited for a few seconds before answering the myriad of questioning statements that had just flown his way. "Well, yes. In fact, I do.... I was just thinking ... you know, I want us to keep out of sight, and ... well, I just thought," Nik said meekly. He winced as he finished and looked a little more affected than the others thought he might. "We are leaving tracks in the snow and have been for days. A seven-year-old could follow those," Nik added, now pointing down the valley at their footprints in the snow. John and Sid felt a little flawed now in their reaction, John most of all, as he generally had the strongest displeasure in his remarks to Nik.

Both Sid and John quickly realized that Nik was thinking about their protocol in being here in 1780–81. Yes, they understood about all the "not be seen or heard" rules they had put in place, but they honestly figured there was no fear of anyone venturing anywhere near this place. The tracks were indisputable; Nik was right.

"They do stick out like a giant white-headed zit on a teenager's face in high school during puberty," added John.

Sid cringed. "Ugh. That's gross, dude. You and your descriptions sometimes!"

Nik now smirked. "Well, kind of ... but it's not really—" he stammered.

"You understand," John interrupted. "And now we understand." John smiled.

They stood for a few more minutes. John somewhat sheepishly continued to yield his position and saved a little face by saying, "Well, if Nik, who hates walking and exercise, thinks it a good idea to hike all the way up the valley and play goat-man for a time up to our CHPS to ensure our invisibility for this time, then, well, it might just be a good idea. After all, he's ... he's been right once or twice so far in this disaster we called a boys' outing—right?"

Sid laughed. "Yes, he has been right. I don't know about twice, but once for sure. No, I understand, and I think we should play it safe. We may have been falling into the lull on this trip back to C-10, and we do need to stay sharp. Although, Nik, your plan may be a little extreme, maybe. It is doable and errs on the side of caution for sure. We should do it."

Nik looked up at the position of C-10 and back behind them down the valley. He shrugged and said, "I was just thinking about not being seen ... or followed."

"You still think there is a chance of that?" asked Sid.

They began to move forward again up the valley. Nik finally responded, "Probably not, but I'd rather be safe than sorry. You know?"

"Yeah, you're right," admitted John. "And this won't take us that long anyway, even if we camp north of the CHPS for the night. What's one more day to C-10?"

That's the spirit! Nik thought to himself, but he kept quiet as they walked.

CHPS Delta, Echo, and Foxtrot came and went as the group trudged onto the thinning area of the valley. Sid pointed, "There! Let's follow this little brook west to the hill right there ... to that rock patch. That's our way up."

Both Nik and John agreed that the route looked good. The boys made sure to stay in the trickle of the brook to mask their tracks in their westward movement. They reached the rocks and began their ascent to higher and hopefully safer ground where they would either camp or continue on to C-10. John felt the need to forage around for some tidbits of food as they made their way up the rocky rise.

"There are things here we can pick up that I wouldn't otherwise scale down to get," John pointed out with a smile. "Look at these frozen berries!"

"Not even the bears or birds ventured up here for a bite!" remarked Sid. The rocks had led them more north than they had wanted, and the boys were now quite far from the bald or even CHPS Lima.

"Hmm, well, it is getting dark, and we have wet and frozen feet," Nik noted. "We need a fire, and we should rest."

"Yeah, sounds good," John agreed. "Look where we came out! It's wonderful!"

They exited the rocks in a lavish and surprisingly green area of pines, winter fern-looking plants, and moss. It was a very level area for the mountains, with a thick canopy of growth, which was very comforting to the group. They had been out in the open (in their opinion) for so long that the cover seemed like a huge improvement; they felt more comfortable and more at home in the mountain setting with a thick forest and believed there was a smaller possibility of being found by anyone of the time.

A fire was quickly started. Nik employed some modern chemistry to quickly facilitate it, and the wind problem they had experienced the past two weeks was virtually nonexistent under the cover of the pine and hardwood canopy. Even though they couldn't wait to get back to their cabin, they really felt good about where they had decided to stop for the night. The temperatures were beginning to drop again, which wasn't unexpected for the mountains—or late January, for that matter. They had the tidbits that John had collected for dinner.

"Well, I have had my share of fruits and nuts today! Fiber in our diet is not a problem!" Sid proclaimed

Nik and John laughed. "It hasn't been for a long time, and the grass soup—oy! Now there's some natural fiber. Blah!" responded Nik.

Nik, Sid, and John remained by the fire and worked on drying their boots, clothes, and feet, even making an additional fire to further facilitate the drying process. Sid figured they weren't too far away from the places they knew and had scouted in the months past and would have no problem finding their way back. He didn't recall any passable access to the bald from this side, so he theorized they would try and start out along the ridge side of the hill that faced the valley below, hoping to run into CHPS Lima along the way.

There was no straggler awake on this night; they were all tired and felt that they had walked deep enough and high enough into the mountains to not be bothered with posting watch or worrying about getting snuck up on. This said, they still slept with loaded pistols and were ready for action if need be. Even Nik, when asked by John if he felt better about things, replied, "Much. We have the high ground, and we are shrouded by nature. It doesn't get any better than this."

They fell asleep in the bliss and security of the forest as they lay on the soft, mossy ground and stayed warm by their two small fires. Sid only woke once or twice during the night to fuel the fire with some more small pine logs.

... 31 ...
Mission Accomplished. C-10 at Last!

Frost was the order of the morning. The landscape was shrouded and encrusted in the stuff, and it almost looked like it may have snowed a little the previous night but didn't accumulate on the ground. It was the tree canopy that caught the brunt of old man winter; white with frost, it almost looked like they were in some heavenly snow plane on a distant ice planet.

The boys smartly broke camp, covering any evidence of their presence there, and pushed over to the ridge area. They traversed the wooded areas for ease of travel, making their way slightly east every so often to look off the ridge for a reference point on where exactly they were. The APS markers were easy enough to see through the binoculars and came in very handy on the way back south through the woods.

"Wow, we did end up farther north than we thought, didn't we?" said John.

"Yeah, no problem, though. We'll get back soon, just a nice walk in the woods now," added Sid.

Nik began. "So what do we want to do once we get back to the cabin?"

The others looked at him and smiled. "Nothing at all!" suggested John.

"Yeah, that sounds good," said Nik, not wanting to start another controversy like he had the other day.

Another hour went by with the boys walking and talking in the woods. Then, Sid finally thought he recognized a patch of tree/ridgeline. It was CHPS Lima! They had reached the plateau of real estate on the side of this lonely hill in the far northwestern part of South Carolina that contained their cabin at the place they called C-10. The boys moved to CHPS Lima and sat down on the makeshift bench they had made out of some rocks and logs many months ago.

"These things remind me of the cinder block and two-by-four shelves we made in college," Nik chuckled, referring to the bench John and Sid were now sitting on.

"Yeah, man, it's a great construction method for college students—very flexible. We made all kinds of things with basically rocks and basic lumber!" Sid exclaimed.

The view was breathtaking—just a peaceful, cool, clear day with full sun and a brisk breeze. "You know," said Nik, "Back in 1997, I dreamed of having a house on a mountain range very similar to this one. Honestly, it could be anywhere in these Appalachian or Blue Ridge Mountain chains; it's just nice up here. We have lived a lot of places in our days, but not in a place like this, not with this view."

The three grew silent with a bit of a chill. John murmured, "Right place, wrong time now.... Dumb, isn't it?"

"Yeah, it sure is," responded Nik.

Sid spoke as he looked up and down the valley with the binoculars, "All clear, and you're right—beautiful views!"

They left CHPS Lima and headed for CHPS Kilo along the small path they had cut back through the woods. Sid had figured back in the summer when he cut these trails that he wanted them to be off the ridge for a hidden movement path. The last thing he wanted back then (and now) was for someone to see these guys darting around on the ridge like it was a vacation spot. The idea of these checkpoints was that they would be overlooks and possible defensive positions if they needed to be.

CHPS Kilo was reached in good time and they spent only a few minutes there. It was as they had created it, nothing had disturbed it over these past weeks. All was similar with CHPS Juliet and

CHPS India. Upon their arrival to CHPS Golf, a similar scene lay in front of them, with one small difference. It was late in the day, and they sat down to admire the view of the now almost glowing valley due to the setting sun to the west. It was cool, and the day was basically about over when Sid spotted something off on the horizon to the south that even he didn't believe. He gave the binoculars to John first, and asked him to look off at about their three o'clock, three thirty, basically due south.

John's mouth hung open, and Nik almost freaked. "What is it?" Nik demanded.

"Well, it looks like smoke ... I guess," John said. "Hard to tell from here, and it's pretty far off."

"Had we ever seen smoke here before, Sid?" asked Nik.

"Not that I remember," he responded.

To Nik, it was like the perfect world of this place had been shattered like plate glass in an explosion. Sid tried to calm things down. "Could be anything, you know," he explained. "We'll keep an eye on it, and it is very far off.... I would say at least two days' hike. We'll take care of things.... It may be nothing at all, maybe a passing wagon train going west or something." Sid was reaching, and he knew it—and Nik knew it. John knew it as well but was slightly less alarmed about the sighting than the others seemed to be.

Nik asked for the binoculars and proceeded to look at the spectacle. "It is very far off; it might even be three or four days off—hard to tell. Let's hope whoever they are, they don't come this way."

"Yeah, there are a lot of directions someone could go from down there. It's fine," John said reassuringly.

"Let's head to the cabin and get situated," said Nik.

They left CHPS Golf, and Sid made a request—well, it was more like an order. "Gentlemen, rifles or pistols? I believe we should still approach our camp carefully and with caution, just in case someone found it and moved in." They agreed, and pistols were chosen for the approach.

They were on edge now—again! After having such a nice, calming evening and day, they were back working on nervous energy. They moved to the canal location and sat for a few moments. Sid moved over to the edge of the small ridge where the canal, if it wasn't stopped up and frozen solid, would spill over its designed course to their cabin area. He peered in the general direction of the encampment and saw nothing out of the ordinary.

With thumbs up, he signaled that the area appeared clear and made his way back to his compatriots. "All looked okay to me. I couldn't see the cabin, but the surrounding area—CHPS Charlie and Delta—looked clear," Sid reported.

"Okay, let's go on to camp. One thing, though, I think I am more comfortable with a rifle doing this. What do you think?" asked John with a concerned look on his face.

"No problem, man. Whatever you want," said Sid. Nik agreed.

They rearmed with rifles, holstering their loaded pistols in their proper and secure places, and moved down the hill to the right of their cabin. They moved slowly, smartly and looked down the trails that connected to the cabin area. All was clear, and Sid moved to the cabin door. He listened, tried the lock, and verified that it was still secure. He motioned for Nik to swing around to the front side of the cabin and verify the window coverings and for John to check the far side by the fireplace and canal side of the cabin. After ten minutes of looking and listening, they called the coast clear and wrapped up their operation.

A last quick physical check down at CHPS Charlie and CHPS Delta completed the day, and the boys opened up the cabin door and sat down.

"Oh my God!" Nik said. "It seems like we have been gone for a year! It's good to be back."

John agreed. "Yes, sir!"

"All the firewood we packed in here before we left is still here, nice and dry! But let's keep the fire small until we know we're good as far as the other smoke source goes," added Sid quietly.

"Good idea," murmured Nik.

"Sleep. We need sleep!" yawned John. "I am done. Lock this place up, and let's go to sleep. No more outside sleeping for a while! We have four walls around us and a roof over our heads." John rambled on.

Sid and Nik laughed in agreement.

... 32 ...
I Wish I *Was* Crazy!

JOHN WAS UP EARLY the next morning. Sid was quick to follow as the sun rose and they continued to "unpack the cabin." The noise woke Nik up, and he was grumpy.

"Guys," Nik moaned, "a man is trying to sleep here!"

"Sorry," a rapidly moving Sid said.

"C'mon, man. Let's go take a look around," John suggested.

"A look around at what?" Nik asked as he yawned and groaned.

"Not sure," John said.

"You're not thinking of going to look for the source of the smoke we saw yesterday afternoon, are you?" Nik questioned, now sitting up with some concern.

"No, not exactly. I just want to see what we can see, now c'mon!" John explained as he repositioned some items in his pockets.

"Okay, okay," Nik grumbled.

They all left with a handful of some old dried berries and water for breakfast; no one was hungry at this point, but they would be soon enough. They hiked out to CHPS Kilo and set up for a time, a time that turned into most of the day. The first measure of business was an immediate glance, inspection really, to the south to look for any smoke or anything else of interest; there was nothing of the sort and all three were pleased for that. The day was nicely moderate in temperature with a slight breeze; it was really the first pleasant day of the new year. They weren't complaining, though; the cold certainly beat the blistering heat of the summer months in the southeastern United States. However, a day that was slightly warmer than freezing was more than welcome. They hung out and talked about all sorts of things from the previous ten months and finally debriefed themselves from the battle at Cowpens.

"How many people did we kill, you think?" John asked bluntly.

A silence persisted for some time. Nik was finally the one who broke it. "We killed plenty; we wounded plenty as well. Did we have a choice?" Silence again. And again, Nik shattered it with, "Yes and *no*!" Sid and John nodded.

Sid followed with, "There was really no choice. The end result was in concrete, and in the opinion of the known history, it had to end with an American win. The Americans needed to be the victors; the fact of that can't be argued."

"How many rounds did we expend, Sid? Did we get a count?" Nik relaxed now as he sat back in the afternoon breeze.

"Well, we took it to 'em for sure. We went through 192 .223 rounds, and I blew through 127 .308 rounds. I had added two extra clips to the engagement. If you figure we hit, on average, two British soldiers per round we fired, that means we wounded or killed 526 men plus or minus, depending on missed shots and singles here and there."

The numbers silenced them again. "The fear we instilled in the other British forces probably sent another five hundred running," Sid continued.

"True," John added.

"Well, what's done is done. The fibers in the tapestry of time have certainly been altered from the true and total history of what was, as we would have known it," Nik pondered aloud.

John looked at Nik and blurted, "*What* in the hell are you blubbering about?"

Sid laughed, and Nik looked at John. "Umm … it's a simple concept dating back to ancient mythology. Each person is a thread or strand in the tapestry of time, like a cloak or sheet."

"I know what a tapestry is!" John interrupted.

"Anyway," Nik continued, now smiling, "my point was that we have no idea who those guys were or what they did after January 17, 1781. Who knows how we changed history by pulling or cutting those threads out of the tapestry of time? You know, what's changed?"

The guys contemplated their actions and still ended up in the same place. "We had to do it," Sid concluded.

"Agreed. I just don't see how we had a choice," John said.

"So," Nik began again, "how are we on ammunition, Sid?"

There was no pause this time. "Ha! We have a ton of ammo!" Sid exclaimed. "All the stuff we brought due to my ridiculous nature of packing for a trip and you two guys packing a ton of just everything else, ammo is what we have the most of, which is really comforting and good, if you ask me. I would say half our weight is ammunition for the weapons we have, and it's fairly evenly distributed; you guys have all the .223, and I have all of the .308. The .50 and .45 is pretty evenly split as well."

Sundown came as if it were a mere hour from when they had arrived at CHPS Kilo. The day was a pleasure and a joy; they wanted and needed nothing, and the three compatriots started out on a leisurely stroll through their CHPS back to the cabin for the night. They saw nothing out of the ordinary that day; the valley was clear, all the APSes were clear, and nothing approached—not even a deer was seen. They collected some water down by the creek before buttoning up the cabin that night, as the canal was still frozen from the chill of January. It wouldn't be long, and it would loosen up just enough to get a trickle flowing down their man-made waterway.

All of the talk and conversation that day left the group short of conversation that night, which generated a very quiet, calm evening. "Sleep is in order!" John proclaimed. "Let's do the same thing tomorrow, weather permitting. Okay?" The others happily agreed, and they all fell over tired with the cabin locked up and the fire crackling quietly in the fireplace.

The next day came as quickly as the last one went, and the boys were found located up at CHPS India sitting on makeshift benches, loitering about and talking like three old women at a bingo tournament. Yes, these past few days were truly carefree pauses in the action they had already gotten themselves into this year. It was the perfect and well-deserved spin down from all the hiking and running they had endured in their Cowpens campaign. The three looked out over the landscape to the east with the valley floor sprawling out in front of them. They sat in no apparent order, with Sid pointed slightly to the north up the valley, John facing straight east at the rolling hills, and Nik looking basically south-southeast down the valley to the south. The concerns after Cowpens had seemingly vanished with the relaxation of the past day and a half, and all apparent short-term worries had vanished.

"So, Nik, I do believe you were on the brink of crazy five days ago, so concerned about the mountain men, our entry wounds on the British, blah, blah, blah," Sid jabbed at Nik.

"Yeah, yeah. Well, you know—" Nik began as John interrupted.

"Man, all the worry. You had me about to lose my mind," John said. "It's good to know you were the crazy one and not us!"

As all the jovial banter circulated around the group, Nik fell silent. Sid and John thought they had hurt his feelings. "Dude," John started, "after all this time, this hurt your—"

Nik moved to his knees now and mumbled, "I wish I was crazy.... Look." As he spoke, he gazed to the south down the valley floor. His mouth now hung open, and a look of disbelief crept across his colorless face.

"What the hell is wrong with you? You know, you can—" Sid began as Nik quickly shushed him and pointed.

John looked first and quietly as possible yelped, "Oh!" He immediately dropped to the ground at CHPS India behind the low rise of rocks they had piled up on the ridgeline.

This had Sid reeling around and dropping to his knees. "What in the hell is that?"

Nik shook his head and sank down, now getting behind the stone rise with the others. "Well, well," Sid remarked, "what do we have here?" The three were now peering through the rocks at dark dots on the valley floor near APS Alpha.

"Probably just some folks passing through the area," John quietly commented.

"I hope so," Nik murmured.

Making sure to stay low, Sid now peered down the valley with the binoculars to see if he could make out any detail. "They are still way out there. Let's see if they approach any closer."

The boys assumed that these specs in the valley were people of one form or another. They kept a straight line up the middle of the valley and didn't appear to waver off in any random direction like wildlife might. "No, these are people for sure; there's no doubt about it," reported Sid.

"Well, we sit and wait—see what they do. We are plenty safe up here for now. You want to load up just in case?" asked Nik of the group.

"I would," said John.

Sid responded, "Me as well—one full magazine."

They loaded a full magazine into their respective rifles without a chambered round and assured their safeties were secured. "All set. Contingency plans?" asked John. "Do we need one?"

"I don't know. Let's see what they do," Nik said. "We stayed off of CHPS Alpha and Beta, so they are not going to see any trace or tracks of us there, except what they might see on the valley floor now, if those tracks are even still visible." Nik was mulling over the unfolding situation aloud.

"We're fine up here," added Sid. "They are not going to run up these hills and surprise us in any way, shape, or form. We own the high ground, and I don't think anyone has any idea we are here."

The three watched the progress of their targets, who were now growing closer to APS Charlie. "Here we go; let's see what they do here." Sid murmured under his breath.

The people moving up the valley had no idea they were passing anything like a checkpoint, but the guys used the markers to gauge the progress of their visitors.

"You don't think they'll see the markers, do you, Sid?" Nik asked.

"No," John answered, "those little sticks? Nah." Sid agreed.

"Well, that's good." Nik breathed a small sigh of relief.

Sid picked up the binoculars and was fairly sure he could pick out some details now from the folks on the ground. "Well, Nik—no, John—take a look." Sid passed the binoculars to John.

John peered through the glass, making the focus correction to clear the image. He was silent. He shook his head and pulled the binoculars away from his face and looked at Nik.

"You, my friend, are one spooky dude." He handed the binoculars over to Nik, so he could see for himself.

Nik looked at his friends and then peered at the spectacle that unfolded through the magnified picture of their reality. "Oh boy." That's all he said.

Sid quickly grabbed the binoculars away from Nik and began to assess their position again. "Those guys! I was afraid of—" Nik began before being cut off by John.

"How in the hell did you know they would follow us? How could they? There is no—" And then Sid cut John off.

"Shh! It doesn't make a difference!" Sid exclaimed. "There were tracks all the way! And that's what Nik was trying to tell us without really telling us." He now looked at Nik. "And that's a problem. You gotta stop that!" Sid now pointed at Nik.

"I know, I know … I just—" Nik stammered.

"I know. Shh." Sid said, cutting off Nik again. "We're fine. They are down there, and we are up here. They have no idea where we are, as 'spooky dude' here had us walk an extra twenty damn miles out of our way—which, by the way, is going to save our entire existence here in the mountains and probably their lives. Let's just be quiet, stay low, and see where these guys go. I don't really want to mess with these guys. Just let them go!"

Sid was correct—the intruders were down on the valley floor, the boys were safe on the high ground, and the mountain men had no idea that anyone was watching them. The art and methods of Nik's paranoia were paying huge dividends this time, as the mountain men had a sparse trail at best, which would eventually lead them to a dead end, and a cold, watery one at that.

Sometime later, they watched the four big men approach APS Delta, which was almost dead east of CHPS India where the boys stayed out of sight and spied on their unwanted guests. The mountain men stopped and looked around; two of them were yelling at each other in that language, a horrible-sounding bark that drove Nik nuts.

"So familiar!" Nik quietly mumbled.

While the two men were having words, the others were scanning the surroundings. They surveyed the ridgeline back and forth, up and down. The boys were now lying down to stay out of sight; they could have withdrawn back into the woods to the west, but they didn't dare move. Also, they didn't want to lose their vantage point for observation of the mountain men.

"Guys, they're looking up here!" whispered John.

"Easy, stay calm. They are just looking around. They have no idea we are here. Stay still and quiet," Sid whispered intently.

The mountain men pointed down at the ground and up the valley; they could obviously make out the tracks that the boys had produced four days earlier as they pushed past APS Delta and on up the valley.

"You were right, Nik. We would have been screwed if we'd left our tracks in the snow all the way past CHPS Alpha, Beta, and Charlie to the cabin. They would be at the cabin right now if we hadn't listened to you," rambled John in a low whisper.

"Just lucky," Nik quietly added.

"No, spooky," finished Sid. "Really spooky."

The mountain men were clearly agitated about something, and the third one was now yelling at the top of his lungs as he pointed down at the snow and signified with his fingers the number three.

"They know we're three. They know there are three of us! Dammit!" Sid continued.

Nik grabbed his friend's arm. "Easy. Who cares? They are down there, we are up here, and they have no idea that we're here," Nik quietly and firmly whispered. "It's no problem.... They'll go away, one way or another—easy."

"I'd love to know who these dudes are and what they are up to!" John said with a whisper.

"Let's be quiet.... Just watch, no more talking. We'll talk later!" Sid demanded.

Minutes turned into hours as they watched the mountain men progress up the valley. They passed APS Foxtrot and were almost out of sight, so the boys moved, via the cover of the woods, to CHPS Lima. Once there, they could see at extreme range the unwanted group arrive at the brook of running water. A few moments went by, and then the boys heard a very loud, bearish scream. It echoed down the valley and off all the valley walls for miles around. The volume of it was without description.

"Ha, he doesn't sound like a happy camper," John smartly and quietly chuckled.

"They just found the dead end we left for them. Nice job, Nik!" said Sid. Nik said nothing. "Let's see what they do now," added Sid.

Yelling and screams bellowed down the valley, a hugely loud discussion was taking place; it was almost as if they were trying to attract attention to themselves. Were the mountain men actually trying to lure the boys out for a confrontation? *An odd ploy*, thought John to himself.

"Can you see them?" John asked. "What are they doing, other than yelling?"

Sid leaned out just enough to see the four men at the brook's edge. "They are standing there, and it looks like … yup … they are … um, yes. They are headed east! Away from us … they are headed back into the hills to the east—toward civilization and away from us! Sweet!"

The boys now sat back in utter relief, while Sid continued to watch long after the mountain men had disappeared into the hills to their northeast far up the valley. The three looked at each other, and John shook his head.

"What else?" John wondered aloud. "What else is going to go on? You know—" But John stopped himself short with a tired and shaken frustration.

"It's okay. We'll watch out again for plenty of time. We are okay. Let's just calm down; it's okay," Nik repeated as he tried to stabilize everyone.

It was getting dark now, and they stumbled back to the cabin in the dim light that was available, stopping at each CHPS along the way as they crept up to the edge of the ridge to look back at the hills off to the northeast. No smoke was seen, and there were no flickers or glowing from any fires. With luck, their unwanted visitors were gone—hopefully never to return. They went with no fire that night; it was cold, but they did what they could to stay warm.

Sid had said, "One night and one day—if we don't see them through all that, we'll be clear for a fire tomorrow night, no problem. Let's just make it through one night and one day." The others nodded their agreement, and they continued to debrief about the day's events long into the night.

The group slept in the next morning and spent the day patrolling the ridge, keeping out of sight and vigilant on their watch. The day was eventless and much less fun than the previous three they'd spent on the ridge before sighting the four mountain men. The day seemed to drag on.

... 33 ...
What's Our Next Step?

"WHAT? REALLY? WE WANT to leave again?" John squealed.

The questions shattered the silence of the group like forty-one tons of dynamite exploding all around them. It had been almost a week since the abrupt sighting and even more abrupt disappearance of the mountain men.

John, now standing up and speaking in a softer tone, said, "I like it here, and we've done ours against the crown and for our country."

Sid nodded. Nik was also nodding his head as if to agree, but with some question in his face. "Yes, yes we have! And we've done a damn good job as well! I just keep thinking there is an event or two we still need to survey ... aaaand, we may have a special mission we might want to embark on if we feel like it," Nik explained with a smile.

Sid finally broke his silence. "What are you thinking about now, Nik?"

"Well, first things first, there is a battle up in North Carolina. Remember? We talked about it before. You know, Guilford Courthouse, where the Americans unfortunately lose, by the way, but not by much! It is where the British win the battle where they should have really lost, and in the process of winning, they lose a ton of men.

"Maybe we go and watch it, and if the situation calls for it, *like the last two battles we've witnessed*, we may have to add a little something if needed. What do you think?" Nik concluded.

A slight pause fell on the area and yielded itself to John, who asked, "And where in North Carolina is this again?"

Nik responded, "Guilford Courthouse. Remember? We talked about this."

"And where is that exactly?" asked Sid.

Nik followed up with a quick answer. "Basically, Greensboro. We have been over all of this. You forgot already? Really?"

John tried to dismiss all of it by saying, "A lot has gone on since we talked about all of that, you know."

After some map drawing in the dirt, Nik stepped back and proclaimed with a frown on his face, "Long walk."

John now sat down. "Yeah, it is."

Sid asked where this all ended, the Revolution that is. "It was up in Virginia, right?"

Nik looked at him. "Yeah, Yorktown, Virginia. You know that— the American forces pin the British against the coast, and our newfound friends, the French, meet them with their navy and shell the hell out of them from the York River."

"The French?" questioned John. "As in, 'We are lovers, not fighters'? As in, 'We are at war with you! Um, we surrender! We surrender! Here, you can have Paris. Would you like some wine with that?' Those French?"

"Yes, those French," Nik confirmed. "Back in the now, they were quite the naval and ground power. Going forward, they could still handle themselves until the early to mid-twentieth century. After that ... eh, not so much. Let's give them credit; in 2010, their government is a hell of a lot more conservative than our own. It's ridiculous! Political correctness, our unprotected borders are an open screen door, social entitlement, spending costs skyrocketing— what a mess!"

Nik's rant made Sid smile. "Oh boy, now you've done it, John!" he chuckled. "You've got him ranting about this stuff again!"

"So Guilford Courthouse is our special mission?" John mumbled.

Nik answered, "No. Like I said, first things first. Guilford Courthouse is first. After that, after seeing what transpires there, we'll see what we feel like. I may have an idea or two that could turn into a special mission."

There was a short pause, followed by a cough from Sid. "Sooooo, what do you think?" Nik asked with a smile.

"Let's think on it tonight," said Sid. "There's no real need to rush, is there, Nik?"

"Nope, we have a few days to make a decision and leave," Nik agreed, now smiling.

"A few days, huh? Oh boy," John sighed. "We better start packing our stuff. I've seen that grin before, and you don't ever help." John was now looking at Sid.

Sid tried to look innocent. "What? Who, me? What?" He smiled as he gathered some water for the evening's drink.

They slept that evening, all of them knowing they were going to leave in short order on another long walk through the countryside. Nik was good with it, as it was his idea, and the thoughts of what could come after Guilford Courthouse intrigued him and his curiosity. He wasn't going to tell Sid or John about his other ideas, because he wasn't sure himself what they were going to do after Guilford Courthouse.

Let's see what happens there first, Nik thought to himself. But he did have some potentially interesting thoughts and just wanted to keep them to himself for now. As far as the hiking, he didn't traditionally enjoy such physical exertion, but these were different times, indeed. He wasn't unemployed anymore (as he had been in 2010), and in some strange way, he now felt he had a job, a direction, even though he didn't know what that direction was exactly. The absence of the static, background noise and rhetoric of society in the year 2010 and the contrasting quiet of 1781 gave his head the clarity to listen to what, to who, was instructing him to make decisions. On the surface, Nik, like all people, felt he and he alone guided his actions to what he did moving forward. He really knew, deep down, that given the temporal circumstances, he was being given direction from something much greater than he would ever be.

Sid rested that night, feeling that whatever they did for the American cause was worth everything—even their lives. He knew this was surely an overstatement, as they hadn't even been noticed yet in their forays in the war effort. He had begun to believe that they were there for a reason; this couldn't all have been some freak act of nature or a random passing black hole, dark space, mumbo jumbo thing; maybe it was an occurrence divine in nature. He pondered this for a long while. But who could know or tell?

Sid had a simple trust in his friend Nik; he felt that Nik, the most unprepared one of the three, could in fact be the most prepared for what was their reality now. Obviously, the three needed *all* of them to survive and carry on, but Nik, he had something else on his side—an insight, a sense, something steering him through things and to things. Sid had always had a strange sense about Nik and his often accidental or whimsical insights, which always seemed to be dead-on correct. They always say that women have "women's intuition." Well, Nik matched that dollar for dollar with his "gut feelings." There were more situations than Sid could recall where Nik had the slimmest chance of producing a correct answer on a subject he had no previous knowledge, exposure, or sense to even be qualified to try and answer and then nailed it with a correct answer. *In a word*, Sid thought, *spooky*.

John was tired of thinking about it all and would stick by his companions to the end. He just wasn't sure what or when the end was. Would they live out their lives here and die in natural time, say around 1800 or 1810? There were too many questions he didn't really want to think about. He was actually motivated to act on the side of the Colonies—the Americans, his people, his nation—however young it still was. He reconstructed their steps from Charleston in his mind and was almost driven to begin writing it down somehow. *What an incredible event this was in their lives*, he thought. *How would this all end, and who would ever know, comprehend, or believe any of it?*

The next day brought a unanimous agreement to go witness the Guilford Courthouse battle, and again, they were only going to watch and document the happenings. Initially, there was no need for rules of engagement, because they were not going to fight. The noninterference role was in play until such time as history was not proceeding as previously described, and then they would discuss what they would do next. Nik had explained that the Americans didn't win this battle exactly, but they did inflict heavy losses on the British, so hopefully, they could remain observers in this engagement.

"Hopeful thinking, Nik. We have seen two situations where history hasn't exactly stuck to its story," snapped John.

Yeah, I know.... Well, maybe this time," Nik said. "Anyway, let's go watch and see what happens; if this one is different, it would be simply unexplainable! I wouldn't know what to tell you. Let's just go see."

"What do you think, Sid?" asked John.

Sid, with a pause, stopped the work he was doing securing the cabin and said, "Well, I don't know. Like Nik said, let's go see.... If worse comes to worst, well, we torch another bunch of bad guys. Best case is we watch, all goes as it's supposed to, and we'll be on our way knowing that at least one battle went according to our proper history. We won't know unless we go see it, right?"

John was now smiling a bit. "I hate when you make sense. I can't argue with it. Okay, when do we leave?"

They all chuckled at John's submission, as the group always relied on one of them to pose a little push-back. It was their form of checks and balances.

The boys left their secured base the next morning and looked back at it as they were leaving with the same sense of loss they had as when they left for Cowpens. They didn't pause this time as they knew, short of capture or death, they would return one day to live out their lives there among the trees, hills, and nature. They all felt assured of one thing—it would be a good walk in the countryside.

... 34 ...
We Have Arrived

THE BOYS HAD SPENT the last thirty days hiking and maneuvering around numerous obstacles in their long trek up to Greensboro, North Carolina, and the site at Guilford Courthouse. They had endured a 245-mile journey northeast up the foothills of the Blue Ridge mountain range then east and around the top of the populated areas in North Carolina (what would have been Winston Salem and Greensboro in 2010).

Nik made a point to remind the boys on March 2 about the adoption of the Articles of Confederation. He explained what Sid and John probably already knew: the Articles of Confederation were rules for the framework of running the newly formed government. They specified and strictly outlined how the government was supposed to function and serve the people. In essence, it was really the first written constitution for the newly formed nation.

"Serve the people. Now that's a new one!" Sid smartly snapped.

"Ha! Yes, it was back in 1781 ... but oh, where the founding thoughts and concepts went after about 1901!" snapped Nik and he continued, "I've told you before, from Theodore Roosevelt and Woodrow Wilson forward, with the creation of the Progressive Party in the United States, policies radically altered our constitutional path. You would think something called 'The Progressive Party' would be good for America and our country! In reality, America would never be the same again; they did horrible things to the country, the people, and the constitutional rule of law and really affected the way many things functioned in government! We took many major steps backward from what we had evolved into as a country. Again, we weren't always perfect, but we usually learned from our mistakes and got back on a constitutional course."

After the history lesson, they dropped into the Guilford Courthouse area from the east and settled on a high, heavily wooded position. They were located approximately five hundred yards behind where Nik thought the American first line would form and approximately 250 yards to the east of where he thought the American second line would form in the days to follow. The site where they settled on building their observation post was perfect—well off the battlefield in a position where they would be able to see all of the various stages of the struggle. If needed, they would be in range to easily commit their firepower to and for the American cause. The structure was quickly and easily assembled using the immense amount of trees and underbrush available all around them on the ridge. The day of March 13 had them in position and provisioned well enough to wait out the events for a few days. If they had to move early, the dense surroundings gave them the flexibility to maneuver in and out of their observation post to the northeast without being seen.

Honestly, they were just happy to sit and watch the buildup to the battle. As they sat there in their observation post, Nik recalled that the Americans' General Greene had some forty-four hundred troops somewhere to the north of them, while Lt. Gen. Charles Cornwallis had around nineteen hundred men somewhere to the south of them massing to bunch up along the road that ran through the area.

Nik pointed out that the road where all the action would be centered came up from the southwest and was called the New Garden Road, he thought. It proceeded to the crossroads and courthouse to their left; all he knew about the road was that it led to some place called Reedy Creek. They huddled now in their lookout to see what was going to happen next. It was quiet until the March 15, and then the positioning of opposing forces began.

March 15, 1781, saw the American forces under General Greene, forty-four hundred strong, begin setting up along their lines in and around Guilford Courthouse. As Nik remembered, the American first line was just behind a rail fence where a field lay; it consisted of around a thousand militia. Nik figured they were probably all from North Carolina. The New Garden Road made the split between the lines, which had some sort of artillery pieces or emplacements of some kind. The boys could not readily identify the future relics, but Sid surmised them to be artillery pieces of some sort. The American second line was also right where Nik's memory put them; they had larger numbers as well. This line was about 350 yards behind the first line and had militia dug into some heavier woods. These troops were about on the same line and 450 yards to the west of the boys. The third American line was hard to see from their location but was partially visible on a bluff of land overlooking the entire battlefield closest to Reedy Creek Road and the courthouse itself.

The boys settled down to wait for the fireworks to start. Sid asked about their load outs. "You know, just in case we need to help out. Two out of three tells me that we will probably need to help our patriot friends."

"Maybe, but let's not project," Nik said. "I personally would like to see history not all screwed up for once, right? *Right?*"

"Yeah, yeah, I know, but humor me. Tell me what you have loaded please," implored Sid with a smirk.

John started off, "You know, the usual—three magazines on standby, one loaded in the gun, thirty rounds each, .223. One well-cleaned and maintained AR-15 all set to go!"

Nik began. "Yup, same here. But you know, Sid, my rifle might not be as clean and as well maintained as John's. You know, I think you might be slip—"

Sid quickly interrupted and defended his cleaning ability, and Nik burst out in quiet laughter. "I'm just kidding! Relax, geez—sooo sensitive!"

Sid rolled his eyes. "Okay, okay … I have the normal as well— four magazines in reserve, twenty rounds each, one *very* well cleaned and *very* well maintained M1A all set to go! Yes, sir, that's right—very clean and very well maintained. And don't you forget it!" More quiet chuckles came from the group.

"So we sit and wait!" John noted. Several minutes later he added, "When does this thing start kicking off, Nik?"

"Well, around one o'clock this afternoon we should be able to see some movement," Nik replied.

They sat and looked at the early spring day now, as they hadn't noticed anything about anything since they trekked in and worked on getting set up in their hideaway. The sun was shining, and it was around fifty-eight degrees Fahrenheit; the grasses and woods were just beginning to bloom and grow in the pleasant early spring season in the southeast United States.

"This is a nice place," John began. "Why are all the fields and orchards turned into battlefields in 1781?"

"What else have they got to fight in? It's not like there are huge cities to ravage and obliterate," Sid noted.

"No, that comes later, in like thirty years," Nik gloomily pointed out. "Oh yeah, and then like fifty years after that, and—ugh—I'm not sure it ever stops, because after we get straight here in the United States, then Europe blows up in 1914 during World War I. And then a short twenty years has them careening into World War II. Will we ever learn?"

With that dose of joy, they sat back and waited for the beginning of whatever was going to transpire that day. They lay positioned on their stomachs, bipods steadying their rifles, and rifle barrels just poking out of their observation post. "I am hoping history is spot-on today, and we just get to sit here, you know?" Nik reiterate to his compatriots.

1:00 p.m. John, using the binoculars, spotted the British forces about three-quarters of a mile to the south and watched their advance. John described what he saw to the others. "They have their artillery in the front and are in two columns, one on each side of the road headed toward the Americans!"

What had been chronicled in the history texts as "one of the most vicious and fiercest battle of the war" was about to take place in front of people of another time. Set to watch the spectacle of the past, the boys were now witnesses to what shouldn't have been.

Were they ready for it? How could it be worse than the carnage they witnessed at Kings Mountain and Cowpens?

It all happened pretty fast, and the boys looked at Nik in wonder. "Was this what it was supposed to look like?" John asked.

Nik, now looking at the advancing British, said, "Yes, I think this is right. The Americans have a lot more forces on the field and will yield the positions to minimize their casualties. The British will win in a fashion but lose five hundred men or more. It was a 20-plus percent troop loss—really bad. The historians almost thought that it was the American plan to lure the British in and not to actually win the battle. That's all theory, of course."

Like clockwork, the British forces proceeded down the road, taking the first volley of American fire. They returned fire and immediately engaged into a bayonet charge toward the American first line. Nik quickly interjected. "Watch this next volley from the Americans at the British bayonet charge. It was noted by some historians that this next American round of fire was the most effective single volley of the war."

The thunderous shots rang out; it was truly a killing strike. The charging British regulars ran headlong into the American fire at almost point-blank range and were utterly destroyed in the face of their miscalculation. The boys reeled back a bit with horror. "Well, we won't be needed here," said Sid in a whispered voice. John all but put his rifle down and sat back, checking their flank to make sure nothing or no one was sneaking up on them.

The fighting continued as the British steadied their ranks and pushed on, while the American first line militia moved off to preserve their relative position on the field. The American second line was up a hill and scattered among trees, which gave them a huge tactical advantage for inflicting great damage. The British, having to fight uphill, had an anemic position on the field, which most certainly aided the disarray in their ranks. This disorganization at the hands of the American second line became an even deadlier position for the British troops.

Nik, Sid, and John sat and watched the forces loyal to the crown get hammered and cut down by the American second line, which continued hiding behind their natural shields. The Americans would pop out in groups from behind trees and thickets, reign death down on their enemies, and then scoot back to the relative safety of their high ground.

"And we lost this battle?" John asked again.

"Yeah, it seems strange, doesn't it? Sitting here watching this, they really could have pushed here and decimated the British. I don't understand," Nik replied.

Sid speculated, "Maybe it was a maneuver to break the back of the British, to demoralize them?"

"Maybe," nodded Nik.

The British now made it to the third line and were immediately repulsed. John reported that it looked like one of the British leads was struck down on that attack, and Nik recalled that it would have been Col. James Webster. The British did breach the American third line for a time, but the American cavalry came up from the rear and sealed the incursion. Now it looked like the American line would hold. Sid, looking back at the British command line, spotted the familiar Tarleton legion from Cowpens and grabbed his rifle. "I'd like a piece of that guy," he said, gritting his teeth and chambering a round in his rifle. As he did, the British opened up on the lines with their artillery.

"An act of desperation?" Nik murmured aloud. "This is correct, though. I remember reading about this—a really ugly maneuver!"

The British shelling was hitting as many British troops as it was American troops; yes, it stopped the American advance, but at a huge cost to their own. At that moment, the Tarleton mounted legion was entering the fight, and Sid was ready to open up on them. Nik stopped him. "No, man, this one is by the book. He won't make the fight before the Americans head down the Reedy Creek Road and make their getaway. It's okay; enough blood has been spilled today."

John began to speak up in an effort to bolster Nik's position. "As much as we hate this Lieutenant Colonel Tarleton and his men, listen to Nik. We are not needed today. Be happy for that. Be happy we are here to witness the event, and let's keep out of it."

Sid calmed down and nodded. "Yeah, you're right," he said with a grumble. "Oh! I want that guy!"

Nik, looking at the battle scene, informed the group. "There they go, and just like that, the Americans have left the field! That's good; they got away and lost very few troops. And look at all the British losses—geez, what a disaster."

Sid sat down and looked around at the field of battle. "Man, oh man, they are not going to be happy about this, are they?"

"How can they be?" added John. "They have a lot of dead guys, a pretty costly defeat if you ask me!"

The boys secured their rifles and made their sidearms handy for the evening's observation and sleep. They made sure they stayed hidden, as the sun was now illuminating their side of the landscape. Sid made mention of this, and John responded with, "There isn't anyone down there looking up here for us for sure. They have enough to worry about."

Sid replied with, "Yeah, you're probably right. We'll just keep well hidden until after sundown."

Moans and cries could be heard from the battlefield that evening, and from what they could see from their hidden location, 90 percent of the dying on the field were British. They could see very few Americans out there; even the militias weren't strewn around as after the previous battles.

"What do you think," asked Sid of the group.

"About what?" asked John.

"Any of it—the battle, the dead. In some strange way it feels weird not to have joined in this time," remarked Sid.

"Well, we didn't have to. For once, the history was correct, and it went exactly the way it went the first time. You know I don't make this stuff up," answered Nik. With that, the boys continued to look and listen until the sun dropped below the horizon, and at last, the peace of darkness fell upon the fallen.

The temperature in mid-March after sundown dropped quickly, and the boys could see steam rising from the battlefield, which was littered with wounded and dead. Some of the wounded had been getting medical assistance, but at an incredibly slow pace. The cleanup would continue well into the night, and the smell of the dead and dying was an unforgettable odor imprinted on the boys' memories from Kings Mountain.

"I don't think I'll ever forget that," remarked John.

"What are you talking about, John?" asked Nik.

"You know, our fifty-one-body mass grave we dug and loaded," John muttered.

"Oh yeah, I was trying to forget about that. Yeah, that is the smell, all right," Nik agreed.

"We'll leave in the morning," Sid spoke up, cutting off the thoughts that were stirring in the group. He didn't figure it helped any purpose to rehash these things. His short-term attitude was, "What's done is done. When we are old, we can talk about it and make peace with our actions."

They secured their rifles and collected their gear to prepare for the pullout in the morning. They wanted to slip out before sunrise in order to avoid anyone who might have an idea of getting an early start on the British side; after all, they were officially in a British-occupied zone now. Nik remembered that the British would fall back to Hillsborough, which was to their south, so he figured they should head out to the north and then decide on their next steps after that. Clouds rolled in after sunset, and the area was trounced in torrential downpours of rain all night.

"Joy, joy," Sid mumbled. "You know, I don't think I'll ever quite get used to just sitting in the rain, let alone trying to sleep in it."

"I second that," grumbled Nik.

"Yup, it sucks! But at least we have some cover—better than those guys out there," John said as he pointed toward the battlefield in the distance.

"Good night, guys. Let's sleep, so we can get out of here first thing," Nik requested.

Sid and John each answered with a simple, "Night."

... 35 ...
And Yet Another Decision

MARCH 16, 1781. THEIR course away from the battle at Guilford Courthouse had them skirting north from the more heavily populated portions of the central piedmont cities in North Carolina. They stopped to rest, gather food and water, and figure out what they were doing going forward. The location was rich in fresh water and hunting opportunities, with a very scenic view and a defensive backdrop. They set up camp nestled against a ridge, which they had scouted earlier in the day. Along this ridgeline, they would be secure, as it was nearly impassable vertically and similarly difficult to traverse.

The events at Guilford Courthouse, which were still fresh in their minds, didn't seem as disturbing as previous encounters they had witnessed. Were they growing accustomed to the killing? Were they becoming sociopathic murderers, or were they simply going with the flow of the times they were now fully embroiled in? They talked among themselves on this subject for a long time that day, and after mulling it over, Sid finally had enough of it all.

"Stop!" Sid yelled. "Listen, this is like watching the news on a cable news network station over and over for an entire day! Stop! We are not psycho killers; we aren't becoming somehow dead to life itself. We are stuck in the American Revolutionary War, and we are our own team!"

They all stopped what they were doing, and Nik and John looked at Sid like he might now be losing his mind. John quietly explained, "Yes, we know we are not psycho killers, we know we are not becoming somehow deadened to the difference between wrong and right, and we are continually reminded and well aware of the fact of where and when we are."

Nik added, "And we are here for us, first and foremost; you know that, Sid."

Sid sat down and nodded in understanding. "So what do we do from here? What do you guys want to do?" he asked. Nik and John both shrugged.

Sid began by poking around at history. "Well, according to what you tell us, Nik, from here, the British are basically screwed. So, we could go back to C-10 and call it a victory and God Bless America."

John, taking a cue from Sid, goaded Nik by adding, "Yeah. You know, our work is done here. Everything is good with the world, you know. We can just go make a farm or something."

Nik looked up at the both of them and nodded his head. "Okay, C-10 would be fine. But make a farm? What are you talking about?" Nik questioned with a sour tone that hung on itself in utter disgust.

Nik knew his friends quite well by now, and this was their way of saying, "Okay, what's next in history for us, and where should we be in the annals of upcoming events?"

Sid was now watching intently, as he knew Nik would most certainly catch onto the blatant request for ideas and suggestions on where they might want to go observe the next altercation.

"Well," Nik said, rubbing his shoulder, "I know a place that history basically forgot."

John now pulled up a stump and smiled. "Aha, I thought so!"

"Well, it's not—" Nik continued. "It's not exactly what you're thinking. It's a place where Cornwallis set up camp with his army on their way to Virginia. I'm not sure how long they were there, but I know he and his army left Wilmington on April 25 and marched their way into Virginia around the eleventh or twelfth of May.

They were at a place called Crowell's Plantation, just outside Rocky Mount, on May 8."

The group sat for a time and pondered their position and what they might want to do. John raised his hand to ask a question, and Nik laughed. "We have been at this for how long now? You don't need to raise your hand—unless you were going to be a smartass by any chance?"

"Yup, that's me," John said with a smile. "So, what were we going to do after we went and found the scariest battle force on the continent?"

Nik, now looking at John, inquired with a smirk on his face, "Well, John, what did you and I do best in our video games in the years 1999 to 2010 when neither you nor I could win?"

John thought for a short minute. "We annoyed everyone else in the game!"

Nik smiled. "Correct!"

Sid cocked his head off to one side as to say, "Uh-huh. Do tell."

Nik hemmed and hawed a bit and then quite expressively began to explain. "Well, maybe we could annoy the you-know-what out of the British patrols or something to, you know, give them a nudge up to Virginia."

"A nudge, huh?" retorted Sid. "What happened to staying out of sight and not affecting history?"

Nik bantered back. "Yes, there is that ... and I feel that we have done an exemplary job in keeping out of the way of history, but—"

"But what?" John jumped into the fray.

"Well, I just feel we have a duty to do now," Nik explained. "I think we need to stick with events and not change any of their results. It's very scary how close some of these battles have been and the things we've seen. History hasn't been very accurate, has it? There have been many occurrences—key happenings—that without our intervention, would have gone the other way, specifically to the British as victories!"

Sid, wanting to add his thoughts, didn't feel the need to raise his hand as he explained himself. "Like Kings Mountain. If we weren't there, the Colonials could have certainly lost. And Cowpens—the Americans were certainly losing until we loosened up the British right flank. That's two "key" battles that *we* directly affected the outcome of in this time line."

John nodded his head and asked, "Why were the events different, I wonder?"

"That's what I am talking about!" agreed Nik.

Sitting down next to the small campfire that night, they continued to discuss the apparent discrepancies in time. It wasn't the same old conversation, so Sid wasn't freaking out. They had found a new issue and all agreed on the odd events they had witnessed.

Nik pondered to himself how it could be that a forgotten dragoon force was present at Kings Mountain in their present time. If that force was there in the history they knew, wouldn't they have engaged back then? Was it a random roll of the dice that they were present in this go-round of history? "Not a chance," murmured Nik and decided to explain his thoughts to the group.

Sid wondered about Cowpens, though, and how it clearly didn't appear to go as planned for the Americans. He also struggled with the sighting of those mountain men at precisely the area where they weakened the British lines and allowed the Americans to successfully perform the double flank maneuver.

"Creepy is what it was," Sid added.

"What about the courthouse battle? Anything odd about it?" John continued. "The British did win, after all, like it historically happened. Right?"

Sid interjected. "The Americans did inflict casualties on them, yes, but they won, which was historically correct."

Nik sat back and began smiling like the Cheshire cat. "Man, oh man, haven't we come far in our historical analysis skills? Here we are, lost souls from the year 2010, commenting on the social, tactical, and political ramifications of battle results in the year 1781—my, oh my."

John, in an attempt to quell Nik's overjoyed state, replied, "Well, you know, just trying to figure it all out—you know."

Nik laughed and told John not to worry about it. He was proud of their progress and was very thankful that they all had brains and had been using them all along. "I do believe that we are quite a force to be reckoned with!" Nik declared.

After a pause, Sid smugly added, "Yeah, in 1781."

Nik conceded, "Yes ... okay, so you got me there. You're right. So, are we up for Operation Nudge?"

The boys pondered it a bit more and agreed that they would set out for Rocky Mount, North Carolina, in the morning.

Sunrise and the breaking of camp was a lesson in efficiency; the group woke up, packed up, and walked east. They discussed the terrain ahead from what they knew about living in the area in 2010 and understood that it would all look drastically different in the 1781 motif. It would be odd seeing the Raleigh-Durham region without highways, roads, convenience stores, supermarkets, or shopping malls. It shouldn't be a surprise to them given the fact that they'd been in 1780 all these months, but these were the areas they called home.

It was odd to them; all this time sort of felt like a long, drawn-out vacation or time away from home. Now they found themselves in their previous home area, only in 1780. They were pleased at the prospect, because they were well aware of the availability of lakes and streams in the region. Yes, the man-made water features were not going to be there, but the construction of these reservoirs were not by accident; in 1780, the many streams and lakes that created these modern structures would be easily found, navigated, and utilized for food and water.

The boys hiked at a fairly brisk pace for the next twenty-one days and really pushed themselves so as to cover enormous distances; it felt, on some days, as if they were driven by something. Nik was pushing the group very hard, and he didn't know why. He hadn't been sleeping well the past few nights, and he couldn't put his finger on the disturbances of the evenings. Sid and John were happy to be tearing up the trail, and for this, Nik was pleased as well.

The group now felt they had a date with destiny and all felt a bit anxious to go on the offensive, as it was loosely described. They quietly talked while they were hiking and reaffirmed that what they were embarking upon was what the group wanted as a whole. There was never any real question; they were in the fight now, and they would "gently aid" the Colonials in their endeavor for independence. Following just south of a predominantly watery area, and after two weeks of traveling east, away from what was going to be the greater Greensboro area of North Carolina, the group all agreed that this area would, in the far future, become the Falls Lake region north of Raleigh.

Midmorning found the group trekking up a small hill after traversing a few streams and tributaries to a local river. This course had them about to go bounding down the opposite side of the hill when Nik stopped abruptly. He was staring to the south and had a look about him that shook the others.

"What is it, man? What do you see?" inquired Sid.

John now scampered back up the hill after having started headlong down it ahead of the group. "What's up?" he asked as he approached the others, a bit out of breath.

Sid quickly said, "Don't know yet. What is it, Nik?"

Nik just continued to look south and was in a sweat now. "Do you see—" he started. "Do you see a small ridgeline down there?" He was pointing to the south and a little west.

John looked and had a hard time finding anything but the small hills of the area. Sid was looking, and John asked for the binoculars. Sid handed them over and continued to squint in the hazy sun of the southeastern spring day. John then quickly blurted, "I see it—it's small, barely there, but it is there."

"Look, Sid, down on the right," John said as he passed the binoculars to Sid. "It runs fairly far south and seems to get slightly lower in elevation. Take a look."

Sid looked at the small ridge and nodded. "Yeah, I think I see it. Okay, so there it is." Sid looked at Nik, needing some more information. "Okay, what are you thinking?"

Nik looked like he was thinking very hard about something. "What's the date today?" he asked John.

John looked down and said, "April 14."

Nik wiped the sweat from his forehead and looked intently at John and Sid, "Do you guys trust me?"

John cocked his head back and stated fairly loudly, "Duh! C'mon, what do you think?"

Sid laughed, thinking Nik had finally lost his mind. "Yes, we trust you, where are we going?" he asked as he pointed east and reiterated. "The fight is that way."

"I know. So, let's take today and go that way," Nik said, now pointing south. "Is that okay?"

"Sure," said John.

"Lead on," added Sid to Nik with a shrug.

They hiked at a blistering speed now. John and Sid wondered what they were running toward and were a bit concerned at what Nik had them moving this quickly toward. Nik, traditionally the one in the party not wanting to kill himself on a trek, was leading the charge and pushing the pace. It was befuddling to Sid and John. The three were in great shape after all these months of walking and running around, but at this pace, they were huffing and puffing as if they were still out-of-shape, fair-weather walkers who had begun this adventure.

Sid, wanting to have some conversation, asked if they were concerned about bumping into anyone as they headed directly toward the city of Raleigh. "Probably not," John puffed. "The town in 1780 is probably pretty small yet, centered downtown of what we know as Raleigh."

Nik stopped for a breath and added, "It wasn't until about 1788 when it was officially named Raleigh."

"After Sir Walter Raleigh," Sid quickly added, not to be outdone.

"Sweet, so we should be good. Where are we heading, Nik?" asked John, now just slightly annoyed.

"Nope, we'll be nowhere close to those folks," said Nik, not answering John's direct question.

They marched on and were quickly back to their breakneck pace. In another hour, Nik, who was just slightly ahead of the group, stopped abruptly at the water's edge, looked around, and shrugged. He ran up and down the bank in the east-west direction and settled on a point of the creek at a bend where it was at its highest point north. He looked north one last time and scampered up the hill.

"What are you doing, Nik? Are you looking for something specific?" asked Sid in a slightly more serious tone.

John caught up to Nik, and as they were hiking up a small grade, asked, "You okay, man?"

Sid now hung back a bit and looked at the surroundings. He wanted to make sure they weren't walking into someone's backyard; just as they had through the entire experience, they didn't really want to meet up with anyone. Nik was now in a little bit of a frenzy; he stopped short and spun around. They had reached a plateau, and Nik was looking around at the heavily wooded area.

Where they stood was a decent-sized flat spot, a table of probably three to five acres or so. The land headed downhill slightly on all sides and then on some sides went back up to other hills. To the south where they had come from, the land continued downhill. On the westward downhill side, Nik scuffled around and found, nestled in a gaggle of typical southeastern pine trees and an accumulation of fallen pine needles, a single oak sapling. He knelt down and looked at it for a few minutes as the sun was now descending behind the small hills—it would soon be dark. Nik stood up and began clearing some of the pine trees and pine needles from around the oak sapling.

"So, we are staying here tonight?" Sid asked as he rejoined the group.

Nik looked up and exclaimed, "Yup, I have a surprise for you!"

John's interest was now piqued. "Will it take long?"

"No, just tonight," Nik assured him.

"Sid, do you have any idea where we are?" Nik asked.

Sid looked confused; they had trekked all over South and North Carolina. He shook his head, smiled, and walked up the hill. "Nope!" he proclaimed. "But I am sure I am going to find out."

They set up a quick camp up away from the now mysterious oak sapling. John asked Sid, "So, is Nik a druid or something, and he just came out of the tree-loving closet?"

Sid laughed and answered, "No, I don't think so."

They finished up their evening cleanup and sat around a small campfire. "So, are you going to tell us what we are doing here now, Nik?" Sid asked.

"Yes. In a few hours, I will tell you everything that I know, which I apologize for in advance. Sadly, it isn't nearly enough."

John was now more curious than before. "A few hours? That's, like, midnight?" he mumbled. "After that marathon, you want to stay awake until midnight?"

"No," Nik assured them, "but could you set your watch to wake us up from a little nap at around 11:30 p.m.?"

Sid, now also curious, utterly confused, and wanting to see what Nik had on his mind, nodded before lying down for a while.

The hours went by, and the boys restlessly stayed quiet as sleep gradually overtook each of them. Awaking around 11:20 p.m., John turned off his wristwatch alarm as he and Sid stretched, yawned, and looked around. Nik was already up and off in the woods to the east-northeast of the oak sapling. John had seen Nik pacing out this position earlier in the day and just figured he was looking for something on the ground. Sid now joined Nik, and John soon followed.

"So, here we are," said Sid.

"Yup, here we are," repeated John.

Nik looked at the small tinderbox in which he had captured some embers from their campfire and transported to this location. He began by asking Sid again, "Do you know where you are now?"

Sid looked confused again. "Nope," he replied.

Nik continued, "You used to live right over there, down the hill and to the left from here. I have had these dreams for the past five nights, and I figured them out this morning," Nik began to explain. "It's Saturday, April 14, 1781, in the year of our Lord. It's Holy Saturday night 1781—the night of the resurrection! What time is it?"

John tried to look at his watch by the light of the now-cooling embers but had to blow on them a little to brighten them up so he could see the numbers. "11:54 p.m." he finally replied.

Nik explained, "We are standing in the spot where the Orthodox Church stands in 2010; 230 years from now, my family and I will be attending the midnight mass, rejoicing the resurrection of our savior, Jesus Christ. My dreams these past evenings were of Christ's journey to Jerusalem—to his death, and his conquering of death. Earlier today I felt that we were very close to this spot, and by the way, you should see that oak tree, in 2010—it's a big one!"

"Time?" Nik quickly asked again.

"11:59:51," John replied.

Nik knelt down and began working the embers and the dry kindling he had collected earlier (which he'd mixed with a few magnesium shavings for effect). At the stroke of midnight a pure white flame leapt up from the spot that seconds before had been dark and lifeless. The light was so bright compared to the total darkness they had been engulfed in for the past several hours that it took a second for their eyes to adjust as the stream of light seemed to reach the heavens. Nik admitted quietly that he wasn't a scholar of theology by any means and couldn't remember much of anything, but he thought he could remember a phrase or two for this occasion.

They fed the light in silent vigil, thinking of what was personal to them and them alone, the light, and the essence of God on this earth. When they all felt an appropriate end to their makeshift midnight mass, Nik quietly murmured the only thing he could honestly put together. "May Christ our true God, who rose from the dead, as a good loving and merciful God, have mercy upon us and save us." Nik ended with, "Χριστός Ανέστη! Christ is Risen!" and a smile.

April 15, 1781, Easter Sunday. The boys slept late that morning, and for the first time, they were sore from the previous day's marathon. Nik and John sat up and chatted, while Sid went off into the woods for an unknown look around.

"How did you possibly find your way here?" John asked Nik. "And how do you know that this is the location where the church will be built?"

"Well," Nik started, "I saw it as we were running down the ridgeline, and it just came to me. I knew we'd hit the water down there, and I knew to find the north pointing elbow in the river and go basically north and uphill to a flat spot."

John, continuing the interrogation, asked, "And how do you know today is Easter?"

A long pause went by before Nik answered. "Somehow I was told. Faith, I guess. I don't really know *how*, but it *is* Easter today, I just know it."

Upon Sid's return, Nik began with an apology; he admitted he should have informed them about what he was up to the previous day. Both Sid and John insisted that it was a very interesting detour with a very moving surprise. He shouldn't apologize; they need all the diversions they can get, and this one was well worth it. They did implore Nik to apologize for the undue beating their bodies took on the high-speed trek that had been foisted upon them, however.

"Please pass the ibuprofen!" insisted the pair.

Nik dropped his head. "I'm sorry."

John looked at Sid and inquired, "Did you find what you were looking for?"

Sid had a short "yup" for a response and then continued with a more in-depth explanation. "This is it, all right. The apartment complex I used to live in will be right over there; it was nestled into a group of hillsides, and it's an odd and unmistakable location. But enough of that," Sid announced. "Is it time to go meet up with our Redcoat friends?"

They were motivated now as they finished breaking down their little camp and proceeded to shove off toward their May destination—the southeastern outskirts of Rocky Mount, North Carolina. Nik looked back at the oak sapling again, waited for a brief moment, and then turned in a somber move away. At the last minute, he went back and cleared an even larger area around the oak sapling to give it the best chance to grow in its first years. Anything could happen, really, but he was sure that this was the huge old oak tree in front of the church in 2010. He thought about burying something near it for retrieval purposes but figured whatever he placed would probably not hold up to the test of time, so he didn't bother. He just walked away. The day was warm and sunny. "Back to the heat!" Nik complained as they made a last-minute scan of the area.

"Okay, let's go," they said in unison as they plied a trail northeast of the camp area. It wasn't very long before they found their stride again. Burlaps and woods (on their rifles) were the order of the day, as they thought they might be walking close to populated areas. They'd had a few people sightings while moving through the countryside of what would become Wake and Nash counties.

The boys had gone back and forth about using burlaps to look like the folks of the day or the camouflage gear they had in an attempt to be invisible in their surroundings. There was a point later in the day when they crossed a trail right in front of a group of locals and weren't even looked at. There was almost numbness about the walk.

"We all doing okay today, guys?" Nik asked, hoping to strike up a conversation; the quiet was bothering him.

"Yeah, man," Sid answered, "just hiking and looking around."

"Tired today," added John. Sid and Nik agreed, and they made their best time to the end of the day.

Camp that night was built light, and the group reflected on the past once again. Nik pulled out the Colonial coins he had found at the homestead and the buttons he had taken off of the dead dragoon's uniforms. He was fascinated with the condition of the coins and intrigued with the fifty-one silver buttons with the marking RP on them. He had pulled a button off of each dead British soldier from Kings Mountain in some sort of commemoration of them or something; he didn't really know.

Sid spoke again of the time line oddities, the mountain men, the dead; John sat quietly and only asked one question: "What are we to do?"

"With what?" Nik looked up and asked him, as it was a very open-ended question.

Sid cut them both off and said rather sharply, "We do whatever we do! Nothing is written, and we are on our own. We do what we can do to help our country. Something isn't right with what we've seen."

Nik agreed and clarified. "Things are very close, though, and there are some very slight turns of history that could have really gone against us, the American forces, in these battles. How do we know these close calls didn't really happen, and they were just lost in the chronicles of time?"

"We don't know, and we'll never know," John blurted. "And we keep talking about it. We need to stop for a while." A silence fell over the camp; no one was sure what to say after John's blunt request.

Nik broke the silence nearly an hour later. "We can change our mode of conversation about all the things that are now. Any suggestions?" he added rather meekly.

John quietly murmured, "No, no … we need to discuss this stuff." Another long pause followed. "It's just … mind-boggling," he continued. "We are computer geeks; we were out-of-shape computer geeks. Well, we're not so out of shape anymore, but—"

Sid added with a smile, "We are computer geeks without computers—ugh! We are officially going through withdrawals!" They all laughed at that. "Okay, so let's sleep and reboot, geeks!" continued Sid.

They lay quietly and all wondered and thought to themselves, pondering the future. Nik felt a bad omen coming now, and for no good reason. They had done well in their plight to go here and there. They'd stayed out of the mainstream, helped history become the way they knew it should be, and aided the peoples of this era in whatever way they could. Nik truly felt they had experienced the joy of Easter in their midnight exercise of faith.

John was so tired that he fell asleep sitting up despite his deep sense of worry—a worry he hadn't felt for many months. Sid was quiet and fell asleep in utter exhaustion but with the anticipation of something; he was feeling an excitement and an anxiety he couldn't explain.

Something was about to change.

... 36 ...
Look to the East

THEY ARRIVED ON THE southwest side of Crowell's plantation at midday on May 6, 1781. The boys were now back in full camouflage, face paint, and awareness so sharp they cut the air as they walked through it. They walked for many days, hoping that their time line would hold fast in reality, so they wouldn't walk into a bad situation when they arrived at their destination.

At the woods' edge now, the boys peered into the fields of the plantation and looked for signs of the British army. So far, all was clear. What was a little eerie was that there was very little activity in the area at all. One would think the people of the plantation would be out doing the business of the day—planting, tilling, something. Had they heard that the British were heading their way? No one could be sure.

Sid suggested they make their way well to the east of the plantation, set up a station there, and wait for the first of the British patrols. They all agreed and quietly moved through the brush to the southeast; a few instances of sounds in front of them kept them moving slowly, their eyes always looking at the farm area and the woods around them.

They passed some creeks and small ponds, which they noted for future reference. Most importantly, they noted which directions the ravines ran and which way the water ran in and out of them. Pressing on, they reached the southernmost point of the plantation's wooded area. Sid raised his hand to signal a quick stop. He knelt down and slid over to the woods' edge. Now pointing to the fields, he was showing John and Nik the farm workers tilling and planting about 450 yards off in the distance.

John whispered, "Look at that. This is only something you see in sketches, not real life."

Nik was concentrating on the real estate behind them, to the south, as Sid pointed to move on. The group quietly faded into the woods and moved to the east again. Proceeding slowly forward, they heard a whimpering scream from a very close distance. "No! Why? I have done all you have asked!" The boys immediately dropped to the ground and scurried into some thicker brush.

"What the hell was that?" John whispered.

"Don't know. Sid, can you see the farm folks?" asked Nik hurriedly.

"Hold on," exclaimed Sid, spinning around to look behind them. "Yes, they are running away from the yelling." The boys moved to where they could see what the commotion was about.

What they had heard was some sort of an altercation involving three British regulars and a civilian man of very slight build. The man was bound and was being pushed around by the three redcoat-adorned men. It didn't look like it was going to end well, as the soldiers looked to be setting the ragged-looking civilian up for his hanging.

"I don't understand!" the man pleaded. "I have helped you in every way you've asked! Please! No! I will do anything, please!"

The boys were not amused. "We're *done* with *ya*! Your Lord can have you now!" said one of the soldiers.

"Oh my God! They are going to hang that guy!" Nik uttered in total surprise.

"What the hell?" came out of John's mouth as his clip entered his rifle's lower receiver.

Sid quickly loaded his M1A with a clip and said, "Umm, we need to do something!"

Nik began contemplating an engagement in broad daylight where someone would survive. His hands seemed to be in automatic mode as they loaded his AR-15 with a clip. "Three of them, three of us. One shot, one kill, guys! Sid, call the shot!" Nik requested.

They quickly set up on their stomachs with their bipods on the ground for added stability and more accurate aiming. The frail man was now screaming, "No, this ... please stop!" The soldiers hoisted the man onto the horse's back facing backward.

Sid began. "Okay, angle is good, the friendly is clear."

John butted in. "Now would be good!"

Nik quickly added, "Range, 151 yards. One shot each, if you please! Land them well!"

Sid now interrupted as the three took aim at their respective targets. "Three, two, one, *fire!*" he ordered. With a deafening sound, all three rifles discharged simultaneously. Once again, the degree of efficiency of the modern rifles stunned the boys, as their targets fell to the ground where they had stood. They had delivered three chest shots, and their targets were simply dead where they fell.

"Oh man!" John said.

The man on the horse was now screaming bloody murder and kicking and thrashing around. He spooked the horse into frenzy. In that instant, the horse bucked up and took off like a shot, leaving the man dangling from the rope around his neck.

Sid yelled, "Oh! Dammit! Nik, scope! Shoot the rope! Shoot the rope!"

"Hurry up!" John demanded.

Nik, listening to the man squealing and suffering under his own weight, broke into a profuse sweat. As if it wasn't stressful enough to have just dispatched three more human beings from the earth, he now had to make some marksman/sniper-like shot to save a man's life. He lined up his scope and fired a three-round burst at the highest point above the man's head where the rope lay draped over the tree limb. The man dropped like a brick and lay on the ground, squirming like a squirrel that had just been hit by a car.

"Oh my God, he's dead!" Nik swore as he rolled over. Sid and John quickly jumped up and ran over to the man, who was now lying still on the ground and breathing very hard. John expertly cut the rope from his neck, hands, and feet and sort of held him down.

"Who? What? Who the devil are you?" the man squealed though his coughing.

Nik, who had now caught up to the scene, grabbed the man by the shirt and quietly said, "Nobody, and you'll forget you ever saw us! Understand?" With that, he threw the man back to the ground. Sid moved between Nik and the rescued civilian and looked at his friend with an odd stare.

"What is your name, and how did you get into this mess today?" John asked. The man began to cry and explained that he had been captured at the siege in Charleston.

"Holy—" uttered John.

"They took me out of there on their move north, and I thought everything was okay," the man continued. "I didn't do anything against us, the colonies, you know. I just helped in menial duties for them—cooking, cleaning, and tending to their ruddy animals. My name is Robert Quinten."

Nik pushed past Sid and began a more calm dialogue. "Well, Mr. Quinten, this was your lucky day! For your own good, I would head to the north and west into Virginia from here. The main body of General Cornwallis's army will be here in a day or so, and I don't think you want to be found around all this," Nik explained as he pointed to the three dead British soldiers.

The man looked heatedly at Nik now. Sid leaned over and said, "Sir, this man just saved your life. Do as he says and forget you ever saw us."

John now explained, "Our favor to you is your life, and your favor to us will be your silence."

Nik, now looking at John, nodded his head and stated, "Nicely said, man."

The man, now looking at who he perceived to be the kindliest member of the three, directed his next question to John. "Mr. Man," he stuttered, "how does he know these things of Lord Cornwallis's army? You killed these soldiers?"

John replied, "Pay no mind to this." He bent down to look him in the eye. "Please do as we ask for your own good, okay?"

Sid took a water skin from one of the soldiers and gave it to Mr. Quinten. Mr. Quinten stood up, brushed himself off, and murmured, "What is this world coming to?"

After that, the frail little man scampered off and disappeared to the north, cursing under his breath all the way. When he was gone, the three dragged the dead soldiers under a thicket and covered them up the best they could in the time they thought they had to spare.

"That's so funny, what Mr. Quinten said about what the world is coming to," said John.

"Little does he know," Sid added.

"No," Nik interjected, "what was funny was that he thought your name was Man, because I referred to you as 'man' when I said to you, 'Nicely said, *man*.' Now that's funny."

The boys had to get to a safer place now, after all the commotion. "We don't need any more company," Nik proclaimed. They probed a bit more south and east and had several more "encounters" that day.

Moving back to the north, the boys identified several locations where they could make camp for the evening. One of the locations was to the east, but a second and better site farther to the northeast was where they decided to camp. This one put just a bit more distance between them and their escapades of the day. Night camp at the more northern site was in a small, dry ravine where they quickly set up a very basic shelter that resembled a bramble of downed trees lying over the ravine. They had grown fond of the downed-tree and brush shelters for their ease of construction and very natural look.

As they lay down to rest, Sid said, "That was a pretty nice shot on the rope, Nik. You hit it with the first round, you know."

Nik sat up and faced Sid. "I don't need that kind of pressure. Why didn't you take the shot?" he asked.

"Well," Sid said, "you had the quickest opportunity from where we were sitting, and you and that rifle of yours—well, it just seemed like your shot to take."

"I guess," grumbled Nik.

John supported Sid by pointing out that they had both stood up, while Nik had stayed on the ground and was ready for a next shot if needed. "Okay, okay, it was a good shot. But way too nerve-racking," Nik admitted, now yielding to the compliments.

The group fell asleep without a fire that night, rifles at the ready, while listening to a far-off thunderstorm and enjoying the cool breeze that it seemed to generate.

"Psst." The noise broke the silence of the very early morning hours. Sid, trying to wake the guys as quietly as possible, tried again. "Psst."

Nik and John woke with a start, which was immediately followed with a quiet *click* of the safeties of their rifles. Sid was now whispering. "Two o'clock. High. British patrol!"

"Are you kidding?" whispered John.

"You loaded?" Sid asked, inquiring on the firing status of the group.

"I'm good," Nik whispered.

"Ready," John replied.

"Wait.... Hold," Sid instructed as they watched the meandering British patrol in the dim dawn lighting of the surrounding wooded area. The soldiers stood in the area for what seemed like hours when, in fact, mere minutes ticked by. They appeared to be looking for something. Apparently, luck was on their side, as the boys were all pointed the proper direction with their rifles pointing toward their feet. Nik was hoping the patrol would just walk by, but he worried about being stuck behind some kind of British line or strategic boundary of sorts. Sid, watching the patrol intently, was fairly relieved that they would move on without discovering them; he was in a sweat now. John tried to get a slightly better angle on things and shifted his weight only slightly, which caused one of the branches under him to break with a loud *crack!* The three cringed and really began to fidget as a voice yelled out, "You there. Stay where you are!"

"Oh geez!" John apologized as the five members of the patrol ran toward their position.

Still whispering, Sid ordered, "Three, two, one, *fire!*"

The members of the Royal Provincial patrol ran right up to the reclined group and their readied rifles. They were dead seconds later. The shots rang out like a siren through the landscape, and the boys jumped up, grabbed their spent cartridges in the early morning light, and converged on their victims. Six total shots were fired at point-blank range; all center mass wounds and a certain instant final result. No suffering, no sounds (except for the shots themselves), and minimum pain—the mercy of the quick kill. The boys briefly waited and listened for any sounds through the woods.

During this time, Nik made sure nothing was left behind at their small encampment, and John checked the soldiers for respiration and heartbeats. None were found.

"We go east. Right now, let's move!" insisted Nik. They all agreed and quickly left the area headed east. After several minutes, they jumped into a dry ravine that ran roughly north-south. There, they waited for some time to listen for anything out of the ordinary. The silence persisted, and the group required their next move. Usually they all would have a fairly good sense about which way they should go, but with all the crazy, hurried actions of the past hour, they wanted a quick response. Sid and John, possessing a weird faith that Nik usually had their course plotted days in advance, looked at Nik for direction now.

"Well," Nik began, "north from here. Let's set up two more stations—one north and a little east and one north and a tinge west, closer to the actual plantation boundary."

Pleased for the course plotted by Nik on the fly, the group started up the ravine to the north, looking and listening for any dangers or obstacles in their way.

The British would probably soon discover their delayed patrol, as several groups of dispatched soldiers littered the woods to the boys' south and west. Sid had briefly inspected the bodies of the deceased soldiers after each engagement and was sure the projectiles from their rifles had easily passed through them. He believed they would not be found. Nik expected more patrols and wanted to be ready for them this time. With the surprise of the morning's events, none of the boys wanted a repeat of any one of them.

The group arrived at a very defendable spot, probably more north than they were figuring. It reminded Nik of the trenches that he had read about outside of Richmond during the Civil War or those used in World War I. The area consisted of a series of much deeper ravines running in all directions; Sid didn't like the irregular nature of them, but they were deep and wide, making them very easy to move within. They would provide for a quick change in position if need be.

After they set up and familiarized themselves with these ramparts, the group moved to the west toward Crowell's plantation. It was now early afternoon, and the boys verified their uniform and load outs. They had full rifles and full clips at the ready. As they approached the woods' edge, Sid and John lay on the ground and crawled up to witness the grand view of the lead expeditionary units of Cornwallis's southern army moving out of the southern perimeter of the plantation. Coupled with this scene, they could see some people of the plantation fleeing to the northwest as the British approached. Nik hung back a bit, kneeling down watching their flank.

"Wow!" exclaimed John. "Look at all those guys!"

"That's an army for sure," admitted Sid.

Nik looked briefly. "We don't want to engage that, and that's not a tenth of them," he said.

John smartly and quietly pointed out, "We'd wipe that army out!"

Sid nodded. "He's right."

Nik now looked quite perturbed. "I know! We are not here to wipe out the southern army under Lord Cornwallis!" After he began, he quickly calmed his tone. "I'm not angry; I'm just saying."

"Well, what the hell are we here for then?" John continued.

Sid, now stepping in, sounded a little concerned. "Let's head back to the ramparts. C'mon ... *c'mon!*"

They got back to the series of ravines and set up a central place where they could look down in as many directions as possible. As they worked, they tried to change the subject and forget the slightly ill mood back on the plantation boundary.

Nik sat down on a rock and began to ponder aloud. "I would almost expect another patrol today or tonight. We need to be ready for it, and I suspect there will be more troops."

John asked, "Should we move farther north and east?"

"We could, but we want to 'nudge' them, don't we?" asked Sid.

There was yet another familiar silence and then Nik spoke up. "Yes, we want to nudge them out of here."

"What time do you think the next patrol will be sent out?" asked John.

Sid figured on another early-morning patrol at first light, much like the one that they'd experienced that morning.

"Possibly a midmorning patrol to cover tomorrow's midday pullout from this area?" theorized John.

"A night patrol or offensive is completely unheard of in these times, so we should be good until first light," offered Sid.

Camp set up for the rest of that evening and night was much like the night before, except they would be pointing in three complementary directions with Nik facing roughly south, Sid pointing southeast, and John southwest. They were resting quietly and hoped they would finally manage a full night's sleep. The night was totally dark without any light from the moon providing a comfort to the boys in the fact that there was no one creeping around or patrolling in the darkness. This, their position and location, in the modern era might be considered a huge mistake, but in 1781, it was a pretty safe bet.

The sleep that night couldn't have been more comfortable, because the weather was cooler and much dryer than normal. The temperature was a huge facilitator for the low insect count, which made it an even better situation for the guys. They had gone off to sleep fairly quickly after dark and were well concealed in the cover of the native brambles. At around 1:25 a.m., a fairly loud clamoring arose to the south. The noise sounded like a gaggle of conversation and the rustling of trees and brush. Still a ways off, the group awoke and positioned themselves against a south-facing rampart (side of a ravine running east-west) and waited for whatever was creating the disturbance.

"Can't be the British—they don't fight at night, right?" John said with a slight questioning sarcasm.

Sid looked at him in the dimness of the evening and responded smartly, "Umm, that's right. Folks didn't fight battles at night in 1781 … very often."

Nik chuckled, "Oy, the qualifier—that makes me nervous. I hate when he does that."

John quickly piped in again. "Well, I'm not laughing! What the—" At that moment, a most unnatural sound began to manifest itself in the dark. The boys now gripped their rifles, released the safeties, and ducked closer to the cover of the bank of the ravine. The sound now evolved into a serenade of hissing, and then an even more unlikely thing occurred.

The boys stood witness to four distinct streams of light climbing into the heavens like threads of lightning, but in reverse. "Flares!" blurted John in an exuberant whisper. "No way! Flares? It can't be!"

There was a long a pause as the boys watched in awe. "Look at the color; look at the burn time and the brightness—no way!" mumbled Sid.

"What in the hell are you talking about, Sid?" John asked, now sounding somewhere between concerned and pissed.

"I have read about these flares before!" snapped Sid.

"Flares? Really? In this time?" John quietly blurted out again. "There are no flares in 1781!"

"No, really. I read about these things in the encyclopedia of the Soviet Navy! In the late 1950s, early 1960s, the Russians developed these really great flares for lighting up battlefields, and they were just awesome! A particular color, hugely long burn times, and the most annoying noise you could imagine."

"Color?" Nik repeated.

"Annoying noise?" John added.

"Yes!" Sid exclaimed as he pointed to the streams of light. "That color … and that noise! They actually stopped using them around land, because they tended to come down burning and usually set everything around them on fire."

"Are you telling me those are Russian flares from the Cold War years?" Nik asked incredulously.

"No," said Sid. "Soviet, and they look and sound just like the flares I was talking about from the Cold War years."

Nik not-so-casually requested the boys to check their clips and get ready. Sid had his M1A, and Nik and John each had their AR-15s. They all had at least four thirty-round clips at the ready. They had just completed the brief task of verifying their ammunition when John asked, "Get ready for what?"

The moment of a simple question yielded a flurry of musket fire ... pointed in their direction! A simultaneous gasp came from the group. The boys now counted seven groups of targets, presumably British regulars, Tories, and others loyal to the crown. They had to think through their immediate plan, and fast, as they ducked behind the embankment, letting the first volley fly by.

"Are they kidding?" Nik exclaimed.

Sid, now assessing the tactical situation, recommended that the groups on either side of them needed to be dealt with first. He then added that he could see four or five groups on their wings that had a better angle on them and were, in fact, firing on their position already. Nik quickly looked and observed two groups of nine or ten men on John's right and two groups of around ten men on Sid's left.

"Any ideas, guys?" John requested.

Sid looked at John and Nik for some agreement with his recommendation to engage the enemy forces on either sides of them. He got it.

"Kill the wings!" Nik ordered.

Gunfire erupted as the second volley of enemy fire came in. They were really in no danger, as it appeared to be a sort of blanket fire with very little direction. John expended the first thirty-round magazines into the right side of the British offensive line and quickly reloaded. Nik assisted for the moment on the right side by covering and clearing out any remaining targets that had eluded John's initial assault. Simultaneously, Sid positioned himself on and almost in the embankment; he aimed left and slightly forward, which allowed him to begin picking off the targets as they came into view. The right side of the offensive now fell quiet, either by the required reloading or dead offenders; they couldn't tell. Nik then pivoted over to the left side, while John watched the right and forward positions.

"Right and forward clear," John reported as the left wing now continued to be dispatched by Sid and Nik.

As a stereo yields a beautiful sound all around you in a concert hall, silence fell to the left and right of the now very smoky battlefield. "Reload!" Sid quietly commanded in a reminder to the group. Nik and John responded with a simple "check." Now quiet, they waited for a short time and looked forward, the light from the flares still illuminating the area and beginning their decent.

"Should we move down the ravine?" Sid wondered aloud.

"Damn risky; all I know is we need to scurry north as quickly as we can after this. These folks are *not* going to be happy with us after all this for sure," Nik remarked.

"Where the hell did they get flares? What about the night fighting tactics? Where did they get that bright idea?" exclaimed John, almost demanding and answer.

"Piss-poor attack, if you ask me," Sid coldly and sternly commented. "They have never done this before, that fact is crystal clear based on the results. A group of sixth graders could have coordinated a better attack in 2010; it's really sad, actually, that these guys had to walk into that slaughter like that—dumb, very dumb."

"We stay here for the moment," Nik suggested. "We have no idea what's out there, although we are probably clear to the north." Just then, a third volley of fire screamed out from the enemy forward position over their heads.

"Let's end this now and be on our way," Sid instructed. They all agreed, and as soon as the bulk of the musket fire subsided, they opened up with all rifles to bear to the south. Nik expended his rounds first and reloaded, looking at the field from left to right. As the others completed the blanketing of the area with their rifle spray, the flares were about past their prime and were now dropping into the trees. With only a moment of light left, Nik caught a shadow of a figure. It was large and moving quickly, as Sid and John quickly picked up the brass from the night's altercations.

Instantly and singularly, Nik's world grew stone still and more quiet than the vacuum of space itself. From the silence of the void in his mind, he heard a voice from what seemed to be a million miles away gently and tenderly requesting of him, *"Flee now ... flee now, brother!"*

"What?" Nik blurted with a jolt, quickly looking around and immediately proclaiming. "We leave now, quickly. Let's move!" In a flash, the boys were escaping north along the ravines on a route they had charted the previous day.

"What did you see, Nik?" Sid asked.

"Not sure! The time ... the light ... is gone? *The light?* It ... it just felt like the time to go."

"Good enough for me," added John. "How many do you think we killed?"

A silence (with heavy breathing from the extended running) transcended the night. At one point, they stopped where their reconnaissance ended, about a mile or so north from where they had been camped. "We killed them all," Sid coldly proclaimed with an edge that was now becoming a very integral sound for him.

They stayed for a bit in a giant grove of trees; it was unnaturally peaceful with a cool breeze and a hint of an oddly familiar smell—a sweet smell that was only there for a moment. *Roses?* Nik thought to himself.

In the distance, a glow could be seen, and soon the smell of burning timber filled the air. "Damn Soviet flares!" John mumbled.

"That is impossible, man. It has to be some kind of unbelievable coincidence," Nik interjected.

Sid, now looking intently at the growing glow on the horizon, asked Nik, "What did you see back there?"

They sat and listened for a long time for any indication of a chase. Nik quietly commented, "We didn't get them all. I saw at least one bogey moving in all the commotion. He looked like a big bastard too, but that could have simply been the reflection of falling flares behind him."

"What was that smell? Did you smell it?" Nik asked the others.

"Yeah, its called burning forest," answered John.

"No, not that smell.... It's ... it's gone now," Nik said, stumbling over his words. "I swear ... I swear I smelled ... a sweet smell ... a familiar smell from my childhood ... and roses. I smelled roses! Before all the wildfire smoke got here, I smelled a very familiar smell from long ago and roses."

Sid changed the subject. "That fire is going to burn up all those guys we dropped; a funeral pyre is what it's turned into."

The thought of all this brought the group's morale down a bit—well, more than a bit. They were annoyed at the *need* to fire on the British. They certainly didn't want to kill so many, they certainly couldn't have given themselves up in the situation they were in, and they certainly couldn't turn their backs on all that had transpired since their transport and arrival into this era.

"We are in it for sure now," John murmured. "We have done some serious damage. It's not like what just happened occurred in 1781. We just knocked down a whole pile of guys, who ... who are feared above no other on this continent."

"True," said Sid. "Let's move on."

They moved steadily the entire next day and made good progress to the north. They did have some trouble navigating what would later be named the Tar River and were not sure why they had so much trouble crossing; it just wasn't a good day for them and water.

"I am a hunter, not a damn mariner!" John protested in a familiar tone from a popular character in a sixties TV show. This wasn't really true, however; they had done very well with crossings before this. The boys may have been very tired, is all.

Nik had remembered that Halifax was the next town where the British would skirmish with American forces, so they decided to settle a bit out of the way at a burned-out building close to a pond near what Nik and John thought was, or would be, the general vicinity of Enfield, North Carolina. They honestly weren't sure exactly where they were, but it was a quiet and desolate location, so they stayed for the evening.

They rummaged around to entertain themselves, and Nik, once again, stumbled across some old, "new" Colonial coinage. He purloined them from the floor of the charcoaled corner of the main structure; there were several more of the silver-dollar-sized coins with the 1776 mint marks on them and also in fairly nice condition. Sid and John couldn't believe it.

"You are drawn to these things, aren't you?" blurted John.

Sid added, "He always found coins everywhere we would go; it's the weirdest thing! Really, we'd be walking into a restaurant, and he'd look down to see an Eisenhower dollar sitting on the ground. We'd go to the range, and he'd find, in the tall grass, quarters and those crazy little quarter-sized dollar coins just lying there. It's just nuts!"

They laughed and cooked up some things John had hunted; it was a good "meat" night. Nik commented, "You know, I'm not sure what this is, but it's good!" Sid agreed and gave his compliments to the hunter and chef.

The evening's conversation turned to where they were going and what had transpired the previous day. "I think we really pissed somebody off," Sid said. "Those kinds of losses have to be frustrating for the old boy—General Cornwallis, I mean."

"If he even cares about his losses," remarked John sharply. "What about the whole flare and night-attack thing? Aren't we worried about that?"

Nik had been thinking about these things and simply had no answers. "It's strange, all right; maybe in this time line they developed something like a musket-launched flare or something such as that?"

"Not a chance," blurted Sid. "There is something else going on. Those were not items of this time, and those guys who attacked us last night, the British, they were not night fighters. It's like they ran into the woods after us with no idea what they were doing, and we cut them down as if they were children. I believe they were utterly baffled."

"Could it have just been our weapon superiority?" John asked.

Nik stood up. "Maybe," he interjected, "but they were clueless out there. They didn't stand a chance, and we ripped them to shreds…. They didn't stand a chance." He ended with a sad note, his voice trailing off.

Sid was now performing a quick field cleaning on the rifles; he wanted to keep them in top form if he could. They had expended sixty-eight .223 rounds out of their AR-15s and twenty-four rounds out of the M1A. They had successfully collected all but one of the .223 shells, as they were in a hurry leaving the scene.

"It shouldn't be a big deal. If someone finds it, they will be curious, and nothing will come of it. Maybe it even burned up in the fire," said Sid, trying to downplay their concern.

"At this point, what would someone of this time say other than, 'What the blimey is this?'" Nik added in his best British voice.

They quietly chuckled for the first time in many days. Things had been too serious, and they needed things to slow down a bit. These guys were not used to getting shot at, and the fact that they had really been "engaged" now for several days running required a much-needed time to disengage and calm their nerves down.

That night wound down with a small fire and small talk, and when night fell, they went to sleep without issue. Even though it stayed quiet that night, each one woke up several times during the night, Sid most of all. He spent extended periods of time just sitting against the most intact wall of the abode, looking around and listening—mostly listening. The sounds of nature had increased, with the evening bug population coming out to do whatever bugs do at night. Make noise mostly, Sid figured. The bug sounds made it hard to listen for any near or distant sounds that might inform them of an approaching soul or animal. He managed to fall asleep around one thirty in the morning.

The morning brought warm, muggy air and dampness on just about everything. They had scanned around a bit and found several paths off to the north of their location. It was May 9, 1781, and the boys knew Cornwallis would be moving into Virginia on May 11. They had done their part for the Colonial forces of their young nation and felt they needed to back off just a bit.

"So much for a nudge," exclaimed John. "We about kicked them in the side ten or twelve times."

"I am sure the action didn't go unnoticed by the British leadership, but they were headed in a particular direction for a reason, and they probably aren't going to stop," Sid surmised aloud.

"Yeah, what happened two nights ago was their attempt at a reaction. I would be pissed at the outcome if I were them!" Nik added. "The Americans and the British will fight several more times in the next few days leading up to the eleventh—all small clashes compared to some of the battles we've seen. We should stay back to the south or off to the east and chill a bit."

Numerous plans and tactics were discussed through the morning, and the boys agreed they'd tack back and forth to the south and behind the forward-marching British Army, just to observe their progression north to Virginia and Yorktown.

"I'd sure like to take pause here and look around a bit. I would love to know what we were dealing with the other night," Sid requested.

John looked at him with a contorted face. "You mean go back there? And look at the results of our battle the other night?"

"No, not exactly. I just want us to pause for a day—get our bearings and see what might pop its head out of the woods," Sid replied.

Nik, who was now interested, asked, "What are you thinking?"

Sid shook his head. "I don't know … just a feeling. Besides, the British could use a day off from us. We can't have them arriving at Yorktown without any troops, right?" They all chuckled and shook their heads.

"Who would ever believe this?" John murmured.

They didn't go back to the previous night's battleground, but they did circle around the pond and abandoned building, making sure not to be anywhere near them during the daylight hours. They searched the woods and edges of the fields for whatever they could see in the area, but nothing of interest was found. They did, however, find a shade-laden pine forest where they sat down during the heat of midafternoon. They arranged themselves again as they often did, each person leaning against a chosen tree, taking up a side, and looking away from each other. They actively scanned the 120 degrees in front of them, making sure nothing walked up on them or surprised them. During this kind of routine walk and survey, they had the burlaps and woods in place, so as to not look too out of place on the off chance that someone were to see them.

"Well, the shade is nice," commented Nik as they actively scanned near and far in their respective directions.

"Yes it is," John replied. They sat there for hours as the breeze kicked up a bit; they simply sat, talked, and enjoyed the day.

It was their first down day in a long time, and they needed it. They discussed the skirmishes they'd had and were happy for saving Mr. Quinten and pushing on the British a bit. The night battle with the flares and all the dead British still worried the group. They just couldn't get over it, and they couldn't figure out what exactly happened and how the invention of the flare had gone unnoticed in history. The idea of flares in 1781—it just didn't add up!

"Something still doesn't make sense, and we may never have the answer," Sid said, giving up on the whole thing. "Forget it; let's not worry about it."

It was now sundown, and they carefully and quietly returned to the pond and damaged building. It had clouded over and looked to be threatening rain.

The boys were seeking a little shelter on this night and were able to climb up to a second-floor perch of the wrecked building. It was a great lookout and a decent place to sleep for the night. Best of all, it had an intact roof. In contrast to the previous evening, everything this evening was quiet through the entire night; it was utterly silent—not a creature was stirring, not even a mouse. It felt a little unnatural to the group, but as they were very quiet, they could hear anything going on around them. They were surprised they couldn't hear any residual sounds from the northward movement of the British army.

"They must have slid east out of our way." Nik thought out loud.

"Good riddance!" John applauded.

The boys settled in quickly for a good, long, uninterrupted night of deep and restful sleep.

... 37 ...

Another Uncommon Occurrence

JULY 13, 1781. THE boys had moved up the coastal plain (well, the east side of North Carolina into Virginia anyway) with ease, shadowing behind the British army all the way. They kept out of sight, and Sid proclaimed, "We are back to our old form! Quiet to all! Light on the land! Ghosts to the whole! Yes, sir!"

"Now, now, let's not get too full of ourselves!" Nik warned, as he had so often in the previous months.

"Yes, yes, I know!" snapped Sid. "I know."

John approbated with, "Did you consider the Rocky Mount happenings as 'quiet to all, light on the land, and ghosts to the whole'? Really?"

Sid replied, "Well, after all that." He couldn't help but smile.

The guys had become so good at spotting the trailing components of Cornwallis's army in the past few weeks moving north that they were able to basically pause and enjoy a time of rest every other day and then move on with a relatively light march the next day to catch up. The boys learned, studied, and became accustomed to the habits and the daily activities of the British southern force in, what seemed to be, perpetual motion up into Virginia from North Carolina.

On the morning move-out of the mass of humanity that was the British southern army, the morning of the fourteenth brought a peculiar difference from the general happenings of the past

---

month, as a small group from the main body remained behind. The boys had witnessed the typical northward exodus of the whole of Cornwallis's army and almost missed the trailing force, which was basically camped out of sight and quite a bit toward the rear of the original encampment. They waited for this force to break camp and proceed with the rest of the British troops, but this didn't come to pass. Sid, Nik, and John waited for several hours and began to think there wasn't anybody at the encampment.

The three, now lying down under some bushes with a small rock face to their right, peered down into the encampment. An hour after getting settled into their observation position, out of one of the three tents came a sight they wouldn't have imagined seeing in another hundred years—or ever! Moving about the encampment roved a large-statured man with huge hands, huge feet, giant arms, and an almost grotesque head and facial features.

John gasped. "Dude! That's … that's … one of those giant mountain men bastards!"

Sid leaned over to get closer look. "Oh my … look what we have here."

Nik peered through the binoculars and noted movement in one of the other tents. The third tent appeared empty, but they couldn't be sure from their vantage point.

Minutes later, a second giant individual showed himself as he emerged from the same tent as the first man and then proceeded to enter into the apparently empty tent. They listened as best they could as the second man, half in and half out of the third tent, began yelling something.

"That damn foreign language again. I can almost recognize it, but …" Nik trailed off.

Sid kept quiet through all of this and was looking at the tactical position they were in. John posed the question, "Do you think all four of those barbarians are down there?"

"That's a good question, John," Sid responded. "Not sure." Sid continued to look at the whole encampment, while Nik scanned the zoomed-in view through the binoculars. Thirty-five or forty minutes went by with little change, and an hour later, all four mountain men were full view, talking among themselves. The final two had come from the second tent on the left side of the camp; the mysterious third tent hadn't yet produced anyone.

It was almost sundown now, and the boys had no idea what they were going to do with this group. They knew what they had witnessed on that mountain trail those many months ago when they worked that family over. Then there was the sighting at the battle at Cowpens and finally in their home sector at their mountain hideaway near C-10.

"These guys inspected what we had done to the British left flank at Cowpens! They knew we were there and just about pointed us out—well, our position anyway. They followed us back to C-10!" John reported. They all knew these facts, of course, but failed to understand who or what these guys were or represented.

"Let's wait through the night and see what they do in the morning. They may move on after tonight," Sid suggested. He then turned to Nik, who had spent quite along time looking at the men through the binoculars. "What are they wearing, Nik?" he asked.

Nik shrugged his shoulders. "Typical stuff—brown, rugged cloth clothes; a little green underneath, like a T-shirt or something."

"John, you looked through the binoculars. Did you see anything out of the ordinary?" asked Sid again.

"No. SSDD," replied John.

"What are you getting at, Sid?" Nik inquired.

"Nothing, really. I was just wondering if anything jumped out at you," Sid continued.

The boys camped down that night, back and away from the ledge where they were spying on the mountain men. It wasn't long after dark when a loud wailing began from the encampment, specifically the third tent. It sounded as though someone or something was being beaten, tortured, and/or murdered down there. The screams filled the night and continued for what seemed to them like an eternity as the boys, now wide awake, were trying to see anything they could. They spent most of the night working to figure out what exactly was transpiring in that third tent. There was light in it, and the shadow of a figure could clearly be seen. The figure was on his knees and was being whipped and kicked, or something such as that. The prisoner, for lack of a better term, appeared to be a male, and his voice sounded almost like he was speaking French, in a way, but it was English. He was barely audible from their vantage point. The mountain men were now speaking English, and it was a travesty at that.

"Dammit! I know that sound! That sound! It is so familiar to me; I hate it!" Nik complained to himself for his inability to identify the sound of the language or dialect.

"They are kicking the tar out of that guy," John lobbied.

Sid, knowing what John wanted, quickly interjected. "We cannot go down there tonight! Not in the dark! An unplanned assault at night on these four guys is not in the cards. There is just no way!" Nik agreed. Unless they had a clear, illuminated set of targets to shoot at, there was no way they could engage them.

"I guess a ground commando-type assault would be out, huh?" John asked again. Nik and Sid just looked at John like he was crazy.

"Did you see how those guys manhandled that family, especially the guy on the mountain pass? I am not in any kind of shape to wrestle that behemoth, are you? Not to mention the fact that there are four of them!" Nik insisted.

John shrugged. "I know."

Sid wanted to immediately end this line of conversation. "Shh, quiet down! If he survives the night, we'll do something tomorrow. Okay?" They all agreed, and the beating continued.

The wailing turned into cries and weeping; they all lay in expectant silence, waiting for the morning, finally getting a little sleep after the noise died down from the camp. It was well past midnight before the torture had ceased for the night, and they fell asleep. Needless to say, it was a long night for all involved.

It seemed like the world was ahead of time that morning as the boys were up and battle-ready at the first hint of the dim morning light. They were in full camouflage, faces painted, no burlaps or woods, with the full expectation of a rumble in the woods. They assumed a prone position along the small ridge they had been using as a listening platform the day before and lined up to wait for their targets and the opportunity to act upon them. They were close enough to each other to hear a whisper of conversation or instruction but far enough apart not to be bunched up and easy to target from below.

The encampment stayed quiet for about an hour, and then a rustle began from the third tent. The occupant appeared to be trying to slip or scoot out of the back of the tent. He appeared to be tied and bound, and anywhere the man's body touched the tent, a streak of redish-yellow soon followed. He wasn't being very quiet, and the boys were wincing for him with his every movement, hoping he would try to be a little quieter in his attempted escape. No luck—he was heard.

"Release safeties!" whispered Nik.

One of the four burly figures had just walked out of the first tent and had a clear view into the now partially occupied third tent. A bold and loud scream could be heard. "Эй, он пытается бежать! [Hey, he is trying to escape!]" one of the mountain men yelled.

"Что! Что! Взять его! [What? What? Get him!]" a second man demanded.

"Here we go. Terminate the first three, and kneecap the last one to keep him from running away from this!" ordered Nik. "We'd like a few words with our mountain man friend."

One was already out ... two ... three little mountain men out of their tents and in the open. "*Go!*" Nik yelled, and the barrage began.

John started off with three quick rounds into number one's chest. Sid and Nik dispatched number two and three in similar fashion.

Sid quickly asked, "Me on four, three ... two ... one!" This was Sid requesting the last of their victims.

Nik and John knew Sid was the best shot of the three of them, and he had the weapon with the bigger round; they simply confirmed his request by each giving a "go."

As soon as the fourth man came out to see his three mortally wounded comrades and their open chest cavities lying on the ground, two M1A shots rang out. And when they did, he looked up and got a visual of the boys on the ridge. The two rounds hit the fourth mountain man, one in each knee—two perfect shots!

"Bingo! Tangos down!" yelled Sid. "That's the way to do it! Damn, are we good!"

At this point, the prisoner from the third tent was mostly out of the back of the tent, spattered in the blood of the first mountain man and screaming to God to help him and save him from the firestorm, which, in his words, "was engulfing this earth."

"Let's go. Keep your weapons drawn!" Sid commanded.

John had already spied a path down to the encampment and was leading the way. Sid was next, and Nik was third. Nik stopped and looked back halfway down the hill; he couldn't believe they were performing another rescue. They arrived on the scene, and Sid poked the downed bodies of targets one, two, and three. He then quickly moved over to the wounded mountain man and gave him a swift kick to the face.

John went over to the prisoner, cut him from his binds, and tried to calm him down. "We are friends. Do you speak English? You are hurt; we can help you."

Nik quickly inspected the three downed men and checked to see if they had died from their wounds. "These guys are finished," he muttered. He then went to inspect the third tent. "Holy—!" he gasped. "It's like a regular medieval torture chamber in here. Good God!"

The freed prisoner was now a bit calmer, seeing three of his previous captors dead on the ground and the fourth screaming at the top of his lungs. Sid was not helping the matter as he continued to taunt and poke the now heavily bleeding mountain man. Nik looked at the fourth man, who was clearly in pain. He was fighting against Sid as he bound the man's hands with the bloody wraps that had held the prisoner from the third tent only minutes before.

Nik sat down and muttered to the man, "How do you like it?"

The man went into a rage, and Sid hit him again. "Calm down! Without us, you're dead!" Sid yelled.

The mountain man, now bound and struggling, was cursing (they thought); spit flew out of his mouth, sweat poured down his face, and his rant would have terrified a saint.

"Pig American!" he screamed.

"Well, well, now that sounds vaguely familiar," Sid questioned with a smile.

The man was now bound to a small stump and was bleeding out of both knees. "You *die!*" he continued to scream.

Nik suddenly looked at Sid. "Dude, you are not going to believe this.... I know that sound now!" Nik immediately stood up and walked into the first tent.

"Gentleman, you are not going to believe this! Not in a million years!" Nik shouted from the tent.

John had moved the French-sounding African man to a makeshift table and was cleaning the wounds on his back, arms, and legs. "I am going to need at least two-thirds of our antibiotic cream for him. He is thrashed," John proclaimed.

Nik exited the tent with a pistol in one hand and a uniform in the other.

"A pistol!" John yelled as Sid moved over to look at the booty.

Nik handed the unloaded firearm over to Sid. "Do you recognize this?" he asked.

"I don't believe it!" Sid began. "You are not going to believe this when I tell you!"

John said quickly, "Try me!"

Sid's face was priceless, and the bound prisoner began to struggle. Sid viciously kicked him again and stated, "This is an old Makarov pistol, circa 1958–59 to 1965, Soviet/Russian Special Forces edition."

Nik bent over the man on the ground, screamed at him, and held the uniform with the red-and-yellow hammer-and-sickle patch to his face. "That's right, *comrade* ... Soviet! ... And who are you, *Ivan*? Who are you, and what the hell are you doing here? We know it isn't something that we would consider helpful and constructive for sure!" Nik was now bellowing in a growing rage.

Sid, who was actually calmer than Nik, looked down to make sure the bindings were holding on their Soviet prisoner. Nik, basically out of control with anger and rage, yelled loudly and asked Sid, "You okay to watch this piece of trash?"

Sid responded, "Yeah, no problem. With pleasure."

Nik looked down at the Soviet soldier. "If he so much as flinches, shoot him!" he ordered Sid.

Nik wiped all the sweat off of his head and face as he tried to calm down. He then joined John and asked if their patient was okay.

"We are going to need to use a lot of our medical stuff on him; otherwise, infection will kill him inside of a month," John reported. Nik was completely opposed to that idea; he glanced at their patient and froze.

"Nik?" John said. "Hey, man, you okay?" When he couldn't get Nik to snap out of his daze, John turned to Sid. "Yo," he called out. "Yo, Sid!"

Sid had become sick of listening to the Soviet prisoner struggle and moan, so he gagged his mouth tightly and moved over to see what Nik's problem was. "Dude, what's wrong?" Sid snapped his fingers in front of Nik's eyes to try to get his attention.

Nik gasped and looked up at his friends. "This just gets stranger and stranger." His face was as white as a sheet, and his mouth drooped open.

The French-sounding African man even asked weakly, "Is ... is your friend okay?"

Nik looked up at John and Sid. "What's the date? The date? John, what is the date?" he asked quickly.

John checked his watch, which was buried deep in a pocket. "Umm, July 15."

Nik sat down on a nearby stump and shook his head. "Just crazier and crazier." He paused and then stated, "Okay, whatever it takes. We have to get Mr. Armistead here back up and into action."

A sudden period of silent and total surprise bubbled from the group. "You know this guy?" Sid blurted out in a hugely surprised voice.

John followed up with, "C'mon, man, you can't possibly—"

Their battered patient interrupted. "Sir, we ... we have never met before.... Sirs, respectfully ... I would have certainly remembered ones such as you, yourselves."

Nik stood up again. "Oh my God! It all makes some sense now! The mountain men, the flares, the British trying to fight at night, the odd, subtle changes in history where if—" Suddenly Nik paused and got choked up for a minute before continuing. "If we didn't 'aid the cause,' all of what was would have changed forever!"

There was another long pause now as Nik swallowed and tried to catch his breath, his mind running a mile a minute. After a few moments, having collected his breath and emotions, Nik cleared his throat and began. "This ... is Mr. James Armistead! He is an African American hero of the American Revolution! Well, he will be anyway ... if we can keep him alive. He is an American or French—I'm not exactly sure—double agent who delivers the news on or about August 25 that Cornwallis is building up a force at York, Virginia. We know it as Yorktown.

"That's why they were here!" Nik pointed to the Soviet special operations corpses. "They were here on some nefarious mission to stop us! To stop *us*, the *United States* from becoming the United States! Holy—"

"How did *they* get here? ... Umm, how did *we* get here?" John muttered.

"Sir, it is imperative we get you well and feeling better and on your way to deliver your information. It is *imperative*," Nik emphasized.

Mr. Armistead's mouth was hanging wide open now, and he began to speak, "How do you know all this? How do you know who I am? How—"

Nik tried to be calm and reassuring. "Sir, we are your friends, and we are most certainly friends of the Revolution and liberty. I can't tell you much more than that, but I can tell you that your information is vital to General Washington, and he needs it as quickly as possible."

Mr. Armistead, still confused, continued muttering. Then Nik continued. "Sir, I don't mean to rush you on this, but do you know where Marquis de Lafayette is? Do you have the information for him? If we can get you feeling better, can you get to Marquis de Lafayette?"

The battered man looked at the boys, and after a minute, answered, "Yes, I can do that. Yes.... Yes, I can do that."

"Guys, I am going to give my entire supply of antibiotic stuff, cream, or whatever to help Mr. Armistead with his wounds. It's up to you on yours," Nik said. "This is a huge piece of the puzzle. Oh man, I can't believe any of this! It just gets more and more complicated!"

The others agreed, and John and Nik went to work on fixing Mr. Armistead up. John also administered four ibuprofen tablets to Mr. Armistead to reduce the swelling; his patient was amazed with John's first aid knowledge, medicines, and techniques.

... 38 ...
Just a Good Soldier

As JOHN AND NIK worked on Mr. Armistead, Sid went over to Soviet special operations agent number four in an attempt to interrogate him. "So what's your deal, comrade? When are you from? Why are you here?" Sid kneeled down and looked at the bullet wounds he'd inflicted on his communist friend.

The Soviet soldier yelled something in Russian and ended his rant with "you capitalist pig!"

Sid sat back a bit from his adversary, chuckled, and stated, "Hmm, they taught you well, didn't they? Listen, comrade! I can take care of your wounds, or I can let them fester, and in a month or so, you'll die of an infection or something similarly as fun—your choice. Your buddies don't have to worry about any of that, of course."

Nik caught wind of the ensuing conversation and walked over to listen to the verbal exchange between Sid and the Soviet. The prisoner began to explain, "You killed my commander! You killed my comrades! You—"

"*Shut up!*" Sid screamed. "You are in *my* country on an apparent espionage mission! You are, *by your own actions*, at war with us. I am sorry, 'sir'! Your commander and *comrades* are casualties of *war*, a war that you and your country are clearly waging on *my* country!" Sid, angrier than the guys had ever seen him, pulled his .45 sidearm, chambered a round, and put it against the Soviet's right temple. At this, the Soviet soldier fixed his eyes on the "Thirteen to Nifty Fifty" flag patch on Sid's arm with a look of shock and disbelief. "You … you are from …" he stuttered.

"The future … like you." Nik interrupted.

"So, *when* exactly are you from, *comrade*?" continued Nik. Nik and Sid were now trying to pinpoint exactly what era the Soviet soldier was from, but it was clear the direct approach wasn't working.

Nik tainted his attack with some blatant antagonism. "So," he began as he rubbed his fists together, "your coward of a leader sent you losers into our past to do what? Mess up our beginnings? Our Revolution? What? Your disaster of a revolution in 1917 wasn't enough for your idiot premier to enslave his peoples, persecute your just religions, and murder some 40 million of your own country's men, women, and children? Is social justice and 'wealth for all' not going so well for you? You want to poison the rest of the world with your impotent stagnation of the 'collective' for 'the people'? *Please!* What a farce! Damn barbarians!"

This line of verbiage sent their prisoner into a rage; he was screaming again in Russian, spitting and thrashing.

"English! We speak English here in America!" Sid taunted.

The thrashing Soviet soldier screamed, "Premier Khrushchev is not a—what you call—a coward!"

"Ah, well, well, our old friend Premier Khrushchev. Now we are getting somewhere! He is a menace and a scourge! His rhetoric at the United Nations, 'We will bury you. We will bury you.' To hell with him!" Sid demonstrably exclaimed as he pulled his pistol away from his captive's head.

A pause in the action yielded the moment to Nik, who began to speak historically. "He's from about 1959–61."

With this, the Soviet soldier looked at the boys and said, "How do you know these things? Where are you from? How did you get here?"

John joined the questioning after he had finished with Mr. Armistead, who was now fixed up and resting on a makeshift table. John asked the Soviet soldier, "Why don't you tell us? When did you begin your mission?"

Silence fell on the scene again—a long silence. Sid quickly dressed the prisoner's gunshot wounds, because he now believed they were far worse than he'd previously thought. He then left the Soviet alone for a while.

Nik, Sid, and John gathered a small distance from their prisoner. "Well, we need to dispose of his buddies, and we'll need to get rid of him as well at some point," Sid began. "And ... he doesn't have long. Those wounds are pretty nasty."

"Agreed," Nik spoke up. "Let's get Mr. Armistead on his way to rendezvous with Lafayette first, and then we'll deal with our commie buddy." Nik then turned his attention to John. "Well, how does he look, John?"

"Good, considering the full-force beating he took last night and, from the looks of it, probably the previous few days before that. I used about half of our antibiotic cream on his wounds, and he'll heal well enough."

"Okay, good. What time is it, John?" asked Nik.

"It's 12:47 p.m." replied John.

"Okay, I am going to talk to Mr. Armistead. Sid, can you go watch our prisoner? John, could you please look around a bit—see if we are still alone. Make sure to look up on the ridge. We don't want to end up like our victims did today."

John nodded, and he was off intently patrolling.

Nik made his way over to the place where Mr. Armistead was resting. He didn't want to wake him up, so he just loitered near the battered man and waited for him to awaken. While he was waiting, Nik looked at his rifle and let his mind wander far into the future to a time when American forces are—or were or will be—fighting in the lands of the sand; those forces, dying for the United States in their war against a global menace. The very same United States that, Nik currently surmised, he and his friends could have very possibly been a key factor in the creation of. The guys would never think about taking any credit for the successful revolution against the British in this time and place, but Nik felt a certain real connection now to these events of 1780 and 1781.

A few hours later, Mr. Armistead arose from his short slumber and sat up, groaning a bit. He looked at Nik, who had been propped up against a stump, leaning on his rifle. Mr. Armistead was looking a lot better than he had just a few hours before, his eyes now clearing from the bloodshot terror of the previous night.

"You and ... your men ... I want to—" he began.

Nik raised his hand so as to politely cut him off. "These are not my men, sir. We are all friends caught in a great mystery of an accident born of a madman. Mr. Armistead, I need your help. This country needs your help. Your original mission ... we need you to complete it. You need to get the information you have to Marquis de Lafayette. It is imperative General Washington receive this information from him by sundown ten days from today."

They sat quietly for a bit, and then from the silence, the wounded man spoke. "Please, sir, call me James. You do not need to be so proper with one such as me."

"James. Nice," Nik sighed. "Well, James, I'm not sure what that exactly means, but know this—we are men, equal to the last fiber of our beings. And you are so much more important than I or our group will ever be in all of this. We need you—"

"I will go," he meekly interjected. "I will go to Lafayette. He is close.... Closer than you think you know. Come, we will go together. We will bring our information to him." Mr. Armistead insisted.

Nik slowly leaned back with this clear invitation to meet some of the most important historical figures of American history. He forced himself to suppress his excitement over the possibilities; they were certainly tempting and tantalizing, and very hard to resist.

"Oh, no ... no, sir.... Don't get me wrong; I would greatly appreciate meeting your compatriots, but it is not my place," Nik explained. *Or time,* he thought to himself. "This is something that we need you to do as you would without us or the knowledge of us."

Nik continued with the hardest of request now. "James, I need to ask you to do just one thing for me and our group. I ask you this with all of my soul." Mr. Armistead now looked very concerned and a little startled. "I need you—*we* need you to go ... go to Marquis de Lafayette and deliver your information. Complete your task as you would have and never speak of what happened here … with us, with your captors."

Mr. Armistead looked a little confused now and said, "I don't understand. You saved me. For this, I am ever indebted to you—"

Nik again gently interrupted him and lobbied, "We cannot be known in this time … *here*," he quickly corrected himself. "Please, will you do this for us?"

A small pause had Nik a bit on the run, thinking Mr. Armistead might actually tell someone about their group. "Please do not speak of us again, ever … ever again." With that, Nik held his hand out. Mr. Armistead, now with a quiver in his chin, a definite trembling of his hand, and a tear rolling down his cheek, extended his hand and strongly shook Nik's hand as he thanked him for what the boys had done. He walked out of the camp that day with a wave and a bow in John and Sid's directions en route to his destiny with history.

~~~~~

James Armistead, a Colonial double agent against the crown, delivered his information to the French and Americans on time and as history would record it. Lafayette's writings later noted these points of James Armistead: he delivered "intelligence from the enemy's camp" and he had performed an "essential service" deserved the "entitlement to every reward his situation can admit of." On January 9, 1787, James Armistead was emancipated, and in 1816 he became a landowner in Virginia where he lived and raised a family. In 1824, he met with Marquis de Lafayette for the last time, never mentioning the boys or the events that allowed him to perform his heroic duties. James Armistead, an enslaved black man in 1780, was truly one of the heroes in the American Revolution!

~~~~~

Nik returned to the others. "Is he going to be okay?" John inquired.

"Yes, he'll be fine; he knows where he's going better than we do, for sure," Nik responded. Nik then turned his attention to their prisoner. "He's looking a little pale, Sid."

Sid looked down. "He's lost a lot of blood, and he has some sort of chest thing going on. I don't think he'll last the night."

"What did we do with his buddies?" Nik inquired.

John answered, "I had dragged them down the hill." He pointed to the northeast. "They ought to be getting pretty ripe about now."

"Oy," Nik grunted as he sat down in front of their withering captive. "You know," Nik began, "you and your comrades would have killed us if you'd had the chance."

The dying soldier nodded. "Da, yes ... we would have."

Sid was now sitting down, and John was leaning against a nearby stump listening and wondering how all this would end. John's honest and sincere request of the prisoner for an explanation must have softened him. The Soviet began to speak freely. "You know, American, you want to hear something funny?"

The boys now all stared at their ever-weakening prisoner with some surprise. "My name, heh ... my ..." and he coughed a bit. "My name *is* Ivan." He began to laugh and cough in a rather laboring way. There was a shocked pause over the boys, and it showed in their faces. "It's okay; you can laugh too. It's funny, you know. You ... you,"—*cough*—"you Americans have no sense of humor, you know that?"

Nik chuckled; Sid and John began to laugh.

They sat in silence for a long time with the sun high in the sky overhead. Ivan coughed, and the boys watched his condition deteriorate in front of their eyes. Nik breached the silence once again and, stuttering a bit, asked Ivan, "So, you and your ... buddies ... what faith—"

Ivan interrupted Nik with a loud coughing, wheezy laugh. "Faith. Ha-ha-ha-ha. Those men you killed? Faith ... they were what you called us—uh, barbarians! Yes, barbarians—yes, yes, that is the word. Their faith was to 'the people, the state, the premier.' No God! No ... they were faithless." Ivan once again began wheezing and coughing.

Nik cringed, winced, and began to inquire. "How about you?" A long pause followed his question.

"I ... I," Ivan began to choke up as he answered. "My—umm, how do you say—parents. My parents and I ... we, we were all ... all, mmm крещеный—how do you say—baptized. Yes, that is it, in secret from ... from the state. You know, American, you know the state does not approve of the church. Did you know that?"

Nik nodded, shrugged, and sighed. "Yes ... I know." Nik now held his head in his hands as he looked at the ground.

Sid next asked the question he knew Nik didn't want to ask of Ivan. "So, are you a Christian?"

Ivan coughed and laughed. "You know ... you guys ... you are smart. Are all you Americans smart like you?" He coughed again.

John leaned forward and answered. "Damn right we are!"

Ivan laughed a huge belly laugh as he coughed and wheezed horribly. He continued with, "I am done here, you know.... You got me ... but it was good to be gotten by you. You make me laugh, you guys, you smart guys."

The boys looked at each other, now feeling really horrible about this particular outcome—Nik especially.

"You know," Ivan began again, "we left home in that foolish machine 426 days ago." A long pause now produced some emotion in Ivan. "I miss my дети—how do you say?" A single tear rolled down Ivan's right cheek. "My children, you know. Do you have children?" Ivan asked.

The boys nodded to confirm their families' existence.

Sid suddenly sprang to his feet. "You're kidding. You can't be serious!" he barked. "We appeared here about that many days ago!" Sid was now moving closer to Ivan. "What machine, Ivan? What are you talking about?"

Ivan now looked up at Sid half smiling and half frowning. "Great Soviet invention. Soviet scientists, they make a time-travel chamber. It killed a great many 'chronmonauts' before it appeared to work, and we stepped into it. We all had the same mission."

"Mission! What mission?" John sternly demanded.

"This man," Ivan said, pointing at Sid. "He was right, you know ... you smart guys, you smart Americans.... Or was it you?" Ivan looked confused now and pointed at Nik. "I forget ... you got it ... our mission was to interfere with the USA. Disrupt you, disrupt your history, stop you from becoming the USA. We were taught your history, you arrogant, capitalist dogs! Ha-ha-ha-ha, how stupid was that thinking."

Ivan began crying. "My детей, my children, how could I leave them for this? For what? Because you love freedom? Because you love this … this liberty? Because our beloved premier wants you dead!"

Ivan was now in a full, uncontrollable sob. "My детей [children], my beautiful жена [wife]!" Ivan cried for many minutes. The boys again felt absolute remorse, which was clear by the look on their faces.

After a time, Ivan recovered his composure. He struggled to get through a sentence without coughing now. "Listen, you guys … you're okay, you know. I don't blame you for this. I am sorry … great Soviet science took you from your—uh, how do you say—families. I hope you see them again … I will not see mine … and I will miss them."

There was more silence now.

Nik, now trying to manufacture some form of distance for Ivan from the espionage mission in his mind, asked the question, "Ivan," Nik winced his face again as he spoke, "did you guys, in any way, aid the British and Loyalist forces in the 429 days of your mission here—in this time?"

Ivan looked down with a drawn face. "Well, um, yes. You could say we aided them, in some ways."

John was unhappy with his answer and politely insisted, "What kind of aid did you give? Try to be specific, please?"

Ivan looked up at John. "You know … you guys, you guys shoot me, beat me. I will die here where I sit … and you ask me questions with 'please.' So strange.… You are good guys, you know."

Sid now chuckled and thought to himself, *I wouldn't have believed this if you showed me the video!* Ivan repositioned himself slightly and coughed again. "I will answer your questions, my friends. Yes, we aided your enemies. We gave them ideas about where they went wrong the first time they tried to defeat you in this day. We didn't exactly tell them like that, you know, but they understood."

Sid rubbed his chin as he thought about it all. "Oh my God—"

Ivan began again. "You know ... we knew about you guys after King-as Mountain ... well, we didn't know it was exactly you ... but we found the mass grave, you know.

"We knew our dragoon plan would be very effective, and when they came up dead in that mass grave, we knew something was very incorrect. We knew you were present and wanted to kill you. You made the others very mad. If we knew your location, they would have certainly attacked you; we looked for you for some time.

"You know, you guys ... there were some big holes in those men. What kind of gun did that?"

Sid rubbed his head and his chin again, as John held out the .50 caliber rifle Nik had brought along. Ivan looked at the hole at the end of the rifle barrel. "That is a big gun ... you know, you guys have nice guns.... What piece of the USA military are you assigned?"

Nik and John looked at Sid, and Sid looked around. "Why do you want *me* to answer that question?" he blurted.

Ivan looked perplexed. "Don't worry. The dead can tell no tales ... and soon, my friends ... soon."

"Well," Sid struggled, "we aren't with the military."

Ivan looked at the group in utter disbelief. He spoke again, coughing every time he paused. "Please, you need to—mmm, how do you say—stop trying to snow the snowman. Ha-ha-ha-ha. You guys ... Really, I promise ... I will tell no one on this Earth in the next ten hours, I promise."

John entered the conversation. "Really, we are all computer technicians and that sort of thing—no military experience, really."

"Look at you guys. You look like G.I. Joe.... Look at your guns ... you continue to snowing the snowman.

"You guys were at the Cowpens place, weren't you? ... What a strange name for a place?"

Sid nodded, and Ivan proclaimed, "I knew it. We tripled the sides of the lines, and they still fell on the left side! More big holes; you guys killed a lot of them, you know. You guys ... for you not being military, you sure do kill—hmm, effectively—you guys.... Yes, sir."

The boys let this go and hoped this part of the conversation would end.

"You … you Americans … you're okay. I am going to sleep now … don't worry for me."

Before the boys moved off to talk over what their next steps were going to be, John brought Ivan a blanket from tent number two and laid it over him. Sid cut the bindings off of Ivan's wrists, legs, and waist and gave him a drink of water and John gently inquired, "How did they plan for you to get home?" Ivan shook his head with a distraught face and shivered slightly. "No way. It was—hmm, how do you say, irreversible. Great Soviet science, it never really has concerns for recovery or the well-being of its subjects, no way back." He began to shiver again.

The boys moved off to the side of their resting, dying captive and began discussing upcoming events. They kept a watch on him, knowing he was in no shape to stand up and walk away on them now.

"How in the world did we get into all this again? I think 1781 could be even more screwed up than 2010!" John proclaimed.

"Your right, man. It's certainly spiraled in some crazy direction, hasn't it?" replied Nik.

"So, what do we do with them?" John asked, pointing over to where he had dragged the other three Soviet soldiers. "Ivan is dead tonight, and the other three—ugh, rigor mortis is certainly setting in by now. When I dragged them down the hill, I pulled them onto a huge pile of brush and downed trees."

Sid nodded and replied, "Good thinking, John!"

John then admitted, "Well, if you must know, the hillside and gravity really put them there. I was barely guiding them as their bodies fell and rolled to rest on that pile. They did all land together, though."

Nik patted him on the shoulder. "Not to sound communist or anything," he began, "but 'it's a means to an end.' In this case, we burn their bodies."

"What about Ivan?" John continued.

Nik now stared at Ivan. "We bury him; in a grave … face up."

Nik selected the site where they would bury Ivan; it would overlook the final fiery end of his comrades. He felt it would sort of be Ivan's justice over his faithless comrades. Additionally, they would lay Ivan to rest facing to the east-southeast, so he would always be facing the light. Sid walked over to where Ivan lay and sat down, since Ivan was now sleeping; it wouldn't be too long before he slipped away into eternity. Nik and John began to slowly and quietly dig Ivan's grave. Shortly, Sid returned and told Nik that he felt they should switch places for the end. Nik handed the little shovel over to Sid and asked John for his watch. He quietly moved over in front of Ivan; the night grew cool but without a wind.

Nik was now sure that Ivan was a Russian Orthodox Christian, whom they'd shot and mortally wounded and was now dying before his eyes.

Russia, Nik thought and shook his head.

~~~~~

Russia was the seat of the Eastern Orthodox Church for almost six hundred years until Communism reared its ugly head in the late 1910s. The earliest and first Christian Church was "the One, Holy, Catholic, and Apostolic Church," which Jesus Christ commissioned his twelve most trusted disciples to form (not to be confused with the Roman Catholic Church; this came *much* later and differed politically and spiritually from the then One Christian Church, which became the Eastern Orthodox Church after the Roman church split away in 1054 AD).

From roughly 33 AD on, followers of Jesus through his disciples formed the church through its liturgy, sacraments, creed, and faith. It was made whole in 325 AD at Nicea and in 381 AD at Constantinople. All but expelled out of their traditional lands and Constantinople in 1453 by the Ottoman Turks (Islam), many Orthodox Christians and their leaders fled to Russia where the oldest Christian religion lived on. Those liturgies, to this day (35, 325, 1781, 2010, or otherwise) survive and live on. On every corner of the globe the scriptures are presented as they were created in the days shortly after the Pentecost. *Every Divine Liturgy today* in the Orthodox Church puts you directly in front of God, in his house, in real time, as it was revealed and taught almost two thousand years ago; it is a living experience that breaches time itself!

~~~~~

Nik reflected on the temporal aspect of their situation and the realness of standing in an Orthodox Church and experiencing God's love and warmth; he now knew why he always got goose bumps and chills at church.

Nik rubbed his hands together tightly with remorse over this unfortunate situation. With the wounding of Ivan, they knew he would die, and there was nothing they could do about it. Nik thought about James as well and hoped his journey would proceed correctly and that he would successfully complete his mission in the weeks to come as history had recorded.

Then Nik's thoughts again returned to Ivan. He thought many things and whispered, "I'd like to tell you that the world is better in our time, but it's not. We could have been friends, you know, about thirty years after you left. Of course, you would have been old, and I would have been around twenty-eight."

Ivan remained quiet and still through all of this. With an abnormally cold gust of wind, a bright white shooting star streaked by in the late evening sky at 11:59 p.m. And with that, Ivan passed with a final deep breath and a shudder that took over his whole body.

Nik sat for a while with Ivan's body and eventually reached over to check for a heartbeat, his hand nervously shaking as it moved over Ivan's cooling neck. He waited again and then positioned the large man flat on his back and in the direction of his grave. He waited several more moments and then went to help dig the last of the grave with his closest friends in the world. *My only friends in the universe,* Nik thought coldly to himself.

"You all right, man?" asked Sid.

Nik looked up at Sid and John and shook his head. "It's much easier when they don't have names."

John nodded. "Amen to that."

3:35 a.m. saw the placement of Ivan's body into his grave. "You know, for the smallest of these guys, he still weighs a ton," proclaimed John as they wrapped Ivan's body with the cover they had given him from the second tent.

Nik placed one of each type of coin he had found into Ivan's pocket and removed any Soviet markings he had on him. "You're a child of God," Nik said. "You were when you were born, you were secretly through life, and you are on your passing into eternity."

The three friends moved his body into the grave, as Nik requested and stood above it, looking down at it by the dim but rising moonlight. Sid moved off to commence the pyre for the other three, and minutes later, they were ablaze. Nik began the burial with a few small shovels of dirt, and Sid and John slowly continued the work as Nik struggled to remember something from his past. His eyes welled over with emotion he began reciting a prayer he had heard a very long time ago:

"Christ our Lord, grant rest to Your servant Ivan among Your Saints, where there is no pain, sorrow, or suffering, but everlasting life.

"With the righteous who have reposed in Your peace, grant rest, Savior, to the soul of Your servant Ivan, and bestow upon him the blessed life which is from You, merciful Lord.

"Lord, remember Your servant, Ivan who has fallen asleep in the hope of the resurrection. Forgive him every transgression he has committed in thought, word, or deed. Grant him peace and refreshment in a place of light where Your glory delights all the Saints. For You are the resurrection, the repose, and the life of Your departed servant Ivan, and to You I give glory, now and forever, Amen."

Nik just stood still and silent by Ivan's grave for a time, and then in the fire's light, the three friends continued moving dirt into the grave atop Ivan's lifeless, lightly wrapped body. They finished burying Ivan as the pyre finally died down, leaving three dead Soviets reduced to ashes and a few small charred bits of bone. With the last shovel of dirt, the sun burst above the horizon in all of its grandness; it shone a single ray of light through the distant trees along the small valley to finally rest on the small stone Nik had placed on Ivan's grave site. The boys slowly backed away from the grave site and sat down to enjoy the sounds of an early summer morning in the woods of Virginia. It was July 16, 1781, and all was quiet and peaceful around them now.

Sid began by solemnly complimenting Nik on his remembering what he thought was a prayer. "That was nice, man. How did you remember that? You've never been able to memorize anything."

"I didn't," Nik explained. "I had heard it before, a very long time ago, and it simply came to me as I was speaking it."

A long moment passed, and Sid felt as if he had to do something, so he began breaking down their rifles for a quick cleaning. John and Nik sat and looked around. They had been up for a solid day, and they were all exhausted from the past few days. They looked around at their newly inherited campsite and shook their heads.

"If we stay here, let's move the camp to the ridge up there. This location didn't work out to well for the last owners," mumbled John with a sigh.

They all agreed with sighs. "And no walking today, okay?" entertained John. There were more sighs of agreement and some tired half murmurs.

Nik sat for hours holding his head, looking at Ivan's final resting place, wondering how he would leave this earth and this plane of conciseness. He was sure he would see Ivan again ... most certainly away from this now most hallowed ground.

... 39 ...
Mopping Up

MIDMORNING BROUGHT SID PROPOSING a shift schedule for sleep. They had been up for a very long time and needed to get some rest but still needed to maintain a watch. He outlined a six-hour, two up, one down schedule that would get them all rested at the maximum and safest rate possible. They had scouted for an hour or so, and John volunteered for the first sleep session with no complaints from the others. Sid was concerned for the group's security and state of readiness, and Nik was simply too numb from the events of the previous two days to care who slept first. John quickly found a spot on the hillside halfway up the ridge, sat down with his hat over his head, and was snoring in minutes.

"He was tired," Nik commented as he yawned himself.

"Yeah, I don't blame him," Sid added. "We have had a really strange time these last—well, three months."

Nik nodded and began looking at the Russian soldiers' encampment. "We need to go over this place with a fine-tooth comb," Nik said, now yawning again.

"Yes we do!" answered Sid. "And we will in time. Let's get all rested up, and then we'll tear this place apart. We have plenty of time, right?"

Nik picked his head up and thought for a second with a pause. "July 16. Yeah, we have plenty of time. Our next thing is in October." Nik struggled with getting his thoughts and words to congeal,

---

which was evident to Sid when Nik referred to their next event as a "thing."

"You know," Sid began, "you can lie down and get some shut-eye as well. I can maintain the lookout for the next five hours."

Nik looked at his friend. "No, man, it's not a problem." A few minutes later, he added. "I'll tell you what. I'll go over here and watch our eastern side. I'll sit against this tree and watch.... Okay?"

Sid waved over to Nik. "Okay, man, no problem," he said, knowing full well Nik wouldn't last ten minutes sitting down in the shade of the trees with no conversation.

Minutes later, Sid strolled over and checked on his now-sleeping compatriot. Nik had sat down on a small flat rock ledge that overlooked the valley below to the east, with Ivan's burial site to his left and behind him and the still-smoldering pyre far below to his left. His rifle, still in his hand, was pointing east, and his head was propped on his knee and shoulder. It almost looked like he was aiming at something, but the slight periodic snore gave him away.

Sid quietly moved off to let his friend sleep and was joined by John a few hours later, He was now awake and fairly fresh and rested. They congregated by the makeshift table where John had patched up Mr. Armistead.

"Where's Nik?" John asked Sid.

Sid put his finger over his mouth and pointed toward Nik's rock ledge perch near the tree and commented. "He was wasted, and I didn't figure we'd need two on guard after all."

John nodded in agreement. "Yeah, this place is behind all the conflict now. Everything has moved on up the way, more north."

The two sat, basically back-to-back, each covering a 180-degree view of their surroundings. "It's quiet now," John said quietly.

"Yeah, we sure turned it up here the past two days.... It's hard to believe any of this is going on," Sid answered.

"You can get some rest if you want to," John told Sid as he stood up and stretched for a moment.

Sid looked at his friend and replied somewhat solemnly, "Nah, I'd rather hang out here and keep you company. The quiet of scouting around alone was, well, odd. We have done everything together for the past year, basically. In all of this—" Both men took a second to look around. "In all of this ... in this time ... I'd rather be awake with you guys, eyes wide open."

John, not sure what to say, replied, "I understand, man.... Let's work on getting rested up, so when Nik wakes up, you can get some rest. In a few days, we'll be back to a normal schedule, and we'll take a look at this stuff." John pointed to the Russian encampment. "There must be something to salvage here—maybe some clues on their mission or something."

Sid nodded as he looked around at the encampment. "Yeah, let's all tackle this together. I'm going to go look up around the high ridge, okay? I'll stay in view and earshot."

John, acknowledging Sid, milled around the flat encampment area, periodically checking on Sid and Nik. Sid came back after a few minutes and reported, "All clear. There isn't a thing in sight."

John looked at Sid and pondered aloud, "I wonder if Mr. Armistead will come and look for us with his French friends."

Sid looked at John with some concern now. "I'm not sure we want to see them."

"Oh, I know.... I was just saying," John explained. "It might be something we need to watch out for." Sid agreed.

Many hours went by, and the light of day began to dim as some summer storms boiled west of them. Nik awoke with a jolt to the sounds of the distant thunder and joined his compatriots in the encampment. He looked at Sid with a frown. "Dude, you need sleep," he said. "I am sorry I was out so long."

Sid shrugged. "It's okay, man. You needed it first ... you and that overactive, imaginative brain of yours. And since you and John are up now, I am going to go over there and fall over." Sid smiled as he felt he had accomplished a secondary or tertiary mission of the day by keeping watch over the place while his friends recharged themselves.

Nik patted him on the shoulder as he shuffled off to a spot that he had spied earlier that day for his eventual slumber. Sid raised his left hand as if to say good-bye; he made his way forward and could be heard groaning. "Man, am I tired.... Good God, my legs feel like—"

John laughed and told Nik about their day hanging out. He also told Nik he was happy Sid had stayed up for as long as he did and relayed Sid's comments about their camaraderie.

Nik looked up at John. "Well, that's good," he said, "and I feel the same way. It's the evening of July 16, 1781. I mean, look at us. What in the hell are we doing here? We—and we alone—are here from our time. We have us, and that's it. Russians? Oh my God ... I don't even know how we debrief from all that. I can hardly believe any of that even went on. But—"

Nik began laughing in a slightly unstable-sounding fashion. "Why should I have been surprised by any of this? We are in 17-friggin-81! That in itself is ... just ... off the charts and in the realm of utter craziness!"

John looked back intently to see where Sid was and to see if he was witnessing Nik's rant. He wanted some help if Nik were to need some calming down. Nik realized how John was feeling, looked at him, and smiled. "I'm fine; I'm just saying ... this is just so ... unbelievable!"

"You're right, man.... This is certainly one for the ages. Ha-ha, Be-dump-bump," John joked.

"I can always count on you, man.... You're hopeless," Nik stated, shaking his head.

Nik perched himself on the makeshift table and peered around, periodically walking the perimeter of the camp. Sid was sound asleep, nestled in a mossy nook in the rock halfway up the ridge from where they had made their assault the previous day. John stayed up for a bit, fell asleep by the tents in the camp area for a while, and awoke again a few hours later to keep Nik company for the rest of the night. Nik took a short catnap between two and three o'clock in the morning, while John kept watch.

The night of the sixteenth and the early morning hours of the seventeenth were stone quiet. Even the birds were silent as the moon traversed the sky. The thunderstorms never made it to their position, and Nik theorized that they might be close enough to the coast that the onshore winds may have kept the weather west and kept them dry. That was just a theory, nothing more, and they honestly didn't have a good idea about where exactly they were in respect to the coast or Yorktown.

"We'll figure it all out tomorrow," Nik assured John around 5:15 a.m.

Sid awoke after a solid eleven hours of sleep. Nik and John each took an additional one-hour nap, and by 10:30 a.m., the three compatriots were awake, fairly chipper, and looking at the campsite for a logical place to start the salvage mission of the next few days. This was quickly put off for more rest and downtime.

So be it. The boys continued to rest and gather themselves and basically ignored everything and anything that didn't include sleep, food, and rest for them. The area around them was quiet for many miles; no one was observed within their self-proclaimed "perimeter" as the boys took turns patrolling, sleeping, talking with each other, and eating. It was like they were taking a small vacation, camping in the woods of Virginia in 1781. It would have been great if it weren't for a very long list of items that made this "vacation" uniquely unusual.

July 23, 1781. The boys decided they were prepared to "get back to business" and started with a salvage operation of the Soviet camp. They began in the least interesting place, which had the fewest number of items in it—tent number three where Mr. Armistead's interrogation and torture had occurred. The boys hadn't even stepped into the tents except for the one instance to find some evidence of whom they were dealing with in the case of their Soviet invaders.

"Ugh," John gasped at the state of the inside of the torture tent. It was simply a mess and had a stench of human sweat and waste. The boys weren't sure how long the Russian group had been camped here before they had arrived on the ridge above. They knew it had been here with the British encampment, but when they stumbled upon it and stayed low to observe, they didn't have a good idea on the age of the camp. This tent was a total loss, and the boys decided they would simply wrap it up without touching most of it and burn it where the three Soviet soldiers had been cremated. The tent, literally wrapped up in a ball, was tied together with the tent bindings, and the whole thing was rolled down the hill to become fuel for a bonfire.

"I figure there will be more for that pile," Sid commented.

"I'm sure we'll have a time sifting through the other two tents, and we will certainly destroy whatever temporal contamination we can," Nik added.

"Temporal contamination, huh?" John piped up. "Fancy words," he added with a smile. "So, how would we identify such a thing? After all, we've done some 'contamination' ourselves, you know?"

A pause formed for a minute before Nik responded. "Well, you're right. At least we know now—if you want to look at it that way—that we didn't start it. Suppose we came to this time without the Russian force here screwing with our history. Suppose we just got here like we did and made our way through things, and the history we knew, without the tampering, just happened. We would what?" Nik now waited for an answer.

Sid replied, "We would have witnessed the history we knew, and everything would have been as it was supposed to be."

"Exactly!" jumped Nik. "But, as it happened, there were these Soviets, there was contamination, there was someone messing with what was supposed to be. Gentlemen, I contend that we are defenders of liberty! I contend that from this day forward, we are not only part of the Continental Army of our fledgling nation of the United States of America, but something else! We are truly an integral piece of history now, this history—we made our commitment to our roles here several times over. And if, in fact, we 'contaminated' the time line to, in effect, preserve what we knew to be, well, true."

A sort of silence fell over group. But in that moment, there was a kind of revelation where they, for the first time (not counting the instances they were engaged in military-type action), felt "in it" and were—well, okay with it.

"So which tent is next?" Sid asked somewhat anticlimactically.

John looked at him and smiled. "Yup, now that we have a role in this time and we have clearly—well, sort of clearly—defined it, we're off to plunder something. Didn't take us a moment."

"Well, it is war, right?" Sid replied.

Nik laughed. "Yeah, but we aren't going to be like those three." He pointed to the area where the unholy Soviet bad guys had met their end in the fires of the early morning pyre.

"No," mumbled John, "certainly not!"

The three moved over to tent number one—the tent Nik had feverishly stormed into to produce the Makarov pistol two days earlier. It was a mess and appeared to be the temporary living arrangement for two of the four Soviet soldiers. There were two makeshift cots constructed out of wood, vines, and pine branches and various small wooden items, like a small stool and a bowl carved from a log. The items of interest that jumped out at them like fireworks on the Fourth of July were two large packs of pretty good bulk.

"We've seen these before," yelled John. "They were wearing these when we saw them on the mountain pass!"

"There we go! Now were talking! Yes, these will certainly prove interesting," Sid added with some excitement. Not wanting to blow the packs apart like presents on Christmas morning, Sid suggested that they set all items of interest from tent one out on the table. There, they would be able to be organized about their search. John and Nik nodded in agreement and set the packs aside to look over the rest of tent one.

In the makeshift cots, the covers were made of crude bedding materials and included a single Russian uniform on each cot. These appeared to be hidden in a fashion, sort of wrapped and weaved into the bedding and covers.

"Guess they were trying to obtain some comfort for sleeping as well, huh? They were also probably trying to keep these hidden at the same time," remarked Sid.

"The uniforms need to go onto the burn pile, right?" asked John.

They looked over the uniforms, which were overalls, really, and assessed whether they should keep them to use. Sid put his hands up and commented, "I vote we burn them. I don't want to put on some heavy, 1960s, cotton-burlap *Soviet* overalls!"

Nik answered, "Yeah, I agree. Ick!"

John shrugged his shoulders and agreed with Sid's thinking. The tents were devoid of anything else, except the actual tents themselves, which were pretty nice as cover went in 1781. They weren't the cabin up at C-10 or the homestead by any means, but they were functional enough. They would revisit the tents themselves later and decide if they wanted to use one or both of them as they moved on.

The packs were brought to the makeshift table and stacked up, allowing them to be investigated one at a time. "What do you think is in these things?" mumbled Nik.

"Only God knows," said Sid.

John yelled, "Stop! Do you think they are booby-trapped?"

The group looked at each other for a second before Sid finally shook his head. "I doubt it. If you were those guys in this time, would you fear anyone, really? Plus, think about this—if anyone knew them, do you think they would break into their bags? And if you didn't know them and had a look at them, would you break into their bags?"

John smiled. "Yeah, I see your point. Okay, let's look in bag number one."

They opened the bag and delicately peered inside. They pulled out some covers of sorts, like bedding but more like light tarp material. They found some additional items of clothing and some furs.

Nik, clearly disappointed, complained. "Okay, this is a complete bust so far! We would like something a little more telling about what the hell—" And at that moment, Sid pulled out a pouch that clinked and clanked with a unique ring.

"Ooh, I like the sound of that! What's that?" John asked excitedly.

The pouch was about seven inches long, as wide as it was tall, and about three-quarters full of something. Speaking more slowly than usual now, Sid exclaimed, "I dunno, but for its size, it sure is hea … heav …heavy." Sid stopped as he looked into it. He then made a space on some of the covers they had put on the table and poured the contents out onto them. With some clinks, clanks, and rings, two handfuls of golden disks fell onto the soft material.

"Whoa! Would you look at this?" Sid blurted.

Nik looked in disbelief as the pieces fell from the bag.

"Are those what they ... they look like?" asked John. "*Wow ...* it's ... they're little disks made of gold!"

"Golden disks," Nik muttered. "What in the world?"

"Money!" Sid blurted. "They used this for money? Right? That would make sense."

"Absolutely, Sid. It makes perfect sense!" Nik stood up, held his head, and continued. "If you were a time traveler, say from 1961, and you were traveling into the past, what would be the one universal thing, here on Earth, you could *always* have with you that you could guarantee would be worth something? What could that something be that you could use to barter for hard currency, goods, services, or whatever since the dawn of time here? What could you bring to be used as a 'barterable' commodity whenever or wherever you were on Earth?"

Almost instantly, John answered, "Gold."

"Yes! And look at it—look at their thicknesses!" Nik said, now boasting and waving his hands.

Sid inspected the disks. "They are all different thicknesses ... to be used as different denominations?"

"Exactly! Are we not the smartest people on the planet right now or what?" Nik congratulated the group for their quick insights.

"This is unbelievable!" muttered John. "They thought of everything, didn't they?" John now had a renewed anger for the Soviet force. "Well," he continued, "we have money now. How did you term it, Nik? A barterable commodity?"

"Yup, a barterable commodity!" he confirmed.

They completed the search through the first bag, including the pouches and pockets.

"Hmm, no rounds for the Makarov?" Sid complained.

"Well, we probably have three more of these bags to go. There might be some in one of the other ones; be patient," replied John with a smile.

The bags were useful, but much heavier than the packs and gear the boys were already using. Nik began with an assessment of the Russian packs. "I suppose if we wanted to store something—say, buried in a location—we could use these bags as protection for the items. They are way too heavy to use."

Sid and John agreed and set the one emptied bag aside. Sid added, "We could use them as mats for sitting on or putting our gear on in wet or messy areas, but I think they will be too heavy to carry with us right now."

"Agreed," they all said, confirming that the packs would be left behind for a possible later pickup.

The second bag yielded similar items and another pouch of golden disks. There weren't as many in this pouch; it was a little less than half full. Sid shrugged again over the absence of rounds for the Russian pistol. It's not like they needed another firearm or more ammunition; it was simply Sid's enjoyment of old weapons and curiosity. They paused for several hours, and John ran down to a small creek where he was looking to harvest something for a snack. He came back with some small shelled critters; they resembled snails or something such as that.

"Ugh," murmured Nik. "All these months of fish and venison, and we have snails today? Kinda depressing. I'm not complaining, of course."

"Yes you are," jabbed John. "It's okay, though. We'd think you were ill if you didn't complain about something."

"True," added Sid as they picked through their meager snack.

They moved onto tent number two and found two more packs similar to the others they'd found in tent number one. There were similar contents with some peculiar differences—fewer clothing and bedding items and more military provisions. They found a fairly large brown, hard plastic box with a lock and some sort of coiled up burlap or material type of apparatus.

Sid picked up the brown box. "Wow, an old-style Soviet field radio. I have only seen pictures of these in books." He worked with what looked like a locking mechanism and wasn't able to open it. "I wonder who they thought they were going to talk to in 1781?" he wondered aloud.

John jumped up at that and almost screamed. "You don't think they have more teams on the ground, do you?"

Nik sat down now and rubbed his chin. "Hmm," he mumbled, "that would suck. You'd figure—and this is just a wild guess—but you'd figure we would have seen them by now? No?"

"I don't know," remarked Sid.

"Ugh, I have a bad feeling about all this," John complained now.

Nik decided he needed to turn the fear off in John. "No, we would have seen them by now if there were other Soviets skulking around. We were brought here by way of their device. Remember the sci-fi of our time or the leading theorists on the subject. Time in a linear reference could run or flow like a stream or a river.... Currents and eddies would tend to lead one down the same or similar path.... We would have seen them by now," Nik insisted, not wholly sure himself what the truth was. "We saw them, and we dispatched the threat. I believe we are alone now in this time, and I am very confident that we will not see any more Soviet forces."

Nik paused, hoping that the others would buy into the certainty of his thoughts. That said, Nik believed what he'd just stated—maybe not quite as certain as he sounded, but he wanted Sid and John, especially John, not to worry about the possibility of other Soviet troops appearing around them. He wasn't trying to deceive them; he simply wanted to eliminate the atmosphere of worry and trepidation that could remain hanging over the group.

"So where's the other radio?" asked Sid.

Nik looked around and admitted, "I don't know.... Maybe it was meant to be used to contact future teams, I don't know. Remember, eddies and currents."

On a positive note, there were two more bags of gold disks. They now had a veritable king's ransom in .999 percent pure gold disk-shaped ingots.

"I have to tell you," John began, "I can't fathom how much this stuff is worth in 2010! We would be in very nice shape! I mean, we have pounds of the stuff."

Nik raised his hand, and Sid announced, "And Nik is now going to tell us how much we'd actually have if—"

Nik interrupted him and said, "I was just going to say that gold was around eleven hundred dollars an ounce, give or take ... sixteen ounces in a pound ... you do the math."

"Yeah, a lot of money!" John blurted.

"Well, maybe we'll get back with some. Who knows?" said Sid, cringing a bit, as he really didn't want to remind the group about the bleakness of their possibility of getting back to their time. As soon as it came out of his mouth, he tried to make his comment disappear. "Sorry, I didn't—"

John patted him on the shoulder. "Dude, no worries. We all thought the same thing, and we know good and well every day how small the chance is for finding our way back to 2010."

"So, let's get back to the stash. What else do we have there, Sid?" John asked.

"Well, look at these. These are those stupid flares I told you about that lit everything on fire a few months ago." Sid held up the six silver tubes, smiled, and added, "These could come in handy."

Nik laughed and answered, "Yeah, if we want to scare the hell out of someone or burn down a forest, sure."

John and Sid laughed as they rummaged through the rest of the last bag. "Well, that's it. Nothing else here," Sid said as he waved his hands.

The boys sat around and looked at the items the Soviets' tents had produced and all thought the same thing.

"They really didn't have much with them," Sid extolled, being exasperated by the fact that there were no rounds found for the Makarov pistol.

As he vented his frustration, John theorized, "Maybe they used them all on some unfortunate folks." The three stood quietly for a moment, pondering the evil that could have been demonstrated by the Makarov on folks of the time. They shook it off and continued about their business. Sid stowed the Soviet pistol along with the bedding and other uninteresting things into the empty bulky packs for storage somewhere.

"Well, I am hungry again," John announced to the group. "I'm going down to the stream again. Maybe I'll catch a few fish or some frogs or a turtle or something—something to eat other than snails."

Nik wandered around, not sure what to do, so he decided to take a quick patrol around. Sid continued to clean up around the lower campsite and move some of the items up to the more protected, higher campsite on the ridge. Nik didn't see much and was partly surprised he didn't see either some militia force charging past in the distance or a British force heading straight for them. He felt as if the war had left them behind, and he thought about Ivan again and leaned against a tree as he looked west at the setting sun. From his vantage point, he could still peer down into the lower camp and easily walk to the upper camp on the ridge. There was a small breeze on the hill where he was standing, and after a fairly long time of utter silence, with only the sounds of nature in the air, he wandered around to the high campsite to check in on Sid and his self-imposed chores.

Sid was moving things up to the high camp and kept an eye on John as he fumbled around the stream, trying to catch dinner. He knew where Nik was but couldn't see him until he arrived from his lookout to the west.

"How's it going?" Nik asked.

Sid shrugged his head. "Okay, just stashing this stuff. I figure we don't need any of this with us. We'll know where it is, and these bags are waterproof; I checked them after you had left on patrol. Did you see anything?"

"Nope, not a soul. It's like we are alone on the planet; it's a little eerie, actually. Should we somehow destroy the Soviet pistol?" Nik asked Sid.

"Well," he shrugged his shoulders again, "there are no rounds for it. I suppose someone could find it and figure out how it should work. What do you think? Take it with us for safe keeping?"

"I don't know. Take it apart and spread the pieces along the trail to Yorktown, or keep it—it probably doesn't make a difference," offered Nik.

After Sid had completed his Sherpa duties, the three met back at the table where John had begun preparing some small fish he'd caught. "They aren't very big, but there are sixteen of them," John exclaimed.

"They look like overgrown minnows," Sid responded.

Nik looked at the little fish. "They'll taste good cooked—they always do, John." Nik wanted to be supportive of John's food-foraging efforts.

John appreciated the comments but never felt unappreciated, even when Sid made fun of some of his more strange attempts at food items. Nik would usually lie and say he wasn't very hungry if he didn't like the look of whatever he had made. Sid, on the other hand, liked to rib John when he could about odd food preparations. It was all good fun, as the mood of the past week finally began to loosen its somber and disturbing grip on the boys and their perceived future—whatever that was.

... 40 ...
A Decision to Move Forward

THAT NIGHT WAS QUIET, and the boys were camped on the ridge now; their entry point into this place where they had been for the better part of a week brought them comfort in the strangest of ways. It reminded them a bit of their camp-cabin area at C-10 with the small ledge and a hardly passable summit behind them; this one had a view of the Soviet camping area off the small ridge to the north. They thought again and again of the reality of the "not so lucky original campers" of that place "down there" where they'd eliminated three servants of the devil and one "good soldier" who had been caught up in an unfortunate turn of events.

These thoughts led to Mr. Armistead. Did he make it to Lafayette? Did he, or will he, successfully deliver his information? Would the Americans meet, pin, and defeat the British at Yorktown like they were supposed to in the history the boys were familiar with? There were many questions asked and no answers to be given. The boys talked about all this at length that night.

"So how will we know we have done our part, and it all turns out the way it's supposed to?" asked John at around ten thirty that night.

Sid rolled over and answered. "Well, I figure we'll hear about it, right?"

"From who?" Nik quickly snapped. "We don't drop by the local eighteenth-century quickie mart or coffee shop to chat with the locals about the happenings of the day! No, we have to go and witness the surrender firsthand. That's the only way we are going to know this ends the way it's supposed to."

"Ha," John laughed, "we are going to just go and be on the battlefield with all the troops, General Washington, this Lafayette guy, the British, the French, and the Germans! You think someone won't pick us out? Even in our best disguises, we don't *really* look like we fit, if you know what I mean. You know what I mean?"

Nik was now quiet and thinking. "Yeah, this will take more thought," he admitted.

"Ya think?" John laughed again.

Sid, quiet to this point, asked John, "So, you like making Nik think like this? You know what we get into when he really plans something, don't you?" Sid chuckled. "John, you are a menace, you know. You're almost challenging him to come up with something so way out there—well, you're a menace, my friend."

"And you," Sid continued, pointing at Nik. "What are you thinking, and more importantly, when are you going to tell us?"

Nik, now the quiet one, mumbled, "Well, I have to go over what Yorktown looked like. Your point is well taken, John. There is basically the entire roll call of players there. What an opportunity to see all the important figures of the times. Washington! Wouldn't you like to meet Gen. George Washington?"

Now both Sid's eyebrows went up. With much sarcasm, he blurted, "Umm, dude. Back to earth.... How do you suppose that would happen?

"'Hey, George. Hey, man.... How's the fam? Doing well here, right on! We're with ya.... Check out this boom stick! Let's take it to those evil British, and by the way, we'll even double down on those nasty Hessians. Wahoo! Hooray for France! But, hey, don't count on them for much longer—this is their finest hour!'"

Nik, no longer humored but chuckling from Sid's rant, muttered, "Ugh. Well, you know, it would be exciting."

John ended with, "Good night. We'll figure it out in the morning." And then he fell asleep. Sid agreed and was soon in a sound slumber on this warm July evening.

Nik, however, was still awake and looked up at the mostly tree-shrouded night sky and pondered the boys' next move in the coming days and weeks. He would certainly like them to witness the surrender of Cornwallis and the British, so they would "really know." But to the others' points, there was a very real danger of being discovered. Something Nik was working on in the back of his mind, though, had him thinking they could, in fact, be there to witness the surrender and not *really* be discovered—and it involved the French. He smiled now, as he hadn't quite gotten the whole plan together but was well on his way to at least having a framework to fashion a plan around.

His thoughts grew quiet now, and he continued to look up to the heavens. He silently asked for help in the decision process on what the group should do moving forward. Although he knew the possibilities were almost endless, he was unsure of the approach going forward and was questioning the thoughts he'd had just minutes ago. It was silent out on this night—not even the insects were making their normal summer nighttime racket.

Nik concentrated on each of the ideas he had thought of, surveying the mental list in his mind. As it happened, when he was thinking of the plan that involved the French, which actually made him chuckle to himself again, another bright white shooting star streaked across the sky. It was much like the one he believed carried Ivan's soul to heaven several nights ago. It lit up the sky like a white-hot beacon, and in his mind, it was an indicator of a well-conceived thought, as it left a smoke trail behind that could be seen in the moonlight. It was then he decided he would spend most of his time working on what he called The French Plan for their endeavor to witness the surrender at Yorktown, if, in fact, the surrender at Yorktown actually occurred at all.

... 41 ...
A Relief and a Renewed Sense of Mission

THE NEXT MORNING WAS stunning. It was mild, very clear, and uncommonly dry for a summer morning—a very unlikely set of weather conditions for the end of July in the southeastern United States. The boys didn't expect it to last. Nik began the morning down by the Soviet campsite looking at the tents and how they might be able to be salvaged. The torture tent wasn't much help, so they literally cut it down, rolled it up, and discarded it over the hillside for burning. Next, Nik fumbled with the flaps and ties, looking for the method by which the tent was secured.

John joined Nik with a giggle and asked him, "What are you doing?"

Nik looked at John and scratched his forehead. "Well," Nik began, "trying to salvage one of these tents, but I am having a time trying to figure out how in the hell it comes apart without destroying it."

John laughed. "Yeah, you're good at destructively disassembling things!"

Nik looked at John and exclaimed, "Yeah, thanks."

John began again. "Listen, Sid is patrolling around and said he wants to talk to you about something."

Nik looked a little surprised. "Hmm, is he mad about something?" he asked. "Do you know what's up?"

"No, nothing like that," John clarified. "I'm sure he is just wondering what we are going to do from here. He doesn't seem like he wants to hang around here anymore. I think he thinks it's time to go."

Nik nodded. "Yes, I agree. I've been working on our approach to Yorktown these past few days. I'll fill you guys in today on what I am thinking. I am going to find Sid."

John quickly added, "Yeah, and I'll work on these tents and properly take them down."

Nik headed up the ridge to look for Sid. He knew he wouldn't be too far from them, as they didn't tend to stray away from the rest of the group. "Psst," rang out from parts unseen. "Psst," Nik heard again.

He looked around and instinctively dropped to the ground. He now saw Sid in a bramble just to the north of him. Sid was pointing to his right, to the west where he'd spied a small regiment of troops, unidentified at this point, moving to the north. Nik made his way over to Sid using a small ledge just to the east and out of sight of anyone from the west.

When he arrived at Sid's location, he asked, "Who are they?"

"Not sure," replied Sid as they spied the formation. "They look like Colonial forces from here."

"Colors are right," added Nik.

Sid fairly quickly broached the conversation with Nik about leaving the area for their next phase or whatever they were going to do. "So, do you have any thoughts on when we are leaving here?"

"Well, in fact I do," Nik said, "and today is the day I will outline what I think we should do. From there, it's up to all of us to decide. How's that sound?"

Sid looked at Nik and said, "You know, you would have made a lousy general."

Nik smirked. "How so?"

Sid quietly explained, "You know where we are going next; you need to just tell us. Drop the diplomacy garbage and tell us where we are going and when we are leaving." Sid said this with levity, but Nik felt the message was a bit sharp and took a little issue with it.

Nonetheless, Nik maintained his way. "This is no time for 'generals,'" he explained. "We're all lieutenants lost in time and feeling around the dark for directions. I may know or feel what I think the next steps should be, but we all have a say in this. Who knows, I may overlook something in a plan of action that could get us killed. We *all* have to think over any idea and agree on our plan of action. It's kept us alive to this point, ya know? Why do we still have these conversations?"

Sid shrugged. "Yeah, yeah, you're right. I'm just picking for no reason. It's just this place, all that we have figured out in the past few weeks—hell, hell past few months—it wears on ya, you know?"

Nik nodded and quietly said as he now looked back at the distant troop movement. "I know. We're leaving this place, and we'll figure it all out."

Nik wondered if Sid was having some confidence issues and continued to support their position. "You have to admit, we've done remarkably well. We foiled a bunch of bad guys' plans, helped our country, helped Mr. Quinten and Mr. Armistead, and found a pile of gold. Short of finding a secret time portal back to 2010, we're doing pretty well!"

Sid sat and thought about all that. "You know," he finally replied, "I didn't think about it like that. All wins minus the time snafu. Who could have seen the time-travel ridiculousness coming? Except, it's not so ridiculous in our realities now!" Sid continued, now gesturing to the northward advancing army, "They are basically past us. Let's get back to camp and get wrapped up here."

Nik was happy to hear Sid's spirits turn positive, so he left it at that. "Yup! I totally agree!"

They arrived back at the lower campsite where John had neatly folded and stacked the two Soviet tents. He looked at Sid and Nik and asked what they had seen on patrol. Sid tried to pick up one of the tent packs to see how heavy one might be to carry and quickly put it down.

"Yeah," John said, "I don't think these will go very far without a horse or mule for transport."

"I think you're right!" Sid agreed. "A mule is a great idea, John!"

John laughed. "I have them once in a while—ideas, not mules. Anyway, I have a surprise for you!"

Sid and Nik sat on the table and looked at John intently. "What's up?" asked Nik.

From behind a rock, John produced a second Soviet radio. This one appeared to be smashed and destroyed.

"It looks like it fell off a mountain or a cliff or something!" John said with a spark of emotion. He was clearly relieved that they could now assume there wasn't another working radio floating around anywhere, potentially with another Soviet infiltration team.

Sid now theorized that if, in fact, there was only one team of Soviet spies, each pair would have had a radio, so they could split up and still communicate with each other. Sid also theorized that his small military scanner/radio probably picked up the Soviet transmission those many months ago back at C-10, and that was why it had stopped scanning on that strange and unfamiliar frequency.

"Sounds reasonable to me," said John.

Nik hadn't been very worried about any more intruders from the future, as he thought Ivan would have probably told them about any additional groups that he might have known about, that was just his gut talking again, he honestly didn't know for sure. He didn't voice this opinion, because he knew what he would have said if Sid or John suggested that very idea—he would have told them that the idea of Ivan telling them everything he knew was utterly ridiculous, and he would have probably been right.

Sid wanted to further diffuse the worry over additional enemy teams. "Well, good. Now that that's put behind us, we'll bury the stuff for possible retrieval later and get a move on!" he announced.

"Oh yeah? Cool. Do tell, where are we headed?" John asked inquisitively.

"I'll tell you our possible plans at dinner, and we'll figure out which one we like the best," Nik explained.

John shook his head. "Still the diplomacy, huh? Haven't you learned, Nik, just tell us where and when. We'll go unless it's stupid or suicidal." John smiled at Nik.

Sid laughed, and Nik shook his head. "You guys are crazy!" Nik said.

The three began digging a hole where they were going to stow all the items, mostly in the large Soviet packs they had emptied and repacked with the items they didn't plan on taking. They first completely searched the items again, one last time, and cut all the labels, as they had done with their other things almost a year ago.

By the end of the day, they had loaded the packs and tents into the storage holes and covered them with rocks, boulders, and debris from the hill and surrounding ridgeline. Nik had kept the radios out and said he had a plan for them, which piqued the interest of Sid and John. He responded to their looks by assuring them that his idea was one that they would like and that would keep the contamination of the future time line to a minimum. They migrated back to their camp on the ridge for a little dinner and a story.

"Okay, so here we are. Story time, Nik," said Sid.

"Yes, do tell what mayhem and trouble you have planned for us now, Nik," John added.

Nik sat down by the small fire and began talking. "Well, after quite a bit of thought on the subject of getting us to Yorktown, I am at a small loss and really only see one way to get us in a position to witness the British surrender."

A silence persisted until John rolled his head around and said, "Okay, based on the silence, our plan, which we haven't heard yet, sounds scary—so let's hear it!"

Sid sat back, knowing he was about to hear a most unorthodox approach to their problem of getting close to the surrendering British and General Cornwallis. Nik had been an expert at the strategy games they had engaged in during their LAN parties of the past, and Sid knew Nik would employ the most unexpected and unorthodox tactics to attain a successful outcome at whatever they attempted. Surprise was always his game, and deviousness was habitual and innate. Nik was simply a sneak—there was nothing more to it. The difference, of course, was that his plans now were not with mere pixels on a computer display; the boys were real and could be easily wounded or killed. *Would he think of this when he unleashed his plans?* Sid thought to himself.

"Okay," Nik began.

"Wait, wait," John interrupted as he ran over to the other side of the camp for a sip of water. "Okay," he said as he returned and sat down. "Oh, one thing," John added as he began to chuckle, "you're not going to employ some crazy computer game, bizarro tactic that has us tunneling up in the British back lines or something, are you?"

Sid also began to laugh now, as he admitted that he'd just had the same thought, recalling a time when Nik had constructed small infiltration tunnels from his base to the rear lines of their bases and wreaked the most unholy and annoying attacks out of those said holes in the ground. John and Sid, now in full hysterics and laughter, almost to the point of tears, looked at Nik and asked him if he remembered what he had done.

Nik just nodded and exclaimed with a frown, "You remember I didn't win that one ... right? As a matter of fact, my army—if you could have called it that—died a miserable, shoeless death."

"Yeah, I do remember that!" John exclaimed, not laughing that hard anymore. Sid, however, cackled even louder, because he had emerged victorious in that particular game.

Nik, slightly bothered by the hilarity, presently requested, "Okay, okay, calm down and listen.... I am not going to get us killed or maimed, but—"

John broke out in laughter again. "Here it comes ... he just said the infamous 'but.'"

Nik, now almost perturbed, snapped, "Dudes! I will get us killed if you don't let me tell you what the hell I am thinking!"

Sid switched gears to now play the peacemaker. "Okay, okay. John, stop and let the man explain how he is going to get us into even more serious trouble.... Again!"

John waved his hand and choked on his drink of water from laughter. "Okay, okay, go ahead, General Custer. How will we meet our fate, sir?"

Nik still looked annoyed and tried to continue without laughing himself, as Sid and John were closer to his plans than they actually knew. "So," Nik began again, "not tunneling, exactly."

A serious look of concern fell over Sid's and John's faces. The concern fell into a silence with a few more smart remarks, and Nik thought he could now, finally, get his thoughts out of his head.

He began. "I call this The French Plan."

"The French Plan?" John gasped. "What the hell kind of name is that for our mission to Yorktown? Are we going to show up and surrender along with the British?"

Sid laughed. "Ha! I don't think that's what he has in mind."

Nik was now shaking his head again and exclaimed, "I think John came to the eighteenth century and got infected by a 'happy and silly bug'—always seeming to be in a great mood, laughing, and making jokes. Well, Mr. Funny Man," Nik continued, "how would you feel if I told you that we are going to witness the surrender of the British and General Cornwallis's army from the very waters where the French Naval Fleet will be barraging them? The York River."

The look from John was priceless, and Sid rolled back and snickered. "You are a sneaky bastard! It's perfect. Who is going to look or care about anyone in the water at that point with all that will be going on toward the coast and the land beyond? We have hearing protection for the potential noise coming from the French fleet and our own firepower to get us clear of any trouble we may encounter."

John interrupted. "Umm, what's to keep the French from shooting at us? You know what I mean? Somehow we'll be near them in the river. They might look at us and think we are going to attack them or something."

Nik and Sid pondered the thought. Nik finally mumbled, "We'll see. We are probably not going to look like a threat to them. We'll certainly hide our hardware; burlaps and woods will be in order.

We'll just look like some crazy colonists with a death wish or something."

Sid asked the obvious question. "So how exactly are we going to get out into the river, Nik?"

Nik answered with a smile. "Ah, the problem of the times. We'll come up with something along the way. Don't worry about it for now."

"Well, I am tired from all the excitement and good cheer," John quietly said. "Now that we know how we are going to die in 1781, I can go to sleep." Sid laughed.

"Oh, stop," Nik said. "We are not going to die!"

Sid now asked for quiet and sleep and reminded the others of their pending trek in the morning. "We *are* still leaving in the morning, aren't we?" he asked.

Nik nodded. "Oh, yes. That sighting today was pretty close. It's time to move on."

John reinforced the plans for departure by going over all the tasks they'd completed that day in preparation for leaving in the morning.

The three retired that evening with a new sense of adventure brewing in their heads. They were leaving this place with a huge amount of information they were not privy to before they had arrived. Who could have predicted any of the happenings of the past three months? Certainly none of the boys! Soviet Troops from circa 1960. The meeting of a true hero of the American Revolution. Piles of gold and the huge realization of the differences between what was and what might have been if they hadn't been around to somehow right the events that had taken such horrible turns in the enemy's favor.

Each of them was pleased with the overall results, minus the death of Ivan, whose intentions, true thoughts, and spirit were unknown to them before being fatally wounded by them. Would they see the surrender of the British at Yorktown as it happened all those years ago? Or would it take a different path where other circumstances force Cornwallis to surrender either at Yorktown or somewhere else? They had so many questions.

... 42 ...
On the Trail Again

MORNING BROUGHT RAIN AND thunder of the sort they hadn't seen for months. Preparing for the trek out of camp that day, Nik was standing in the pouring rain looking at Ivan's final resting place once again. The group had no idea if they would get back to this place, either on their way back to C-10 or from wherever. The rain was cool amid the warmth and humidity of July, and there was little wind, allowing gravity to pelt its victims straight from the sky.

Sid moved over to Nik and slowly prodded him away from Ivan's grave. "C'mon, we've got plenty of walking to do today. He'll be here; he's fine. You saw to that."

John watched the scene unfold with Sid and Nik and was moved by his emotion over Ivan. He checked around to make sure they hadn't missed or left anything at either site that would give them away to the common hiker or onlooker.

"Okay, let's go," mumbled Nik.

"That's the spirit," encouraged Sid. "We don't have to kill ourselves with the walk today. Let's just get six or seven hours down the trail at a comfortable pace, and we'll look for a place to relax and bed down for the evening. We'll start slow and build up from there."

The three headed east across the small valley they had admired for the better part of two or three weeks; it turned out to be bigger than they thought—much bigger. It was covered in small streams and brooks, none more than a significant trickle of water, with one main "river," if you wanted to call it that. They were good on their supply of water, and places like this gave the group ample opportunity to gather usable items as they traveled, most notably, edible items such as berries, grasses, and, of course, the random fish John could easily snare. The boys made steady progress that day, adhering to the "comfortable pace" Sid had promised. They didn't need to break themselves back into the mode of hiking, they didn't need to rush where they were going, and Sid suspected that Nik was still plotting their course and would find it easier to do so without thinking about a brisk hike.

They reached the river's bank and stopped for a break as they looked back on their path up to the area of the small ridge. "I can barely see where we started with all the trees. It all looks the same," said Sid. "We've made good progress."

John looked back too. "This valley didn't look this wide from where we were before," he noted. "I think we must have dipped down some small hills several times walking down to the river—sure adds to the feel of the walk."

Nik looked back and noticed several spots where they appeared to have dropped slightly in elevation, which would explain the misperception of actual walking distance. "It's no big deal. We're walking, and it's all the same when we get to where we're going," Nik added.

"And other than Yorktown, where would we be going, actually?" John asked, now spooling up his playfully smart aleck tone.

Nik looked at him and chuckled. "I'll tell you at dinner," he barked.

Sid laughed and uttered, "That's right, John. You cook, and Nik will pontificate while eating—a perfect combination."

Nik shook his head, wiped the sweat off of his forehead, and said, "No, it's not like that—"

John quickly jumped in. "I know, man. Don't sweat it—ha-ha, no pun intended!"

Sid mumbled, "Oh boy, more wit. Trapped in 1781 with a band of traveling comedians."

They rested for an hour or so, drank some water, and headed east again, stopping about six o'clock that evening to camp for the night. There were some trees and cover to bed down in, and it just seemed like a comfortable place for the boys to stop. They spent an hour or so preparing their overnight accommodations and the rest of the dusk period to get a bite to eat and discuss the path forward.

Sid was trying to find some material to add to the pouches of golden disks to quiet them down, as they created quite a bit of clanking noise while the boys walked. He complained about the noise throughout the day. "This will never do! How the hell will we be able to sneak around with these things making this commotion?"

They had combined all of the disks into one pouch, thinking they would be able to better contain them and keep them quieter than if there were three packages of gold clanking around; they were sadly mistaken.

John and Nik rustled around the area for something that Sid could use as packing material and came up with the fluffy material from cattail plants. They figured it could be packed into the pouches of gold and tied up with vine or twine to keep it all together. Sid thought this was a great find. "It's perfect!" he exclaimed. "Good deal, and we are going back to three pouches. I thought about it, and I think we need to each have a supply, as is with everything else we have on us, in case of an unforeseen happening where we get separated."

John and Nik nodded and began dumping the cattails out for Sid to process and pack into their gold pouches. He counted out the gold bullion as evenly as possible, prepared the three bundles, handed them out to Nik and John, and proclaimed, "I wash my hands of the golden noise! Now ... let's eat!"

Sid was particularly hungry on this night, but unfortunately, there wasn't much to feast on. They hadn't spent too much time really foraging around for food, so it was a pretty lean dinner. John had caught some small fish in some of the streams, and the group had collectively passed up on two medium-sized turtles; they could have done something with them for dinner but didn't like the idea of eating a turtle.

"We should have grabbed the turtles and maybe roasted a leg or made soup or something," mumbled Sid.

Nik replied, "Eh, I would have felt bad eating a turtle. Here, man, have my portion of the fish. I am not that hungry tonight. We'll find something tomorrow for us to feast on; I'm sure of it. All this time, and I really can't remember a time we went hungry. Yeah, there were some lean moments, but we never starved."

John piped up with an exuberant, "Yeah, tomorrow will bring food. We'll actually spend some time looking for food tomorrow."

The three settled down and discussed the path forward and how they would have liked to be back at C-10. Nick outlined the path east. The basic plan was to move east to the coast and figure out how to move up to Yorktown.

Sid looked at Nik inquisitively. "Move up to Yorktown? Isn't there a bunch of water between the coast and there?"

A pause yielded to John adding, "Uh, yeah, shouldn't we probably head north and approach Yorktown from the west? I know you have The French Plan and all, but that sounds a little risky."

Sid, wanting to add his voice of concern for the plan that put them on the "high seas" with the French fleet, somewhat weakly offered the idea of a reconnaissance mission to explore the land route to the Yorktown battlefield.

Nik sat down now and began to draw a map in the dirt. "Yeah, I thought of that, but the area is completely covered with humanity—British, Hessians, and Tories on the coast of the York River and all forms of American and French on the land side for as far as the eye can see.

"This entire area, all the way up to the battlefield at Yorktown," Nik explained, now pointing at his map, "is, or will be, totally covered in troops and people. We wouldn't stand a chance of going unnoticed in all of this."

The others pondered the problem, and Nik offered a compromise. "We can edge north for the next few days and see what we observe. If it's clear, we can continue until we either get there or we get stopped by a massive amount of humanity of whatever form it might take. Sound good?"

"That's okay, but how badly does that screw up what you had planned, Nik?" Sid asked.

"It doesn't," Nik replied. "Not at this point. But at some point, we'll have to make a decision to go one way or the other or potentially lose our chance to see the white flag rise over Cornwallis's war-ravaged headquarters on the York River—not that that's actually what happens, but you know what I'm saying. Also, depending on how far we go, we may have to double back some distance along our path to get to where we need to be."

The boys figured they were at least two or three weeks away from that decision and didn't worry about a little "erratic navigation" at this point. It was July 25, and the boys spent the next twenty-seven days zigzagging all around the eastern Virginia countryside attempting to move north while avoiding British and American forces. They were persistent in their task, but it appeared hopeless, because the number of British, Tory, and Hessian forces to their north, east, and west, coupled with groups of American forces moving into the area to their west, was exposing their flank to the point of becoming very dangerous. At one point, they were pinned between seven groups of mixed forces, which were jockeying for position in the developing central Virginia battlefield areas.

"Okay, dumb idea!" Sid began. "I am tired of playing tag with these guys!"

John sat down on a log. "Well, at least they don't know we are here," he tried to happily convey.

Sid shrugged. "True."

Nik stayed quiet—not on purpose, he just couldn't add anything to the somewhat depressing conversation. Sid continued by complaining again. "We have beaten ourselves up in this quagmire! I officially dislike the swamps in Virginia!"

The boys had been traveling in predominantly wet areas for the past few weeks, and it was taking a toll on them. It was hard work while tromping around squishy ground, and they knew they had been spoiled with their first year in the past, because they spent a majority of their time in more mountainous terrain and areas with a much more solid footing.

"So, what do we do?" John asked abruptly.

A pause fell on the group for a minute before Sid spoke up. "We go to the—what did you call it Nik?—the 'I am French, and I am surrendering plan'?"

John laughed, and Nik looked up a bit surprised. "Ha-ha," John blurted. "Yeah, that would be the one."

Nik shook his head. "No, it's called The French Plan," he corrected Sid. "Well, I am slightly confused on where exactly we are," Nik admitted. "We have bobbed and weaved so much in our course; I couldn't even begin to guess exactly which direction to head. I would say, though … we should head east, and if we need to, we can edge slightly south to eventually make the coast."

John immediately asked, "Do we want to take a day to get our bearings and try to dry out our lower bodies a bit?"

There was almost instant agreement, and they now began to move to some slightly higher ground they had spotted a few days before. They knew enough to realize they had moved in a sort of circle and were near those small hills again. It was also observed that this area had recently become devoid of any other humanity, so they thought. In any event, they were safe for a few days.

John and Nik looked for items in their immediate surroundings for dinner, while Sid looked around their proposed camp area and set up some snap traps for alarms during the night. He thought of their place at C-10—cabin, running water, all the comforts that 1781 could offer them. He now wanted to return back there sooner rather than later.

After a small dinner, the boys continued to discuss the day and the events of the past few weeks. Sid was frustrated with the attempts they had made to move farther north and was surprised at the number of groups and frequency at which they continued running into gaggles of people. John was equally bothered by it all and shared Sid's annoyance with the areas they had been traversing over and over again. Nik was all of these things and more, given that he was generally unhappy (even after all this time) with the whole "being outside" thing. He had a notion that the "traffic" was going to be fairly heavy and quite a challenge moving north, but it had been even worse than he thought.

"So we slide east?" John asked. "To where?"

"Well, I am at a bit of a loss right now," Nik admitted. "We need to move east and see what we find in the way of coastal access. I am hoping that the farther east we move away from some of these major thruways, the better we can get our bearing on where we need to be and figure out a way to get there. It's just so busy around here. I remember that Norfolk, north of us on the coast of a bay, is basically connected to the Chesapeake. It is most likely a decent size and a busy place by this time in history. We certainly do not want to go there via land; now if we are on the water, we would probably go unnoticed—I think."

John frowned. "Oh, I don't like a thought ending with 'I think'!"

"Unfortunately, we are in for some more wetlands walking," John added, "but with that, we will be in a different mode, I think."

"Different mode?" questioned Sid.

"Yeah, you'll see. It'll be pretty cool," replied Nik.

"Okay, okay, ye land lubbers. Get some sleep! We head east at first light!" Sid comically ordered in a pirate-ish sort of voice.

... 43 ...
East and the Way Out?

AND HEAD OUT THEY did. During the next thirteen days, they got serious—seriously lost, frustrated, agitated, and tired. They had left the major traffic of all the human contact behind, which was a great thing. The unfortunate part of the past two weeks was that they had hiked their way into an area of swamp and muck, east of their start point. The boys were still staunchly a team, but they were utterly exhausted from the miserable waste they had been laboring through.

John began to yell in frustration. "Does this ever end? We have been stuck in this for weeks! Have we been going straight? I am so pissed, I can't think!"

Sid joined in, attempting a comical tone. "I know, man. It's okay ... we'll figure a way—"

"*No!* We need to get out of this—*now!* I can't stand it!" John interrupted Sid in a not so comical snap.

They stopped now on a "high spot" in the swamp. "Okay, here you are John; we are officially out of the swamp," Nik said trying to be light and jovial.

"*No!* We are not out of this stinking mess. Wow, do I hate this place!" John continued. John now dropped his gear and announced that he had to go "pee on this place" that he hated so much "with all of his soul." Sid and Nik laughed, and Nik asked him not to go too far, as they didn't want to lose him in the mucky quagmire.

Minutes later, Sid began to telling Nik about staying there for the evening when a great screaming and splashing erupted from the swamp in John's general direction. Sid pulled his pistol and chambered a round as the two took off toward the commotion. They met John less than halfway back to their dry location.

"Guys! Holy—! Guys, you need to—" John yelled. Nik caught John as Sid moved several steps forward, looking for the immediate suspected peril that might make John ramp up to the energy level he had.

"What, man? What are you so spooked about?" Nik asked quickly.

John, still standing in the swampy muck, ranted. "Dude! Good word for it—spooked! You are not going to believe this, really, I wouldn't have run back like … Where's my stuff?"

Sid and Nik looked at each other and glanced back in the direction of the hump. "Guys! You left my stuff?"

Sid now requested—no, demanded—they return quickly to the dry area where John's gear had been left, and then they would listen to what had John so freaked out. They quickly arrived back at John's gear and knelt down to rest.

Sid rapidly began the interrogation. "What was all that yelling? Do you want to get us found?"

"No, no, but you won't believe what I saw," John began. "You are not going to believe it!"

Nik wanted John to calm down and catch his breath. "Okay, okay. Are you okay? Did you get bitten by something?"

John looked at Nik. "What? Stop! No, it's nothing like that! It's … you are not going to believe it!"

"Then what the hell is it?" Sid yelled, now getting pissed and waving his pistol in the air. "Do I need this or not?"

John looked at him strangely. "No." John then turned to look at Nik. "Why does he have his pistol out?"

Nik started laughing. "Because you started yelling and running like the giant swamp monster from Mars was after you."

"No, no monster," John quickly said. "Pirate ship!"

Sid holstered his pistol. "Did you hit your head on something? What the hell are you talking about? Pirate ship?"

John looked at Sid. "Really. Really, I'm not creative enough to dream up something like this." He looked at Nik and smiled. "That's Nik's department."

Nik, knowing the tension had subsided, yelled back, "Hey! Hey, keep that down. I only want you guys to know I'm crazy."

John continued. "There is no one around, but right over there," John pointed to the southeast, "is a big, wooden ship, just sitting there in the mud of the swamp."

"Really?" asked Sid. "You're not kidding?"

John now stood up. "Really! I kid you not—follow me. This is the thing we've been looking for!"

Nik retorted in a mumble, "We were looking for a pirate ship?"

They began trudging back through the swamp where John had gone to relieve his bladder, and just beyond a decent-sized thicket of swamp trees stood a mast pointing straight up out of the swamp. The boys moved closer to the apparent shipwreck and were able to get a better look at the large mast sticking out of an unexpectedly large, grounded hull of an apparently previously ocean-worthy sailing vessel.

"You have got to be kidding," mumbled Sid, his pistol now coming back out of its holster. "Would you look at that?"

Nik stopped and also armed himself. "It's probably abandoned, but better safe than sorry. Right?"

John commented, as he pulled his sidearm out as well, "Well, if they didn't hear us yet, they probably aren't there. Right?"

Sid looked at John. "Umm, yeah. Next time please be 'very, very quiet,' like your 'hunting wabbits' or something and come and get us. Okay?"

John smiled and nodded. "Sorry."

Stopped now, they spent more than a few minutes looking over the spectacle that lay in front of them. "You guys think it's safe to board?" John asked.

Nik began the theory session with, "Probably. It's huge and sitting perfectly upright in the mud."

"Yeah, almost like it was beached there on purpose—or built there," Sid muttered. This comment brought a silence and gave Nik the chills. They pondered their next move for a few more minutes and decided to circumnavigate the hull, looking for any signs of life and a possible way aboard. An hour went by without a sign of life on the vessel, and the boys had inspected all but the very back of the wreck.

The approach to this area of the wreck was totally overgrown and very dense with vegetation. Sid did point out, however, that if they were unable to gain access any other way, they may be able to scale up the dense overgrowth to get up and into the beached remains of the ship. They spent a few more minutes looking for an easy way up into the ship and decided to go to Sid's plan B.

"You would think a wrecked ship would have a hole or something in it that we could just walk into," John said with a grunt.

"We could make a door," Nik suggested.

"Nah," said Sid. "Let's get up via the trees back there. Who knows, maybe she's seaworthy! If we make a hole in the hull, we won't be able to sail it out to see the French and the surrender of the British."

Nik looked at Sid with the perfect "What the hell are you thinking?" stare, gawked, and said, "Stop it!"

Sid smiled and replied, "I was just sayin'."

"Yeah, I know. You were just saying ... sometimes, man." Nik said, now shaking his head in disbelief.

John laughed and started looking at the bramble of vegetation on the backside of the ship. He started up one of the taller pieces of tree-type flora and made it about halfway up and stopped; he froze at an opening in the hull they hadn't seen from ground level.

"You okay, John?" Nik inquired.

There was a pause before John replied with a shaky, "Yeah, I was just surprised by this overgrown porthole.... It's open but pretty small. It's pitch black in there. I can't see any light or breaks in the decking."

Sid began to climb up the lowest part of a connection tree, and Nik was now a bit on edge. John continued up, and although it looked like the climb became more difficult, he made good time to the top where he could see over the edge of the gunwale and onto the deck of the ship.

Nik yelled up to John. "Don't step too hard out onto the deck ... who knows if it's solid."

"No worries. I'll tread lightly," John yelled back down to Nik.

Sid insisted of John. "Dude, take only one step onto the deck. Don't go wandering around—wait for us."

John disappeared over the side with a small struggle, and Sid made quick work of shimmying up the swamp vegetation. Nik chuckled, as he figured that Sid didn't believe John on his word that he wouldn't stay put at the top and wait for them. As Sid worked his way over the side of the boat and onto the deck, he yelled down to Nik. "C'mon, man."

Nik wasn't exactly a climber. Steep hills and ridges, no problem; ropes and trees, not so much. It took Nik a few tries to begin the ascent, jockey around for a better position and footholds, and then start up a bit more. He finally made it up in a sweat and gasped. "Okay, that sucked!" As he picked his head up from being exhausted, he couldn't believe the view.

The three stood fairly close together and looked around. They were positioned high enough to be able to see over the entire swamp and to all points beyond. John pointed at Nik and then pointed to the north. "Look, man. What's that look like?"

Nik peered a little over to the right side of the vessel to get a full view to where John had pointed. "Looks like a lot of water, the ocean maybe?" Nik quietly mumbled.

John excitedly responded, "Yup, that's what it looks like. We found our way out to Yorktown! Sweet!"

Sid now looked, squinting to see what he could see. "Well, I don't know about that, but we sure do have a nice perch up here."

The three stood almost paralyzed for a time, just looking around and studying their surroundings. It appeared they were actually standing on a portion of the ship that had been covered at one time; it looked like an area that had several decks or levels, based on the scant remaining structure, which was now missing most of its walls, floors, and support beams. These missing pieces were nowhere to be found, except in a location with a sort of recessed or sunken pile of rubble that had filled in and appeared to be a possible way down into the ship.

John took a few steps out and away from the side where they had been standing. "Feels solid," he exclaimed, taking a few more steps.

Sid now took a few steps in another direction and reported the same thing. "Amazing! Who knows how long this thing has been sitting here like this! It is still in good shape structurally."

Nik looked down off the edge they had climbed up; he didn't like heights—*at all!* He turned to find Sid and John almost all the way to the bow of the boat. "Hey, guys, wait up!" And then he muttered to himself, "Watch, I'll fall through the decking."

He didn't, and all three converged on front of the beached and aging hulk of a vessel, joking about "moving this thing out onto the open waters." They all knew that wasn't happening, but it was a fun discussion. John looked around and was pleased to be out of the swamp, as Sid now commented, "So, we going below deck?" A quiet came about the team.

Nik meekly said, "Let's just look and see what we can see from up here."

"Ha! C'mon, Nik, where's your spirit of adventure? It'll be fine" Sid joked.

John came to Nik's defense, in a way, by mentioning that the deck appeared sound, but what he saw of the below deck areas looked to be in far worse shape. Nik sharply responded, "Adventure will get you hurt or killed, my friend. You know my theory on luck."

Nik had explained his "cup of luck" theory many months ago to Sid and John. It was a bit odd, for sure, but it had always kept Nik on the safer (and boring) side of life. His theory and "law to live by" went something like this: every time you take a risk or do something that is clearly stupid, careless, or reckless, you rattle or shake your "cup of luck." In the cup of luck are "luck chips," and if you rattle them too much, one—or a few—fall out, and you lose them. When you run out of your luck chips—in Nik's mind—you're done. You have no luck left, and the next time dumbness crosses your mind, real dumbness, you're really done.

Yes, it sounded odd, and over the years, Sid had called Nik many things for his theory, which would have (in the twenty-first century) had Nik committed to various wards with little white padded rooms and little white jackets. There was really no harm in his theory of luck. It just made for a more boring life for one adhering to such things. Either that, or it assured you a better chance of a longer life. It all depended on how you looked at it.

It was September 3, 1781, at around five forty in the evening, and the guys just sat high on the deck of the ship discussing their camping plans for the upcoming night. They were a bit uncomfortable with how exposed they felt out in the open without the trees and woods around them, as they had grown very accustomed to the cover of the mountains or forest during the past year or so. They decided to investigate the only remaining intact piece of the vessel left, which was on the deck and above the deck level. It looked to be two stories, but it might have been three or four originally. It had probably met the same fate the other deck structures had on the rear of the ship; they either slid or blew off into the sea or the marsh during a hurricane or some other strong wind event. There was no way they could know for sure.

The small structure was fairly battered, and John hoped to find a way to the area below deck. No such luck—the entire area of the item was strictly above the deck and was in pretty bad shape structurally. Sid carefully scampered up to the second level and moved to the back of the area. He paused for a little while and then whispered down to Nik and John. "Psst. Hey, guys, come look at this!"

Nik and John made their way up to where Sid was and found him pointing at a large rowboat-looking craft. John happily exclaimed, "It's a longboat, or at least a large dinghy! It would be perfect for our plans—The French Plan." And then he laughed. "I'm sorry, man. It just sounds like a silly idea some modern-day British comedian would come up with."

Nik moved over to the boat, which was lying upside down on the second-level mezzanine floor. "Do I dare stick my hands under this thing to lift it up?" Nik asked with a slight nervous tone in his voice.

Sid moved over to the boat. "Let me pick it up," he offered. "Stand back." Sid now pried up the front side of the boat and began to get under it.

"Well, nothing ran out from underneath it. That's a good sign," mumbled John as Nik laughed at the comment. Sid didn't find the humor in it and completed his action to position the boat on its side.

Nik moved closer to the boat and inspected the wood and joints. "Boy, they knew how to put these things together," Nik said. "Looks like it's in really good shape."

"We won't know until we get it into that water," Sid noted.

Sid and John were able to guide the boat down to the first level of the small covered area. "Let's leave this here for now. We'll figure out what to do with it tomorrow," suggested John.

"Yeah, that sounds like a good plan," replied Sid.

At that moment, John announced he was going down to get some branches and material to make bedding material for the evening. Sid offered to help and asked Nik to follow them to the edge, stay on the boat, and pull up the brambles of material they were going to collect.

"Sure." Nik nodded in agreement.

Sid didn't want Nik to go back down to the swamp floor, remembering the trouble he'd had getting up onto the boat the first time. Sid thought about the past year or so. *Nik is as sure-footed as a goat in the hills, but he can't climb without the good earth under him for anything.* He chuckled at the thought.

John stopped again and peered into the porthole on the rear of the ship that had surprised him hours before. When Sid reached the same level, John said with a smile, "We need to look in there. You never know what we'll find."

"Yeah," Sid began, "tomorrow." That response drew a "party pooper" comment from John. They continued down and collected what appeared to Nik to be an entire jungle of undergrowth, branches, and leafy coverings.

After the fifteenth load, Nik yelled down, "Umm, what are we creating up here? A world-famous botanical garden or something?"

Sid looked up. "Quiet up there! Keep pulling this stuff up—geez," he yelled and then laughed as he scampered back off into the swampy woods. After several more trips, Sid and John climbed back up on deck, and the three proceeded to set up some snap traps made of sticks, much like Sid had at the thicket near Charleston. They placed the traps in clear and obvious locations near where they had climbed up. There was no other apparent easy way to gain access to the deck from the swamp short of using a grappling device and rope, so this area was well covered with the noise-making brambles of sticks.

The boys created a mat of brush and slept under the stars—no trees, no bushes, no cover at all, not even clouds in the night sky. It was the first time in a long time they were simply out in the open, flat on their backs, and totally exposed. They didn't feel too worried about it, as they were now comfortable on their raised platform above the swamp floor. Conversation was slight, since they were tired from the day's events and, really, from the previous week's events.

Sid mumbled to his compatriots, "So we get our boat down tomorrow and see if it's seaworthy?"

"I don't see why not," John answered. "What do you think, Nik?"

A snore came from Nik's direction. "Ha, he must have been dead tired," John chuckled.

Sid sat up and looked around, "Yeah, we have been traipsing all around the state of Virginia for the past month. It probably caught up to him. Hell, I think we are all tired."

John sat up now and looked around at the little he could see in the moonlight. "You think we'll ever get out of here, Sid?"

Sid nodded. "One way or another, I guess. It's not like we can walk through time. This may be our time now. We may find ourselves walking back to C-10 in two or three months and watching each other grow old. I'm not sure what else to think or say. Chuckles over there," Sid said, pointing at the slumbering Nik, "he's your theory guy—not me."

John accepted that and now understood that Sid was beginning to get used to the idea of living out the rest of his days in this time.

It was a sobering thought for John. He said good night to Sid and rolled over for the night's sleep.

Sid continued to sit up and stare at the moonlit swampland, wondering if he really believed what he'd just told his friend. After a few minutes of pondering it all, he figured that the finality of their lives was up to a higher power, and he would do the best he could for himself and his compatriots. He sat quietly and as still as possible now—a chill came over him, and he looked up to the heavens for an answer.

A short time later he felt very tired, and he lay down for the night. He didn't have any answers, but he was looking forward to water-testing the rowboat and getting on with their adventure—their mission.

... 44 ...
Possibilities of Deliverance

Banging, slamming, crashing, and the absolutely horrific sounds of splintering lumber abruptly shattered Nik's deep sleep. He sprung up and reached for his pistol, expecting to find the grounded hulk, which they were camped upon, in a state of collapse. He quickly gained his senses and whirled around to look for Sid and John; he finally found them tearing apart the remains of the two-story structure.

"What in the hell are you guys doing?" Nik yelled. As he looked around, he realized it was still pretty early in the morning.

Sid apologized for the noise. "We are making a planking system to get this boat down to the ground," he explained.

Nik rubbed his eyes and complained. "You scared the daylights out of me! I thought the whole ship was collapsing—with us on it. Talk about a bad dream."

Nik wandered over to the new construction zone, scratched his head, and looked down and their handiwork. "Okay, that might work," he said. "Man, I could go for some bacon. I'm starving!"

John put down the boards he was holding. "You want me to go find something for breakfast?" he asked.

Sid put down his armload of debris and joined in. "Yeah, let's eat. I saw some turtles and lizards down there yesterday."

Nik smirked, "Blaahhhh! I asked for bacon, and he talks about lizards.... What happened to birds or fish ... eggs, bacon ... toast?"

Nik shrugged and continued. "I'll get a small fire going." With that, he walked off.

Sid and John just looked at each other. "He'll cheer up," John said.

Sid chuckled. "Yup … after he wakes up."

The three convened around the campfire Nik had built on a dry hump of land near the front of the mud-bogged vessel. Sid and John had wrestled a small assortment of critters for their morning meal—two small birds (which John cleaned very quickly), a turtle, and some type of eggs (which made Nik frown, because when he'd mentioned eggs before, he was really talking about chicken eggs and not mystery eggs). John announced he had dibs on the snake he had caught and cleaned. Again, Nik wondered how he had made it this long "camping" in the eighteenth century. Sid didn't seem to really care what he ate and began disassembling the turtle.

"So we get this longboat down from the ship and into the water today?" Sid asked, hoping the answer was yes.

Nik and John both nodded. "Let's get this show on the road!" Nik agreed. "We have a little more than a month to get to the York River and hopefully see the British defeat."

John asked the obvious question. "How far are we by sea to where we want to go?"

Nik paused for a moment and then concluded, "I have no idea, but I bet you we have walked further than we need to paddle." After another short pause, Nik asked, "Speaking of paddling, how are we going to move this thing, assuming it floats?"

Sid sat back now as he roasted two of what he thought were turtle eggs over the fire and squinted a bit. "Yeah, I have been thinking about that. We'll need to fabricate some paddles or something."

"Maybe a sail or something if we have wind," John mentioned.

"All good ideas—we are thinking like we need to!" Nik bellowed. "I'll look around after breakfast for something to use for paddle and or sail material."

More ideas for the trip and its progression surfaced as they sat and worked while eating breakfast—where they were heading and how they would make their way, where they should camp, how they would avoid other boats and folks on the shores, and on it went on for what seemed like the entire day.

After they were done eating, John and Sid went right to work on the ramp to get the boat down from the ship's deck, while Nik went looking for items useful for the propulsion of their new swamp/lake/ocean-going chariot. Soon the rowboat was sliding down the ramp under some control from vines and branches that John had tied to it. Sid and Nik were lowering it in a sort of controlled fashion using the makeshift ropes, but John rather intelligently wasn't standing under it as it came down. It made its journey down safely, and Sid ran down off the boat to see if it would float.

Sid wanted to be the first in the boat out on the small piece of marsh. He enjoyed the status of being first at things, no matter how silly.

Nik chuckled at his friend. "So predictable," he said with a smile. "John! Get the boat down to the water and jump in before Sid gets down there."

"No, no! Wait," Sid yelled, "I have to be the one who sinks if it's going to sink!"

Nik yelled back. "Dude, that's stupid! What sense does that make?"

As Sid ran along, he continued yelling at Nik. "Hey, who knows? Maybe I am the key! Remember, I ran ahead on the bald. Maybe I'll do this and open the stupid hole in time and get us home!"

John burst out laughing. "Ha, you have lost your mind! Be my guest," he invited Sid, as he pointed to the craft sitting on the floor of the swamp.

All three of them were needed to move the rowboat over the floor of the marshy swamp to the water's edge, so they stood and waited for Nik to come and help. Nik, taking a quick look off the front of the ship to get his bearings on exactly where the large body of water was, started down to meet up with John and Sid. His arrival brought jeers from Sid: "C'mon, you're slow as a—"

Nik sat down and relayed just how far they needed to move the boat to actually be able to make it out of the misery of the swamp and get to the lake, which led to the bay, which led to the ocean. "It's not just over the hill, you know. We probably have several miles to carry this thing before we get it into water that we can navigate to where we want to be."

"Crud! I never thought of that," said Sid. "I was in too big of a hurry to get in and test the worthiness of this thing."

Nik, not wanting to bring Sid down, bellowed, "And you shall, my captain! Just not right at this moment!"

John motioned over to a bigger area of marshy, liquid goo water and said, "Sid, we can drag the boat over here, and you can test it in this puddle of wonderful, smelly, brown, puke-looking liquid."

They all laughed at that. "Yeah, you can do that," Nik said. "I mean, we should test it before we huff it out all that way to the actual lake, or bay, or whatever connects this mud pit to the ocean, right?"

Sid, now looking more upbeat, began moving over to the boat, and before they knew it, the craft that held all their hopes and ideas of navigating north to the York River was floating with a proud Sid standing in it. John quickly jumped in after seeing that it wasn't going to sink, and Nik just watched from the shore of the "goo pit" as Sid and John jumped up and down in the rocking boat.

"Well, it's water tight!" Nik jovially reported after some inspection. "Okay, don't break the damn thing! We need it to get where we're going."

John and Sid stopped their tomfoolery and jumped back onto dry land. They dragged the boat to a dry area and looked around.

"So, which direction is it?" asked John.

Nik, expecting this question, pointed north. "That way," he announced. "A few miles, and we'll be at water's edge. Then, days and weeks, maybe even a month of rowing, who knows.... That way," he reiterated.

Sid smirked. "Wow. Mr. Exacto today, huh?"

Nik honestly had no idea how far they needed to paddle. He could make a guess at the mileage over land, but nautical estimates were beyond him unless he made many assumptions, which he felt would be an utter waste of time. In an effort to appease his friends, he began with, "Well, I would assume that it's basically the same distance as a land route, but time-wise I have no idea, because we'll be paddling. The wind could be against us, at our backs, or anything in between. It's hard to say."

John nodded. "We know. We're just giving you a hard time."

Nik began walking away. "So when do you want to leave?" Nik asked.

Sid jumped at this and quickly answered Nik's question. "Today! We leave today!"

John followed up with, "Yeah, man, let's go!"

Nik stopped and looked at his friends. "Really? You don't want to bask in this wonderful swamp? It's so lovely here.... We even have our own private accommodations in the nautical suite and fun room."

Sid and John weren't sure if Nik was serious about staying, and Sid looked confused. "Huh?" he started.

"Just kidding," Nik said. "Let's get our stuff and get out of here."

John, now relieved, began pulling the boat to a point on their northern route out of their present camp location.

They returned to the deck of the ship and collected their things. There wasn't that much scattered around, as they had only been there for one night. Nik looked around at the ship and wondered if it was still there, like this, in 2010. He'd never know unless they could find a way back to their time. *A long shot to impossible*, he thought to himself. He would never verbalize his thoughts on the subject, though; he knew they all missed their families and just didn't want to bring it up. He figured they'd cross that path when they got back to C-10 and then all have a good cry, but for now, it was time for stiff upper lip and to move forward.

Sid quickly gathered his things and packed the brush they'd collected into the small covered area where they found the boat. He figured if they came this way again, it would make for a good resource. His thoughts were of their trek forward and their future on the water. They were not sailors or seafaring folks. He wasn't even sure John could swim. Then, after thinking on that for a bit, Sid felt stupid. He was pretty sure with all the outdoor activities John was involved in back in 2010, that he could swim just fine. *What was I thinking?* Sid thought to himself again.

"C'mon, ye matey," Sid yelled to the others in his best pirate voice. "Move yer arrrsses now!"

Nik looked at Sid as if he were demented and smiled.

John jumped up. "What in the hell is wrong with you?" He couldn't help but laugh as he hoisted his gear and climbed over the side of the grounded, aging hulk of the ship. He was happy to leave the swamp and wondered what it would be like on the water. He figured they would basically follow the shorelines for the most part and camp along the water's edge in the evenings. They didn't have an anchor, so they couldn't stay on the water at night without someone staying awake; that just wasn't going to happen. John casually assumed they would figure it out, and he was just happy to get going to somewhere, anywhere at this point. He hated the swamp.

... 45 ...
No Easy Task

A NEARLY THREE-MILE HIKE lay ahead of the boys as they carried the boat they had unloaded from the beached ship. Minutes into the hike, John blurted, "This is not going to be easy."

"Nope," Nik replied. "We'll drag it, carry it, maybe use some logs to put it on and hoist it up on our shoulders or something. We have a month and a week or so to get this thing and us to the York River. This will be the hardest part, I think." As he spoke, Nik secretly crossed his fingers. The three looked at the boat for a few minutes, picked it up again, and began walking north with it flipped upside down and hoisted up on their shoulders.

"Okay, this sucks," Nik began.

Sid and John both grunted, and Sid retorted, "Let's get as far as we can and then rest a bit."

John tried to reassure the group that this would pass; they just had to push through it and get to a main body of water. He was right, but it was going to be brutal, as they were not used to carrying something as bulky as the boat. They had enough already with their gear and the few things they had picked up and kept along the way.

The spent many, many days (seven to be exact) trudging through the swampy areas with the boat in tow. At one point they even used some logs to drag the boat along their route. Only a few areas were wet enough to fully float the craft along its way.

Finally, on September 11, their grand expedition reached the banks of the major expanse of water they had seen from the deck of the landlocked shipwreck.

"This is it," Sid announced. "This has to be the large bay we saw from the shipwreck. Thank God!"

Nik agreed. "Yes, I think it is. In theory, all we have to do is row north, and we should reach an inlet that gets us out to the ocean/ Chesapeake Bay."

John interrupted the thought. "Do we want to spend a night— or two or three—here and fabricate some paddles, get some dinner, and enjoy a good night's sleep before we leave in morning? I don't know about you, but I'm dead tired and, um, sore as hell!"

They all agreed and spent the rest of the day finding food, building a fire, and looking for suitable lumber out of which to fabricate a set of paddles.

By five o'clock that evening, they had secured dinner in the form of fresh fish, as John had outdone himself once again. Sid and Nik identified and harvested a dozen suitable pieces of green lumber that could appropriately be shaped for use as a set of oars. They weren't very big, but they'd do the job, even though they'd most likely pose a challenge in the forming of an actual paddle. They sat near the fire on the bank and admired their surroundings.

"You would never know by sitting here that just over there," John now pointed south and west, "is a stinky, nasty swamp full of yuck and bugs!"

"Yeah, it's pretty nice here," admitted Sid. It was a cool evening with a slight breeze and a very low insect count along the huge expanse of water in front of them as they watched the sun drop behind the trees in the western sky.

The shade had been a lifesaver during the past weeks. Except for the short time on the deck of the ship, the swamp and forest cover had made the waning summer heat of the American southeast bearable. Sitting on the bank of this mass of water was a little like heaven—quiet, cooler, serene-looking, and calming by all definition of the word.

"So," Sid started, "these oars might take us a day or so to get right. We may have to work hard on these and make several sets— you know, just in case."

The three smiled. "Uh-huh," Nik mumbled.

The guys retrieved their knives out of their packs and went to work on the lumber. They found that flattening out the round logs was a challenge; the diameter reduction for creating the handle areas was far easier. To Nik, this seemed counterintuitive, but he wasn't skilled at, or even familiar with, wood carving or woodworking.

Whatever, Nik thought to himself, *like any of us are skilled Colonial anything. Stuck in 1781, oy!*

John looked at Nik, saw that he was thinking or pondering something, and asked him what was up. Nik looked up and relayed his thoughts to his friends.

"Yeah, you're right, but we've done okay for *who* and *when* we are," Sid said.

"Oh, I know you're right—just funny thoughts as we sit here and whittle or carve or whatever we're doing to get these things ready for our waterborne adventure," Nik added.

Sid wasn't much of a water-oriented individual. He could swim without a problem, but boating? *Ha,* he thought as he continued to shape his piece of wood.

John was fine with it all, as he had many stories of kayaking, canoeing, white-water rafting, falling off all of the above, and surviving to tell his tales. The stories kept them entertained during their time in the past; none of them cared if they were totally true or a work of complete fiction. Sid and Nik were pretty sure that John did all the things he talked about and probably more, and they hoped his stories didn't ever stop, as they were stories that they certainly, short of this adventure in time, would never have for themselves.

The fire dimmed as the sun went down; they kept it purposefully low now. There was no need or desire to draw any attention, as was the rule for basically the past year and more. Sid had carved two oars, and John had completed three in the time they had been relaxing and conversing about this and that. Nik was just finishing up his first one and looked dejected at the losing count. John proposed that they had whittled at just the correct speeds for an even number of oars, giving them three sets to use on their journey. It made Nik feel better about his lackluster carving performance, and Sid thought it an excellent stopping point for the evening.

"I figure we'll use these and take the other pieces of lumber with us, in case we need them for something," Sid commented, looking for approval.

The boat was plenty long enough for all their gear and the lumber, so they were basically set to start off in the morning on the water, bound for the waters to the north and the Chesapeake Bay. Nik and John nodded in agreement and sat back to enjoy the rest of the cooling evening, finally nodding off. Sid followed suit, and they were all quickly and comfortably asleep for the night.

The next morning came quickly, as the three arose and began to think about their journey ahead. The evening went well and was utterly eventless; they slept so soundly and, well, it appeared to the boys that a turn was in the air. Nik thought it was that autumn was just around the corner, John felt the impending British surrender was somehow changing the feeling among the group, and Sid just felt alive. Sid dragged their craft to the bank of the lake in preparation for their pending departure, while John scattered the residue of the campfire and Nik loaded their belongings into the boat.

"You guys ready?" asked Sid. "Forget staying here any longer. Let's get going."

"I can be in a few minutes," John answered, not expecting the "go" order today.

Nik just looked back into the woods toward the swamp. He looked frozen for a second and peered around, intently scanning the area from which they had walked just the day before. John and Sid unsheathed their rifles and moved over next to Nik.

"What's up?" John inquired.

Nik shook his head to indicate "nothing" and said, "It's okay. Let's go.... I don't see anything; I'm just a little spooked. Let's get on the water."

John became a bit rattled now. "Your spooked means trouble, even if you don't see anything," John explained. "I've grown to trust your 'spooked-ness.' Let's go, I don't like it here anymore!"

They pushed off from the shore and affixed their homemade oars into the places where traditional oars would go. Overall, they were a decent fit with only the occasional slipping out of position—they would make due. Their journey would take them north to the inlet where Lynn Haven Roads would be in 2010, well west of Cape Henry. Then they would hug the coast to the south of them. Every evening, they would go ashore in some "hopefully" inconspicuous place and camp quietly, only to leave early the next morning.

As they traveled, there were a few occasions when they were in an area where, if someone really cared to look up and notice them, they could have. They were in full burlaps, and their 2010 gear was on the logs in the boat, which they had brought along from the swamp's edge. The logs came in very handy for keeping their provisions and weapons raised off the bottom of the boat where water occasionally collected from their day of plying the water toward the goal.

The boys pondered over, only for the shortest of times, traveling by night and camping and sleeping by day. This idea was quickly discounted because of the experiences they'd had on land during daylight in this area of Virginia; there were huge numbers of people about. This area, near the James River, was one of the first places the English settled to pursue trade and development. Of all the places they had been, this was the most populated by far. Honestly, if a passerby saw three men in a rowboat on the coast of a river or bay, no one would have thought the wiser of it. It was a nonevent in most folks' eyes in 1781.

They reached a spot on September 20 where the coast to the south turned away from the boys, and they had to make a decision. "So, we are at the proverbial turning point," Nik began. "We can turn north and move across the James River inlet here to a location close to Hampton Virginia. From there, we will probably have to work pretty damn hard to get to the other side where there will be some French and or British naval vessels stationed. Or we can move farther west and take on the James as the actual river. This could be an easier row and may give us a greater chance of success. But it also may add time onto our trip—potentially significant time—or, well, a major workout. Those are our choices."

Peering at Nik, Sid and John had the "Oh good, it's Mr. Sunshine again!" looks on their faces. Nik wanted to chuckle, but he felt it would probably get him hit or thrown overboard at some point.

A silence fell upon the small craft, the likes of they hadn't seen to date; the small boat now gently drifted with the current. The usually pleasant sound of surf splashing onto the side of their craft posted an almost metronome-like beat that now intensely bothered all the boys instead of relaxing them.

John broke the silence. "Well, we can't just sit here. It's fairly calm out there from what I can see, and we need to make the best time we can. I say we go north toward Hampton."

Nik nodded and looked at Sid. "So? What do you think?"

Sid suggested they leave in the very early hours of the next morning. "I have noticed in the past fifteen days," he explained, "that the water has been the calmest during that part of the day."

Nik agreed. "I have noticed that as well. That gets my vote."

John, agreeing heartily, quickly added, "Sounds good to me!"

They navigated south to a stretch of beach where they landed and camped for the night, and, as the entire voyage on the water went, fish was for dinner. A small fire was created, and quite a few small to medium-sized fish that John had caught were sizzled along with some kind of seaweed John said was edible. Sid frowned at the greens. It was great, even the seaweed was surprisingly good.

"I don't know a whole lot about water or nautical anything, but the survival guy on television taught me about seaweed," Sid admitted. "It just looks nasty."

Nik shrugged. "Whatever it takes. At this point, I think we'll try most things if we know they won't kill us, you know?"

They kept quiet and heard nothing around them other than the water and the birds.

"So, I have noticed that the birds near the ocean don't fall into my bird traps nearly as much as the mountain or land birds do," John noted.

Sid laughed. "You could write a book or something. Or better yet, you could become the world's first bird physiologist or whatever you would call it!" Sid then began quietly laughing at John's expense.

Nik butted in. "Dude, cut it out. I think that is an interesting observation.... I wonder if they taste any different?"

"Ha-ha-ha!" laughed John. And they all settled in for bed, theorizing about the taste of sea birds versus mountain or prairie birds.

Before they all fell asleep, Sid asked Nik, "So, how far is this crossing we have to make?"

Nik delayed his answer and then replied, "Mmm, pretty far. It may take us more than the daylight hours tomorrow to get across. I have an idea, though, so no worries yet. If what I remember should be lying ahead, actually lies ahead, we will see the light, and it will guide us through the darkness."

John rolled over. "Oh ... I hate when he talks like that. It either means he doesn't have a clue, and we are in for some unforeseen problem, or we'll be engaging a British warship in a dinghy out in the middle of the ocean—a damn knife to a damn gun fight! Sweet dreams ... yeah, right!"

Sid chuckled, because he knew what John was saying was so true—not in its exact translation, but he had summed it up pretty well. Sid supported Nik, though. "Eh, we've got it covered," he said with a chuckle before falling asleep.

A final "Oh boy!" came from John as he rolled over and went to sleep.

Nik was fairly sure of his plan now. He hoped the "light" would be there for them, and he felt a certain calm about their chances. He knew the crossing of the James River inlet would take more than twelve hours and hoped the winds or currents would help them along. If the winds or currents went against them, it would be a very long few days, or they would be blown hopelessly off course and have to return to try again.

Ugh, he thought. Suddenly, Nik developed a stomachache, which made for very poor rest that night.

... 46 ...
The Crossing and Time Served

MORNING'S FIRST LIGHT CAME with overcast skies and ominous-looking seas. John gazed at the chop on the water and expressed his deep and growing angst. "I think I'm going to be ill, and we're not even on the water yet!"

Sid agreed. "Oh, this doesn't look like a good day to do this!" he moaned.

Nik was staring intently at the conditions, tossed some sea grasses he picked into the air, and exclaimed, "Gentlemen, this is exactly what we needed! Let's go—right now!"

John and Sid looked at Nik like he had lost his marbles. "Are you kidding?" Sid retorted.

John entered the conversation with, "Nik, it's rough as hell out there."

Nik stopped. "I know, but I have a hunch. If worse comes to worst, we can come back and try tomorrow, right?"

"Well, I guess ... if we don't drown in the process," John whined.

"Nah! I think we'll be fine," Nik stated. "C'mon, c'mon! Let's go."

Sid, now annoyed, asked, "What the hell is the hurry anyway?" After receiving a sharp glare from Nik, he finally agreed. "Okay, okay ... we're coming. Geez."

The group hurried to put their stuff on board. John was scattering the campfire residue when Nik barked at him. "Forget that ... who cares if someone knows that someone camped here. Where we are going, no one will care about this camp! C'mon!"

"What the hell has gotten into you this morning?" Sid now complained to Nik.

"A free ride!" blurted Nik.

They paddled their way toward the northwest, and after an hour, their labor became, well, a little less laborious; actually, it became a lot less laborious.

"You sneaky—!" John blurted. "You're letting Mother Nature take us where we want to go."

Sid now put two and two together. "Aha. The wind ... and the current—they're going our way, aren't they?"

Nik sat back. "Yup. We needed this kind of luck. It may still take us two days to get where we are trying to go, but we won't be quite as worn out when we get there. And I think we have a better chance of getting there as well."

Nik now began to fidget with one of the packs, and in a few minutes, he had pulled the Soviet box radios and the Soviet pistol out from their storage locations. "This is about as good a place as any for these things," he commented.

Sid smiled. "You're going to dump them out here in the salt water, aren't you?"

Nik nodded. "Yup!"

John looked slightly perplexed but simply assumed that they would never be found at the depths of the straight, and that was good enough for him. Sid explained that the saltwater would very quickly corrode the electronics and basically the entire shell of the radios and parts of the pistol, leaving little to nothing in very short order.

"These things will be gone in a few years; there will be no trace of them ... never to be discovered by anyone moving forward," said Nik as he tossed them overboard.

John nodded and smiled. "One less piece of time-line contamination we have to worry about!"

At around two o'clock that afternoon, a shoreline was in sight in the distance, and the winds had died down. Outlines of some larger vessels were clear on the horizon directly to the northeast and east. Nik could make out the turn of the land ahead but couldn't see the bay near Hampton, Virginia. Sid kept a lookout behind them, just as a precaution. He knew full well that in 1781 nothing was going to sneak up on them, but being out in the open had him feeling like he needed to remain vigilant somehow. John manned the oars, course-corrected when needed, and paddled some to maintain their general direction.

Each member of the group spent some time peering through the binoculars at whatever he could see. The boats in the extreme distance were a spectacle and almost an unbelievable sight to each of them. Among the three of them, they thought they could make out between three and nine vessels in the distance at any one time, and they appeared to be moving in and out of sight. They could clearly make out the sails and masts and the existence of the flag they were flying. Unfortunately, the haze in the air and the odd glare of the water made it impossible to identify what country the vessels belonged to.

"British ships?" Sid asked.

"Maybe, but by this time, let's hope they are French. Otherwise, we may be in for a surprise," Nik replied.

The light, erratic winds and a flowing current were steering their small craft north where they would, if Nik had remembered correctly, run into the beaches of the future Hampton Roads area and the very land mass where all the excitement would occur in less than a month's time.

Four o'clock came and went. Five thirty had them drifting slightly west, so they had to start rowing more briskly for a proper landing on the beaches near an area the British called Point Comfort. Nik explained that there was a fort (built around 1820) just north of where he thought they might make a landing.

Additionally, he added, "For some reason I thought that back in the days of the Jamestown settlement, on that very sight of the 1820 fort, was another fort. It began with Al- … Alger- … Algernosomething.... Oh, I don't remember. Needless to say, there is a Colonial presence on the peninsula where we are going to land."

"Hmm, more comforting thoughts—*not!* I wish we were up at our mountain retreat again," John moaned.

"Honestly, being here in this chop, floating along in a really small boat, I'm with you," admitted Sid.

Nik understood and wanted to say something positive, but in all reality, he would also love to be at C-10 in their nice "home sector" with a big fire and the relative security of their hideaway in the mountains. They kept rowing and noticed a new blanket of overcast sky moving in on the area.

"We have to get there; otherwise, we'll be spending the night floating without a clue," John insisted. Just then, John remarked energetically, "Is that the sound of breaking waves?"

The three quickly looked forward in the ever-dimming light of the day. The overcast conditions weren't helping, and they all felt they were in for a rough ride and a possible crash-landing, hopefully on a soft beach versus a rocky shore. John sat down at the oars now and asked the other two to sit down—one forward and one aft, because he was going to "drive this thing into shore."

"How do you know it's the 'correct' shore?" Nik asked.

John replied quickly, "It's getting dark, and we've been on the water all day, moving at a pretty good clip for more than twelve hours. If it ain't the right piece of land we were aiming for, then it'll do till morning. We'll figure out where we are at first light."

This explanation made sense in all of the raucousness of the moment. Sid added smartly, "Please don't break the boat. This has been much easier than walking, and there will be way too many people where we are going to walk to the battle."

Their landing was less than smooth, with the waves breaking prematurely on a few unseen sandbars. The boat never bottomed out, but the ride through the white water was turbulent, and they almost tipped several times. John rowed hard and ended up breaking one of the paddle's ends off, while Nik and Sid shifted their weight to keep the craft balanced. Sid was able to change out the broken oar with a new one almost instantly, as they were slightly closer to him on the floor of their boat—and John rowed on. Nik wasn't sure they were doing much to help, but with the single oar placement on the boat, there wasn't much Sid or Nik could really do.

They made it through to the other side of the sandbars where the waves were smaller and easier to navigate. Sid looked for the end of the journey and reported to John, "Straight ahead. I think I see the beach!"

This was John's cue to row harder, and in a minute or two, they were on shore. What shore, they weren't sure, but solid land it was.

"Sweet!" John rolled out of the boat with excitement.

Sid hopped out and began hurriedly dragging the craft out of the surf, and Nik and John quickly joined in. As they made it to a dryer position, Sid whispered, "Quiet down!"

They all looked around for signs of life. A few minutes of the sounds of the surf, the wind, the seagulls, and no visible indications of human life around had them standing upright and moving to a more covered area.

John began the first real conversation on the beachhead by asking, "I think we should move the boat up and away from the shore and, honestly, all the way to wherever we make camp."

Sid agreed, and Nik said, "Okay, sounds good to me!"

They scanned the area and found a suitable place to settle down for the night; Sid and Nik positioned the boat based on wind direction, so it could be used as a windbreak; the wind had picked up again and was quite stiff and constant off the water. Sid stood up for a moment and announced that it was time for a small patrol mission in the immediate area, just to make sure they had it all to themselves.

"We don't need to be surprised, and we are not going to be here very long," Sid noted. "I just want to be on the safe side."

The three guys moved off to the north and circled all around their camp about a quarter-mile walk with no indications of troops or human development. John inquired about the need to worry about Indians here, and Nik responded after a brief delay. "No, the Jamestown era and expansion for trade, trapping, and such pretty much pushed the Indians out of this area. We are standing in, or within, twenty or thirty miles of what's basically the very area where the British landed and began their first attempts at surviving the New World. There were other settlements, but Jamestown and this area was really the first to make its mark on history."

Camp was cool and loud due to the wind, and a fire was going to be nearly impossible to keep lit or safely contained. That said, Nik and Sid worked on one anyway and had a small, smoldering pile that grew into a small fire after the winds died back around ten twenty that night. Sid was not happy with the really horrible defensive nature of their camp and surroundings and announced that they wouldn't be staying for more than the night. Sleep was difficult as well; they were not very comfortable and, honestly, were just miserable.

"Okay, we've had better camps," John reminded Sid and Nik. They agreed and lay awake listening to the constant noise around them. John suggested using their hearing protection to block out the noise, so they could at least get some sleep, but Sid wouldn't have it. "We have to at least to hear if someone or something is walking up on us." He was right, and the evening ended with that.

They spent the next twenty-five days tacking around the coastal areas south and east of Yorktown, avoiding humanity as well as ground and naval patrols, and staying out of sight. It wasn't horrible, but it wasn't relaxing either, as the tension of what they hoped was coming on October 19 wore on their nerves. The discussions about their active intervention in battles of the American Revolution filled the days ahead. Long evenings dissecting their activities, which had turned armed struggles for an almost clear defeat of the Americans into victory in the name of the history they knew, filled their minds. They considered an outcome, any outcome, different from the surrender of the British Army at Yorktown as a loss to them at this point. A change of the proper history by the Soviets could, and very well might, lead to the "unfounding" of *their* United States.

In those days, there were a couple of occasions the boys witnessed a few distant naval encounters, presumably between naval elements of DeGrasse's French fleet and the remaining British fleet. Sid, Nik, and John couldn't believe, even after being in the past for all this time, the way man waged war in the eighteenth century. It was honestly a lost art; yes, they succeeded in hitting and killing their respective enemies, but with a great amount of time, energy, and inefficiency. The knowledge and use of modern weapons and their destructive power were hugely more effective and devastating for utterly blasting your enemy and his position.

"They'll learn," Nik mumbled.

"Yes they will," Sid acknowledged. "And we Americans will become quite proficient in the ways of war in the upcoming centuries."

They knew without ever really admitting to it or talking about it that they—the three individuals Nik, Sid, and John—could have been considered the strongest army on the continent, if someone of the time actually knew they were there. The Soviets certainly could have had a standing in the force category, but they appeared to have little in the way of modern weaponry with them. The boys scoured their camp and found only the round-less pistol; their mission was clearly one of "military advising" to the unknowing British.

Sid dwelled on the fact that the boys had only been at three battles and repeatedly posed the question, "What if the Soviets were at other points of conflict that we weren't at to help the Colonies? What then?"

Nik, somewhat meekly, held to his present and active theory of time travel (at least how he felt it pertained to their situation) and described time as a flow like the flow of a stream or river. The same currents that brought them to this specific area in 1780 probably brought the Soviet team whom they'd dispatched a month before.

Nik also reminded Sid that they intervened in several nonbattle situations. Mr. Armistead for sure was important, but what of Mr. Quinten? Or the family at the homestead? Or even the family on the mountain road? Even though they didn't engage the Soviets there, they were ready to.

John, after a time in America's past and many repeated conversations, found these talks almost humorous and would keep Sid and Nik on track if one forgot part of their side of the discussion, as they had trudged over the same banter many times. Sid believed that John somehow wrote down the separate arguments on paper somewhere and used the notes to good-naturedly fuel the next debate.

The battlefield was well established by now; it had been for some weeks, and the boys had to stay well away from land routes that they had identified earlier as even lightly used by the peoples of the time, as they would become very busy throughways with the growing conflict. They could hear indications of the fight in the form of what they thought were naval shelling from the York River and artillery fire from the battlefield itself.

It was October 10, 1781, and the boys had scouted their route from where they had been hiding for a little less than a week now and were ready for that day to come—October 19, 1781, the day the Americans initially win their independence from King George and the British Empire. In eight or nine days, they would row out to a point between Yorktown and Gloucester on the York River and hopefully witness the surrender.

Nik admitted he wasn't sure if they would be able to see any of the formal surrender from their small, sea level position on the river. The indication to them of the cease-fire and surrender would probably come in the reality of a cessation of the naval and land-based artillery and siege batteries, which, he figured, would still be peppering the enemy military, support, and command and control positions.

... 47 ...
Time Would Tell of the End ... or Not

DAILY RUNS WERE PROPOSED for the next week, as the boys wanted to ease out into the area between Yorktown and Gloucester where the French frigates were (or would be) posted. In some odd fashion, Sid thought it would be a good idea for the French naval forces to see them every day and "get used to their presence."

"You think?" asked John. "I dunno. It seems a little risky to me."

"Yeah, me too," Sid answered quickly, "but if we don't see the reaction today, we might get our back ends shot off on the day of the surrender and—"

"So we get fatally shot today instead of four days from now? That makes no sense. How does that help?" John continued his grievance.

They both looked at Nik, and Nik put his hands up. "Don't look at me. I'm enjoying watching you guys going back and forth for once. For once, you guys aren't teeing off on me for coming up with some plan that you might think odd or obtuse. Pass the popcorn!" Nik smiled as he happily sat down to enjoy the party.

"That's great," protested John. "What happened to we all help make the plan on where and what we do?"

Nik answered, "Well, we are. Sid has an idea, and we are discussing it. Right?"

A silence fell over their camp, and John answered, "Well, yeah."

Sid continued. "Well, let's see what happens."

It was agreed. They would set out midmorning to see what the waters would show them. The boys donned their burlaps and woods and fashioned fishing poles to use as cover. Fishing was probably a normal thing folks did up and down the York River in 1781. The rifles were kept out of sight, as they didn't want to spook anyone or alert them to their standing out of time. They wanted to look like simple fisher folk who were just—well, trying to fish in a war zone? Okay, they'd have to work on that.

The sounds of battle could be heard in the distance, both on land and from the York River. They assumed that such barrages and gunfire would be a common occurrence up until the surrender, and they hoped they could stay clear of any of the heavy military action. Sid handed out the hearing protection they would have used for shooting at the rifle range and masked the plastic material with burlap and feathers.

"They kind of look like earmuffs now," John giggled.

"Great. Three guys in a rowboat wearing earmuffs—that'll be a sight," murmured Nik.

"We'll only need these if we get close to a ship firing its cannons or if we decide to beat feet (or paddle) into a battle zone to the northwest of here," Sid clarified to the group.

They pushed off and could make out other, much larger vessels in the water to the north, which they hoped were French vessels. Well, they guessed they hoped they were French. Who knew, maybe the British would leave them alone as well; after all, they weren't much of a threat so far as they knew. The first trip out to sea was quick and lasted only an hour with the boys venturing out to where they could, in fact, see the French flagged ships formed up on the York, trolling for enemy resistance. They thought they may have been spotted in their tiny craft by the French, but they really couldn't be sure. Another trip was taken that afternoon. The second expedition brought them just a bit closer to the French fleet that they had seen earlier that morning; this trip lasted a half hour longer, and they were able to demonstrate, to anyone who was paying attention, their fishing cover with all the details, including a few caught fish—by John, of course.

They had pondered, for a time, an attempt to row a bit east into the swampy area they had settled in. Nik had recalled a series of creeks that he thought could get them very close to the actual battlefield near York. He kept this to himself, as he quickly realized they might actually row past the American-Franco lines and end up in British-held areas. None of these possibilities were of any interest to him and were wholly too risky for them. They could certainly defend themselves if needed, but they needed to maintain their anonymity in this time and place.

Their prime mission ruled the day, and they would follow it and stay out of sight of the forces on the battleground near Yorktown. The boys continued moving closer and closer to the ships on the river with little or no attention being shown in their direction. They were able to see some of the American-Franco lines from their tiny vessel in the York River. It wasn't much, as they were quite a distance away, but the frenzy of the lines was the same—gun and artillery fire with men scurrying around doing the deeds of battle.

The morning they spent on the York River on October 12, 1781, was pleasantly comfortable for their tasks. The boys planned their fishing charade and wasted little time getting on station as the days grew closer to the date of surrender. Their voyage proceeded as it had on the many days before this one—row a bit toward the French fleet, fish a bit, and become part of the scenery, which happened to be one of our nation's defining conflicts—the battle for freedom and independence at Yorktown, Virginia.

On this day, though, the boys noted one difference as the wind blew stiffly out of the northeast; the brackish water of the river danced turbulently around their small vessel.

"It's a ship!" blurted Sid. "To the northeast—just one, and she's British!"

A small, lone British naval vessel, apparently caught north behind the French blockade weeks before, was swiftly heading south to run the blockade and escape to the freedom of the Chesapeake and the open seas.

"It's suicide," remarked Nik. "That captain doesn't have a prayer running this armada." As he spoke, the French fleet expertly began forming up for the engagement.

"They are making incredible time!" John now nervously warned. "If we don't move quickly—" *Boom! Boom!* The northernmost French vessels were already firing on the incoming enemy vessel.

"Options, guys?" asked Sid with the full realization that they would be at the center of the battle in mere moments. The British ship had used the stiff wind and wind direction to move at an incredible rate of speed down the York River and was now almost engaged with the French fleet nearest to the boys' position. There was no time for the boys, in their small boat, to move out of the way. The battle was upon them. The boys could see elements of the northernmost French fleet turning southward, adding their fire to the area.

The French cannons were firing from the front and to the entire right side of the boys now, as they secured their rifles and gear onto the small craft. The noise was deafening. The heavy, choking smoke of gunpowder and the concussion of the cannon fire in such close quarters was utterly debilitating to the boys, as the naval barrage continued to spray its deadly reports into the skies above them.

"We weren't counting on this!" yelled John.

"Row, row!" yelled Sid, as the boys came to the full realization that they were now directly in the path of the fleeing British vessel and the French cannon fire. The concussion and fire that the British vessel had experienced down the line of the French fleet had altered its course slightly south, putting it on a collision course with the boys' small craft.

"Holy—!" John yelled. "It's headed right for us! You might have finally succeeded in killing us this time, Nik!"

Sid was still yelling for them to row, while Nik quickly finished the tie off of his gear. "Prepare for a broadside hit!" Nik ordered. "Jump out of the right side of the boat! It doesn't look like—" And just then the burning British vessel rushed by the boys, upending their craft and tossing them into the river.

The boys surfaced as quickly as they could, as the pull of the fleeing British ship forcefully and uncontrollably towed them under the murky and cold river water. They managed to come together a half mile down river with the final detonation and sinking of the British vessel well beyond them. The boys were left hanging on to their overturned craft.

As water dripped down his face into his eyes and mouth, Sid took a deep breath and asked, in an extraordinarily calm voice, "So, how did we get into all this again?"

After taking a day off from the unwelcome "action" on the twelfth and getting cleaned up and dried off, the boys meekly got their sea legs back and ventured out on October 14. The only "action" they saw that day were some taunts that were yelled at them mixed with laughter and hand motions from some French sailors; the boys just smiled and waved back with outward humor and inward annoyance.

Sid snarled, "I'd like to show them something … laughing at us. We could board that ship and take the damn thing over, hoist our own flag, and sail off into the sunset. Pompous—!"

"Relax," Nik quietly urged still, waving and smiling at the French. "They know not what they do, my friend." Nik now sounded very fifteenth-century British.

"Let them have their fun, and besides, they aren't our problem," Nik continued. "Getting to witness the surrender is our concern, not the antics of some lonely French sailors who are two thousand miles from their homeland."

John laughed. "Ewwww, lonely French dudes—bad visions. By the way, Sid, sailing off into the sunset with that boat and no crew … we'd have a very hard time!"

"Yeah, yeah. Okay, stop with the political, social, and technical commentary on my frustration. I don't like being in this little boat. It's a rowboat, for God's sake! I see us as more of a land unit—you know, ground-pounders, not naval folks."

They all agreed to this, as they had performed well in their land escapades since landing in this time. "You're right," Nik admitted, "we are not a naval force by any means, but we're not trying to be one. We are simple fishermen just hanging around—fishing."

John asked Nik, "The next few days … what are we looking at?"

Nik shrugged his shoulders. "Well, we do this some more. Maybe we'll take a day off, row out here on the seventeenth, and hope the shooting stops."

"That's it?" jabbed Sid.

"That's it," answered Nik.

"Not like the movies, huh?" mumbled John.

"Nope, it's all pretty mellow.... A surrender isn't a wanted, noble, or happy moment for the surrendering side, even in 1781," Nik answered.

The boys didn't row out the next day and took the sixteenth off—a day of rest and anticipation. They had more fish than they knew what to do with and basically ate all day and evening. They repacked anything that might have been unpacked to lighten their load on the boat. Their hope was that surrender would be signaled and the war would be correctly and truly over with an American defeat of the British forces at Yorktown in the coming days.

"We won't know until it happens," said John. "It's going to be strange when it happens."

Sid looked up and stepped into John's usual "devil's advocate" role. "It'll be stranger if it doesn't happen."

That drew Nik's sharp attention, as he raised his left eyebrow. Before Nik could say anything, John quickly looked at Nik and responded. "What do we do then?"

Nik paused and looked back over at John. "I don't know."

The pause was long, and the silence was longer—only broken by the sound of zippers and Velcro. Sid felt bad now for pulling a "John" on such a serious subject. *Ugh*, he thought to himself, *I need to stick to lighter topics when trying to joke around.*

"Well," Nik began, feeling like he had to say something on the "no surrender" situation even though he knew it would probably sound plainly obvious, "we would need to row back here and devise a plan moving forward."

"Back to C-10!" said John.

"That isn't a bad plan," Nik answered and nodded.

Sid, who wanted to make up for his earlier foot-in-mouth maneuver and entertain his friends a bit, proclaimed proudly, "No, we'll board and seize one of the French vessels, enslave its crew, and order it to sail around the tip of South America and north to Alaska where we will live in peace and quiet for the rest of our lives!"

They laughed most of the night about Sid's proclamation and added commentary as they saw fit.

"You don't like the sea, remember? A trip around South America and up to Alaska? You'd be sea-crazy by then!" John poked at Sid.

Nik comically dwelled on the enslaving of "lonely French sailors." He simply muttered and shook his head with a look on his face like he had just witnessed a most disturbing event.

"Okay, okay," Sid yielded. "I was just trying to make light of an otherwise dismal event."

Nik nodded in acknowledgment about what Sid was saying, and John laughably added, "Yes, yes, we know you want to enslave lonely French sailors and drive them to the point of mutiny and a walk on a plank."

This banter fell off with the ten o'clock hour, and drifted off to sleep in the cooling breezes of the fall on the mid-Atlantic coast line. Sid and John pondered the events of the next day as they lay down and fell off to sleep. Nik was not so lucky with his attempt at sleep. He couldn't stop thinking about the question of what they would they do if the surrender didn't take place. Numerous ideas filled his mind—sure they could go back to C-10, or they could row up the Chesapeake or down to Florida. They could do whatever they really wanted, as the possibilities were endless. But what was the correct choice?

Nik believed that if the historically correct happening of a British request of parley actually took place the next day, the eighteenth would bring a quiet that would yield to the American and French cheers and uproar of the full surrender of the British. All of this would mark the end of the American Revolutionary War on October 19, and that would be that, as they say.

If (commonly known as the "smallest, biggest word in the English language")—that was the $64,000 question! *If* the events would actually happen! Nik was in a sweat now, as he thought of this not happening like it was supposed to. Well after midnight, to the snores of his compatriots, Nik fell asleep in an uneasy state after vomiting in a far-off bramble with worry and anxiety.

The boys awoke relatively early, with Nik rising last.

"Didn't sleep well, Nik?" Sid asked, looking at his friend.

"No…. I am just sick," he answered.

John walked over. "Sick?" he asked. "How sick? What are you feeling; what doesn't feel right?"

Nik shook his head and frowned. "I'm not sick, as in a cold or the flu. I am sick with angst and anxiety. I used to get this way before I took tests in school—it's awful."

John backed up. "Well, I can't help that. Sid, did you bring any antianxiety medicine?" John asked, despite the fact that he knew full well he hadn't

"Nope, no prescription stuff. Sorry," Sid responded.

"I'll be fine," Nik insisted. "Let's get going…. It is supposed to happen this morning! I want to see once and for all if we or the Soviets screwed up all of history. C'mon, chop, chop!"

Sid and John didn't respond to the ill attitude of Nik, as they knew he meant well. He was just having a time of it this morning. They shoved off at 7:45 a.m. and made sure they had all of their items. Just in case things didn't go as hoped, they could make an exit from the theater as quickly as they could row themselves out of there.

"You know," Sid remarked, "it just struck me—we never made it to the area between York and Gloucester. I know the military action was just too intense, but does that screw up our plan today?"

John answered. "Nah. If, in fact, everyone stops shooting, we'll know something's gone down, and well, I suppose we'll figure out what happened then. Right?"

"Yeah, basically," added Nik. "We'll know."

They rowed for a while and noticed the attacks continuing. They waited off the coast, far off the coast, of what Nik thought was the Moore House, although he wasn't sure of this landmark and had endeavored to verify this fact without any real or assured success.

"So, how are they—the British—going to surrender, exactly?" John asked Nik. "I mean, look at all of that—a big battlefield, men and cannons everywhere."

Sid joked, "They raise a white flag, stupid. How else?"

Nik began. "Well actually, in Yorktown, at around ten o'clock on the morning of the seventeenth, the British sent out a single party that consisted of a single drummer and a single officer waving a white handkerchief or something of the sorts. The drummer gets sent back, and the officer works out the details from what I understood of it. From there, the British lay down their arms tomorrow, and they all go home. And officially, it all ends on the nineteenth."

The three floated on the boat awhile, until John broke their silence (although the sounds of war still pierced the air). "They all go home?" he murmured.

"Well, that was a little more simplistic than what actually happens, but for us sitting on the York River in 1781 just before the surrender of Cornwallis, it'll do," Nik noted. "Let us not forget that in a few relatively short years, like thirty-one years from now, it all starts again. America's second revolution—the War of 1812."

There was more silence. "We'll be like seventy years old, give or take three or four years. Ugh," moaned John.

Sid reassured his friend. "We'll all be old and in the hills near C-10 living out our lives and enjoying the mountains and … perishing in peace by ourselves."

Again, silence filled the air, although the sounds of war were still ever-present. And then Nik responded to Sid's comment. "Well, while that is a bit grim, we can take solace that we won't be embroiled in the next conflict here in America. At seventy years old, we won't be fighting anyone, and C-10 is very far away and off the beaten path from any fighting that occurred in 1812."

"Time?" asked Nik.

John knew Nik was asking him for the time and responded, "It's 10:02 a.m."

Nik seemed puzzled and looked at Sid. "Can you see anything over there?" he asked, now pointing at their ten o'clock position toward the shore, which was near the town of York, and the battlefield areas. "Look at the building near the river," Nik added.

A long pause led to Sid jockeying in a futile action for position in the small boat. "Nope … still looking," Sid noted. Nik and John waited for Sid to hopefully report something, when finally he said, somewhat anticlimactically, that there was a difference in the lines.

"I can't tell what is going on, but there is a change in the posture of the lines we've been looking at over the past week," Sid explained.

"How so?" John asked with a concerned sound.

"I don't know," he said slowly. "Just a lot of looking and not a lot of the typical mayhem." Moments later, Sid reported, "They are looking at something for sure." And that's when the world all seemed to make sense.

In a matter of seconds, all the siege guns, artillery batteries, and cannon fire from the French fleet came to a screeching, sudden, thumping, complete halt. Both land and sea heavy weapon discharges ceased and became a gentle and windless silence. The rifle and arms fire off all of the visible redoubts and offensive American positions fell quiet just as quickly, and the whole world appeared to have hit the mute button.

"Is it happening?" asked John, hardly able to keep his voice down.

"It is happening. They are—" Sid held his thoughts, waiting for some additional evidence of the apparent fruition for the historically expected surrender of the British.

Nik hoped it was what he thought it was and didn't know how to recognize for sure that the British had parleyed surrender. From their vantage point, they couldn't see a thing on any low points on the field of battle or its surroundings.

"Dammit! We can't see the … " Nik now frustrated. And again, it seemed like their prayers had been answered. A huge roll of noise resonated off the distant fields. There were cheers—American cheers! American cheers followed by French cheers! The three could not contain themselves; they raised their hands and arms and cheered with huge, booming voices.

The French on the nearby ship looked over at them for a second, and Nik yelled, "Liberty! Wahooo!" And the French began to cheer, again clapping and waving their hands and kissing to the sky.

It was such an intense scene to them that the boys grew quiet; they wanted to soak in what they could see of the event now that they had gathered their emotions and spirit. "It's done; it happened like it was supposed to. All that we have been through and have seen, all that we intervened with in the hope of maintaining our history. I know it was really small in the grand realm of this enormous continental conflict, but what we got into ... serious—" Nik rambled.

Sid leaned forward and looked all around. The sounds of the distant silence and the commotion on the French vessels had him slightly spooked. He looked at the French ships to verify their status, raised his arms, smiled, and clapped his hands. This brought a round of deep cheers from the vessels crew, which then rolled away from their position through the French fleet.

"Hey, man, that was like a wave at a stadium," John said. "You started the world's first wave-type cheer!" John proceeded to try and initiate another. He stood up, raised his hands in the air, and cheered, looking at the closest French ship. The French responded in kind, and the cheer rolled through the fleet once again in deep, loud revelry. Sid, John, and Nik smiled and laughed at the merriment now occurring on the York River.

Nik began to slowly row, moving the boys' boat away from the French with the intentions of leaving the scene. John now insisted on taking the rows and sat back for just a moment to watch the French ships. Then he quickly peered through the binoculars toward the shores of both York and Gloucester.

"I can't believe we are here!" John exclaimed. "1781, Yorktown, Virginia, the surrender of the British—are you kidding? Soviet chronmonauts—time travelers who tried to stop the creation of the United States. And we—us, the three of us—tried to go camping and shooting at a range in January up in the mountains for some dumb reason. And we're here?"

Sid asked John if he was okay. "Yes, I think so," John responded.

The reality of everything they had been through hit all three of them now; these events that they had witnessed and been a part of were still, at this moment, unbelievable to them. Sid looked around and soaked in the environment. He felt great that history had played out the way they'd wanted it to, the way they'd needed it to, and he was content to leave now. He could leave now, knowing that the United States, at the present time, was on its way to "forming a more perfect union." That was good enough for him.

Honestly, that was good enough for all of them. They looked at each other, all with deep-seated emotion pasted across their faces; the roller coaster of the last seventeen months began to well from inside them. A rush of thoughts hit each of them, pacing them through their reality in the past and all of their memories from their lives in their time—their wives, kids, and families—what of them now? What of the boys? Would they return to C-10 and pass into the annals of time as the "hermits on the hill"?

John had gone into autopilot mode and was paddling to the southeast as hard as the others had ever seen him, all the while mumbling to himself. Sid and Nik listened and understood his emotion. They consoled each other in their personal emotion as the nation around them—their nation—cheered over its independence, its freedom, its newfound liberty.

The sun would set on an ever-changed planet, one that saw the defeat of a great empire and the creation of a greater republic ... the United States of America!

... 48 ...
A Hard Pill to Swallow

SOMEWHERE IN TIME, IN a frigid, smoke-filled, darkened room, sits a man behind a large solid office desk. The gloomy, stagnant air is pierced only by the light of a cracked window shade and a pale-yellow incandescent light dimly glowing in the corner. Into the room rushes a small-statured man, nervously wringing his hands.

The man behind the desk, who has a large, sweat-beaded forehead under his thin crown of white hair, blows cigar smoke through the remarkably large space between his two front teeth.

"What is it?" the man demands. "What have you come to tell me? What news of our special unit?"

"Premier ... our—" The messenger is abruptly cut off by the seated man.

"What news? Tell me, tell me *now!*" he yells.

The small man starts again, shaking slightly and stammering, "Premier ... our telemetry ... our preliminary telemetry shows—"

Once again, the seated man interrupts. "What does it show? Come closer, Georgi, come closer!"

"Sir, our preliminary telemetry indicates ... it indicates a firming up of the temporal signature. We—"

Again, Georgi is interrupted. "What does this mean?" The seated man's fist now hits the desk in front of him.

Georgi timidly moves slightly closer to the desk. "It ... it is our belief ... our belief is that our team has failed." The small man winces slightly now. "We have failed in our mission."

At that moment, the seated man bounds out of his seat and lunges forward, his chair bouncing off the wall behind him. He grabs the small man by the throat as he begins to scream.

"*No!* We must not fail! We must not fail! What of the device? Make it work! Send—"

Georgi, now gasping for air, attempts to explain the status of their operation. "The device ... the device is showing ... it indicates an anomaly! We ... we cannot—"

"*No!*" the seated man yells. "*No!* I do not care about any ... anomaly! Prepare the device!" The balding man throws Georgi to the ground as he continues screaming, sneering, and slamming his fists on the desk.

"Send in Team 2! Send in Team 2 *now!*"

Epilogue

October 24, 2011. As a note for the reader moving forward, in Nik's town, many businesses both small and large have closed, including his gas station/coffee venue. Please understand, many more have lost their jobs, and the economic upheaval has not become "better." Neither have the national and global strains been eased. The institutions that define mainstream economic information for us have skewed data and the results to show and project to us a better picture.

One clear and obvious example to anyone in the world is the cost of food and fuel. You would expect that these very necessary items, which we all require and purchase on a very regular basis, would be included in the economic indicators reported to us. In fact, they are excluded from economic indicators that tell us, the citizens, how things are doing economically. Don't believe what you hear; investigate for yourselves. We are not being given the true state of things. We are being "nudged" into a place we do not want to be.

The present practice of Keynesian economics has not worked—it has never worked throughout all of history. In simple terms, it is this: if you owe money and are in debt, you spend more money to spark growth to get yourself out of debt. Common sense tells us otherwise. If you owe money and are in debt, you can't spend or create money to spend to get yourself out of debt. You need to cut, or reduce, spending. It's simple common sense. The leaders who make policy in our day believe in the practice of Keynesian economics and are shaping every aspect of our lives with it. Was this the intentions of our founders? How has life, liberty, and the pursuit of happiness become laws that are more than 2,500 and 4,000 pages in length and written in language best left to lawyers and judges?

You decide. Is freedom what you want? *Or* would you rather be told, for the rest of your life, what to do, when to do it, how to do it and, most importantly, if you can do it? Do you want to live in the empty world of subjugation—basically slavery—to your government and its "elected" officials?

Wake up, America! Wake up! We are being played! There is an evil in the world, and it's trying to break our way of life. Don't let your freedom and liberty be legislated and litigated away from you!

One final note on Communism, Marxism, and Fascism (which are really one and the same thing; don't be fooled by this either)—over the past one hundred years. You can thank the various forms of these governments around the world for the deaths of roughly 120 million innocent persons, often by starvation, exhaustion, a mockery of a trial and subsequent death sentence, or a bullet. Do we want to give up our freedom and liberty for this?

The End

About the Author

ART THEOCLES WAS BORN and raised in western Massachusetts. He has a bachelor of science degree in aeronautical engineering, and he has always been fond of American and world history. He currently lives in North Carolina.